D1205996

"**I need to give you a little lecture now.** Please bear with me," Kenntnis said. "There's a war being fought, much older than the 'war on terrorism' or our current adventures worldwide, but tied to them in a dark and fundamental way. This ancient war is being waged for the spirit of humanity. If my side wins, mankind literally inherits the stars. If *they* win, gateways between universes will be fully opened again and the earth and all of her six billion inhabitants will enter a new Dark Age with all the attendant ignorance, superstition, suffering and death."

He stared into Oort's eyes trying to read the reaction, but there was nothing to read. The man hid well and offered no encouragement.

"Our weapons are science, technology, rational thought," Kenntnis continued. "Their weapons are superstition, religion and . . . magic. You encountered a touch of it last night." Oort stirred in his chair. Kenntnis anticipated the question. "No, it's not common for it to be used so overtly or openly in this modern world. Which either means they are very close to opening the gates and allowing a flood of Old Ones back into the world, or there is a power-drunk child wielding the power. Neither of which is good news."

"And what or who are these Old Ones when they're at home?" Oort asked.

"Every dark myth and monster you can think of." Kenntnis paused, then said it. "And *every* god you can name."

That got a reaction. Oort stiffened. "I think you should know . . . I'm a person of faith."

Kenntnis hesitated, weighing what to say. "We can negotiate about that later."

The policeman advanced on Kenntnis. "It's not subject to negotiation."

"I think it might be when you understand a little better."

The
EDGE of
REASON

MELINDA SNODGRASS

TOR®
fantasy

A TOM DOHERTY ASSOCIATES BOOK
NEW YORK

This is a work of fiction. All of the characters, organizations, and events portrayed in this novel are either products of the author's imagination or are used fictitiously.

THE EDGE OF REASON

Edited by Patrick Nielson Hayden

A Tor Book
Published by Tom Doherty Associates, LLC.
175 Fifth Avenue
New York, NY 10010

www.tor-forge.com

Tor® is a registered trademark of Tom Doherty Associates, LLC.

ISBN 978-0-7653-5420-4

First Edition: May 2008
First Mass Market Edition: June 2009

Printed in the United States of America

0 9 8 7 6 5 4 3 2 1

*For Carl D. Keim, who always believed in me,
and therefore made everything possible*

Acknowledgments

Thanks to the writers of Critical Mass, that indefatigable writers group that has offered so much help and guidance on this book.

And special thanks to the brilliant men and women around the world who work each day to bring us to a fuller understanding of ourselves, our world, and universe; from the smallest atomic particle to galaxies beyond measure. Theirs is truly the "divine" fire.

Any mistakes are entirely the fault of the author, and apologies in advance.

From the sleep of reason monsters are born.

Francisco José de Goya y Lucientes

The
EDGE *of*
REASON

Chapter

ONE

In her misery Rhiana Davinovitch decided she wanted to die. She had been running for three hours now. Her hunters were slow, which meant she kept well ahead, but unlike her human muscles and tendons, they never tired. Eventually they would wear her down and she would die. That time had just about arrived.

Rhiana drew in a shuddering breath across a throat made tight and sore from exhaustion and raked the hair out of her eyes. Despite the chill of the mid-November night, her hair was moist and slick against fingertips aching with cold.

For the first time in an hour she looked up from the sidewalk, where her gaze had been desperately focused, as she tried to place each foot carefully in front of the other without tripping or falling, or without losing the steady rhythm of her half-walk half-run.

She was surprised to find herself in the uptown business plaza set between Albuquerque's two main shopping malls. She stood in the median of Uptown Boulevard, which ran between the Morgan Stanley office on the north and the City Center and Uptown Center buildings on the south.

She had escaped from the trailer in the South Valley in the early evening. They had been keeping her, hoping she'd finish the work, but after her escape they seemed to have decided that silencing her was more important. So they'd summoned the hunters. She'd tried hitchhiking, but no one would stop. Once she reached the populated areas of Albuquerque she had hammered on doors, but no one had answered. She realized that the creatures who hunted her had trapped her in a field of darkness and fear that no human would enter. No one could help her.

She reckoned she had covered somewhere between fifteen and seventeen miles. She could go no further. Without volition her hand went into the pocket of her coat. The metal of the pennies was sharply cold against her skin. If she could feed she might be able to fight, but there were no people nearby for her to use. A wave of cold brushed against the exposed skin of her face and hands. She glanced up at the bare branches of the trees. They stretched motionless toward the cloud-filled sky. Rhiana looked to the west and watched as one streetlight after another blinked out. The exterior lights on the Uptown City building faded and died.

They were coming.

✷

Officer Richard Oort had been following the winding trail of darkness from Rio Bravo in Albuquerque's South Valley. He kept checking with PNM, New Mexico's electric and gas company, who kept assuring him the power was on and running even as he sat in darkness. He was doing that now from his position in the parking lot of the Morgan Stanley building.

"I'm telling you there's a power outage." The plastic of the handheld mike smelled faintly of hamburgers. Richard wrinkled his nose against the stale odor and pulled the mike away from his face.

The voice of the dispatcher came crackling back over the car's radio. "Our computers don't show a problem."

"Well, I've got a news flash for your computers. I'm now up on Louisiana and it's black as sin. No streetlights, no traffic lights, no lights in any of the buildings. . . ." He broke off and peered through the breath-frosted front window of his parked car. It didn't seem possible, but he said it anyway.

"Even my headlights are fading."

"You never . . ." Static obliterated the word. ". . . that before," said the dispatcher.

"It hasn't happened before," Richard replied.

"Having . . . say . . . again."

The headlights failed, the engine coughed and the car shuddered as it died. Richard tried the key and nothing happened.

The hinges on the car door creaked as he pushed it open. He stepped out and took a three-sixty look. His breath puffed in white streamers. It seemed that every streetlight within a five-block radius was out.

He picked up his mobile radio from the car seat and keyed APD dispatch. "Hi, Dolores, I'm leaving the vehicle and taking a look around."

A burst of static made him jerk the radio away from his ear. Faintly he heard Dolores ask, "What . . . there?"

He made a guess at what she'd said. "I don't know. Right now there's nothing here but dark. Look, if I don't check back within ten minutes send some backup."

There was another sharp burst of static obliterating her first words. He barely heard her "Be careful."

He slipped the radio into its Velcro holder on his vest. The microphone crackled on his left shoulder. Thrusting his nightstick through the loop on his belt, he grabbed the flashlight and headed off down the sidewalk. The weight of the belt festooned with cuffs, stick and pistol left him feeling awkward.

He flashed the beam from the flashlight from side to side. Spindly trees encased in concrete seemed to jump toward him as the light caught them. The landscaping was professional modern, sand grass and chamisa thrusting through the gravel-filled verges between the sidewalks and the tree coffins.

As he walked a carpet of dry leaves whispered around his shoes and crackled underfoot, releasing a rich musty smell that raised childhood memories of lit fireplaces and warm cider. The light of his flashlight danced and glittered in the windows. Everything seemed fine at the Morgan Stanley building and at the small strip mall which held the bank, offices and a couple of low-end restaurants. They were cheap and convenient which meant he'd eaten in both of them.

He stopped so the crunch of the leaves wouldn't be the predominant sound. To the south he heard the occasional whine of tires and rumble of the motor of a car traveling on I-40. Otherwise there was the leaden quiet that precedes a snowstorm. He crossed the street toward the twin buildings which housed the APS Service Center.

An icy wind came sighing down from Tijeras Canyon. He pulled his coat closer around his body and crossed the street. The beam from his heavy black cop's flashlight washed across the empty parking lot. He walked toward the buildings. The click of his metal toe taps echoed off the glass, steel and concrete looming in front of him. He blinked, trying to focus, and realized that the light from the flashlight was dying.

"Well, drat." A sharp slap of the body of the light against his gloved palm produced no result. The light continued to fade with each step he took toward the building. A few moments later it died.

It was inexplicable, a feeling more than a conscious thought, but Richard found himself thumbing up the holster guard and loosening the Browning high-power pistol where it rested at his side. Immediately he felt like a fool. He had only fired the weapon at the range. Never drawn it in the three years he had served on the force. His rational mind argued with primal fear, but he couldn't quite lift his hand from the pistol's grip.

A sharp cry of pain came from deep between the buildings. Richard jerked upright and keyed the radio. It was as dead as the flashlight. He drew his gun as he ran down the incline between the two buildings.

Now he could hear harsh breaths, and the sound of blows connecting with flesh. His eyes adjusted to the gloom, and he saw three hulking figures surrounding a smaller figure who was fighting hard, throwing kicks and punches that seemed to have no effect on the attackers.

He dropped into the approved two-handed-grip horse stance and drew down on the assailants. "Police! Back off!" There was no reaction from the three attackers. For an instant he dithered. Nothing in the manual or his experience had prepared him for this.

He raised the pistol over his head and snapped off a shot into the air. The report, trapped between the two tall buildings, was deafening, and the muzzle flash allowed him to get a look at the focus of the attack.

It was a girl. Late teens at the most. Long hair swirled darkly about her face. Sweat glistened on her skin, and her features were twisted with pain and terror. A pocket on her leather coat was torn loose. All he could tell about her attackers was that they were enormous and dressed in something dark and formfitting. They were as unimpressed with the gunshot as they had been with his shrill command.

The girl ducked under a ponderous roundhouse blow from one of her attackers. There was no more time for warnings. Richard's palms were wet with sweat and he was grateful he had the gloves to help steady his hold on the Browning. He was breathing in sharp, shallow pants. He forced himself to hold his breath, took careful aim at the back of one of the muggers and double-tapped two rounds.

The first bullet fired but the muzzle flash was substantially reduced and the kick against his palm much gentler than it should have been.

Richard's attention was distracted from his target to his pistol because the second round wasn't firing. Richard had a sense it was lodged in the chamber of the pistol, and he tossed the gun away before it could explode in his face. He looked down the alley to see the results of his one shot and felt the breath stop in the back of his throat because the man was continuing the attack as if he hadn't been hit.

There was a hollow sense in his gut warning him that this was eerie and scary and he ought to run the other way, but he couldn't abandon her. It was like twisting ice-covered rope to force the muscles in his legs to move. He managed to break into a staggering run and headed toward the girl.

"Hang on, I'm coming," Richard yelled. His voice sounded stretched and thin and more soprano than tenor.

"HELP!" She screamed. "Help me! Help . . . me. . . ." She gasped down a breath, and ducked beneath the encircling arms.

Richard felt something under the soles of his shoes, and he realized the ground was littered with pennies.

The eye finds patterns and the mind supplies the expected description. Since he couldn't see the bulk of clothes his mind had provided the explanation of a formfitting jumpsuit. It wasn't until Richard launched himself onto the back of one of the attackers that his brain finally accepted the reality . . . *they weren't wearing clothes*. But now he was on the guy's back, and his brain had a whole new series of sensations to process.

There were odd bumps under Richard's knees, and he found himself sliding as if the man were greased. He gripped tighter with his right hand, and punched hard at the man's temple with his left. His fist sunk three inches into the man's head, and something oozed between his fingers.

He yelled in disgust, his legs lost the battle to hang on, and he slid to the ground. Lightning shot up his spine as his tailbone connected hard with the pavement.

One of the other attackers came lumbering around to face Richard. "Oh, God!" he whimpered, because what faced him wasn't a man. It was a monster.

It was constructed of mud and sticks with a featureless blank where its face should have been. It leaned over, slow and ponderous, and reached for Richard. Ice had again encased his muscles and his mind. The only thing filling his head was a little voice frantically yammering the Lord's Prayer, except he couldn't remember any of the words past "Our Father, who art in Heaven." Another voice replaced the panicked, stammered prayer.

"When you're down you gotta roll clear so you gotta chance to get to your feet. Now roll, you motherfuckers."

The gravel voice of Sergeant Jerry Hernandez echoed through his head. Richard rolled frantically away, as a fist the size of a coal scuttle smashed into the asphalt next to his head. The monster got a grip on the back of Richard's coat. There was intense pressure in his armpits before the fabric gave way. He was left wearing the arms while the creature threw aside the body of the coat.

Change went skipping and dancing on the asphalt. The girl flung herself across Richard. Her knee hit him in the diaphragm, and he gulped like a fish as the air went out of him. At first he thought she was trying to shield him, then he realized she was scrambling after the coins.

She grabbed up a penny and balanced it on her outstretched palm. Richard had the sudden and very unpleasant sensation that something cold and wet had just been dragged across the inside of his skull. The girl stared at him with an expression that included confusion, dismay and anger. She shook her head, sucked in a deep breath, and called out in a strange language. The penny began to spin and glow, throwing out copper-colored sparks. The girl tossed the penny into the air. It hung spinning like a tiny firework.

She batted the penny toward one of their attackers. The coin struck the monster in the chest, and there was suddenly a wall of flame. Richard threw an arm over his face as the blast of heat singed his eyebrows. The other monsters reeled away from their companion. The flames died away. The creature didn't move. The girl jumped to her feet, and kicked it hard. The creature shattered.

Richard staggered to his feet. A thread of air was beginning to trickle into his chest. He spotted the roundhouse sweeping toward the girl's head. She didn't.

He wrapped his arms around her waist, and dove sideways. He barked an elbow on the pavement. His shirt tore and his skin with it. The cut on his elbow stung like crazy and blood began trickling down his arm. The girl was on top of him. Her hair, damp with perspiration and smelling of sweat and sandalwood, snaked across his face and mouth. He noticed, distantly, that one ear held a number of earrings stretching from lobe to tip.

Richard got one knee underneath him, shoved himself upright, lifting the girl with him. It wasn't easy because she was taller than he was.

"Come on, let's get out of here!" Richard said.

"They'll just keep coming," she sobbed.

Suddenly the girl jammed her hands into his chest and shoved, hard. Richard went tottering backwards as an enormous fist cut the air in front of him. Goblets of mud spattered against his face. He came up against the side of a building; there was a window to his left. He raised his uninjured elbow, smashed it against the glass, and howled. It always looked easy in the movies. The glass broke, the hero leaped through. In fact the glass remained firmly in place and the hero's elbow hurt like hell. Richard yanked out his nightstick and swung hard. This time the glass shattered.

"Come on!"

He felt the words ripping along his throat, and he beckoned frantically to her. She darted between the monsters and ran to him. He was going to boost her through, but she braced a foot high on his thigh, the heel grinding into the muscle, grabbed his shoulder, and climbed him like a stepladder. Her heard her land inside. Which left him outside. With the monsters.

Richard grabbed the windowsill. The edges of the broken glass cut through his gloves and into his palms. He gritted his teeth against the pain, planted a toe of his heavy shoe against the wall and boosted into a handstand flip. He landed on his feet in the office and felt the jar from his shins to the top of his head. It had been a long time since he'd done any serious gymnastics.

"Ow, ow, ow, ow, ow," he groaned as he surveyed their surroundings.

It was some kind of nondescript office space. Computers on metal desks, chairs on casters, and office cubicles formed from carpeted panels. Briefly he wondered why the alarms weren't working, decided it was all part of the lack of light and firepower, then forgot it all as sausage-sized fingers gripped the windowsill, dripping mud from their blunt tips onto the industrial carpet. The monster hauled itself through.

"PENNY!" the girl screamed. Richard dug into his pants pocket and pulled out a handful of change. The girl frantically sorted through and emerged with three pennies.

The second monster was through the window.

The girl huddled over the pennies cupped in the palm of her hands. She muttered in that strange language again. The pennies began to spin and burn. She tossed one into the air, and batted it at the attacker. Flames exploded around the monster. The girl tottered. Richard got an arm around her, and realized they were propping each other up. Then technology decided to work. The automatic sprinkler system kicked to life, and doused the flames.

"Oh . . . damn," Richard said.

The monsters advanced.

The girl lifted her head. Water ran out of her hair and across her skin. Richard ran forward and head-butted the lead creature. If his fist had been gross, this was disgusting, and he didn't shift the monster by an inch. He lifted his head, shaking mud from his hair, and saw a fist. It connected, snapping his head around. His cheek felt like he was chewing ground glass and his neck became a column of pain. He went staggering across the room, hit the wall and fell down.

The girl held up a penny and began to chant, but she was trembling, forcing the words past chattering teeth. A small section of mud slid off the thigh of a monster carried in water from the sprinklers. A thin thread of hope formed. Richard scanned the walls, and spotted the glass fire box with its extinguisher and coiled fire hose about ten feet to his left.

It was like moving through wet concrete, but Richard got to his feet. He tried to run, and managed a shuffle. Still it carried him to the fire box. He moaned, clenched his teeth, and broke the glass with his less-sore elbow. Icy water ran through his hair, and dripped off the end of his nose. The monsters were a foot from the girl.

He uncoiled the fire hose, turned the spigot, and nearly lost his footing as high-pressure water gushed from the nozzle. Holding hard with both hands, he brought the stream of water onto the chest of one of the monsters. Despite the lack of a mouth, a high-pitched howl emanated from the creature, weird and inhuman. Mud went washing down its chest, carrying twigs and branches with it.

Richard aimed the water at the other creature. It also produced the horrible cry. He alternated the water back and forth between them. Rivulets of filthy water sluiced around their feet as they melted. He had a wild image of the scene at the witch's castle in *The Wizard of Oz*, and couldn't believe he was doing this. Eventually all that remained was a floor awash with brown water and floating sticks.

Abruptly the alarms began to howl and all the computers sprang to life and began an automatic reboot. Outside the streetlights snapped back on and there was a sharp explosion as the unfired cartridge in the chamber of his gun detonated. Richard began laughing hysterically. Behind him he could hear the girl's choking sobs.

A dark figure lunged through the window. The laughter died as his air choked off in fear and Richard brought the fire hose to bear. The shock of the water elicited a long string of curses in a number of languages, only three of which Richard recognized. He pulled the hose aside, and stared at the face lifting cautiously back over the windowsill. Water plastered the man's long hair to his skull and dripped from his beard. Judging from the patched and dirty coat and the layers of sweaters it was some homeless guy in search of a quick profit.

"Forget it, buddy. There are going to be no free computers tonight," Richard croaked, his throat raw from exertion and yelling. Water squelched between the soles of his feet and his shoes and lapped around his ankles. He was losing sensation in his toes. Now that he had stopped exerting himself he felt the sweat trickling down his back and chest like rivulets of ice. He managed to turn the spigot and the gusher of water died to a trickle.

"How the hell did you get in here?" the homeless man asked. The voice was youthful and he spoke in a normal tone of voice. Richard couldn't understand why he was able to hear the man clearly over the din of the alarms. "You should not have been able to walk in darkness. . . ."

The words were oddly ominous and a clattering filled Richard's ears as his teeth began to chatter.

Yea though I walk through the valley of darkness.

He was back in Sunday school at the strict Lutheran church his family attended. At six years old the words were parroted, meaningless and incomprehensible. Today he was twenty-seven and he was afraid.

The man looked closely at Richard. "Oh, I see what you are."

Richard's breath stopped in his throat and his gut clenched down tight. Instinctively Richard wrapped his arms across his chest and belly in defense against this body blow. It was a secret carefully kept, which haunted his nights. It had sent him fleeing from the East Coast to this nondescript city in a poor and obscure state, and into a new career, and now this man had perceived it.

Another sound joined the yammering of the alarms. Police sirens wailing in the distance.

The bum was breaking off the shards of glass sticking up from the frame like jagged teeth in a steel jaw. He ran a hand across the casement to verify it was clear, then leaned his elbows companionably on the windowsill like a neighbor talking across a narrow tenement street.

"We have a decision to make," the man said. "I was sent here for her." A jerk of the chin toward the girl who knelt in the water sobbing softly. "But then I find you, and you're not supposed to be here. I could take her, but I think she'll be safer with you. They can't see her when she's with you."

The sirens were very close now. Headlights and light bars danced white, red and amber through the windows as police cars came wheeling into the parking lot.

"What are you talking about?" Richard asked.

"I'll get back to you on that. Right now I've got to go before your brethren arrive. Remember, don't leave her. She's only safe with you."

The man spun away from the window. Richard lunged after him. "Hey. Wait. What do you mean?" He was yelling after the man's retreating back as the man ran up the alley.

His coats ballooned around his body, giving the effect of wings. "You mean I have to . . . take . . . her . . . home?"

Richard turned back to survey the rescued. Her clothes were drenched, her black hair plastered to her cheeks. Despite the bruises and the blood-coated split lip she was the most beautiful woman Richard had ever seen. She had pale, pale skin, and winged eyebrows over green eyes with epicanthic folds.

"I need you to stay quiet. Follow my lead. Okay?" The girl nodded. Richard looked around the room and spotted a copper glow. A penny. Still spinning. Still on fire. He picked it up and deposited it in his pocket.

He couldn't do much about the mud and the sticks. They would have to remain, but in a state where a body found in the trunk of a car, hands tied behind the back and six bullet holes had been ruled a suicide Richard didn't think anyone would inquire too closely. There were reasons he'd selected New Mexico to begin his career with the police; this was one of them.

The alarms cut off. Someone had reached the control box. The abrupt cessation of sound was almost painful. Flashlight beams were playing across the walls opposite the window. Richard pulled off his badge and held it out. The other hand he held prudently over his head. A gun and flashlight were thrust through the window. A head peeked cautiously around.

"*Freeze* . . . oh," the cop said.

Chapter

TWO

The Browning, its barrel peeled back like a newly opened daylily, rested in the center of Lieutenant Damon Weber's desk. It was unfortunate that Weber was on duty tonight because he was smart and conscientious. The battered old PC on the desk sent up a dull hum, and the blast of tepid air from the heat register ruffled the edges of the paper piles which were stacked on every available flat surface.

"I observed three . . . men beating up the lady." Richard hoped Weber hadn't noticed the minute hesitation. "I ordered them to stop. They didn't, so I fired a warning shot," Richard said. It hurt to talk. His jaw didn't want to open and his neck had stiffened into a column of pain. He could turn it but only an inch to either side.

Somebody was heating a tamale in the microwave and the smoke and bitter smell of the red chile had him salivating. Too many hours and too much exertion had left him limp and empty. At least he'd been allowed to change out of his soaked uniform and into street clothes before he faced Weber's gimlet stare. So now he was just scared, hurting, tired and hungry instead of scared, hurting, tired, hungry, *cold and wet*.

"And that didn't produce asses and elbows?" Weber asked, and rubbed his fingers over the deep acne scars running along his jaw line.

Richard had noticed the lieutenant did that a lot. He wondered if the older man was embarrassed by the blemishes? He shouldn't be. Damon was a handsome man. Richard forced himself back to the moment.

"No, sir. Since I felt the victim was in imminent danger I shot at one of them."

"And?"

It was hard because it was going to look bad and send him back to the range for many more hours of practice. Richard swallowed. "I missed. I went to fire again but the gun jammed. I got us into the building and then the cavalry arrived."

"And the assailants?"

"Ran."

"All three of them?" Richard nodded. He was nervous at the sharp tone of inquiry in the lieutenant's voice.

"Our guys only spotted one person fleeing the scene," Weber said.

"Maybe they split up," Richard offered.

There was a long silence as the two policemen regarded one another. Beyond the frosted glass door phones rang and men's voices rumbled like the basso stops on a powerful organ. Occasionally a woman's flute-like tones would add a counterpoint to the bass.

The lieutenant looked at the girl sitting silently in the chair next to Richard. She was swallowed by the shirt and pants provided by Lucile, one of the dispatchers, who had had a change of clothes in her locker. Lucille was a lush lady, and her oversized clothes made the girl look even younger, like a child playing dress-up.

She's such a baby, Richard thought. *I wonder how old she is?*

"Is that pretty much how it came down, Miss Davinovitch?" he asked her.

So that's her name, Richard thought. *They must have talked to her while I was changing.*

"Yes, sir." The voice was low with a husky catch at the end of the words. Richard wondered if she sounded like that normally or if it was the residue of a night of screaming.

"I'd like you to sit down with a sketch—"

"No," the girl broke in. Weber reared back in his chair

startled by the ferocity. "I mean I couldn't do any good. It was so . . . dark. I didn't see anything."

"You have family we can call?" Weber asked.

"No, my family's out west. I was going to school here. I'll be all right. I just want to go home." It emerged in a breathless rush.

Richard stood. "I'll type up my report."

"No," said Weber. "We're fifteen minutes from shift change. Go home."

"Yes, sir."

Weber nodded toward the destroyed Browning. "You got a spare?"

"Yes, sir, at home."

Weber stood. "Okay." He turned to Rhiana. "We'll arrange a ride for you."

"Could he, Officer Oort, take me home?" the girl asked quickly as she jumped to her feet.

Richard flushed as Weber tried to hide a grin. "Sure. Don't see why not." Richard opened the door and stepped aside for the girl to pass. As he started to leave Weber leaned down from his six feet until his lips were level with Richard's ear, and with a leer whispered, "And another one bites the dust."

"With all due respect, sir . . . shut up," Richard responded, and he followed the girl out.

The main bullpen was awash with people trying to prepare for the shift change. Most were typing and filing frantically, but all of them paused to look as Richard and the girl emerged from the lieutenant's office. Richard understood why. From his early childhood Richard had known that his looks had an effect on people—male and female. He had learned to live with the stares, the whispers, the come-ons. Now he was standing next to a woman who matched his extraordinary looks. *And I wonder if it's been as much of a burden to her as it has been for me?*

Lucile bustled over, her arms filled with a bulging white plastic garbage bag. "I got your clothes, honey. They're still soaked so I put 'em in a bag. Just keep my things until tomorrow. Rich can bring them back."

"Richard," Richard corrected, knowing he wouldn't be heeded, but needing to try anyway. Davinovitch accepted the sack.

"Thank you."

"You're welcome. We're just glad you're okay. It just gets worse and worse out there."

The girl's face was bleak as she said, "Yes . . . yes, it does." She clutched the plastic bundle to her chest and followed Richard out the door of the bullpen, and into the hall. He hesitated for a moment, looking from the door to the stairwell and the elevators. Finally he led her to the elevators and punched the call button.

"You usually walk, huh?" she asked.

He nodded. "I'm pretty sure we don't need any more exercise." The elevator arrived with an anemic "ding." The doors slid reluctantly open and they stepped inside. Richard punched the first floor and the elevator shook, groaned, and began lurching downward. "So where do you live, Ms. Davinovitch?" he continued.

"Rhiana, call me Rhiana, and I'm going home with you."

"I beg your pardon?"

"He told you to stay with me," she said.

"Well, yes, but . . . if we're talking about the same *he* . . . he was a bum."

"He's not a bum," the girl answered.

"Okay, then what is he?"

"I don't know . . . exactly. Maybe a familiar," she mused.

The elevator stopped with a jar. Richard's teeth clacked lightly together and a white hot poker jabbed up from his battered jaw to emerge somewhere over his right eye. From Rhiana's expression she was experiencing something similar.

"So are you going to pretend it didn't happen?" Rhiana said as she followed him out of the elevator.

"I haven't decided yet," Richard said.

"I hope you don't because that won't help me much. I need you to believe if you're going to keep me safe."

The metal bar on the front doors was cold against his palms as Richard thrust it open. "Believe what?"

"That what happened tonight really happened."

They locked stares. Richard broke first, disquieted as much by the sooty lashes framing her beautiful eyes as by the lurking terror in their green depths. He turned and went clattering down the concrete steps and into the parking lot behind APD headquarters. Her footsteps pattered after him. It was very dark. This late in the fall the sun wouldn't rise over the rocky pinnacle of the Sandia Mountains until seven o'clock.

Taillights flared red as the morning shift pulled into the lot, braked and parked. Richard thrust the key into the door of his used Volvo. He looked back over his shoulder at Rhiana who stood a few feet behind him with the tentative air of a wistful child.

"So, what were those things?" Richard asked.

"I don't know. Not exactly. They were sort of like golems, but . . ." Her voice trailed away and she shrugged.

"Is there anything that you do know?" Richard demanded.

"I know that they're going to kill me if you don't let me come home with you."

As the hours passed Kenntnis decided that Cross had failed. The girl was dead. The sun climbed over the stony shoulders of the Sandias. Kenntnis's desk was situated to look up at the gray and rocky face of the towering mountains. He swiveled slowly in his chair, and keyed the control for the western shutters. Hydraulics purred and the shutters slid up into the wall over the vast picture window which offered him a view across the city to the Three Sisters, extinct volcanoes on the western edge of Albuquerque. Beyond them the mesa rolled away flat and brown. At the distant end of sight the snowcapped peak of Mount Taylor thrust glinting in the sunlight some sixty miles away.

He had lived in many places. None had the clear skies of New Mexico (though they were less clear in recent years), and the state's lack of moisture and low scrubby trees did little to obscure the view. It was a foolish whimsy, but in these early days of the twenty-first century he wanted to be able to see into the distance since he didn't seem able to see into the future. He had thought mankind would be so much further ahead. Instead they seemed to be sliding back into—

The hum of the elevator broke into his thoughts. He couldn't help himself. He left the office and stood waiting in the outer office for the elevator door to open. The polished stainless steel threw back his reflection. He stood over six feet tall and well over three hundred pounds, with features that were an amalgamation of the features of all the human races. Cross stepped out. The hairs of his mustache and beard glittered where his breath had condensed and frozen in the frigid morning air. He was alone.

"She's dead," Kenntnis said heavily. Cross shook his head. "Then where is she?"

"There was a cop in the mix," Cross said as he walked into the private office and over to the untouched breakfast tray sitting on an inlaid onyx table near the floor-to-ceiling bookcases. He settled into a chair, removed the covers from the plates, and began to eat. "I left her with him."

"Excuse me?"

"He was undeterred by darkness. He even finished off

two of the hunters," Cross mumbled around a mouthful of toast.

"Whose piece is he?" Kenntnis asked as he sat down opposite the homeless man.

Cross paused with a spoonful of soft-boiled egg halfway to his mouth. "Nobody's. His own. The name on the tag was Oort. Funny name." He shoved in the spoon, his lips snapping closed around the silver. Kenntnis leaned back against the desk. The polished granite was slick and cool beneath his palms. "Does Grenier know this Oort has her?"

"He'll think she's dead," Cross mumbled around a mouthful.

"No," Kenntnis corrected. "He'll know his constructs were destroyed. He won't assume success." Kenntnis fell silent, weighing the options.

Smacking and slurping filled the silence. His concentration broken, Kenntnis glared at Cross. Even after all these years in human form, the Old One still hadn't grasped the most basic of manners.

"You'll have to go get her," Kenntnis said, sharper than he'd intended. The creature had annoyed him.

Cross's head swung up and he presented Kenntnis with a view of half-chewed food as his mouth hung open. "From a cop? No way. This one's on you."

"I don't work that way. I don't get involved anymore."

"Well, you better fucking get involved. We've got the Clash of Civilizations coming, Armageddon, the New Dark Age." Cross's voice provided the capitals. "You keep dithering and I'm going to fucking end up on the other side."

Kenntnis knew it wasn't a threat, just a statement of fact. If the concepts of tolerance, love and forgiveness continued to erode between religions and races the Old One's darker nature would reassert itself.

"Okay, I'll call the mayor."

"By the way, the cop's one of the empty ones," Cross said as he poured out a fresh cup of coffee.

Kenntnis turned slowly to stare at him. "And you didn't think this was relevant and significant?"

"Not particularly," Cross said. He blew hard across the coffee. Steam bent and danced under the assault. "What are you gonna do? Arm him with the sword? It's not 800 A.D. anymore." The creature paused, considering. "Although he might be willing to use it on me." There was a hopeful note in the final words.

"As I keep telling you, the only part of you that would die is the part that's useful to me. So, no."

Swinging behind his desk, Kenntnis pulled the computer out of sleep mode. He would investigate the background of this paladin before he actually contacted the man. But the arrival of an empty one at just this juncture and the symbolism of the policeman's shield wasn't lost on Kenntnis, though it represented a level of coincidence which made him decidedly uncomfortable. Fate was not normally a player in Kenntnis's plans. In fact she was usually a downright bitch.

They hadn't talked during the twenty-minute drive from downtown to Apartment Row out north on Montgomery. Her face throbbed in time to the beating of her heart and exhaustion dragged at every limb. Rhiana rested her head against the back of the seat and let the music pouring from the radio lull her. It was something soft and classical. She didn't know anything about that kind of music.

She awoke, unsettled, from a sleep she hadn't intended to take. It had been the jouncing of the car passing over a speed bump that woke her. As they pulled into the parking lot of an apartment complex, Rhiana noted it was one of the nicer units nestled close to the foothills, and built in a pseudo-Spanish style with tiled roofs and bright stucco on the walls.

She waited by the car as the policeman opened the trunk and removed a shotgun. She noted the bulletproof vest with its ceramic inserts lying on the floor of the trunk. *That won't help him against what's coming,* she thought.

Nausea took her as the fear returned. The slamming of the trunk brought her back. Oort was indicating the way with a gesture of his long, slender hand, allowing her to go first. Was it manners or did he want to keep that shotgun at her back? She started up the path from the parking lot.

He had a ground floor unit. He unlocked the door and stepped aside for her to enter. The cheap carpet was the usual apartment beige, but everything else was unexpected. The room was dominated by a grand piano set near the sliding glass doors leading onto the minuscule patio. There was a metal and white leather sofa of a very modern design arranged in front of a small television, an armchair, a glass coffee table with a few books scattered on the top. There was no dining table. It appeared he ate at the tiny counter that separated the kitchen from the living room.

A Bose stereo system sat against one wall. On the other wall was a tall bookcase. It was filled with books and sheet music, CDs, a signed baseball, and a NY Yankees World Series mug. On one shelf in a modern silver Nambe frame was a family photo. A stern-looking man with gray hair and amazing dark blue eyes looked out. Next to him stood two young women—one with light brown hair, the other with dark blond—both attractive without being beautiful. In front of the older man stood a slender and delicately beautiful older woman with white blond hair and gray eyes. The man had his hand on her shoulder, but it looked more controlling than affectionate. Rhiana didn't have to ask if this was Oort's mother. Her features were etched in his face. The cop was also in the photo, but he wasn't looking at the camera. His gaze was on his father's face with an inscrutable expression.

There were a few paintings on the wall. All abstract. All icy cool in shades of white, gray and pale blues. Everything was excruciatingly neat. The only evidence of use was an open book of music on the piano's stand.

She couldn't help but compare it with her family's home, cluttered with piles of old newspapers and *People* magazines, reeking of dog pee which had permeated the cheap carpet, and filled with the competing noise of four televisions in four rooms all tuned to different channels. It made her feel awkward and low class. She felt the embarrassment transform to resentment against the cop.

Oort propped the shotgun against the wall near the front door. He crossed the room. He had an economical way of moving and an upright posture. Rhiana realized it was not the erect stance of military service but more reminiscent of dancers or gymnasts. He twitched shut the curtains over the sliding glass door.

"Are you hungry?" he asked.

The reminder had saliva bursting across her tongue and her stomach clenching. She nodded. The interior of the refrigerator was as neat as the rest of the apartment, and equally as spare. Milk, eggs, a carton of plain yogurt and various kinds of fresh fruit in the crisper drawers.

"I drink a yogurt shake in the mornings," Richard said. "I also have oatmeal, if that sounds more appealing."

"Oatmeal," Rhiana said. She expected the usual microwaveable packet, but instead he took down a package of steel-cut Scottish oats from a cabinet. While the oatmeal cooked he dumped yogurt, honey, fruit, wheat germ and milk into a blender and whipped the mixture to a froth.

The oatmeal was set before her on the counter along with the milk, honey and a package of extremely tiny raisins. Rhiana surreptitiously turned the package to read the label. Zante Currants. So that's what currants looked like. She had read about them, but they hadn't been a staple in the Davinovitch household.

An experimental taste of the oats revealed a far richer, nuttier flavor than conventional oatmeal. The local New Mexico mesquite honey had an almost bitter aftertaste. The policeman stood in the kitchen, his shoulders propped against the front of the refrigerator, and sipped his drink. There was a frown between his pale brows. Finally he reached into his pants pocket and deposited the penny on the counter.

It sat spinning and glowing. Rhiana's throat was suddenly too tight to swallow. She set down her spoon and met the icy blue eyes of her host.

"Now I need to have a few questions answered," he said in his soft tenor. His expression was worried and vulnerable.

"O . . ." Her voice broke. Rhiana coughed and tried again. "Okay."

"What did you do to it?" He indicated the penny.

"Activated it so it could carry a spell for me." She saw no point in holding back. He was her only hope for staying alive.

"A spell?"

Furrows formed in the oatmeal and filled with milk as she dragged her spoon through her cereal. "When you do magic you need a focusing device. Some people use wands. Others use crystals. I use pennies. It's whatever works for you."

"And those . . . monsters, they're magical too?" Richard asked.

"Created by magic. They're not magical creatures. They were just sticks and mud animated by magic." She worried this was too much information, but his expression was still attentive.

"And they were sent to kill you?"

"Yes," Rhiana said.

"A gun would have been easier," Richard said.

"But guns need someone to shoot them, and people and guns can be traced. You can't trace mud and sticks."

"So who created and sent these things?" he asked.

"I'm not sure. Maybe the man who's been funding us. Maybe the group, but I didn't think they had the power for something like this."

"Does this man who's funding you have a name?"

"I don't know it. Josh never let any of the rest of us deal with him."

"And what was the funding for?"

This was getting dangerously close to the heart of the matter. "Magical stuff . . . work."

"And why do they want to kill you?"

And now they were to it. The million-dollar question. If she answered, it would slam her ass in jail and remove her from the protection of this man. In jail she would die and she didn't want to die.

Rhiana slid off the barstool and walked into the living room, playing for time and seeking inspiration. "It's complicated," she said slowly as her gaze flew across the books on the shelves, the books on the coffee table. One was open. Gilt-edged pages glinted and she realized from the minute type and the almost translucent pages that it was a Bible. Suddenly the other titles on the shelves snapped into focus. Works by Aquinas and Augustine set alongside an array of forensic books and psychology texts.

She whirled to face the policeman. "It's because I wanted to leave the coven." It wasn't a lie. She had, but not for the reasons this man would assume.

"All right," he said. Richard laid a hand on the edge of the oatmeal bowl. "Are you finished?"

"Yes, thanks."

He picked up the bowl and his glass and moved to the sink. They were quickly rinsed and deposited in the dishwasher. Rhiana drifted back toward the kitchen.

"You're not denying it. Pretending it didn't happen. Telling me you don't believe in magic," she said as Richard dried his hands.

He glanced at the glowing, spinning penny. He then opened the freezer and pulled out a couple of cold packs. He tossed one to Rhiana. She instinctively caught it. He laid his against his jaw and sucked in a quick gasp.

"The evidence is pretty incontrovertible," he said.

Rhiana laid the cold pack against the side of her head where one of the monster's fists had connected. Her gasp echoed his. They stood staring at each other across the breakfast bar.

"So what do we do now?" Rhiana asked.

"Sleep," came the reply.

The memory of Josh's pawing hands and how he always managed to press his crotch against her when they were working filled her mouth with a sour taste. Granted this man's slim body was a vast improvement over Josh's pendulous belly, but . . .

"You take the bed," he said. She looked into his beautiful face and realized he had sensed her dismay. "I'll sleep on the couch."

Tears pricked hot and moist against her eyelids and hung on her lashes. Rhiana nodded and headed toward the bedroom door.

"And the door locks," he added.

She looked back and wondered what fate had placed her in such gentle care. She found a small and nervous smile curving her lips. "I don't think I'm going to need that."

Her dreams were filled with burning people running down cavernous streets. Her horror was tempered by the tingle of power arcing along her nerve endings. Twisting shadows pushed through mirrors. Her legs cramped, sending pain shooting through her muscles, as she tried to run from their advance. Each time it happened she awoke with a gasp, and had to reorient herself in the strange room. At some point she was so exhausted that neither dreams nor pain could penetrate.

It was the furtive *snap* of the bathroom door closing which returned Rhiana to consciousness. Pushing back the tangle of her hair, Rhiana rolled over and squinted at the luminous numbers on the alarm clock. Ten a.m. There was the sound of water trickling from a tap. Rhiana rolled out of bed and wrapped the sheet around her body before crossing to the bathroom door.

"Just a minute," the policeman called in answer to her light knock.

"Don't you sleep in after a night shift?" Rhiana asked.

"Not on Sunday," came the muffled reply. She heard the sharp rattle of the shower against a plastic curtain. "Go back to bed. I'm going to church."

"Not without me," she said to the door and gathered her clothes.

The church was drab. Plain glass windows offered a view of the brilliant blue New Mexico sky. The promise of snow had not materialized. Wooden pews. Wooden altar. Plain wooden cross. There was the smell of lemon-scented wood polish rather than incense. A small portable organ in the back corner of the church wheezed out a seemingly random series of scales as people filed in the doors. The men wore coats and ties and almost every woman wore a dress. There were very few Hispanic faces and no blacks.

"Is your family religious?" Richard whispered as they walked to a pew near the middle. Some of the woman were staring at her hiking boots and leather jacket.

"Holiday Catholics," she replied.

The wood was cold through the fabric of her jeans. Slumping down, she took the strain from her sore back onto her tailbone. The cop sat straight, holding his Bible between long, slender fingers. The bruise on his jaw was livid against his white, white skin.

People were still staring at them, and Rhiana lightly touched her own bruised face. She dropped her head allowing her hair to fall forward and veil her injuries. *People probably think we either had really rough sex last night or a really big fight,* Rhiana thought. She wanted to scream out what really happened and shake up their very white, very ordered lives.

The service began with an opening hymn. Next to her a soaring tenor rose above the congregation. Rhiana turned and stared at the cop. Her aunt Judy liked to think of herself as sophisticated, and always had classical music playing whenever her brother came over. Rhiana had only heard voices like this on the records her aunt played.

The only familiar thing was the Lord's Prayer. Rhiana could mumble along with the rest of them on that one. As the minutes ticked slowly past, Rhiana alternated between flipping through the hymnal and glancing at her companion's profile. He never felt her gaze, never looked at her. During the prayers his eyes were tightly closed, but his expression wasn't one of joy.

Based on the sermon there was plenty of reason to be grim. The minister seemed generally pissed about the state of the world and each and every person in it. Once Rhiana had the drift of his remarks she allowed her mind to wander. She wondered about the others. Did they know Josh had sent things to kill her? Did Josh know she hadn't died? Based on the homeless guy's remark that seemed likely. She had felt confident that they wouldn't use ordinary weapons against her, but that might have changed since her escape. The cop might be able to hide her from the darkness, but he couldn't stop a bullet or a hit-and-run driver, or a knife, or a fire. Her lungs felt clogged. She choked and struggled for breath.

Richard's fingers closed over her wrist. "Are you all right? Do you need to leave and get some air?" he whispered.

The realization that he had been aware of her, and seemed worried and concerned about her, created a lump in her throat. Tears blossomed wet and warm against her lower lids. She brushed them away with the backs of her hands and nodded. Richard took her under the arm, and helped her out of the pew and out the doors.

"I'm sorry," she said once they stood in the parking lot.

"It's okay, the service was almost over."

"What are we going to do now?"

"Go home. I need a little more sleep."

But that plan didn't work out. When they got back to the apartment there was a message on the answering machine from the mayor's Chief of Staff, requesting that Officer Oort go to a meeting with a Mr. Kenntnis of Lumina Enterprises at three that afternoon.

Chapter

THREE

The Internet was a wonderful tool. While Officer Oort might have an unpublished number and a fake name attached to his address, all the real information was easily captured on the Web. The chair creaked under his bulk as Kenntnis leaned back and stared at the thirty-two-inch monitor.

Richard Noel Oort, twenty-seven, born on Christmas Day (Kenntnis assumed that was the source of the middle name) in Newport, Rhode Island. His father was a federal court judge. Two older sisters. Amelia, thirty-four, a surgeon. Pamela, thirty-one, a lawyer. Mother a homemaker.

The youngest Oort had obtained his undergraduate degree at Cornell majoring in fine arts—music. He had been on the gymnastic team, joined the fencing club, the ski club. In his youth he and his father periodically entered yacht races and finished modestly well.

He did his graduate work at the Rome Conservatory, focusing on piano and voice. He'd returned home and joined a Wall Street brokerage firm and lasted three months. There was no record of him for six months until he turned up in the police academy in Albuquerque, New Mexico. He was unmarried, and he carried a staggering amount of credit card debt, much of it incurred buying clothes and art.

Kenntnis was still working on the missing six months, but either way it was a strange background for a beat cop in an undistinguished city in the poorest state in the Union.

It was annoying that it was Sunday, but Kenntnis had the mayor's home telephone number. A large contribution and the taxes generated by his building and company meant that Kenntnis's calls were answered and his requests met. His current request was that a young officer by the name of Richard Oort be assigned to help Kenntnis form a security force for a subsidiary company he was planning to relocate to New Mexico that would employ one thousand people. An appointment was set for 3:00 p.m. that day. Kenntnis checked his watch. Only a few minutes from now.

The Internet search meant he had tipped his hand, but the timing was so fast that he doubted his opponents could have arranged anything. Levering himself up on the palms of his hands, Kenntnis looked out through the window. The telephone line below his office sagged under the weight of the birds waiting to intercept his every call. Technology was his ally and he had long ago replaced his land lines with cell phones. It was now time to go to wireless Internet service as well. He couldn't understand why the Old Ones continued to rely almost totally on magic rather than wiretaps, shotgun mikes and all the other panoply of modern snooping technologies. Kenntnis assumed it was something psychological and hoped it would continue. Kenntnis then gave a rueful smile: of course he had an Old One standing guard, watching for any magical attack.

The westering sun slanted through the wide windows. A touch on a switch and the blinds rolled into place. He left the slats tilted so light laddered across the Persian carpet, bringing the blues and reds into high relief. He knew where Oort lived, so early in the day he had sent Cross to keep watch on the girl. The Old One reported that the pair had gone out around ten-thirty and been gone for a little over an hour. The most recent report established that the girl had a fine sense of self-preservation. According to Cross there had been a spirited argument in the parking lot which ended with the girl ensconced in the front seat of the car next to a disgruntled policeman. Thus the girl ended up where Kenntnis had intended, if some hours later than he could have wished.

His secretary's voice came over the intercom. "Mr. Oort is here to see you, sir."

"Send him in."

The massive carved wood and frosted glass panel of the door swung open. Kenntnis lowered his eyes to locate his visitor. He was a small man, no more than five foot four, and very slim. The camel overcoat over a blue cashmere sweater gave bulk to his slender frame. Perfectly tailored gray pants broke on his instep, and cufflinks glinted on the cuffs of the shirt worn beneath the sweater. Kenntnis now understood the level of debt. The clothing was all designer quality.

He transferred his attention to Oort's face. The policeman flushed under Kenntnis's intense scrutiny. Despite the bruise blooming across the right cheek it was a face of almost unearthly beauty, and beauty was the right word

despite the gender. This was simply the handsomest man
Kenntnis had ever seen. Silver gilt hair combed neatly
back. Pale white skin so translucent that he could see the
blue veins at Oort's temples. High cheekbones narrowing
to a pointed chin, and unique eyes. The interior of the irises
were ice blue, but haloed by a blue so dark that it seemed
almost purple. The surface expression was polite and a bit
aloof, but deeper there was a sweetness and a vulnerability
in those eyes, and Kenntnis wondered again at the career
choice.

"Officer Oort, pleased to meet you." Kenntnis rose from
behind his desk and extended his hand.

It was taken in a firm grip, the pale skin seeming even
whiter against the ebony of Kenntnis's skin, but very
quickly released, almost an avoidance of physical contact.
Kenntnis took note of those hands—long and slender with
tapering fingers ending in buffed and manicured nails. The
young man wore one piece of jewelry, an elaborate gold
signet ring on the little finger of the right hand. It looked
old.

"Thank you for coming on such short notice," Kenntnis
said.

"It appeared from my captain to be a request that I
couldn't refuse," came the soft reply. The words were iced
with an achingly monied East Coast accent.

"I have clout," Kenntnis said.

The blue-eyed gaze roved around the office, noting the
collection of glass in the lighted cabinet, and the eighteenth-
century French clock, and the Reynolds hanging over the
fireplace.

"Evidently." There was a dry edge to the words.

Kenntnis indicated the chair in front of his desk and Oort
sank down warily. Kenntnis came around and sat on the
edge of the desk in front of Oort. The wariness intensified
until the policeman had his back pressed against the chair.
They regarded each other. The hum of the computer, the

ticking of the antique clock, and the man's breath all seemed very loud.

"A few years ago I would have played the charade," Kenntnis began conversationally. "I would have set up a new company, formed a security force, wooed you with enough money so you would come to work for me—"

"You would have failed."

"Really?"

"I'm a police officer. I don't want any other career." There was something in the tone that made Kenntnis think this was part of a long-running discussion. Kenntnis wondered with whom?

"All right. Well, perhaps the work we do here would interest you."

The man's eyes narrowed. "Probably not. But make your case."

The response pleased Kenntnis. Not the annoying and meaningless *I don't understand,* or the nervous babble of a man off-balance.

"I need to give you a little lecture now. Please bear with me," Kenntnis said. He drew in a deep breath and mentally looked over what he needed to impart. It loomed vast and unwieldy, an ocean of information in the era of the sound bite and MTV.

"There's a war being fought, much older than the 'war on terrorism' or our current adventures worldwide, but tied to them in a dark and fundamental way. And I use that word, fundamental, quite deliberately, as you will see. This ancient war is being waged for the spirit of humanity. I don't use the word 'soul' because it's too loaded, too charged, and it's one of *their* words. If my side wins, mankind literally inherits the stars. If *they* win, gateways between universes will be fully opened again and the earth and all of her six billion inhabitants will enter a new Dark Age with all the attendant ignorance, superstition, suffering and death."

He stared into Oort's eyes trying to read the reaction, but there was nothing to read. The man hid his thoughts and emotions well and offered no encouragement.

"Our weapons are science, technology, rational thought," Kenntnis continued. "Their weapons are superstition, religion and . . . magic. You encountered a touch of it last night." Oort stirred in his chair. Kenntnis anticipated the question. "No, it's not common for it to be used so overtly or openly in this modern world. Which either means they are very close to opening the gates and allowing a flood of Old Ones back into the world, or there is a power-drunk child wielding the power. Neither of which is good news." Kenntnis paused to encourage comment or reaction. All he got were two words, thin and tight with tension.

"Go on."

"Let me explain a bit about magic. It bends and warps natural law, and that takes enormous power. Power as in will, not in the physics sense of mass and energy. The Old Ones and the humans who serve them feed on human emotion. The more powerful the emotion, the deeper they can reach into our minds. Dark and negative emotions are easier to evoke than joy. Humans are utterly unique in what brings them joy. There's nothing unique in how they experience grief, pain, fear and death.

"We're at a crossroad here, Richard," Kenntnis continued. "We're on the verge of sharing technology, medicine and science worldwide, and if that happens it will kill forever the chance for the magic to return. But there are forces at work, human and otherwise, who tell us that it's too much information, that there is some knowledge that man was not meant to know—the origins of the universe, for example, or genetic engineering. They argue that the exploration of these questions undermines our values.

"They can no longer argue that science is the work of the devil so they offer us bad science—global warming is natural, condoms don't prevent disease, birth control is a sin but destroying the environment through overpopulation isn't, homosexuality is sin rather than a naturally occurring trait, creation science and intelligent design rather than evolution and Big Bang theory. We're raising a generation of truculent devout dunces inhabiting the wealthiest country on earth, with the most powerful army on earth." Kenntnis was both enraged and depressed by the litany. "It's a recipe for disaster for us, and a banquet of death for our foes."

Long, slender hands clutched at the arms of the chair and the policeman was on his feet. He came to rest across the room from Kenntnis with his back to the fireplace. It was a retreat, but only a partial one.

"And what or who are these Old Ones when they're at home?" Oort asked.

"Every dark myth and monster you can think of." Kenntnis paused, then said it. "And *every* god you can name."

That got a reaction. Oort stiffened. *He's not making the mistake of thinking that I'm only talking about safe, ancient pagan gods.*

"I think you should know . . . I'm a person of faith."

Kenntnis hesitated, weighing what to say. "We can negotiate about that later."

The policeman advanced on Kenntnis. "It's not subject to negotiation."

"I think it might be when you understand a little better."

They were only inches apart. Blue eyes lifted to meet his. A whiff of aftershave reached Kenntnis, spicy and rich.

"What happened last night?" Oort demanded.

"Our opponents tried to kill a girl. And I owe you my thanks. The girl you saved is important to us."

"Stop assuming we're united in any way. What makes this girl so dangerous that someone would want to kill her? Aside from the fact she can make pennies light up and spin, and make sheets of flame?"

"You don't think that's enough?" asked Kenntnis, his sense of the absurd and ironic momentarily overcoming his good sense and very real worry.

He managed to offend his guest. Oort cloaked himself in dignity "Every tenet of my world has been thrown into question. I don't need flippant horseshit from you. So either answer my question, or I'm going home and get some sleep before I have to go back on shift."

"I'm sorry," Kenntnis said sincerely. "Sometimes you just have to see the absurd in all this or you'd lose your mind. Would you like some coffee?" Kenntnis asked, partly out of politeness and partly because he needed to marshal his thoughts.

"No, thank you. I don't drink coffee," came the reply.

Kenntnis regarded his guest quizzically. "You really are in the wrong business."

"So many people have said."

It was meant to be neutral, even lightly ironic, but Kenntnis heard the resentment just below the surface of the words. Kenntnis suspected it was not so many people as *one* particular person. He again wondered, who?

Leaving the desk, Kenntnis crossed to the south wall and opened the hidden cabinet doors on the polished slate. Tucked away in the cabinet was an elaborate espresso machine. The body was a gleaming iridescent red tricked out in brass. "I do drink coffee," Kenntnis tossed back over his shoulder to the policeman.

Oort joined him. A small smile played at the cop's mouth. "I'd venture that's an understatement. This looks like an altar."

Over the grinding beans Kenntnis asked, "So where was I?"

"Ms. Davinovitch."

Kenntnis poured the grounds into the portafilter and tamped them down with the weighted metal tamp. He screwed it into place, and set a tiny cup underneath. The espresso machine began to hiss like a disgruntled dragon as he pulled a shot.

"Ms. Davinovitch is a physics major at the university. She's also at that age where one searches for spiritual meaning. She fell in with a group promising enlightenment and a return of magic into the world. Given that some current physics theories sound like magic it probably wasn't a big step." The thick dark liquid ceased falling into the cup. Kenntnis placed a cube of raw sugar between his teeth and drew in a sip of coffee.

"My opponents trawl for people like this. Most are harmless, though they all add to the general silliness in the world, but some, like Rhiana, have real power to be tapped. Now I'm going to have to make some assumptions, at least until we talk to Ms. Davinovitch, but my guess is that Rhiana realized the real goal of this group—to construct a nuclear bomb—and she ran."

Kenntnis caught Oort by the wrist as he pulled out his cell phone. The bones were fragile beneath Kenntnis's fingers, and he could feel the man's pulse racing.

"What in God's name are you doing?" Richard demanded. "We've got to call . . ."

"The police?" Kenntnis interrupted. "I'm talking to them."

"I'm a beat cop. This needs to go way higher than me."

"Wait. Hear me out. At the moment we've pulled their fangs because we have Rhiana and they don't have fissionable material. She was their bang."

"I don't understand," Oort said.

"Rhiana possesses enormous magical aptitude. Properly fed and nurtured she would have the power to manipulate matter, but you play with that at your peril. Eventually there would have been a catastrophe. Of course Rhiana wouldn't have survived, but at that point hell truly would have been released because all the evidence would point to Islamic fundamentalists. Then equally evil Christian fundamentalists would cry for holy war, and it would begin. We have some time because it won't be easy for them to replace Rhiana, and meantime . . ." He paused, a calculated effect. "I have *you*."

It was as Kenntnis had expected. Oort was bright, aware of subtleties, and he hadn't missed the emphasis.

"And what am I?" The tone was low and wary. Whatever Kenntnis was going to say, the man was not anticipating it with any pleasure.

"A genetic freak, a human utterly devoid of magic."

Cross, out in the street, saw it coming. A silver-gray feather against the deep blue New Mexico sky. It arched toward the building. Birds blew skyward with a clapping of wings. There was no time to enter the building, take the elevator and issue the warning. Cross pulled a knife and plunged it into his palm. Blood streamed toward the sidewalk, but never hit. It dissolved into red swirls and vanished. Only then did Cross run for the side door of the building.

Kenntnis's words fell like a blow. Once again he had come up lacking. *You're a disappointment to the family . . . I get you a job and then you quit . . . A policeman? . . . Do you really think you've got the grit for this? You've been very sheltered. What a waste of education.* The big man sensed Richard's distress. His large hand was warm and heavy on his shoulder. "No. Lacking magic is a *good* thing. Almost unique."

Kenntnis broke off abruptly. Richard looked up and found the older man staring at his desk. The bowl of the ornamental fountain was steaming and the ceramic sides of the bowl flashed as swirling opalescent colors chased each other around the rim. Kenntnis flung himself at the desk. Richard was close behind. The water burbling from the pump hung frozen in space and the water in the bowl showed an image of the stone and glass exterior of the building in which they currently stood. It also showed something about to break like a gray wave over the building.

Kenntnis grabbed Richard by the shoulders and propelled him through the door of the office and into the waiting room. Rhiana sat on a chair nervously flipping through a magazine. Her eyes were unfocused. She was seeing nothing but the inside of her head.

"Take cover," Kenntnis snapped at the older woman behind the desk. Without question or panic she dropped beneath the desk.

Kenntnis swooped down on Rhiana, collected her under one long arm, and threw both Richard and Rhiana to the floor, covering them with his body. As the weight fell onto Richard, yammering panic filled his head. He began to struggle desperately and violently. Kenntnis grunted as a fist found flesh.

"Shit! Be still! This will be over. . . ."

The rest of the sentence vanished in the shattering explosion. Numbing silence filled his head. For an instant Richard feared he had gone deaf. Slowly sound penetrated. It consisted of frightened queries, sobs of pain and terror. Breath also returned as Kenntnis rolled away.

Richard heard Kenntnis order, "Call emergency services!"

Richard slowly pushed to his knees and then to his feet. He offered a hand to Rhiana. Once she was up Richard walked slowly to the office door. He pulled it open. The metal slats from the shutters lay like twisted silver crepe paper across the floor of the office. A few slats were embedded in the wood of the door along with splinters of glass from the windows. It looked like a madman's version of modern art. The upholstery on the sofa and desk chair was shredded and stuffing peeked pale and white through the rents. If he had been in the room he would have been flayed.

Richard became aware of Kenntnis at his side. He glanced up at the older man. "Thank you."

"De nada."

Richard glanced over at Rhiana. She stood with her back pressed defensively against a wall of the outer office. "Is this a continuation of the fun from last night?" Richard asked.

Kenntnis didn't really answer. "What are they planning that they're being so overt?" His frowning focus was turned inward. He gave himself a shake, a tectonic movement of those massive shoulders. "I need to see to my employees. Fortunately Cross got the warning to us in time. . . ." His voice trailed away.

"What do you want us to do?" Richard asked.

"Wait," Kenntnis threw back over his shoulder as he stepped onto the elevator.

Through the broken glass of the front doors Richard watched Kenntnis climb into the back of an ambulance with the receptionist from the ground floor. She was the most severely injured and he wanted to accompany her to the hospital. The polished granite top of the horseshoe-shaped desk was spattered with blood. Richard shivered and tried to blame it on the icy wind whistling through the broken doors. Light from the ambulance splashed across the stainless steel and black marble walls, and the wail of the siren faded as it drove swiftly away.

Glass littered the floor of the lobby and crunched underfoot as Rhiana joined him. She came so close that her arm pressed lightly against his shoulder. Exhaustion clogged

Richard's head, making his thoughts sluggish and disjointed. Though he longed to lie prone on one of the couches down in the main lobby there was work to be done. It was time he and the girl had a Come to Jesus conversation.

"So tell me about this bomb," Richard said.

Rhiana jerked back from him, but not too far. "B-bomb," she stuttered. She must have seen something in his face because as quickly as she started the pretense she dropped it.

"We were building it in a trailer down in South Valley. Josh put around that it was a meth lab so nobody bothered us."

Which says a lot about Albuquerque, thought Richard. "And you never thought to call the police?"

Rhiana trudged over to a couch and collapsed as if her body had lost its skeleton. "By the time I figured out that this wasn't your typical coven they had me locked up."

"Give me the address," Richard ordered. She did.

🙢

He should have called his lieutenant, taken backup, but he was a terrible liar, and he couldn't find a way to explain why an off-duty police officer should be interfering in the South Valley. Before heading out he pulled the shotgun out of the trunk and propped it against the passenger seat. He had started to roll out of the parking lot when the passenger door was yanked open and Rhiana jumped in.

"You are not leaving me."

Richard's peripheral vision caught a glimpse of the backdoor swinging open and a ragged figure jumping in. Richard slammed on the brakes and heard an aggrieved "Ow" from behind him. Looking around he stared into the dark eyes of the homeless man. He was nursing his nose with both hands.

"Excuse me!" The last pieces of Richard's patience frayed and snapped. "Get out of my car."

"You have to protect me."

"You might need my help."

His unwanted passengers said it in chorus.

"Look, this is not some f . . ." He bit back the profanity and swallowed hard. "Some game."

"You're wasting time," said Homeless.

And indeed, driving seemed more profitable than arguing.

Chapter

FOUR

They flew south on the freeway, the sun hanging red and swollen on the horizon. The barrel of the shotgun was cold and bumped uncomfortably against Rhiana's knee as they bounced over New Mexico's famously bad roads.

She had learned that the homeless man was called Cross. *Just Cross,* he'd said when the policeman pushed for more. She learned that every button on the radio was tuned to the classical station and that Oort wouldn't permit smoking in his car. The tape in the deck was a mystery novel.

She glanced over at the driver. Oort's skin was white and taut over his cheekbones and blue shadows hung beneath his eyes. She sensed she didn't look much better. They had only managed two hours of sleep.

She guided him past the two prisons, across the railroad tracks and down a narrow dirt road. Trailers sat on dusty one-acre plots. Often the area around the trailers was dotted with dead cars on blocks, broken washing machines and various kinds of farm equipment. Mixed breed dogs, most of them chained in front of peeling doghouses, sent up an ululating chorus as they bounced across the washboard surface of the road.

"If anybody's still there they sure know we're coming," remarked Cross from the backseat.

Oort's mouth tightened into a thin line, and his grip on the steering wheel turned his knuckles white. At first Rhiana thought he was angry at the homeless man. Then she realized he was scared. She sympathized. She had spent days afraid, locked in that trailer.

It loomed up ahead of them now, unique from its fellows in the total absence of yard clutter. She sagged with relief. It seemed that Josh and the others had decamped. Oort parked on the side of the road outside the drooping barbwire fence. Taking the shotgun, he climbed out. His hands opened and closed around the butt of the shotgun as he eyed the seemingly empty trailer. He then moved to the back of his car, opened the trunk and pulled out the bulletproof vest. Cross looked on approvingly.

"You're a cautious guy. That's good."

Oort stared at him for a moment, then shook his head and said, "Stay here with the car." He tossed his cell phone to Rhiana. "If something happens call for help."

"If something happens I'm going to run," she said.

"That's okay too. Just call at some point so maybe I can get some help," said Richard as he stripped off the overcoat and jacket and shrugged into the vest. He pulled his badge out of his coat pocket and clipped it onto his belt. He looked down at the ground for a moment and drew in a slow breath, as if he were trying to gather his nerve.

Rhiana and Cross watched as Oort made his way in quickly toward the trailer. He was careful to stay out of the line of sight from the windows and the front door. Cross started after him.

"Hey, wait," hissed Rhiana. "He said to stay here."

Cross looked back over his shoulder at her. "It's incredibly liberating when you can't be killed."

"Yeah, well, *I* can be killed."

"I think you'll be okay for a few minutes," came the comfortless reply.

Oort reached the side of the trailer. There were three steps leading up to the front door. Rhiana watched as Richard stood well off to the side of them, and stretched out an arm, but he was too short to reach the door. He reversed his hold on the shotgun, and pounded on the door with the wooden butt.

"Police! Open up!"

The only response was the door swinging open under the first blow, and the cop nearly losing his grip on the barrel of the shotgun at the unexpected removal of resistance.

Cross appeared in the doorway and peered down at Richard. "They've cleared out, but you've got to see what our resident sorceress has done. You've got some serious mojo, girl," the homeless man called out to Rhiana.

Embarrassed, she hustled over to join the men.

"I thought I told you to stay with the car," Richard said angrily.

"I ignored you," said Cross.

The blunt challenge seemed to fluster him. Richard opened and closed his mouth a few times, then said weakly, "Well, this is a potential crime scene so don't touch anything."

"Her fingerprints are probably all over the place," Cross pointed out. "And I don't have fingerprints."

"Of course you do. Everybody does," Richard said. Rhiana followed him up the stairs and into the trailer. "Unless you've burned them off with acid or something."

Cross thrust out his hand, palm up. Richard inspected the tips of his fingers while Rhiana peered over his shoulder. The palms were smooth but with an old scar in the center of one and a fresh wound on the other. The fingertips were as smooth as a mannequins. Richard didn't just drop the other man's hand. He threw it away, and took a couple of steps back.

He jerked his head toward Cross's hands. "Those are stigmata."

"This one is," said Cross, pointing at the old wound. "This one was me and a knife."

"What caused the other one?" Rhiana asked.

Cross laid a hand on his chest. "Look, kiddies, this is a construct. How it looks depends on what folks are focusing on. Fingerprints have never been a big part of the vision, but stigmata . . ." He gave a thumbs up. "Very big with the religious crowd." He sighed. "It's a drag."

"I don't understand," said Richard.

"Of course you don't, but this is a bad time for explanations," said Cross. "How about we save it until after we've looked for clues." He made quote marks in the air as he said the final word.

It seemed sensible so they searched. They found some cut electronics wire, and a soldering gun which had fallen behind the battered green couch in the living room. There was a stack of videotapes from Blockbuster next to the old fifteen-inch television and the VCR. There was food in the refrigerator and Richard pointed at the half-filled pot of coffee sitting on its stand in the maker. The group had forgotten to turn it off and the smell of scorched coffee hung in the air.

"They left in a hurry," said Richard as he turned off the coffee maker with the tip of a pen from his coat pocket.

They checked the first bedroom and found the bed rumpled and unmade, a few clothes in the closet and a suitcase fallen open on the floor. Shirts and pants hung like tongues over the sides of the open bag. The mirror over the dresser had a gray sheen instead of the twisting colors, but Rhiana jerked her gaze away, afraid it would draw *their* attention.

The second bedroom was much the same except that light was pouring in through the open bathroom door.

They stood in the doorway and stared at the back wall of the trailer. A portion of it had crumbled into fluffy ash. The portion that remained was crisscrossed with fine gray lines like a spider's web.

"Like I said—mojo," said Cross.

The blue eyes locked on her. "You did this?" Richard asked.

"I had to get out." There was the faint smell of an unpumped septic system overlaid with the tropical fruit smell of an overturned bottle of shampoo. It caught in the back of Rhiana's throat and her stomach heaved. She swallowed hard.

"What did you do?"

"I deconstructed the molecular structure."

"Could you do this to anything?" he pressed.

"With enough time and enough energy to draw on." Rhiana caught a glimpse of herself in the medicine cabinet mirror, distorted by the silvering of the mirror. Dark circles hung beneath her eyes and her hair trailed in rattails over her shoulders. She jerked her gaze away. *They might still be there.* She pulled her thoughts away from the mirrors and faced Richard. "Of . . . of course there's a size limit. I couldn't bring down a building. . . . At least I don't think so."

"Don't test it," said Richard. He led them back to the living room.

As they walked Cross asked, "How did you draw the power without them noticing?"

"Naomi and Alice were so scared they weren't noticing much," said Rhiana in an undertone. She didn't want the policeman to hear and realize that she'd tried to feed on him.

Richard pulled a Palm Pilot from his coat pocket and set it on the scratched end table. Next he removed a handkerchief from his pocket, picked up the phone receiver and with the tip of a pen dialed in *69. He listened, then hung up the phone and wrote a number in the Palm. He took a slow turn, carefully inspecting the living room. He squatted on his heels and inspected the rectangular impression in the bilious green carpet.

"We need evidence techs," he said. "And I need a plausible story to get them."

"Our employer will get you whatever you need," said Cross.

"*My* employer is the Albuquerque Police Department." He turned to Rhiana. "Give me the names of the people involved in this," he ordered.

"Josh Delay, Alice Rangold, Naomi Parsons and Dan Douglas." She followed the swift flourishes of the stylus.

"How did you all get together?" Richard asked.

"There was a notice in the Sub at UNM."

"So you were all students?"

"Me and Alice, Naomi and Dan were. I don't know about Josh. I'm not entirely certain that was his real name."

"Another reason we need evidence techs. It doesn't look like any of you were wearing gloves, and this place hasn't been wiped."

"Yeah, and I can't wait to see what your police techs are going to make of the magically disintegrated wall," said Cross. "You really ought to keep this in the family, so to speak." Rhiana could tell from Richard's expression that he hadn't considered this aspect. "Are you going to call the number?" Cross continued.

"No, I'm going to find out who it belongs to first."

There was an aggressive pounding on the front door and all of them jumped. "Hey!" a voice yelled from outside. "We told you to get the fuck out of here. What are you doing back?" The accent was the lilting cadence of a New Mexico Spanish speaker.

"I'm a police officer," Richard called. "Please open the door and show yourself."

The door swung open. Standing on the top step was a

smooth-faced young man with sleek black hair and deep
brown eyes. In one hand he held a statue of the Virgin of
Guadalupe and in the other a .357 magnum. In the dirt
yard behind him were a number of Hispanic males ranging
in age from the mid-teens to their seventies. They were all
armed.

"I'm going to show you my ID. Okay?" Richard said.

The young man nodded tense and tight. Richard
reached slowly down to his belt and unclipped his badge,
holding it up high so as many as possible could see it.

"It's okay, he's not one of them. He's a cop," the young
man called back to the crowd. They surged forward to the
foot of the steps.

"What happened here?" Richard asked.

The answers battered at them. *Strange lights. Weird
noises.* The oldest male moved forward, the others giving
before him with the lightest touch from his parchment-thin
hand.

"My grandfather used to go into the mountains and
wrestle demons. They were walking last night." The old
man stared at Rhiana with cataract-clouded eyes. "And I
saw La Llorona, the Weeping Lady, last night." Rhiana
shifted sideways until she stood behind Cross and Richard
and hoped she wouldn't be recognized.

Cross cast her a sardonic look, and muttered out of the
side of his mouth. "Hey, you've been upgraded from sorceress to demon."

"Shut up."

"So we came over this morning and told the *brujos* to
get out," said the young man.

"So they left because of your request?" Richard asked.

"No, sir, they were already packing. We just didn't let
them finish."

Two spots of color blossomed in Richard's cheeks.
"Then you saw what they were driving?"

"Oh yeah, couple of minivans."

"Brand new," offered a heavyset man.

"All tricked out too," said a teenager enviously.

Out came the Palm and within minutes Richard had detailed descriptions of both vans, including the temporary tags.

"Look, we need to make sure this place is secure and nothing gets touched." The policeman gave the neighbors a sweet and sincere smile. "But there's this big hole in the back wall, so I was wondering if you would keep an eye on things until I can get some evidence techs out here."

"Like those guys on those *CSI* shows," said the young man with the shotgun.

"Exactly like that."

"Cool. Yeah, we'll watch it."

"We wouldn't touch anything anyway," said the old man with a warning frown to the assembly. "Get yourself cursed."

"Great. Thanks so much." Richard checked his watch. "We've got to go."

They piled back into the Volvo. "Can you drop me back at the office?" Cross asked as they pulled back onto paved road and headed for the freeway.

"Sure."

"What about me?" Rhiana asked.

"I don't know. Taking you to work with me would be tough," said Richard with a frown between his pale brows.

"You can stay with us," said Cross.

"Forgive me, but whatever else you might be, right now you seem to be a homeless bum, and your boss is . . . well, I don't know what he is, and somebody attacked the building. . . ."

"I think they were gunning for him." Cross jerked his head toward Richard. "Not you."

"Me!? Why?" the cop blurted, and he had gone even whiter if that was possible.

"Look, both of you should just relax. You're with me and Kenntnis now, and we're the pros from Dover," said Cross.

"Pros at what?" Richard asked. "What does Kenntnis do?"

"Controls one of the great fortunes of the world. He endows universities, funds scientific research, supports Doctors without Borders, finances politicians, puts computers in grade schools, donates money to the United Nations Fund for Population Activities. . . . How long do you want me to go on?"

Richard glanced back over his shoulder at the homeless man. "Until you get to the point. He does all these things, but what's the ultimate goal?"

"They're not worthy in and of themselves?"

"Of course they are, but no one does this without an agenda. He seems to be asking me to join in, but I don't sign on until I know what's behind the curtain."

They were driving north on the freeway and making good time. The tires thrummed on the asphalt and the headlights formed a necklace of light stretching south. Ahead of them taillights glowed red.

"We should wait for Kenntnis. He can explain this better than I can," hedged Cross.

"Why are you with him?" asked Rhiana.

"Because I want to die," he said simply.

Rhiana's neck jerked as Richard abruptly braked the car, and looked back at the other man.

"You told me you couldn't be killed," she accused.

"Yes, which is why the dying part is hard."

"Explain, please," said Richard. Each word was very, very carefully enunciated as the policeman hung onto the ragged edge of control.

"Okay, but you're going to need a history lesson, and it goes back thousands and thousands of years."

It wasn't like him; the ostentatious lifting of the arm, shaking back the cuff and looking at the watch face, but Richard was nearing the end of his frayed and exhausted patience. "Can we do this in the next twenty minutes? Or can we have the CliffsNotes?" Richard asked sweetly.

"Okay, asshole," said Cross. "Riding in the backseat of your car is Jesus Christ." He jammed a dirty forefinger against his chest and gave them a smirking grin.

Rhiana slid her gaze to the left and met Richard's eyes. He suspected that his expression was mirrored on her face. She pressed her lips together, but a bubble of laughter escaped. It broke the policeman's control and then they were both whooping with laughter.

For Richard it was the release of almost twenty-four hours of confusion and tension. The curtain had been pulled back and the Great and Powerful Oz had been revealed to be a poor deluded head case. The world began to settle back into normal patterns. Somewhere there were logical explanations for the earlier events, and like the homeless man they would be found and understood.

A new sound cut like a bass continuo through their laughter. Guttural gasps were coming from the backseat. Neck muscles twanging, Richard snapped his head around. Cross was arched as if he was trying to touch his feet with the back of his head. Blood suffused his face, turning it almost black. Foam speckled his lips. Richard jerked the wheel and with a squealing of tires sent them careening across three lanes of traffic. Horns blared. It was too dark to see the fingers being thrown, but he could imagine. They came to a halt on the shoulder. Richard tossed his cell phone to Rhiana.

"Call nine one one," he ordered as he jumped out.

He had the back door open and pulled Cross out of the car and laid him down on the cold pavement. The seizures were continuing. Richard laid his head on Cross's chest. He wasn't breathing. The man's neck was so rigid Richard had to struggle to position Cross's head for CPR. Richard feared the teeth were too tightly clenched to open and that proved to be the case. As he pinched the hinge of the jaws, trying to force them open, a weird witch light rose like fog from the man's body. Richard's eardrums suddenly hurt as if pressure had suddenly been lost in an airplane's cabin. He realized the cause was a sound at the upper limit of human hearing, but powerful enough to be felt.

Cross's body began to shake; then there was the disorienting vision of multiple faces strobing across the core face. It was like watching an animation artist riffle pages of a drawing, causing it to flicker and dance. The sound became unbearable. Richard clapped his hands over his ears and fell back. From the corner of his eye he could see Rhiana doubled over in pain, the cell phone falling from her nerveless fingers.

Cross's body flew into multiple figures. Transparent images of myriad men flew in all directions and then shot away, becoming streaks of light. Richard stared at the empty pavement where moments before a man . . . no, where *something* had lain.

Richard looked over at Rhiana, who was also staring at the ground. A shivering settled into the pit of his stomach. "Do you have any idea what the hell just happened?" he asked with elaborate care.

Wordlessly she shook her head.

Chapter

FIVE

They stood before him, looking like Hansel and Gretel when they discovered the birds had eaten the bread crumbs. Their hands were almost touching. Kenntnis suspected that if he growled they'd be holding hands.

The building echoed to the sounds of hammering and power saws as contractors began the repairs. "Let's go in the conference room," Kenntnis shouted over the din. The door fell shut behind them and the sound abruptly cut off.

A wave of his hand over the wall switch brought up the lights and started the ornamental fountain on the stone bar at the far end of the room. Richard and Rhiana looked like they could use some relaxation. Kenntnis settled into the large chair at the far end of the hexagonal table. He waved the couple toward chairs. They didn't take him up on the implied invitation.

"So what's up?" But the man and girl didn't move. Instead they exchanged glances. Each seemed to be urging the other to speak. The silence dragged.

Finally Rhiana blurted out, "We broke your homeless guy."

"Or lost him," Richard added. "Or both."

They both looked absurdly young and so painfully tired and confused that Kenntnis realized they couldn't handle a full explanation.

"Look, you didn't do anything. He'll be all right and he'll make his way back to us over the next few days." It was a calculated risk. As long as Cross was splintered there was a chance that one of the less benign fractals would make its way to Richard, but Kenntnis feared if a full understanding of Cross was presented he'd lose the policeman. And he needed him.

"What happened to him?" Richard asked.

"He was attacked. He'll recover. He's tougher than he looks."

Rhiana swayed and caught herself by pressing a hand on the table. Richard's arm went around her waist to steady her, but he didn't look much better. His cheekbones were prominent blades and his eyes had sunk into hollows.

Kenntnis stood and came toward them. "Look, I have a private suite in the building. Why don't you both get some rest?"

"I have to get to work. I'm going to be late as it is," said Richard.

Kenntnis waved a calming hand at Richard. "I've

gotten you out of work, and you're handling the investigation."

"What investigation?" the policeman asked.

"The attack on my building. I'm trying to keep anyone from categorizing it as a terrorist attack. We've got quite enough hysteria on that front without me adding to the din. Now, where have you been?"

"We went to check out the trailer," Rhiana answered.

"What did you learn?" Kenntnis asked, looking to Richard.

"Well, for starters the people in the trailer are gone. I've got a good description of the vehicles they left in, and partial information on the temporary tags. We've got the neighbors watching the trailer, but we need evidence techs."

"So order them."

"I'm a beat cop."

"Oh, sorry, forgot to mention it—you've been promoted to detective." Kenntnis was surprised to see dismay wash across Richard's face.

"Oh, great, I'm going to be even more popular now," Richard said very quietly.

"You want me to have them take it back?" Kenntnis asked.

"No . . . no. . . . I just wanted to earn it."

"You were going to get there. It just happened a little faster than normal. So what are you going to do?"

"We have to give some explanation for what hit your building. Whether you like it or not I'm going to call it a bomb, call the people in the trailer suspects, and issue a four-state bolo. Since none of them are even remotely of Middle Eastern descent we should be able to avoid the kind of hysteria you're worried about."

"Sounds good," said Kenntnis. He stood. "Why don't you get that in motion and then get some rest? We won't know anything for several hours."

"I'll go with you," Rhiana said to Richard.

Exhaustion was probably the cause, but Oort's patience snapped. "Am I stuck with you for life?" he demanded. Rhiana shrank in on herself. The policeman didn't miss it. "I'm sorry, but I need some time to myself. Some time to think."

Kenntnis moved to Rhiana's side and laid a gentling hand on her shoulder. "You're magically opaque when you're with him, but you need to learn to do it on your own. He can't always be with you, and he might die." Now it was Richard's turn to shrink back. "Let me teach you."

Rhiana sagged as if the slight pressure from his hand had leeched all the strength from her.

"You'll keep her safe?" Richard demanded.

"I swear it."

❦

Richard had forgotten to turn on any lights when they'd left at 2:30 that afternoon. He felt foolish, but he drew his service pistol as he opened the door. Light flared in the living room as he hit the switch. The apartment was empty and serene. After locking the door behind him he swung through the kitchen for a glass of milk and a handful of crackers. He had the sensation he was having to search for the floor with his feet, a symptom of exhaustion, but nonetheless disconcerting.

He had ordered the bolo and sent criminalistics to the South Valley while he drove home. He kept waiting for someone to shout "Fraud!," but his requests had been met without comment.

He stood numbly in the center off the living room trying to decide what to do. Television? He shuddered when he contemplated the noise. A book? He was pretty sure that nothing would penetrate the fog wrapped around his brain. Music? He looked from the collection of CDs to the piano.

The piano won. But what to play? Chopin required too much emotion. Right now he needed to try and think. The mathematical perfection of Bach was the best choice. The resistance of the keys against the pads of his fingers helped ground him back in his body. The body of the big Bösendorfer amplified the hammer strikes against the wires and the sound seemed to struggle against the confines of the small room.

Guiltily he checked his watch, but it was only a little after 8:00 p.m. No one would object. He ate a few crackers, took a sip of milk, and resumed the sonata. The mistakes gave him an opportunity to pause and eat. Eventually, though, the mistakes became too irritating. He knew they were happening because he was tired, but the music was no longer soothing. If he couldn't play any better than this he needed to stop.

Richard took the gun with him into the bedroom. He made certain no round was chambered and he placed the gun on the bedside table away from the side of the bed on which he slept. It might be an urban legend, the story of the man who'd picked up his pistol instead of the phone and blown his ear off, but he didn't want to test the possibility.

Switching off the light, he laid his head against the Tempur-Pedic pillow and waited for the heat from his body to soften the foam. It wrapped softly around his neck and shoulders. He was falling headlong toward sleep. He blinked, holding it at bay. If ever there was a night for devotions this was one. He began the Lord's Prayer, but he kept seeing Cross's face reflected in the rearview mirror and hearing Kenntnis say *"and every god you can name."*

He fell asleep before he reached the end of the prayer.

Rhiana looked about curiously. Kenntnis's living quarters occupied the entire top floor of the seven-story building. Windows to the east looked out on the bleak and rugged face of the Sandia Mountains. Monstrous boulders humped just beyond the wide glass windows like the shoulders of long-buried leviathans. They were close enough to touch if one were to lean out the window. She turned away from the forbidding view to the splendor of the living room.

A fire burned in a central glass fireplace. Comfortable furniture with butter-like leather upholstery clustered about the crackling warmth. The thick beige carpet caressed and cushioned her feet. Wafer-thin speakers suspended near the ceiling filled the room with low music. A Celtic harp rested near the bookcases on one wall. She thought she'd heard the strings give a soft musical sigh when she and Kenntnis entered. Pictures filled every available area of the remaining walls. She had the uncomfortable feeling that she had seen some of the paintings in art books. On the polished tabletops were more objets d'art—curved knives from the Middle East, a tiny carved marble statuette of a horse and rider that looked Greek, Lalique glass—it was an overwhelming display.

As had happened at Richard's apartment, Rhiana suddenly had the discomforting sense of standing in two places at once, for her mind's eye had overlaid the living room of her family's home in Van Nuys. There were no bookcases, no art, just one wall dominated by a big-screen TV that they couldn't really afford, the stuffing protruding from the arms of the sofa sleeper where the dogs had chewed off the upholstery, the smell of cooking grease and an overflowing garbage can.

She felt ashamed and awkward so she glared at Kenntnis when he bustled in. The harp strings sighed again. He checked in the doorway.

"What?"

"Nothing," Rhiana snapped. Then, unable to help herself, she added, "How much money do you people have?"

"A lot," came the uninformative reply. "Are you ready to learn some control?"

"Will it keep me safe?"

"That's the goal," said Kenntnis. He beckoned her over to the sofa. Rhiana sat down warily at one end. Kenntnis sat at the other. "Cross says you're a lighthouse, a veritable flare of magic energy."

"Is that unusual?" Rhiana asked.

"Yes. Almost all humans have a touch of magic. I think it was laid down in your genes by the Old Ones so they could always keep a foothold in this dimension, but you have an extraordinary amount of it. Fortunately you also have a scientific aptitude." Kenntnis frowned. "Which is also pretty unusual, but it will help us now so we'll worry about the why later."

"Why do you rely so much on Cross?" Rhiana asked. "You seem to be the big shot around here."

"Cross can see magic before the spell is actually unleashed. I can't."

"But you fight it?"

He smiled at her. It enfolded her, warm and affectionate. "Yes."

"So you must really dislike me."

"You can't help what you are, and you could be very useful to us if you were willing to help. That's why I sent Cross out after you the other night."

"So you'd use magic to fight magic?"

"I'll use anything." He clapped his hands suddenly together. "So, let's get you protected. Do you read music?"

"No."

"Hmm, that's too bad. Breaking a song down to its mathematical components is an easy way to do this."

Rhiana moved to a table and inspected the collection of small stone jars. They looked Egyptian. "I don't really like music." She turned back to find Kenntnis regarding her quizically. "What?"

"That's a trait of the Old Ones. Interesting."

It felt like criticism. Rhiana felt herself flush. "Look, could you give me the big outline on how this works?"

"Oh, yeah, sorry, that might help. Emotion is the tool of magic. Tamp it down and you start to blind them. Go to the most rational and logical of the sciences. . . ."

"Math," Rhiana said.

"Right, and you disappear. None of their spells can locate you."

"But they can still see me?"

"Oh, yes. Light enters through the pupil, strikes the retina, travels down the optic nerve to the brain, and voilà, sight. The natural laws of the universe continue to function."

"So I just keep a mathematical formula running through my mind?"

"Exactly. At first it will be a strain, but eventually you'll have it running subconsciously. And we'll keep a little Bach playing, just to help you along."

Rhiana stood up and stepped closer to the glassed-in fireplace. She rubbed her hands together, hearing the rasp of chapped skin. "Could I actually become invisible?"

"Average people wouldn't be able to see you, but the folks who want to kill you would spot you in a heartbeat. It would also take a tremendous amount of energy, and while you're under my protection you don't get to feed."

"If you want me to do magic I've got to draw power from somewhere."

"Use yourself."

"I had to do that Saturday night. It sucked."

"Tough. That's the deal. Take it and be safe with me. Leave it and go out there and face them alone." The callousness of the reply left Rhiana breathless. "You tried to use Richard, didn't you?"

Rhiana swallowed hard, then forced herself to face him. "Yeah, but I couldn't get anything. He was really scared. It should have worked."

"He's an Empty One. He can't be used in that way. But I reiterate, no feeding."

The confidence with which the order was issued pissed her off. Rhiana set her hands on her hips and glared at Kenntnis.

"And if I do?"

"The world can do with a little less magic."

She had to force herself not to retreat. "So, you'd kill me." She shook her head, disgusted. "I thought you were supposed to be the fucking good guy."

"First, I never said anything about killing you, but there is a way to prevent someone from using magic and I won't hesitate to use it if it becomes necessary." He paused and stared intently at her. "And I am the fucking good guy."

Rhiana turned away petulantly and gave him her shoulder. "Yeah, right."

His hand on her shoulder was gentle. "Rhiana, you've touched what waits on the other side of the barrier. They want them in this world. I don't. Doesn't that make me the good guy?"

Rhiana remembered the coiling and nauseating colors that filled every reflective surface in the trailer and the way they had sometimes coalesced into terrifying and horrifying faces. Shudders shook her and Kenntnis was at her side holding her comfortingly close.

"I'm sorry. I'm putting too much pressure on you. Today just let me teach you how to stay safe. Later we'll talk about the future."

"Hey, Oort, the captain wants to see you," the desk sergeant said as Richard arrived at APD headquarters that morning. He stared curiously at him as Richard signed in.

"Okay. What about?"

"Probably your promotion," and there was no hiding the jealousy and resentment edging the words.

Richard ducked his head and walked into the squad room. Conversations stopped, then resumed and the looks seemed to strike against his skin. He was a beat cop. He'd been in the captain's office once—when he had been welcomed onto the force. He forced himself to walk briskly to the frosted-glass door. Then his nerve failed and he tapped tentatively on the glass beneath the stenciled name.

"Come in," Captain Ortiz called through the door. Richard entered and closed the door behind him, to the disappointment of the watchers in the squad room.

"So, congratulations are in order, Richard," said Ortiz. He was a burly man in his late forties with gray-streaked black hair and a conquistador's spade beard and mustache.

"I guess, sir," Richard stammered and felt himself blushing.

"So, somebody pulled a string. You're not the first and you won't be the last. And you've done your three years, you've taken the exam. You're eligible for detective." The captain slid a gold badge across the desk to Richard. "We found a desk for you." Ortiz stood and held out his hand. Richard shook it. "And hang the uniform in the closet. You're only going to need it now for funerals and disasters."

It was the opportunity to mention the bomb, but Kenntnis had said it wasn't really a nuclear bomb. It could only go nuclear by the use of Rhiana's magical powers. Richard decided to wait until he heard back from the evidence techs he had dispatched. If they found evidence of radiation. . . . *But geiger counters aren't normally part of an evidence kit*, intruded an uncomfortable and unpleasant thought. *Or maybe they were after 9/11*. He didn't know. He'd need to find out.

Richard and the captain stepped back into the squad room. The ringing of phones and the pecking of computer keyboards, the smell of cheap coffee and equally cheap aftershave assailed his senses. This was the real world. How did he tell his captain that a sorceress/witch had been tapped to turn an ordinary run-of-the-mill bomb into a radiological disaster? Answer: He didn't.

A desk had been squeezed into the area designated for plain clothes. It was easily recognizable as his because of the surface, naked except for a telephone. The other detectives' desks sported computers and coffee cups and stacks of paper and folders. A few of the detectives nodded to him. Most didn't. Richard wondered how many people had been passed over for him to get this promotion. He realized he had set his teeth and a sharp twinge between the shoulder blades reminded him he had braced. He shook off the tension, both physical and emotional. He pushed back the night stick, and heard the cuffs rattle as he sat down. It was going to be strange not to have the weight of the belt, stick, holster and pistol, and cuffs hanging at his waist. He realized he would need to buy a shoulder holster. Or was that too James Bond? Maybe it would be better to stick with a belt holster? But he had the start of arthritis in his hips from years of gymnastics, and it would be nice not to have the dragging weight of a pistol on his hip.

Stop accessorizing, he ordered, and pulled himself up to the desk.

The casters on the chair rattled over the uneven linoleum. Lieutenant Weber was on the telephone. He looked up and lifted a hand to Richard. Dale Snyder, who was closing in on twenty years, glared and turned his back.

Richard's stomach tightened at the blatant rejection. *I'll work hard. I'll win their acceptance.*

"What's up?" Richard quietly asked Joe Torres, a heavy jowled Hispanic whose five o'clock shadow appeared at eight a.m.

"Guy got cranked on his own product. Shot the six friends he was partying with, his wife and two kids, then decided he could fly. Took a header off an overpass and splattered himself all over Tramway Boulevard. Not exactly heavy lifting on this one. Just a shitload of paperwork," Torres grunted and turned away.

Richard went to work. A call quickly established that there was as yet no response to his four-state bolo. Pulling out his Palm he checked the number he'd obtained at the trailer against an Internet database. It belonged to a pay phone in Detroit. That was way outside his jurisdiction. A call to criminalistics earned him a sharp rebuke to the effect that they had only finished processing the trailer at 3:00 a.m. and tests took time to run.

He drummed his fingers on his desk until an exasperated *Shut up* from Snyder sent him in search of notepads and pens. He drew a line down the center of a sheet of yellow legal paper. One one side he wrote "Cops." On the other he wrote "Magic." Or started to. He glanced left and right and crossed through the three letters he'd written. Underneath he wrote "Imponderables."

Under Imponderables he wrote: *What is Cross? Who is Kenntnis? Can Rhiana be controlled? Where do her loyalties lie? Where do mine lie?* Irritated, he drew an X through the notes and turned to the other half of the page. And then he knew what to do. He had the make on the vans. He knew they were new. He knew they had been purchased yesterday. He grabbed the phone and called the Honda dealership.

Chapter

SIX

Yeah, I remember them. Church group," said the young salesman at Garcia Honda. He was a lean young Hispanic in a slightly shiny suit indicating long wear and insufficient funds to replace it. They stood in the glass-walled showroom surrounded by automobiles. The indulgent scent of new car filled the air.

The information that there was a religious connection was unwelcome to Richard. "Are you sure about that?"

"Well, they said they needed the vans to take folks up to a Bible study retreat in Colorado at a sister church in C. Springs."

"Do you still have the check or has it been posted?"

"They paid cash."

"Isn't that a little unusual?" Richard asked.

"Yes and no. You know churches. Some are swimming in cash. Others scraping along asking for donated junkers. This was one of those fundamentalist groups. They seem to swim. Me, I'm Catholic. The church is rich, the parishes poor."

"Is there anything else you can tell me?"

"They were gringos, no offense."

"None taken. Accents?" Richard suggested.

"Kind of Texan," said the young man. He frowned and worried at his lower lip with his teeth. "They bought three car seats from us. That was a little strange; normally people have their own if they've got kids."

Richard now understood why he hadn't gotten a response to his bolo. He thanked the salesman and went outside and stood beneath the brilliant and famous New Mexico turquoise sky. He pulled out his cell phone and called the Colorado State Police. It was as he had feared.

The Staties had stopped the vans just outside Colorado Springs, and learned they were with the Faith in the Rock Church on their way to a retreat. Seeing two men and four women with attendant toddlers rather than the two men and two women described in Richard's bolo, they had sent them on their way. It had been the perfect cover.

He assumed it was a made-up church, but just to be certain he went back into the dealership and asked for the Yellow Pages. He then stared in disbelief at the listing for Faith in the Rock. There was a quarter-page picture ad with a smiling pastor in front of a utilitarian building adorned with a cross. More shocking was the small notice at the bottom of the ad that the church was affiliated with the World Wide Christian Alliance.

Richard's family was active in charitable work so they had crossed paths with the WWCA. Because of the Oorts' Washington connections they had even met its founder, Mark Grenier. Richard tried to recall what he could of the man.

Grenier had risen to public prominence some fifteen years back when one of his parishioners had become president. Grenier had become the presidential spiritual adviser, displacing the Graham family. He had actively and agressively pursued the title of the "Face of American Christianity" in the press. Grenier led worldwide crusades bringing the Word of God to millions, and funneled millions to conservative causes. Though they were devout, the Oorts were a liberal family, which put them at odds with the fundamentalism currently sweeping the country. Richard was well aware of Grenier's efforts to stop funding for stem-cell research and how WWCA lobbied against various pure science projects like the super-collider.

And now an affiliated church in Albuquerque had knowingly or unknowingly transported a bomb to a sister church in Colorado Springs.

It seemed to support the view of reality described by Kenntnis, and Richard didn't like that reality at all.

There was a call from criminalistics when Richard got back to the office. They had some preliminary findings. He went down to the lab. It was next door to the morgue and the scent of formaldehyde and dead flesh came out of the heating vents. During the walk Richard had realized he was hungry. The smells in the lab took care of that.

Since he'd been a beat cop he hadn't had any occasion to deal with the chief coroner, but he had heard the stories. He found Angela Armandariz in her office. It was a temple to paper, both bound and unbound. Books crammed the utilitarian metal shelves, files formed stalagmites rising from the cracked linoleum floor and towers on the desk. Single sheets of paper fluttered like the wings of dismayed birds as Richard pushed the door open. Armandariz flipped the pages of a report with one hand while with the other she wielded chopsticks shoveling lo mein into her mouth. The noodles hung briefly over her chin like a walrus's mustache, then were quickly sucked into the bud-like mouth with a loud slurp. It was amazing that such a tiny person could produce such an amount of noise.

Richard stared down at the elfin figure curled in the big office chair. Armandariz glared up at him from beneath dark brown bangs, and defiantly sucked in another mouthful of noodles. "What?" she demanded. She had a cute round face, rich cocoa-colored skin, the cheeks tinged with russet, and deep brown eyes.

"I had a message. You had some results for me."

"And who the fuck are you?" The voice drilled out.

"Oort."

"Any relation to the astronomer?" she asked.

Richard was surprised. Most people just reacted to his unusual name, never connecting it to the Dutch astronomer who had discovered the cometary cloud at the outermost edges of the solar system.

"Some kind of distant relation. My family's been in the country awhile."

"I'd bet a long while based on that candy-ass accent you've got." She pushed aside the noodles and opened a file in front of her. He caught a brief glimpse of a photograph of the disintegrated trailer wall, and packets containing ash, tufts of the stained green carpet, the trimmed wires, and other less identifiable substances and objects.

"Okay, so we found definite traces of C4 in the joint. The glass in all the mirrors had been silvered. Don't know what caused that." She raised her dark gaze to meet his and spun the photo of the trailer's back wall across the tops of several files. He caught it before it launched itself off the desk. "And I have no fucking clue what did that. Despite the ash there's no trace of heat damage. No explosive residue. The wall just fell down. That help?"

"Not particularly. Did you find any matches on the prints?"

"One young woman, Naomi Parsons, took the LSATs. Not your usual profile for a mad bomber."

"I think most of them were students," Richard said.

"Then I'd go talk to UNM," Armandariz suggested.

"Oh, right, duh." Richard could feel the blush.

The criminologist suddenly grinned, revealing the thin line of a retainer. "Promoted today, I hear."

"Yeah, looks like I have a big learning curve."

"Bigger than you think, Dutch. My team didn't have a warrant." Sudden nausea filled the back of Richard's throat. Some of the shame and guilt must have shown on his face because Armandariz's expression softened. "I caught it last night, and we found Judge Blackman and got the paper."

"Oh, God, thank you."

"You're welcome, but now you owe me." It was more than just a simple remark, significance rode on every word.

"Okay, and what's the payment?"

"If you find out what took down that wall, let me know. It isn't often I come across something new, interesting and puzzling."

⚕

By the time Richard finished at UNM it was pushing four-thirty. It had been a productive few hours. He had addresses for Alice Rangold, Naomi Parsons and Dan Douglas and, having learned his lesson, he had requested that APD's judicial liaison make the request for search warrants. He had family contact information and he had a list of their classes. Of Josh Delay there was no record. He had put in a call to Social Security, but it would be tomorrow before he learned if Delay had a number.

He sat on the edge of the dry fountain in the quadrangle between Popejoy Hall and Johnson Gym, and the brick was chill through the fabric of his pants. Brown brick and flagstone set in patterns swept away to meet the brown stucco walls of the buildings. After three years in New Mex-ico, he was beginning to appreciate adobe architecture, but UNM's faux-adobe style didn't really work. In fact he thought many of the buildings looked like dirt clods dropped randomly across the campus.

Reviewing his notes he noticed that the two girls had been in a comparative religion class together. Richard decided to see if the professor was in his office. As the sun set, the cold intensified. He decided to cut through the music building and get out of the cold. The New Mexico Symphony performed in Popejoy so he knew the building well.

He turned down a hall leading away from the concert halls. He was walking past practice rooms, and since the soundproofing wasn't very good he moved in and out of pockets of muted music. Violin, piano, and then a soaring baritone voice practicing the death aria from *Don Carlos*. Grief tightened his chest and he leaned back against a wall.

If he'd had more courage maybe he could have resisted the familial demand that he amount to something and this would have been his life. For an instant Richard was back in Professor Zanetti's office in Rome, lost in the music and the caress of the keys beneath his fingers and the stretch of the muscles across the back of his hands as he reached for the chords. He had been a good singer, but an exceptional pianist, and standing in the dim hallway of a second-rate university music department he suddenly realized why. He had felt safe behind the barricade of the piano. When he sang there was nothing between him and the world. Richard turned that revelation, studying it from every angle, and wondered if it would have made a difference in his singing if he'd come to that understanding earlier. A sharp head shake dislodged the regrets. He had chosen his course.

⚜

Professor Bernard was a spare, ascetic-looking man with shoulder-length brown hair and deep brown eyes. A jutting blade of a nose divided the face. Deep lines cut on either side of his mouth. Richard thought they suggested a life lived in pain, and then noticed the metal crutches propped against a filing cabinet. The office was the size of a large walk-in closet and the walls lined with bookcases and books gave the sense they were teetering and about to fall inwards under the weight of paper and binding.

"This is rather eccentric," Bernard said as he studied Richard's uniform. The voice was dark velvet so warm and rich that it left the listener feeling breathless. Richard dropped his gaze from those amazing brown eyes. "Am I in trouble?"

"No, sir, I just wanted to ask you about a couple of your students. Naomi Parsons and Alice Rangold."

Bernard closed his eyes briefly and his brow furrowed. "Oh yes, Tuesdays and Thursdays 9:00 to 10:30 a.m. They haven't been in class for the past two weeks."

"Any idea why?" Richard asked.

"They're big kids. I let them make their own choices and mistakes."

"Could you give me a sense of them?"

"Desperate to have meaning," the professor replied dryly.

"How is that different from anyone?" Richard asked with equal dryness.

Bernard blinked several times and then seemed to actually focus on Richard. "You're an odd sort of policeman. I rather thought you would say *huh*."

"And you're making assumptions based on intellectual superiority and stereotypes," Richard said gently.

"Fair enough, officer. My impression is that Ms. Parsons and Ms. Rangold came into my class seeking answers and a support for faith, but faith shouldn't require either support or proof. If it did then it wouldn't be faith, would it? They didn't like the fact that my course deconstructs religions, shows the fundamental similarities and traces how religions change based on human and societal development."

"The idea that man creates God in his own image?" Richard asked.

"In a nutshell, yes."

"So I take it they didn't find meaning from you?"

"No, but they found it somewhere. The last few times they were in class they were positively argumentative and they had the air of people who shared a great big secret that put them well up on everyone else."

"Can you be more specific?"

Bernard looked thoughtfully off into space for a moment, then nodded. "We were discussing Abraham and Isaac. They argued that rather than being a testament to faith on Abraham's part or an example of mankind moving away from the idea of a capricious, bloodthirsty god, this was an example of a man shying away from true understanding and great power because he couldn't make the hard choice. Alice said that sometimes sacrifice was necessary if humanity was going to take the next evolutionary step. I confess to being rather sarcastic. I pointed out that she might not feel so sanguine about human sacrifice if she were the sacrificee rather than the sacrificor. They walked out in a huff." Bernard's eyes darkened. "I remember they stopped at the doors, looked back at me, and laughed. At the time I was annoyed. In retrospect I realize it was all rather threatening."

"And you don't know the root of this?"

"No, sorry."

❦

Lean Cuisine hefted light in the hand as if the contents of the package were as cardboard as the box. Richard hooked open the crisper drawer of the refrigerator with the toe of his shoe. Fresh bok choy, peppers and ginger flashed color and guilt at him. He would cook. While the microwave hummed, defrosting chicken, he slowly chopped up the vegetables. He was glad he was making the effort; it was helping with the memory of his last phone call before leaving work that evening.

Emma Parsons's valiant effort to mask terror and desperation under a bright insouciance had been heartbreaking. No, she hadn't known where her daughter was right now, but *you know young people. You've got to give them the opportunity to try their wings even if they fall and bump their noses.*

She described Naomi as passionate and spiritual, always seeking the hidden meaning. According to her mother,

Naomi was dissatisfied with what she called the sterility of the Presbyterian Church. She had opted for a more fundamentalist church. Richard hadn't been surprised to hear it was Faith in the Rock. Emma told Richard that three months ago her daughter had told her that she had been one of the select few to attend a retreat where many of her questions had been answered. She was evasive about just what those answers had been, and began to drift away from her mother. But Emma wasn't worried. It was perfectly natural. Then had come the question and the fear had shown through.

"Do you know where my daughter is? Is she all right?" And Richard hadn't had an answer for either question.

He splashed sesame oil into the wok and set it to heating while he went to the bedroom to change. There was a sharp pang of regret and fear as he hung up the uniform. Truth was he was finding his first day as a detective harder and more emotionally draining than fantasy had made it. As a beat cop he issued tickets, responded to wrecks, bar fights, domestic disturbances. Upsetting, sometimes sickening, but he rarely dealt with the collateral damage caused by the fight or the wreck. Now he was searching for three lost children, and their parents' desperation was like a physical blow.

He set his pistol on top of the dresser, dressed quickly, and returned to the kitchen. Passion, rage and fear had driven him into police work. Because it was so much more than a job he needed it to be pure, almost a sacred calling. That many of the men and some of the women who joined the police did so because they liked to drive fast, beat up people and shoot off guns, as Lieutenant Weber had said, had been a sobering and depressing realization. But despite it all Richard still believed that the police held back the darkness.

"I just thought the darkness was the evil living in the

soul of every person," Richard muttered aloud to the kitchen. "But no . . . there have to be monsters too."

The oil was heating in the wok, the brown rice was in the steamer. Richard selected a CD of Schubert lieder and dropped it into the Bose. The first song began and he realized that unconsciously he had selected the song known as "Death and the Maiden." He stood frozen in the kitchen listening to the words and the music with the growing sense that Naomi Parsons was dead. From there his thoughts went to another girl who had brushed death. He wondered how Rhiana was doing, and decided that after dinner he would call and check on her. It was while listening to the German lyrics that something suddenly clicked for Richard.

Kenntnis means knowledge in German. The realization set the hairs on the back of his neck to pricking.

The doorbell broke through his whirling thoughts. For an instant Richard hesitated. His holstered pistol was on the dresser in the bedroom, but it seemed absurd to answer the door holding a gun. The bell rang again. A glance through the peephole revealed Cross. The hood of his sweatshirt was pulled up, and he was shivering. Richard opened the door.

"Thanks. Cold out there," the homeless man said as he brushed past.

"What happened to you?" Richard asked.

"Kenntnis didn't explain?" Richard shook his head. Cross smiled. "Hey, what's for dinner?" he asked.

"I don't recall inviting you."

"Charity begins at home." Cross was prowling around the living room. He threw back the lid on the piano and banged on the keys with a forefinger. Two strides had Richard across the room and shutting the lid. "Wow, touchy."

"It's very hard to keep the piano in tune in this climate. It has to be handled carefully." Richard returned to the kitchen. "If you need a ride back to Kenntnis I can call a cab."

"And here I thought you'd take me yourself." Cross's voice came from close behind him.

"Look, I've had kind of a long day, and I'd like some time to myself. . . ." Richard popped open the door of the microwave. As the reflective surface swung past him Richard saw Cross, the cleaver upraised, moving rapidly up behind him.

Reflexes honed in hours of gymnastic training kicked in. Richard flung himself to the side as the cleaver cut the air where his skull had been. The linoleum's polished surface turned the lunge into a slip. Richard went with it, tucked and rolled. Using his hands he increased momentum and flipped back onto his feet. Cross grabbed a long butcher knife from the block. Cleaver and blade wove a deadly pattern before Richard's eyes. The hood of the sweatshirt had fallen back, revealing long dark golden hair and blue eyes. The Cross in the car had had brown hair and brown eyes, but the features were essentially the same. What wasn't the same was the murderous intent reflected in the blue eyes.

Fear hammered in Richard's throat, cutting off breath. A trembling in the pit of his stomach threatened to spread to his legs. He had always been terrible in his hand-to-hand combat training. He wanted to turn and run for the bedroom and his Firestar. He knew if he did he'd die.

He looked frantically around the kitchen, searching for a weapon. The knife block was behind Cross. A few pots hung from a rack overhead and Richard needed the footstool to reach them. Cross lunged, Richard dodged and a burning brand seemed to have been laid across his ribs. Warm and sticky blood flowed down his side. His frantic dodge left him leaning against the stove. The flames on the gas burner licked at his sleeve.

Richard grabbed the wok by its handles. The hot metal

seared the soft skin of his palms. Teeth gritted against the
pain, Richard tipped it forward until the oil just touched
the open flames of the gas burner. The oil exploded, the
flames shooting past Richard's face. He whirled and flung
the burning oil over Cross. The thick fair hair went up like
a hay rick. The oil permeated the sweatshirt, setting it
ablaze. Richard ran backwards as the burning figure came
after him, swinging the cleaver and thrusting with the
knife.

They were in the living room now. Bits of burning material dropped onto the carpet, starting it smoldering.
Richard was almost at the bedroom door. Just a few more
steps and he'd have his gun. There was a stunning crash as
a dark figure, surrounded by shards of glittering glass and
dripping blood from a multitude of cuts, burst through the
patio door.

It was Cross. The Cross Richard knew, or so he hoped.
The burning man turned to face his doppelganger. They
both let out bone-chilling shrieks and leaped at each other.
Locked chest to chest they rocked back and forth. Flames
licked at the fringes of Cross's hair. Blood smeared against
his opponent. The cleaver bit deep into the rescuer Cross's
shoulder. Richard cried out as blood fountained from the
wound.

He ran into the bedroom. It required only a few seconds
to have the pistol out of its holster. He thumbed off the
safety as he ran and yanked back the slide, chambering a
round.

The scene in the living room had changed. The flames
were out. The cleaver lay discarded on the stained and
burned carpet. The butcher knife quivered in the wall. The
attacker held in the circle of Cross's arms seemed to be
smaller. Appreciably smaller. Richard swiped the back of
his hand across his eyes. It wasn't an illusion. The anti-
Cross was shrinking not only in height but in girth. Within
seconds he was a wraithlike figure. Cross bent and locked

his mouth over the other's. His throat worked and he swallowed the other Cross. Richard gasped, gagged and vomited. Cross, singed and smeared in gore, turned to face him.

Richard's knees were shaking, the muscles in his thighs shivering with strain and terror, but his hands were rock-steady as he squeezed the trigger and proceeded to empty the entire clip into Cross's chest. Each of the nine bullets forced Cross back a step. The roar of the shots left Richard deafened, and the recoil sent agony lancing through his burned hands.

"Well, that's a hell of a thank you," Cross said. The words were muffled and seemed distant because of the ringing in Richard's ears. "Now we're going to have the cops on us again. Get to Kenntnis as soon as you can. And if you see any more of me wandering around . . . well, try to keep them from killing you."

And he was gone, back through the shattered door. An icy wind sent the drapes billowing into the room. Richard sat down abruptly on the floor and shook.

Chapter

SEVEN

Muffled in bandages, his hands felt paw-like on the steering wheel. The flare from approaching headlights burned in his eyes, and there was a throbbing point of pain at the hinges of his jaw. Richard forcibly parted his teeth and tried to relax as he once again drove toward Kenntnis's building.

"Missed again?" The memory of Weber's dry question sent another stab of pain through Richard's jaw as he ground his teeth together.

THE EDGE OF REASON

Then there was the apartment manager's blustering statement that this kind of thing wasn't covered in the damage deposit, and Richard was going to have to pay to have the carpet replaced and the walls repainted to deal with the smoke damage. It was all he needed given the state of his credit cards.

And finally there were the lies . . . lies upon lies. The tale he had spun tonight was about a man hopped up on PCPs breaking into the apartment and attacking him. Weber had just looked at him, but how could the lieutenant argue? There was the shattered sliding-glass door, the knife in the wall, the bloodstains on the carpet, Richard's burned hands and the wound over his ribs.

An ambulance had been called and he'd been driven to the St. Joseph's emergency room just down the street from his apartment. A wounded cop never waits. Within moments of arriving he was seated in a curtained cubicle having the cut on his side stitched and his hands bandaged. They admitted him for "observation," but after availing himself of the bathroom and eating the sandwich sent up from the cafeteria, Richard checked himself out and walked back to his apartment to get his car.

As he drove up the winding road toward the foothills of the Sandias, Richard saw lights only in the top floor of Kenntnis's building. He called directory assistance and got the number for Lumina Enterprises. The phone rang five times before shunting him to voice mail, where a cultured voice gave him the office hours and suggested he call back during those hours. Richard didn't know how he was going to get in, but he was going to get in, find Kenntnis and throttle him.

He parked in the empty lot and walked to the front doors. He noted that they and the west-facing windows had been replaced. The doors were locked and there was neither buzzer nor intercom. Richard turned and looked out over the city's lights. They ran down to the river, which formed a ribbon of darkness. The lights resumed on the other side, climbing high onto the sandy mesas. Far off to the west the setting moon struck white against the snowcapped peak of Mount Taylor some sixty miles away.

He began a circuit of the building. In the back, nestled against a Dumpster, was a large cardboard box. Light leaked around the edges of a piece of cloth that served as a door and Richard heard the low hiss of a propane lantern. Suddenly footsteps rushed him and an arm was thrown across his throat. Gasping, clawing at the arm, Richard kicked back trying to connect with his assailant's shin. A violent shove from behind sent him sprawling onto the pavement. He caught himself on his hands. Even with the cushion of the bandages it hurt like hell. The fall also ripped the knees out of his slacks and skinned his other knee. He somersaulted back onto his feet and drew his pistol.

"Not cautious. Not cautious at all," said Cross. "Don't assume you're safe here. You're not safe anywhere."

"Why? Because of you? Because of Kenntnis?"

"Because of what you are, and because we found you." Cross started toward a door set in the back wall of the building. "Come on, we've been expecting you."

Pique and humiliation almost drove Richard back to his car, but he needed answers. Logic prevailed and he followed Cross into the building.

The private elevator deposited them in a marble foyer. Through an archway Richard saw flames dancing in a glass fireplace. He marched into the living room, leaving Cross to hurry after him. Kenntnis sat on the leather sofa, sipping brandy and watching the fire.

"Get the man a drink," he ordered Cross.

"I don't drink," said Richard, biting off the words.

"You don't? Why not?" Cross asked.

"No head for it."

Kenntnis cranked himself around to look at Richard

over the back of the sofa. "And your mother spent time in rehab," said Kenntnis.

The statement was made matter-of-factly, but it unleashed a torrent of memory and emotion. His mother, tiny and fragile, kneeling in front of him with a suitcase at her side. The perfect bow of her lips curved in a smile, and her voice was light and caressing.

"You be a good boy, and do what Ellen tells you, and don't worry. Your papa is here to care for you. I'll be home so soon you won't even know I've been gone."

But even at seven he recognized fear and shame, and he saw them glistening in her gray eyes and felt them echoed in his chest. He raised his eyes to his father waiting at the front door. His father's gaze raked across him and he knew it was somehow his fault that Mama was going away.

With a snap Richard was back in Kenntnis's palatial living room. Anger clogged his throat and left a rank taste on the back of his tongue. "You son-of-a-bitch. How dare you! How dare you dig at me!"

Kenntnis stood up and bore down on Richard. "Oh, stop it! Of course I investigated you. I couldn't risk letting you close without knowing what you were. And by the way, it's nice to see that something can penetrate those perfect manners of yours. I need you to be angry. It's the only way you can stand up to the fear. Now sit down and let's get your questions answered."

Richard wasn't sure why he took the indicated chair. Maybe because he wasn't certain he'd survive another day without guidance and understanding in a world gone mad. Cross bent solicitously over the arm of the big chair and said, with a jerk of the head toward Kenntnis, "He's got almost anything you'd want. Fruit juice? Milk? Tea?"

"Milk," said Richard.

Cross left. Kenntnis stood, hands clasped behind his back, bouncing lightly on the balls of his feet, and stared down at Richard. Richard looked away and around the room. He recognized a Caravaggio on one wall and a Picasso on the other. He sensed the other works of art were equally rare and valuable, but he didn't have time for a thorough look because Cross returned carrying a tray with a glass of milk and a gigantic slice of chocolate cake and chocolate milk for himself.

"That going to hold you for awhile?" Kenntnis asked the homeless man with some exasperation, and then Richard realized that Cross wasn't exactly homeless. He referred to Kenntnis as his boss and lived in a box behind Kenntnis's building.

"So, why doesn't he live in the building?" The question emerged almost without volition. Cross and Kenntnis looked at him.

"Because of his episodes. I don't really need all those fractals caroming around the building. And some of them aren't terribly well disposed toward people . . . and *you* in particular . . . as you discovered tonight," said Kenntnis.

The milk was cold and thick across his tongue and laid down a soothing wash over Richard's burning gut. "Does everything in your universe want to kill me?"

"In a word . . . yes. Well, strictly speaking, it's not my universe, it's his." Kenntnis inclined his head toward Cross.

"Yeah, but you're not exactly innocent in all this," Cross mumbled around an enormous mouthful of cake. "Because once you found Richard he became a target." Crumbs blew between his lips, littering his lap.

"So, all I have to do is get away from you," Richard said to Kenntnis. "And I'll be fine?"

"No, you're too valuable a piece. Now you either have to play or be eliminated."

Richard's stomach twisted and the milk suddenly tasted sour. He set aside the glass on the Italian inlaid wood table at his elbow. Kenntnis rested his hand on the back of the armchair and leaned in over Richard. The smell of the older man's aftershave was bright and sharp. "Tonight you get answers, as many as you want."

Richard sat in silence gazing at the unwieldy mass of confusion and questions. He couldn't get his arms around it, much less frame a coherent question.

Cross leaned forward from his seat on the couch and laid a hand on Richard's knee. He left a chocolate thumb print on the fabric just above the rip. "You probably want to start with me," he said. Richard didn't answer. He just stared down at the ruin of his pants. His lips tightened in annoyance.

Kenntnis laughed. "I'll buy you a new pair. And I'll take care of the repairs at your apartment."

"Fine."

"Why did you shoot me?" Cross suddenly asked.

The fear and horror returned, only slightly dulled by the passage of a few hours. "You swallowed somebody . . . thing."

"Just stickin' the parts back together," said Cross.

"You're confusing him," Kenntnis interrupted. Kenntnis sat down on the coffee table directly in front of Richard and looked him in the eye. "The forces we're opposing aren't native to this world."

"Now we're going to talk about aliens?" said Richard faintly.

"Good move," said Cross sarcastically to Kenntnis.

Kenntnis waved his hands back and forth as if scattering the earlier words. "Erase that. Let's start with physics. There's a theory that there are twenty-seven folded multiverses. The theory's correct—partly—there are actually twenty-three. Anyway, they're densely compacted, touching at multiple points. We're native to this universe." Kenntnis pointed at Cross. "He's not."

"So, why are you here?" Richard asked Cross, deciding to just go along with the craziness.

"Because a few million years ago one of your distant

ancestors left the trees, stood upright, and began the evolutionary scrabble toward intelligence. It doesn't happen very often and when it does it attracts us; like sharks to blood, or bees to flowers." Cross smacked his lips, and Richard didn't think he was tasting chocolate any longer.

"Add to that that humans are relatively unique," Kenntnis broke in. "You have this wild, almost chaotic, creativity and deeply rooted and very powerful emotions. You represent a source of sustenance to these creatures in the other multiverses."

"And you eat emotions, that's what Kenntnis said." Richard looked over at Cross.

"Well, not exactly. It's more complex than that. We feed off your life energy, force, however you want to say it. Emotions are the easiest way to feed, and dark emotions are the easiest of all. Early man was a scared little sucker. I was one of the watchers and every time some chimp got spooked by lightning, or lost a kid, the fear just poured out. We would suck it in, and soon we were tearing open the peep holes. A few of us wriggled through and helped you establish religion. The bloodier the better. We noticed you had a tendency to distrust anything different. We worked to promote that, and got some tasty wars rolling. With that much power we were able to turn the rips in the fabric of spacetime into full-blown gates, and more and more of us arrived." Cross jerked a thumb at Kenntnis. "Then he came along and spoiled the party."

"How? By doing what?" Richard asked.

Kenntnis smoothed a hand across his hair, tugged at his upper lip. He frowned, then finally said, "By promoting rational and scientific thought, and trying to wean you off religion and superstition."

"Eating of the fruit of the tree of the knowledge of good and evil," Richard said almost to himself.

"He had an effect—humans began to question, and Ken-

ntnis and his paladins—" There was a throat clearing from
Kenntnis. "The *Lumina*." Cross stressed the word, and
nodded at Kenntnis in some kind of private exchange that
Richard didn't understand. "Killed some of us. We were
weakened and we couldn't keep the true gates open. But
we could encourage you monkeys to keep the superstition
train rolling, and we could keep opening tears into this dimension and those of us already here could keep feeding
as long as you kept killing and hating."

"Since I wasn't able to eradicate gods and religion I
tried a stopgap measure," Kenntnis said. "I fostered the
idea of loving and compassionate gods hoping that would
weaken them further until we could push them back out of
your world."

Cross joined back in. "Religion's about obedience and
fear, and your early ones were real lip smackers. Blood
sacrifice. Good stuff. But he," a gesture to Kenntnis, "was
having an effect. Human sacrifice gave way to animal sacrifice, polytheism was pretty damn tolerant. So us Old Ones
got together and fucked him good."

"How?" Richard asked

"We encouraged the One Bookers," said Cross. "They've
been a magnificent disaster."

"Wha . . . what?" stuttered Richard.

"Monotheism. The second worst idea after religion,"
Kenntnis said, and he pinched the bridge of his nose as if
his head pained him. "Now everybody has the 'one true
god' and the Old Ones have religious hatred and religious
wars on which to feed. Two thousand years of crusade, ji-
had, inquisition, pogrom . . ." Kenntnis sighed and he
seemed to be looking across a vast distance. For the
briefest instant Richard thought he saw whirling lights in
the profound darkness of Kenntnis's eyes. Then Kenntnis
blinked and the lights were gone.

"Then Scripture is—" Richard began.

"Bullshit," Cross interrupted. "Well, it's not totally untrue. You humans actually wrote down some of the unbelievably horrible shit we did—killing every firstborn son. Fucking over Job, ordering you to war with your neighbors. Actually read what '*God*,'" Cross provided the quotation marks with quick flicks of his fingers, "ordered Joshua to do to Jericho. And what's really amazing is how you humans try to justify it and find some holy meaning instead of saying, *Wow, these gods are crazy murderous psychopaths who like to watch us suffer. Why would I believe in this?*" Cross seemed to be working himself up into a rage.

Kenntnis rubbed a hand over his face and he looked unimaginably tired. "Anyway, I thought the grand march toward secular humanism was a dismal failure and then Cross showed up—the schizophrenic god. He had been supping on human emotions and there had actually been enough people who accepted and tried to live by these compassionate ideals that it began to affect this particular Old One." Kenntnis turned and stared at Cross and reluctantly Richard did the same.

When set beside this incredible explanation Cross's constantly changing appearance began to make a degree of sense.

"So you reflect back the vision of the faithful," Richard said slowly.

"Yeah, but it depends on which faithful. For some I'm a pretty blond Jesus. For others I'm Allah, and for others, Yahweh." The homeless man stopped frowning and preened a bit. "Not to be immodest, but I was the source for three world religions."

Memories of prayers and services spun through Richard's head. There was the feeling of an emotional snap and the core from which he guided his life seemed suddenly empty. The loss overwhelmed him, and he no longer heard them talking.

Slowly he became aware of Cross's voice again.

". . . got me with a triple whammy. A bombing in Tel Aviv, a retaliation in Gaza, and a gay bashing in America, and a massacre of Hindus in India. Guess that's actually four, but anyway they split me."

"That was deliberate?" Richard asked.

"Oh, yeah, they wanted to get me away from you and release some of the fractals so they could kill you."

"Why?" Richard cried.

"Because your presence at my side gives me an advantage in the struggle," Kenntnis said gently.

"How did they find out about me?" Richard cried.

"They watch me just as I watch them."

Richard looked at Cross. "You said you wanted to die. If Kenntnis wins will you die?"

"Yes."

"And the other aspects of you want to prevent that," Richard continued.

"Well, duh. That whole Kenntnis wins thing . . . not really good for our . . . their side."

"If Cross dies will it affect the rest of them?" Richard asked.

Cross perked up and looked hopeful. "Kid's got a point. Maybe it would weaken them. He could use the sw—" Kenntnis glared and Cross subsided.

"You are too useful to me, and I'm afraid it will make them even more powerful without your moderating influence. So, no," Kenntnis said firmly. Cross slumped.

"I don't understand how you can be all these creatures—" Richard began.

Cross made a rude noise. "Oh, please, you said you were a believer. That means you've accepted this shit for years—Father, Son, Holy Ghost."

"But we're not talking about faith now," Richard said. The effort to keep his voice level made his throat hurt. He fought back the rage. "I'm talking biology."

"There are examples even in this world—amoebas,

atoms. His kind evolved in a different universe, under different conditions," said Kenntnis.

"Then you contain Allah and Yahveh . . . ?" Richard began.

Cross shook his head. "Not the big ones. They split off totally a few hundred years ago. And it's a damn good thing one of them, including the Big J, didn't try to come and croak you last night. If they had, you'd be dead." There was another significant look between Cross and Kenntnis. Kenntnis gave an almost imperceptible head shake. "What I try to keep pasted together are all the little Jesusi created by small but passionate nut bag Christian sects, and the little Allahs created by equally nutty Moslem sects, and the little Yahvehs created by Jewish nuts."

Richard stood and looked down at Kenntnis. "You're trying to enlist me in a war on God."

"No, I'm trying to enlist you in a war on invading creatures who will enslave your kind, turn this world into a living hell and sink you in a darkness from which there is no morning."

"And what happens if you win?"

"I give you the stars," said Kenntnis simply.

They left it there. It was Richard himself who ended the discussion, saying he was too tired and too disturbed to properly evaluate what he'd heard. He needed time to process. Kenntnis offered a guest room and this time it was accepted. Kenntnis thought that was a pretty major victory. The policeman had so many barriers around himself. This was the first sign they were breaking through.

The attack on his own building had shaken Kenntnis. He had to assume it was an overzealous subordinate, but if it had been Grenier himself it meant he and his masters were far too confident for Kenntnis's peace of mind. So he set

Cross patrolling inside and outside the building, watching for magic. At least they'd managed to damp down Rhiana so she didn't interfere with the task.

Kenntnis lit a candle in one of the antique silver candlesticks in the dining room. It was an archaic gesture considering how deeply he revered and nurtured science and technology, but there was a power in the symbolism of the flame. Shielding the fluttering tongue of fire with his hand, Kenntnis went to the bedroom where Rhiana slept.

A fall of pale peach-colored muslin hung from a hook in the ceiling and draped, tent-like, over the graceful sleigh bed. Kenntnis caught a glimpse of himself reflected and refracted in the three mirrors in the vanity. Delicate Limoges boxes dotted the polished wood surface of the vanity. The Bose was set so low that the music of the Bach fugue was more an impression than any real sound. Nervous, Kenntnis checked to make certain it was still set for continuous play.

Reassured, he moved to the bed and drew back the veiling muslin. The light fell flickering over her extraordinary features. The high points of her cheekbones narrowed down to the pointed chin. Sooty lashes swept the top of those cheekbones. In the candlelight her skin seemed luminescent. The long black hair fanned across the pillow and cascaded over her shoulders. She slept with wanton abandon, sprawled across the entire bed, one arm thrown behind her head, one foot escaping from beneath the covers.

What was she? Kenntnis wondered. It had been long, long since this much power had walked in human form. Tomorrow he would begin investigating her and try to find some answers.

He left Rhiana and moved down the hall to where Richard slept. It was a simpler space with twin beds, a dresser and a large armchair set in front of a fireplace. The closet door was open and Kenntnis could see the coat, slacks and shirt carefully hung, the shoes set neatly on the floor beneath the clothes. The policeman's underwear was folded on the dresser. Next to it lay his empty holster. Kenntnis looked for the gun and found it lying on the table between the beds.

Richard slept curled tightly on his side. One hand was beneath the pillow, the other clenched beneath his chin. The white-gold hair had escaped from its perfect part, forming a soft fringe across his forehead. There was a furrow between the pale brows. If he had dreams they weren't pleasant.

A shadow on the wrist caught Kenntnis's attention. At first he thought it was a line formed by the sheet, but then he realized there was a scar running across Richard's wrist. Kenntnis craned to look down at the other arm. The skin was unblemished. Disturbed, Kenntnis stepped back and considered this development. *Old, but not terribly old.* Kenntnis wondered if this was the source of the missing months. Suddenly the man seemed terribly small and frail to be the repository for Kenntnis's hopes and the bulwark against his fears.

Kenntnis started for the door. Richard's voice stopped him before he reached it. "Who are you?"

Kenntnis turned back slowly. "Why did you try to kill yourself?"

"A piece of rope caught around my wrist during a yacht race," said Richard. His look dared Kenntnis to disagree. Kenntnis took the dare.

"And the examiners at the police academy bought that load of shit?"

"Albuquerque has a profound shortage of police," said Richard placidly.

They stared at one another in silence for a few moments.

"I need to know if you're strong enough to take this. Why did you try to kill yourself?"

"I only discuss personal matters with friends," said Richard. "Who are you?" he repeated.

"And I only give my name to friends," answered Kenntnis. As a barb it missed its mark. Richard just smiled.

"So I guess we'll keep our secrets." Kenntnis frowned, realizing he'd been trumped and hating it. Richard chuckled, a rich musical sound, and Kenntnis realized this was the first time he'd ever heard the policeman's laugh. "I think you're too used to getting your own way."

"You planning on teaching me humility?" asked Kenntnis.

"No, just pricking your arrogance now and then."

"Are you going to work for me?" Kenntnis demanded.

"I don't know yet," Richard replied.

"Don't take too long. Events are moving with or without you," Kenntnis warned.

Chapter

EIGHT

In the morning Richard had found a box of non-adhesive bandages, medical tape and scissors sitting in the bathroom. He wanted to return to his apartment for a shower and clean clothes, but the bandages were a stark reminder that he needed another person to wrap his hands. The shower was stocked with high-end bath products scented with sandalwood. In a drawer by the sink he found an antique straight razor with a mother of pearl handle and shaving soap and a brush in a Limoges cup.

Given the attention to detail he'd found in the bathroom, Richard half expected to find a change of clothes in the closet, but only his torn and dirty clothes were there. He dressed, gathered up the antibiotic ointment and bandages and went in search of help.

The smells of freshly baked bread, ham and coffee led him into a large, aggressively modern kitchen. Rhiana was at a table set in the bay of a window. Covered chafing dishes stood on a buffet. Winter sunlight blazed through the glass and danced across the chrome and steel appliances. Flecks of what looked like opal glittered in the granite counter-tops. She was perusing a textbook, her chin propped in her hand.

Richard glanced curiously at the open page. There were a lot of mathematical formulae. The only thing he could read said,

A Bose-Einstein condensate is a gaseous superfluid phase formed by atoms cooled to temperatures very near to absolute zero. A rotating Bose-Einstein condensate could be used as a model black hole, allowing light to enter but not to escape. For a popularized version of this theory see the science fiction story "Light of Other Days," by Bob Shaw, which introduced a condensate as "slow glass."

It was a stomach-aching reminder of how he'd struggled to pull out a C in Calculus. Richard returned his attention to a more pleasant subject, the girl. The sun sparked highlights of blue and even deep purple from her hair. A dirty plate sat nearby.

"Good morning," Richard said.

She jumped and looked up. "I didn't know you were here," she blurted.

"I arrived pretty late," Richard said.

"Kenntnis should have woken me up."

Richard walked to the table. "Look, I was wondering . . ." He gestured with the box, tube and scissors.

"Sure." He sat down, and she took his hands in hers and

gently turned them palms up. There was a hiss of quickly indrawn breath. "What happened?"

"I got burned."

"How?"

"It's a long story, and I really need to get to work. May I tell you tonight?"

"Yeah. Okay."

She opened the tube of ointment and spread it gently across the raw blisters on his palms. The tips of her fingers were cool and very soft. Three of the fingernails, two on one hand, one on the other, were broken. The rest were long, perfect ovals carefully polished.

"Did you break them the other night?" he found himself asking inanely.

Rhiana nodded and laid a gauze pad over his palm. Her hair fell forward, brushing lightly across his wrists. The tang of citrus wafted to his nostrils. Desire shivered down his nerves. The reactions spreading through his body were unexpected. It had been a long time since he'd experienced any type of physical arousal.

Sex had been his greatest vice. His dirty secret. It had caused most of the problems in his life, and he hadn't slept with anyone for four years. It hadn't been hard, his injuries had been so bad and his fear so great, but now he was faced with Rhiana. He pictured them in bed, skin to skin, sweat slick and burning hot, and a stab of blinding panic gripped his chest. For a moment he writhed, pierced by two divergent, almost painful drives—passion and panic. Panic won and the bulge in his crotch subsided.

Rhiana shook back her hair and looked at him. "I never thanked you for saving me."

"*De nada*," he said.

Her words made him very glad the desire had drained away. If he had acted on his attraction it would have seemed as if he expected her to respond out of gratitude.

And she was awfully young, he would be taking advantage.

She shot him an impish grin and said in a deadpan tone, "Just doing my job, ma'am."

"Not quite *that* sanguine," Richard said. "It fell just a tad outside my job description."

Rhiana finished bandaging his hands and jumped to her feet. She nodded toward the chafing dishes. "What can I get you? There's just about everything."

She started lifting lids to reveal eggs poached, fried and scrambled. Beneath another gleaming lid was sausage, ham and bacon. There were waffles and pancakes, toast, fresh fruit and porridge.

Rhiana wrinkled her nose as she lifted the last lid. "And these weird little fish thingees."

"Kippers," said Richard automatically.

Rhiana flushed, saying quickly and aggressively. "I knew that."

But Richard hadn't been a psych minor for nothing. "Just some fruit and a slice of ham," he said quickly to get them past the moment.

It was pretty evident that the physics text no longer had any lure, so Richard resigned himself to breakfast conversation. "So, where are you from?" he asked, knowing that most people like to talk about themselves and if he asked the questions he would be able to eat. He bit into a piece of honeydew melon. The rich, sweet flavor exploded across his tongue. Definitely not from a local market.

"Van Nuys."

"And that's where?"

"Oh, California. My dad's a trucker. Mom works for a company that manufactures medical equipment."

"Brothers? Sisters?"

"Three brothers. Two sisters. But four of us are adopted."

"Oh." Richard paused and speared a large blackberry.

He wasn't sure how to respond. *That's nice. How noble of your parents.* He settled for another question. "And how did you end up in New Mexico?"

"They gave me a full scholarship—encouraging women in science, you know. I'm the first one in my family to go to college." She was babbling with nervousness. Richard wondered if it was him and what he had done to elicit this reaction.

"Congratulations, that's a major accomplishment." He smiled over at her, and she blushed brightly.

"Thanks." She twisted a strand of hair between her fingers. "That wasn't my folks' reaction. All they could focus on was how the grant only paid for tuition and books, not housing. I had to take out a loan for that. They wouldn't help at all. Well, maybe they really couldn't, but still . . ." She frowned at the memory. She looked up and her brow cleared. "And anyway, I don't think they understand why I wanted to do it."

"Forgive me, Rhiana, I know this is impertinent, but how old are you?" She hesitated and fiddled with her napkin.

"I'm almost eighteen," she said.

"Wow."

"I skipped a couple of grades."

"I'm impressed." A glance at his watch sent him out of his chair. "I've got to go. I've got to go by the apartment for a change of clothes before I go to work."

"Okay. See you tonight."

"Right."

As he drove down Montgomery, Richard reflected on how odd human beings were. He was defensive because of his family's money and social position. Rhiana was defensive for the exact opposite reason. Maybe nobody was ever content and secure.

The stink of wet, burned carpet caught in the throat as Richard pushed open the door of the apartment. He stepped in and froze at the sight of the slender man seated on the couch.

Justice Robert Oort looked up over the rims of his half-moon glasses. The dark blue eyes were cool and emotionless. He set aside the book he had been reading. A year's absence made Richard aware of how his father's iron-gray hair had turned to silver. He wondered if it was him or his mother who'd caused that, or could he not feel guilty and assume it was just the passage of time?

"Sir," Richard said.

"The manager let me in," the older man said in answer to a question that hadn't been asked.

"But why are you . . . ?" Richard began.

"Your lieutenant informed us you'd been hurt. I flew out on the red eye and went to the hospital only to find out you had checked yourself out."

"Sorry, sir." It was stupid and inane to apologize but that was the nature of the relationship.

"That was not wise."

"Yes, you're right, sir."

"Where did you go?"

"Friends," he almost said automatically, but he caught himself. He didn't want an inquiry into the identity of the friends. "Hotel," he answered instead.

The judge checked his Rolex. "You're going to be late if you don't start changing."

Richard walked into the bedroom. His father followed. Richard selected a coppery brown suit and a dark gold shirt. His fingers were trembling as he flicked through the dozens of ties hanging on the electric racks in the closet.

"Your lieutenant also told me that you were promoted."

"Yes, sir," Richard said as he pulled shoe trees out of a pair of brown loafers.

"You didn't think that deserved a phone call?"

He turned to face his father, and found himself unable to meet the judge's intensely dark blue eyes. Instead he studied the ugly Berber carpet. "It . . ." He paused to clear his throat. "It happened very suddenly."

"So I gathered. I talked with Captain Murphy in Newport and he indicated that it was almost unheard of for a young officer with so little experience to be promoted to detective without strings being pulled." The judge's voice provided the interrogatory.

Richard's stomach began to ache. He forced himself to relax his fingers, which had clenched tightly around the material of his shirt.

"You'd have to ask my captain," Richard said.

"You have no idea why you were promoted?" his father pressed.

Richard considered the events of the past three days and the conversation he'd had last night with Kenntnis and shook his head. He also realized that his father's arrival had little to do with concern over Richard and a lot to do with distrust of the mysterious patron.

"I'm concerned that you're mishandling this career as well."

"I thought you didn't approve of my becoming a policeman."

His father sighed. "It wasn't what I'd hoped for, but you lacked the . . ." He paused and then resumed. "Temperament for law or medicine, and after your . . . illness you chose to quit Drew's firm rather than return. You needed to do something."

His stomach was pressed up hard against his lungs and Richard felt as if he had only inches with which to breathe. "I was good at music."

"You told us that only one tenth of one percent actually succeed in having a professional career. I didn't like those odds. And you told me yourself you weren't certain you had the talent. I wanted you to have something secure to fall back on. So I got you the job."

"But you seem to be objecting when someone makes an

effort on my behalf in this career," Richard said, and felt the breath freeze in his chest at his father's look.

"I don't know who's acting on your behalf, and I want to make certain you're not doing anything that could blow back on me. I'm on the Federal bench. I have to be careful, and your judgment hasn't always impressed me."

Richard knew the force of his father's personality and will. Captain Ortiz would tell him who had made the request. "He's a businessman named Kenntnis. He owns a company called Lumina Enterprises."

"I find it disturbing when you lie to me. Did you think I would actually believe that you accomplished this on your own?"

The nausea was increasing. If he'd just told the truth initially he might have avoided this rebuke.

Robert Oort shook his head. "I don't understand you at all. I raised you to be better than this." Richard didn't respond. "Well, it's apparent you are determined to set your own course." The older man turned and walked to the door of the bedroom. He paused and looked back. "You might want to instruct them to inform someone else next time you come to grief. I'm a long ways away."

Richard heard the front door fall closed. Dropping the shirt, he ran for the bathroom, hoping to reach the toilet before he vomited.

ॐ

The ribbing started in the parking lot outside APD headquarters and continued all the way up to the bullpen. Various officers—plainclothes and uniforms—commented about the shootout at Richard's apartment the night before and his seeming inability to hit anything. After the encounter with his father Richard was finding it hard to maintain his equilibrium, but it was fatal with cops if you reacted. Like wolves, they sensed weakness.

Richard kept smiling, but his cheeks were burning by the time he reached his desk. He pulled out his notebook and Palm indicating dismissal, and eventually the pack wandered away. He tried to concentrate on transferring his notes, but his thoughts returned over and over to the conversation with his father. *If only he'd told him about Kenntnis initially. There was nothing wrong with having help. Why did he need his dad to be proud of him? The judge had never been proud of anything he'd done before. It wasn't going to change now.*

A shadow fell across the desk. He looked up at Lieutenant Weber. "Could I talk to you for a minute?" Weber asked.

Richard nodded and followed the other man into an empty conference room. Weber shut the door behind them and sat down at the round table. Richard remained standing. A hard knot formed again in Richard's stomach as Weber stared up at him.

"Sit down. You're not in trouble," Weber said, as if he'd read Richard's mind. Richard sat cautiously on the front edge of the indicated chair. "I sent evidence techs over to your place last night."

"And?" said Richard brightly.

"Whatever you shot at, you didn't miss," said Weber. His expression was somber, his brown eyes wary and confused. "There were no holes in the walls."

"He was in front of the sliding doors."

"I checked outside. There's a seven-foot cedar fence around your patio. You didn't hit that either. And we didn't find any bullets out in the commons area."

"Why is this important?" Richard asked, swallowing hard, trying to force back the dread.

Weber ran a hand through his thick mat of wavy brown hair, leaving it looking like a disturbed haystack. "Because I found out yesterday that you were at the building that got bombed. The chief had sent you over there for an interview. Who's after you? And what have you done to set them on you?" Weber asked.

"I'm not dirty," Richard said, assuming that was what Weber was thinking.

"Oh shit, I know that. You're a fucking boy scout." Weber left his chair and came around to sit on the edge of the table near Richard. He laid a hand on Richard's shoulder. Richard noticed a faint dusting of freckles across the back of Weber's wrist and the powerful muscles and tendons.

"It's pretty damn obvious that you're in some kind of trouble, and I wanted you to know that if I can help I will. You're a good cop and we'd . . . *I'd* hate to lose you."

The support and honest concern were unexpected and terribly welcome after his earlier encounter. Richard felt a glow of pleasure that this decorated officer thought well of him.

The phone in the conference room chirped. Weber leaned over, picked up the receiver, listened and handed it over to Richard.

"Richard Oort," he said.

"Detective, this is Sergeant Vallis in Denver." Richard felt the pulse beating in his throat. "You had an APB out on some kids?"

"Yes."

"Well we've got three of 'em in the morgue up here."

"Which three?"

"Naomi Parsons, Dan Douglas and Alice Rangold."

You know how kids are, Emma Parsons had said. *They all want to try their wings.* Well, Naomi had tried and they'd failed her. Panic and dread overtook him as Richard realized that he'd have to break the news to this mother . . . to all their mothers. It had him so agitated that he momentarily lost the thread of what Vallis was saying. By the time he could focus again, he heard Vallis say, ". . . got caught up in a drive-by."

"They were shot?" Surprise sent his voice up an octave.

"Yeah, that's what I just said," answered Vallis.

"Were they the only fatalities?" Richard asked.

"Nah, four bangers got hit, too. It's been a long time since we've seen it this bad. Will you be comin' up?"

"Yes, I think I better." Richard handed the phone over to Weber to hang up.

"Bad?" the lieutenant asked.

"Yes." Richard stood and started for the door. A new and unwelcome thought intruded. "Can I go to Denver?"

"Sure, if it's part of an ongoing investigation."

"It is. The bombing that's now become a homicide."

Richard got as far as the door, then hesitated, his hand gripping the doorknob. "Do I . . . am I the one who tells the families?"

"Some cops do it themselves. Me, I call the chaplain and have him deliver the news," Weber said, trying to sound matter-of-fact and failing.

"I . . . I think I'll do that."

Chapter

NINE

Vallis was a heavyset man in his midfifties. He sported ostrich cowboy boots and a belt buckle the size of a dinner plate wedged up his sagging belly. He nursed a big bottle of water, and periodically he would sniff at an open jar of carmex. Richard felt like Vallis looked, after the turbulent flight up from Albuquerque aboard one of Mesa Airlines' twelve-seater prop jobs. The plane didn't handle the mountain updrafts terribly well. Richard took a companionable sip from his own bottle of Evian. Vallis stuck the water bottle under his arm and held out a shovel-sized hand.

"Glad you could get up here this fast. I've got the parents due to arrive in the next few hours and they all want to take their kids."

"Understandable," Richard said.

"Don't get many beat cops coming to take a look," said Vallis.

"I just made detective. . . ."

"Congratulations."

"Thank you. Anyway, I've tried to get at least a journeyman's knowledge about various aspects of police work so I've read a lot of forensic books over the past few years."

"Well, this one is pretty damn cut and dried," said Vallis over his shoulder as he led Richard through the office cubicles and the big double metal doors into the morgue itself.

Vallis choked out a cough and stuffed blobs of carmex into each nostril. Richard looked at the older man curiously. There actually wasn't much odor in the morgue. Giant exhaust fans beat out a rhythm, moving the very chilly air. Richard wondered if Vallis had gotten a whiff he couldn't forget, and now his mind provided the stench whenever he was near a body. And there were a lot of bodies. Denver was a much bigger and richer city than Albuquerque so there were three coroners at work and a couple of assistants. A body on one table had been cracked open, rib bones starkly white against the red and yellow of the viscera and muscles. There was the sound of gurgling water running constantly down the length of the steel table carrying away the waste.

An assistant spotted them. "Who you here for?" he asked.

"The drive-bys," Vallis croaked out, trying to breathe through his mouth and talk at the same time.

The assistant nodded and led the way to the lockers set in the far wall. The drawers slid out with a rumble of metal on metal. Richard pulled thin surgical gloves over his bandages, and twitched back the first sheet to reveal the waxy pale face of a young man. Dark blond hair fell limply across his forehead. Richard steeled himself and pulled again until the torso could be seen. There were four wounds like tiny mouths in the dead boy's chest and stomach. Richard covered the body and moved to the next.

The girl in the next drawer had soft brown hair cut to chin length. She had a wound in the side of her neck and two in the chest. The final drawer held a zaftig dark brunette with more torso wounds. He felt ghoulish, but he checked the toe tag. The zaftig brunette was Naomi.

"Okay?" Vallis asked.

Richard nodded and pulled the sheet back up. The coroner's assistant rolled the brunette back into the wall. The man's hands closed around the end of the slab. There was a large bruise across the back of one hand and something snapped into focus.

"Wait!" Richard pulled the sheet back down from the first girl's body and stared at the neck wound.

"Could you get a coroner over here, please?" he asked the assistant. The man looked bored and irritated, but he nodded and walked away.

"What?" Vallis asked in an aggrieved tone.

"This bullet went in on an angle." Richard gently touched the ragged edges of the neck wound. "It had to have hit either the carotid or the jugular or maybe both. There should be a huge swelling from the hemorrhage."

Vallis bent forward, but Richard noticed that he never actually focused on the girl's throat. His eyes kept sliding away.

"Okay, so?"

"Let's see what the coroner says," Richard replied cautiously and turned to greet the white-haired, paunchy man approaching them. He was snapping his heels down hard as if to emphasize his annoyance at the interruption.

"Yes? Danny said you had a question," said the coroner.

"More of an observation," said Richard, and he repeated what he had told Vallis.

"Obviously it didn't hit either the vein or the artery." Impatience and superiority made each word hit like a dart.

"Could you just take a look?" Richard asked, since the coroner hadn't once glanced at the body.

The coroner's eyes slid off the body and focused on the far wall. "It's what I would expect from this kind of wound. We've done the autopsies."

Richard blinked at the coroner. He looked back at the smooth, unblemished body of the girl. "But . . . but you haven't," he said weakly.

"Are you insinuating that I and my staff haven't done our work?"

"Well, no . . . yes."

The man's face was a mottled red. "If you'll excuse me. You can find your way out." The coroner turned and walked away.

"There hasn't been an autopsy," said Richard, appealing to Vallis.

"Of course there has," said Vallis. "Look, I gotta get back to the precinct."

He walked to the door. Richard followed, his mind whirling.

Just outside the door he caught Vallis by the arm. "Are you releasing the bodies to a mortuary?"

"Yeah, the Davis Funeral Home."

"When?" asked Richard.

Vallis looked at his watch. "Well, now that you've had a look, probably within the hour."

"Thanks," said Richard. He waited until Vallis cleared the front doors before he pulled out his cell phone and placed a call to Albuquerque.

Richard waited on the sidewalk out front of the Davis Mortuary. A redbrick building with white trim and wide bay windows with mullioned panes, it looked more like a house than a funeral parlor, as if the sting of death could be eased with Colonial respectability. His breath puffed white streamers in front of his face. Frost sparkled on the sidewalk where the light of the street lamps pooled. Occasionally he heard a car pass on the larger street behind him. He checked his watch. 11:43. Armandariz's plane had been due to land at 9:20. *I wonder if she's thought better of it and isn't coming after all,* he thought. *What I'm asking is completely out of line.* The icy air bit at the skin of his exposed wrist. Richard quickly shook the cuffs of his shirt, suit coat and topcoat back down, and pulled up his glove. He paced a slow circle.

A car turned the corner, the headlights sweeping across the darkened facades of the buildings. The Neon rolled into the curb and stopped. The lights and engine died and Armandariz stepped out wrapped in a bulky white parka with a fur-trimmed hood. The pale fur set off her dark skin. She had a medical bag in one hand and a Styrofoam cup in the other. The cup added its steam to their mingled breaths.

"Okay, you told me if I came I might get some answers about the ash in the trailer," Armandariz said.

Richard held up a hand. "That's not exactly what I said. I said you might find something as intriguing as the ash."

"So I get more questions and no answers?" asked Armandariz.

"Possibly . . . probably. Or I misinterpreted what I saw and wasted your time and my money."

The coroner nodded, accepting his caveats. "Okay, let's do it."

Richard led her around to the back of the mortuary. Two hearses and two white limos were parked in the lot near a Dumpster. "Tacky," Armandariz opined as they walked past the limos. "They should be black."

They reached the double doors set in the center of the back wall. Richard knocked softly.

"How did you get them to agree to this?" Armandariz asked.

"I waited until the owners had gone home, and I wooed the night staff with a flash of a badge and a hint of *Silence of the Lambs*. Todd liked the idea of being part of something bigger than a night spent embalming."

"Yeah, I could see where that would enliven his evening," said Armandariz, and she blew on her exposed fingers.

The locks clicked, and one door opened. Todd looked cautiously around the parking lot, and waved them in. He was a small man only an inch or so taller than Richard, but softly round.

"Todd, this is Dr. Armandariz. Doctor, Todd Aikens."

"So pleased to meet you," said Todd in a hushed tone as he pumped Armandariz's hand.

"We can't thank you enough for this," Richard said.

"Not at all. I knew when I saw them I had to do something. They looked so sad." He turned and led them down the hall.

Armandariz rolled her eyes at Richard and whispered, "What they look is dead."

"You're a cynic," said Richard.

The bodies, discreetly draped with sheets, were laid out on tables. On shelves lay the mortician's tools of the trade—putty, wax, jugs of bright pink and orange fluid. Richard stared at the neon colors in confusion.

"It takes a lot of pumped-in orange and pink to turn corpses back toward normal color," said Armandariz.

Richard had been expecting the reek of formaldehyde, but the room smelled of a floral air freshener. Armandariz shed the parka, pulled a long apron and a pair of surgical gloves out of her case, and donned them. Next she set out her instruments. Richard leaned against a wall to watch.

But the Albuquerque coroner was skittish. She pulled down a sheet, then turned away to fuss with her instruments without ever looking at the corpse. She picked up a scalpel, then asked Todd about the prospects for the Colorado Rockies in the upcoming season. Richard watched closely, trying to analyze what was happening.

Armandariz flung down her scalpel. It hit the side of the table with a metallic *ting* and went bouncing away across the tile floor. Todd ran to pick it up.

"Todd, I'm really tired. You got anything with caffeine around this place?" the coroner asked.

"There's coffee in the kitchen," Todd answered, handing the scalpel back.

"Would you get me a cup? Black." The mortician nodded. As soon as he'd cleared the room Armandariz rounded on Richard. "What the fuck is wrong with me?" she demanded.

"What do you mean?" said Richard, and he made his tone as noncommittal as possible.

Armandariz glared at him. "It's going to sound crazy."

"I won't hold it against you," Richard said.

She hesitated, then blurted out, "I can't look at these bodies, and I've never had a problem looking at bodies. It's like they're repelling any kind of close inspection."

Richard nodded. "I don't think that's crazy. I think it's the only explanation for why a professional coroner would fail to autopsy homicide victims." Armandariz stared at him. Richard stepped forward and took another pair of surgical gloves out of her case. He blew in them and pulled them on, working his fingers to smooth out any wrinkles. Taking the scalpel out of her hand, he said, "Tell me what to do. I'll do it."

"So you don't feel it?" Richard shook his head. Armandariz glanced down at the girl's body. Her eyes started to slide away, but she forced her gaze back to the neck wound. "Make a cut here," she ordered curtly, and indicated the line with the tip of her finger. A trickle of sweat slipped from beneath the hair at her temple, and ran across her cheek.

Todd returned with the coffee. Armandariz took the cup and gulped down a large mouthful. The smell of the coffee was dark and bitter, vanquishing the floral air fresheners.

The flesh parted under the knife. "Hold it open," she ordered. Richard clenched his teeth, worked his fingers into the cut and spread it open. Armandariz pulled a small, powerful halogen flashlight out of her bag and inspected the interior of the wound. She stepped back with a nod and pulled off her gloves with a sharp snap. "I'm done. You can have them," she said to Todd.

"So, what did you find?" the mortician asked with an eager glitter in his eyes.

"Sorry, Todd, you're not cleared for that," Armandariz said portentously.

Todd managed to look both disappointed and excited at the same time. "This is big, isn't it?" he whispered.

"Yes, *X Files* big, and we couldn't have done it without you," said Armandariz. The coroner closed her case and jerked her head toward Richard and the door.

Richard paused to shake Todd's hand again. "Thank you again, and please, please, keep this entirely between us."

"You can depend on me."

Outside Richard sucked in several lungfuls of fresh air so cold it burned his throat. "So, what did you find?" he asked, repeating Todd's question.

"They were shot post mortem, they need to be autopsied, and the cops need to look for somebody other than the bangers."

"I don't think they're going to," said Richard. "And here's why." He pulled the rolled-up papers from the pocket of his top coat and handed them to Armandariz. "This is a copy of the police report complete with the testimony from the only surviving gang member. Start at paragraph six."

Armandariz pulled the flashlight out of her case. The powerful beam illuminated the page to a stark white. She read quickly, then looked over at Richard, and slapped the back of her hand sharply against the page. "I want to hear this straight from this *pendejo*'s mouth."

"No," said Richard. "You answered my question. You do not want to be involved in this."

"The fuck I don't! Get your ass in the car."

Richard looked, shook his head. "We won't be able to see him now."

"Fine. We grab a hotel, get some sleep and see him in the morning."

"Okay, but I'll drive myself. I have my own car." Richard waved toward his rental parked across the street.

"No. You are not ditching me."

She had anticipated him. Richard felt his jaw slide forward, ready to fight, but then just sighed. He was secretly relieved to have someone else around to verify and document the craziness.

"Okay, just let me get my case."

Richard retrieved his overnight case and tossed it into the trunk. He then opened the driver's side door for the coroner, Armandariz gave him a strange look, then shook her head and got in.

🔱

It was partly because she was hungry and partly because she wanted to spend more time with the enigma that was Richard Oort that Angela Armandariz insisted they stop for food. They found a twenty-four-hour Carrow's and were led by a frowning, gum-chewing teenager to a booth. Angela used the menu as a screen as she leaned across the table and said softly, "When I was her age I had to have the homework done and be in bed by ten." He smiled and Angela felt dazzled. She realized this was the first time she'd seen the detective not looking stressed, confused, or grim.

"Careful, you're showing your age," he whispered back. "But I have to agree. Where are their parents?"

"And you be careful. You're about to imply that women need to stay at home and raise the kids." She shook a finger under his nose and he sat back like a startled puppy.

"No, not at all. I was raised in that kind of home, but my parents encouraged all of us to get an education and pursue our interests," Richard said.

"And who's all of us?"

"My two sisters. One's a doctor and the other's a lawyer."

"And you didn't become an Indian chief," Angela quipped, and glanced at him from beneath her lashes to see how he would react. He chuckled.

"I've heard how you enjoy getting under people's skin." He paused and lined up his silverware. "Are you from New Mexico?" he asked.

"Yeah, I'm a rarity—a native—a twelve-generation native, or thereabouts, at least on my mom's side. I'm one of the crypto-Jews of northern New Mexico."

He scanned her face as if searching for the joke. "I beg your pardon?" said Richard.

"Jews fleeing the Inquisition in Spain. A number of them fled as far as was physically possible, which was the mountains of New Mexico. They were passing as Catholics, and over the years they became assimilated, but certain eccentric rituals survived. I can remember my great-grandmother bringing out the candles on Friday evening, covering her head and praying to the Virgin."

"So are you Jewish or Catholic?"

"Neither. I flirted with converting to Judaism, but I found out it was just as shitty toward women as Catholicism so I opted for agnosticism. It seemed a safer bet than out-and-out atheism."

She had touched some nerve. The policeman was looking grim again. Angela paused for a long sip of her coffee. "Look, if I've offended you . . . well, tough. Some people believe. Some don't. I don't."

"It's not that, it's . . . well, it's an odd echo of . . . well . . . things that are happening in my life," Richard said.

"Want to talk about it?" Angela asked, and mentally kicked herself as she watched him shift down and away from her.

"No," he said, tempering it with a smile. "I'd really like to hear about New Mexico before it became trendy."

The teenager returned and they ordered. While they ate, Richard a salad and a glass of milk, Angela pancakes, eggs, ham, sausage and bacon, she launched into stories about the family, the big house on Rio Grande Boulevard, the ranch outside of Taos, the horses, crawdad hunting in the ditches. Her six siblings and her parents.

"It wasn't easy for them," she said. "Dad was in the Air Force, stationed out at Kirtland. The women in our family tend not to marry outsiders, and Dad was *way* outside."

"Because he's African-American?" Richard asked.

"Yeah. That whole Rainbow Coalition thing . . . not so much in New Mexico. The Hispanic and the black communities don't generally mix."

"But your last name is Hispanic."

"My paternal grandfather was from Cuba. Like the Indians in New Mexico with their Spanish names, well, the same thing happened to the slaves in the Caribbean."

"But your folks, they made it work? They're still together?"

"Yeah." Angela smiled fondly at the memories. "Love really can bridge all differences. Sorry, that sounds really corny."

"I think it sounds nice."

Angela grinned. "The irony is that Dad's actually Jewish. His mom is Jewish."

He insisted on paying, but didn't make it about being a gentleman. "You came up here to help me out on a case. I'll get reimbursed."

While he took a tip back to the table, Angela checked the phone book for a nearby motel. She tried to figure out how he had dodged talking about himself, and kicked herself for babbling like a teenager. She studied his ass as he walked away, the cut of his coat across his shoulders, and gave herself permission to feel like a teenager. Richard tossed down the money, turned and started back to her. Damn, he was gorgeous and without the swagger that incredibly handsome men usually possessed. It was also nice that he wasn't very tall. At five feet nothing she got very tired of always looking up.

"Ready?" he asked.

"Yeah. I found a Motel Six," she said.

"Excellent."

He held the door for her again.

&

Richard could hear the television from Angela's room next door. It stayed on for almost an hour after they checked in. He wondered if she'd actually be able to sleep after the three cups of coffee she'd drunk at dinner.

He had tried but each time he closed his eyes he saw the pale, slack faces of the dead, and replayed the conversations with their families. Soon they would be coming to Denver to collect their children and take them home. In the morning he would meet the sole survivor of the gun battle, a Hispanic kid who would undoubtedly be charged with felony murder, and there would be another grieving family to mourn the loss of a child. Whoever had actually murdered Alice, Naomi and Drew had a lot to answer for, and he was going to see to it that they did. Which meant he needed help.

He lifted his wallet out of the breast pocket of his coat and pulled out Kenntnis's card. For a long time he sat on the foot of the bed holding his cell phone, staring at the card, and feeling his stomach clench down into a tight, painful ball.

Kenntnis answered on the first ring, and there was no hint of sleepiness in the voice.

"Okay, I'm with you," Richard said without preamble.

"Why?" Kenntnis asked with equal directness.

"They killed those kids, at least three of them. We need to find the fourth, this Josh Delay. Perhaps you can make inquiries through less formal channels."

"All right. You need to be careful. I think this Delay is the one who threw the spell at the building. He's a pretty major sorcerer."

The incongruity of the words seemed to beat in time with his throbbing headache. Richard covered his eyes. "I can't believe I'm doing this."

"Do you think it's the right thing to do?" Kenntnis asked.

"I don't know what I feel . . . ," Richard began.

"Don't feel," Kenntnis interrupted sharply. "I want you to think."

"I'm human. I feel," Richard said with matching sharpness.

"That's fine, feel all you want on your own time. With me, you think," Kenntnis replied.

Chapter

TEN

The interrogation room at the county's juvenile facility was painted a bilious shade of green. The predominant smells were disinfectant, coffee and bacon. Angela glared at Richard.

"Damn, you had an actual change of clothes."

"Yes. What did you think I had in that bag?"

"I assumed you were like most cops and had a razor, a pair of socks and a pair of clean underwear."

"Sorry to disappoint."

"You just make me look bad. I hung my pantsuit up in the bathroom while I showered, and hoped," Angela said.

"It didn't work," Richard said, but smiled.

"Yes, I know that."

Shuffling footsteps and the rattle of metal on metal interrupted them. A guard escorted Danny Sisneros into the room. The guard removed the handcuffs but left the ankle fetters.

"Knock when you're finished," the guard said, and left.

Sisneros was a burly kid with a long scrawny neck, like a straw balancing the square head on broad, blocky shoulders. His prominent Adam's apple bobbed up and down the length of throat like a cartoon character. His left leg was in a cast and thrust out stiffly along the side of the table. He stared at them bleary-eyed and kept rubbing his cheeks. The scratch of skin on stubble was loud in the interrogation room.

"Is this gonna take long, man?"

"No," said Richard. "I just want to hear what happened night before last."

"I didn't shoot nobody," Danny said with some urgency.

"We know that."

"In fact, you got shot," said Angela encouragingly.

The boy's lower lip drooped in a pout. "Yeah, and somebody's gonna pay for that. Not like you think," Danny hastened to add.

He had that *oh shit I shouldn't have said that* look that Richard had seen far too many times on suspects. Richard looked away toward the dingy pale green walls. He didn't enjoy witnessing the general stupidity and low impulse control of most criminals. He couldn't forget how much of it was due to trauma in the womb from drug-addicted mothers, and the violence and grind of poverty after they entered the world. Richard's was not a popular view in law enforcement, which is why he kept it to himself.

"Maybe we'll sue 'em," Sisneros added belligerently.

"Yeah, you hold that thought, sport," said Armandariz. "Now answer the nice policeman's questions." Richard threw Angela an exasperated look. She shrugged an apology.

"Please," he said gently.

"We were dealing . . . like big surprise."

Richard threw up his hand to stop the flow of words. "Have you said this before and have you seen an attorney?" He caught Angela's look of surprise out of the corner of his eye.

"There was like shit all over the sidewalk, and the PD said the dope was like the least of my problems."

"All right then, go on."

"I was down the street about half a block on lookout. Everything seemed to be smooth. Johnny had the shit and Juan had the money. Then these Anglo assholes come walking around the corner at the other end of the street. Right into the middle of the deal. Next thing I know everybody's shootin'."

"And why was that?" Richard asked. "Did the Anglos do anything to provoke it?"

"I couldn't see. Me, I think Juan decided they were cops and Johnny had ratted him out, so he pulled his piece." He paused and massaged his face with his palms again. Richard waited and pinched his nose to briefly shut out the smell of scrambled eggs and old grease. "It was weird, though. Everybody else was diving for cover or running, but these dumb fucks just stood there in the middle of a gunfight."

Richard stood. "Thank you, Danny."

"That's it?"

"Yes, thanks."

Richard was pleased that Armandariz kept silent all the way back to the car. Dark gray and white clouds hung heavy in the sky and there was the smell of moisture in the air. He opened the driver's door for Angela, but she paused, leaned her folded arms along the top and stared at Richard.

"Dead people don't walk," she said.

"I warned you not to get involved," Richard replied.

"You're pretty cool about all this."

He didn't respond, just stepped into the car. Armandariz turned on the ignition and backed them out of the parking space. The heater was roaring. "Let's hope we can get to the airport before the snow hits," she said.

"I've got to pick up my car," said Richard. "Drop me back at the mortuary."

As she climbed the narrow steps into the Mesa plane Angela cursed Richard mentally in English and Spanish. Despite her best efforts he had managed to ditch her. She had waited until the absolute final call for the flight and kept ringing his cell phone every fifteen minutes only to get his voice mail. She had finally left a message; simple, short and to the point. *"I'm in. Like it or not, I'm in."*

During the short flight back to Albuquerque, she considered. She needed details on the case, and she knew enough people within the police that it shouldn't be a problem. She didn't stop at home for clean clothes but went to APD headquarters.

She spotted Oort's desk immediately. It had the same neat economy as the man himself. There were only two detectives in at this hour. One of them was Snyder. Angela knew his reputation from friends on the force. He was a grumbler who always felt underappreciated.

She hailed him. "Hey, Snyder." He looked up from his newspaper. Powdered sugar from the open box of donuts coated his fingers. Angela sighed. Cops resented being stereotyped, but they were often total clichés.

"Doc," he said, and waved his coffee mug at her.

"The lab's doing tests for Oort, and he's fucked up some documents." It was absolutely the right tack to take. Snyder beamed.

"Little asshole. He's either got pictures of the chief fucking a chimp or he's fucking the chief."

"So may I look through his files?" Angela asked.

"Be my guest," Snyder said, and waved a hand grandly at Oort's desk.

Angela settled into the chair, and read quickly through the handwritten notes, noting the small and precise handwriting and the distinctive lefthander's tilt. It didn't take her long to realize that the trailer whose evidence she'd analyzed was step two in a trail that began with an explosion at Lumina Enterprises.

She had never paid much attention to the elegant modern building with its multiple angles placed on a knoll at the foot of the mountains. Now she studied it closely as she wound her way up the hill and pulled into the parking lot. It reminded her of the prow of some fantastic ship preparing to sail out across the river valley far below.

There was a security guard as well as a receptionist in the lobby. The walls sent back the echoes from her heels tapping on the black and silver marble floor. She showed her credentials to the receptionist.

"I want to see Mr. Kenntnis."

"Who should I say is calling?" the woman asked.

"Doctor Armandariz." The woman turned aside and spoke so softly into a throat mike that Angela didn't catch a word.

Angela wandered around the lobby. Drew a hand across the butter-soft leather upholstery on the sofas and the chairs. Flipped through the assortment of magazines and newspapers, both scientific and business and not all of them American or even in English. The security guard watched her sleepy-eyed, but his physical stance told her he was very much awake. The perfectly coifed young woman answered the gentle chimes of the phone. Bored, Angela wandered up to the security guard and indicated the alternating dark silver panels on the walls and the dark floor with its swirls of silver.

"You know, if Darth Vader had an office it would be in a building like this."

"What makes you think he doesn't?" rumbled a basso voice.

Angela whirled, grasping for her scattering composure. She hadn't heard the elevator. The man who was stepping off and into the lobby was massive and African-American. She hadn't expected that. Then on closer inspection she realized his face was a fascinating mix of racial types. He thrust out a hand.

"I'm Kenntnis."

"Dr. Armandariz."

"Please come upstairs to my office."

The elevator doors sighed shut. "You wouldn't know a bomb exploded here three days ago," Angela said conversationally.

"Considering there hasn't been any news to that effect I'm wondering how you knew," Kenntnis said. His eyes had narrowed and he took a step back from her. The retreat seemed odd from a man so large and powerful.

"I read Oort's file this morning."

"Now you are beginning to interest and alarm me a great deal," Kenntnis said.

"Hey, relax. I'm a good guy."

"I would feel so much better if Richard were here to tell me that."

"So you haven't been able to reach him either," Angela said.

Kenntnis reached out and hit the stop button on the elevator. "Who are you, and what is your interest in this?"

"I'm the County Coroner and I think Richard's in trouble," Angela said simply.

"Why?"

"I think he's still investigating in Denver and it's never a good idea to work a high-wire act solo."

"You act as if this investigation is dangerous," Kenntnis said, clearly probing.

"Considering three dead people managed to walk down a street and get shot I think it's way past dangerous and into fucking surreal. Now can we get this elevator moving and finish this conversation sitting down? I had three hours of sleep last night."

Suddenly Kenntnis was grinning down at her. It made her feel that shiver of joy reminiscent of when her father had praised her efforts after a track meet or the grades arrived. Kenntnis jammed the button down and the elevator hummed back into motion.

"How did you find me?"

"Richard's notes."

"You wouldn't happen to have a copy of those, would you?"

"Hell, no." She paused and enjoyed his discomfort. "I have the originals."

This time Kenntnis laughed out loud. The elevator sighed to a stop and they stepped into an elegant outer office. Kenntnis began flipping through the pages, his eyes scanning quickly down the lines. Suddenly he stiffened and stopped walking.

"We need to go someplace more secure," he said, and turning on his heel, he led Angela back into the elevator. It took a key override to ascend to the topmost floor.

He was walking so quickly that Angela had only an instant to react to the marble parquet floor and the intricate plaster work. As they pushed through a pair of double doors Kenntnis called out, "Rhiana, if you're doing anything unnatural, please stop."

A stunningly beautiful girl looked up, startled, as they walked in. Angela registered the seven or eight tennis balls spinning like a green nimbus around the girl's head and shoulders before they fell onto the thick oriental carpet and went rolling in all directions.

Kenntnis glanced over at Angela. "How are you holding up?"

Angela made a rude noise. "Telekinesis? Please, that's kid stuff compared to zombies."

Kenntnis looked at her approvingly. "You'll do."

"Who is she?" the girl called Rhiana asked, and she didn't sound real happy.

"Someone Richard has pulled in on his line."

Rhiana stood up. "How do you know we can trust her?"

"Because there's no coincidence, just convergence. Work out the math," said Kenntnis shortly. He turned back to Angela. "Now, do you think Richard has gone to this church?" He slapped the file with the back of his hand.

"Yeah, but I wouldn't worry about the church. . . ."

"Oh, I'm very worried about the church," Kenntnis interrupted. He looked at Rhiana. "Do you think you're ready to confront some of the faces in the mirrors?"

The sentence was nonsense to Angela, but it had a profound impact on the girl. The pale skin grayed as the blood retreated from her face and her lips thinned to a tight line. "He saved your life," Kenntnis said softly.

The girl shuddered and clenched her fists at her sides. "Payback time," she said almost to herself. She raised green and frightened eyes to Kenntnis's face. "Am I strong enough?" she asked.

"Yes. And you won't be alone. Cross and I will be there."

"And me," Angela chimed in, though she had no idea where they were going or what she was getting into.

ELEVEN

H is first impulse had been to drive directly to the Faith in the Rock Church in Castle Rock, but Richard thought about it and acknowledged that he was exhausted and hungry. He checked into a Super Eight, and walked to a nearby café for lunch. Castle Rock had become a bedroom community for both Denver and Colorado Springs, but it still maintained its charm. The downtown held nineteenth-century redbrick buildings and there was a stretch of cobblestone on a few streets. He was seated at a window table that gave him a view of the rock formation that provided the name for the town.

His waitress was a gawky girl with long straight brown hair, a long torso and equally long legs. She was also chatty, and she told him about the restaurant that used to be open on the top of the rock, but rattlesnakes had infested the walls and slithered out to the dismay of the diners. Despite Kenntnis's disdain for feelings, it still felt like an omen to Richard.

After returning to the hotel Richard called the church and made an appointment with the pastor for five o'clock. He changed into pajamas. Like many cops he kept a big bottle of generic aspirin close at hand. He shook out three pills and dry-swallowed them. He also had a wider range of pharmacopeia available. The Xanax bottle came easily to his hand. Richard checked the expiration date. It was a few months past the date. He hadn't needed the drug for a long time. He bounced the bottle on the palm of his hand and considered. No doubt he was stressed. No doubt he needed to rest. He placed the bottle back in the overnight case and climbed into bed. It felt like a victory.

The Faith in the Rock Church was at the north end of

Castle Rock in an industrial area. In fact the church looked like it was housed in a converted warehouse. There were only a few cars in the enormous parking lot. Either they got a lot of worshippers or they were really hopeful.

The lobby area held the usual array of flyers listing the times of worship. The pastor, a blow-dried young man in a light blue suit, grinned out from the front cover. He was posed seated with an open Bible resting on his knee. The air held the dusty smell of cheap paper and candle wax. A sign on the wall of a hallway read "Office." Richard headed down the hall. His heels echoed against the bright blue linoleum floor. He reached a door. Etched on the glass was "Reverend Darryl Hines." Richard knocked.

"Come in."

The voice was deeper and more cultured than Richard had expected. He entered and understood why the voice didn't match the picture of the man on the flyer. It was Mark Grenier seated behind the broad desk. The presence of this counselor and comforter of presidents in a seedy, makeshift church in Castle Rock, Colorado, suddenly made Kenntnis's claims a great deal more credible. A cold hand seemed to brush across the back of Richard's neck. He shuddered.

"Welcome. Do come in," Grenier repeated as he unfolded the long, spare length of his body from the chair. He indicated a chair in front of the desk with an elegant turn of wrist and hand.

He was as tall as Kenntnis but lacked the bulk. Where Kenntnis's hair was black and thick, Grenier's was iron gray shading to white over the temples and it formed a close cap across his skull. His features were aquiline. He had hazel eyes, and he boasted a perfect tan achieved on a variety of expensive and exclusive golf courses.

Richard felt off-balance both from Grenier's presence and from his physical similarities to Richard's father. The policeman retreated to rote, using it like a security blanket.

Pulling out his badge in its leather holder, he held it out, saying, "I'm Detective Richard Oort of the Albuquerque Police. . . ."

Grenier waved a hand dismissively. "Oh, do let's dispense with all this. I know why you're here. And more importantly I know *what* you are, which is why I made the trip out here so I could meet with you in person." Grenier was fiddling with a pair of thin reading glasses. There was something odd about them, and then Richard noticed that the lenses weren't clear but silvered.

To cover his confusion Richard glanced around the office. There were a surprising number of mirrors on the walls; the top of the desk was glass, as was the top of the coffee table. He noted the same silver-graying of the glass in the mirrors he had seen in the trailer in the South Valley of Albuquerque.

Ignoring the proffered chair, Richard went to the naugahyde sofa and sat down. It forced Grenier to cross to him and bought him a few more seconds to think. It was Richard's nature to wait and allow others to make the opening move. For some reason that didn't seem safe this time.

"Kenntnis says you're evil," Richard said bluntly as Grenier sank into the chair on the other side of the coffee table.

"And I say he's evil," Grenier replied. "Now you have a dilemma. Which one of us do you believe?"

"No, you don't get off that easy. He made his case. Let me hear yours," said Richard.

Grenier threw back his head and laughed. "You're a cool one, aren't you?"

Richard was glad the veneer was working, because he could feel his heart beating in his throat and the air didn't seem to want to reach his lungs.

"I'm sure Kenntnis has been railing against the evils and dangers of faith and feeling, and extolling the virtues of science and rationality. I'm sure he's nattered on about the stars, but never mentioned the flip side of all his wonderful technology. Somehow he always turns a blind eye to pollution, extinction, resistive bacteria, not to mention rush hour and gridlock." Grenier paused and smiled at Richard. It was a practiced smile exuding warmth and charm, but it never reached his eyes.

"All that's true," said Richard, then added, "but why have you opposed beneficial research such as the work with stem cells and research for the sake of pure knowledge like the super-collider?"

"My, my, we have done our homework," said Grenier, and there seemed to be a bit of an edge to the smile this time. "Because, while worthy, these things are like tiny pebbles shaken loose on a cliff's edge that will eventually lead to a catastrophic avalanche. Think about the end point of Kenntnis's position. It's sterile, cold logic, and utterly confining. The universe as clockwork and humans trapped without choice or free will. Think how horrifying."

Richard crossed his legs, and straightened the crease on his pants before answering. "You've picked the wrong argument with me. I was raised in the Dutch Reformed Church, the closest thing to old-fashioned Calvinism still around. I've grown up with the idea of predestination. Free will seems a luxury." Richard forced himself to meet Grenier's gaze. "Shall we try another?"

Grenier surprised him by laughing and this time it sounded genuine. "All right, let's talk about magic. . . ."

"Let's not," Richard interrupted. "It doesn't seem to be terribly relevant since I apparently don't have any."

Grenier leaned forward avidly, his hands closing tightly around the reading glasses. "Ah, so Kenntnis has told you that."

"Yes. . . ."

"So, he's no doubt told you other things." The man's eyes were intent, and he leaned completely across the coffee table, his hand reaching for Richard's knee.

At the edge of his vision Richard thought he caught a glimpse of color roiling turgidly through the glass tabletop and an answering flash of color in the lenses of the glasses. A stab of fear sent minute shivers through the muscles in Richard's arms and legs. He jerked his knee away from Grenier and stood up.

"Look, why don't we come to the point. What do you want from me? You wouldn't have come here yourself unless you wanted something."

Grenier also stood up and stared down at Richard. "Kenntnis gave you something or soon will. We want it."

He almost blurted out, *No he hasn't,* but his usual caution reasserted itself. "Why?" he said instead.

"We need it."

"Well, that's a compelling argument," Richard said.

Grenier didn't react to the sarcasm. Instead he took the time to fold and refold the ear pieces of his glasses, wipe the silvered lenses. "Let's break this down into advantages and disadvantages. First, no one who's ever borne this thing lives very long, but I expect that won't mean much to you. You have the look of the martyr. My allies will suck you dry and kill you. But before you die I can make your life quite unpleasant." Grenier stood and strolled back over to the desk where he picked up a thick file folder.

"I have a large, well organized and well financed organization. We've dug into every aspect of your life." He paused and flipped through a few pages. "Your mother is certainly a weak reed, isn't she?" Grenier lifted his head and smiled at Richard. "And secrets . . . my, you have more than your fair share. Believe me when I tell you that I won't hesitate to disseminate them in the places where they will do the most harm."

Panic stopped the air in his lungs. Richard found himself gripping his wrists with either hand. He couldn't feel the scar on his right arm through the bandages and the material of his shirt and coat, but the memory of hours of pain, humiliation, and betrayal that had led to the suicide attempt crashed across his mind and swept away all rational thought.

The memory of a voice surfaced through the black memories and desperate shame. *"Face the monsters who hurt you, and don't let others like 'em hurt anybody else."*

Four months later Danny McGowan had found Richard in his apartment, leaking blood from his right wrist into the warm waters of the bathtub and trying to keep a grip on the knife handle, his hand so slippery with blood that he couldn't slash the other. Danny had been a medic in Vietnam and he'd sewn up the wrist, keeping Richard out of the hospital so no one would know he'd tried suicide. Richard asked the older man if he didn't think he needed a shrink. It was McGowan's answer that now pushed back the fear raised by Grenier.

Officer Danny McGowan, sturdy and round as a boulder, his face seamed with wrinkles and his head crowned with a thatch of thick white hair: He was the reason Richard had become a cop. McGowan found Richard dumped in an alley, took him to the hospital, and visited him for weeks after, trying to get Richard to say who'd assaulted him. Richard never had. But a deep friendship had formed, and McGowan had continued to monitor the younger man.

"No, boy, I think you need to need to make a difference. Face the monsters who hurt you, and don't let others like 'em hurt anybody else."

Richard slowly lifted his eyes. Whatever Grenier saw there made him take a half-step backward.

Grenier said hurriedly, "Look, all you have to do is give us what we want, and we'll support you in any and all of your goals. Chief of Detectives for New York? Director of the FBI? A brilliant concert career? A contract with the Met?"

"You could do all that?" Richard asked softly.

"Yes." Grenier stepped in closer, gripped Richard's shoulders in both hands and drew him to his feet. Richard tried to step away, but Grenier tightened his grip. "Listen to me. Our world is not so terrible. . . ."

"The parents of Naomi and Dan and Alice wouldn't agree," said Richard.

"Ask the dead at Hiroshima if Kenntnis's path doesn't exact a price." Grenier gave an angry wave with his glasses. "You can't counter the faith of millions. Even now, you want to believe. Go back to that. Worship. Live your life. Be safe and we will give you anything you want. The only cost is that you turn aside, and leave this unwinnable fight to others."

"Excuse me. Those are traditionally *my* lines," came Kenntnis's voice from the doorway.

Richard and Grenier whirled. Kenntnis pushed his shoulders off the doorframe where he had been lounging and strolled into the room. Cross, Rhiana and Angela appeared from behind Kenntnis's camouflaging bulk.

"A rescue." Grenier's lips skinned back from his teeth in a parody of a smile that he turned on Richard. "Which tells me all I needed to know."

"He's throwing a spell!" Cross yelled, and he flung himself between Richard and Grenier.

Richard had the briefest glimpse of color flashing in the lenses of the reading glasses before electricity arced from the overhead light and from the lamp on the desk heading straight at him. Cross took one bolt full in the chest, then pirouetted and threw himself sideways to intercept the other. He lay on the floor, his clothes smoldering, and grinned thinly up at Grenier.

"Shot your wad, asshole," he said.

"Not quite," said Grenier calmly, and reached into his coat pocket.

Richard heard a woman scream in wordless warning.

The barrel of the gun looked enormous at such close range.

⚜

Angela jerked at Rhiana's shrill scream, and then registered the gun leveling at Richard. *No time! No time!* her mind yammered as Richard flung himself sideways. The deafening report of the pistol crashed off the walls of the room. The impact of the bullet sent Richard tumbling into the coffee table. The top broke into a thousand glittering shards, leaving the policeman tangled in the metal frame. Cross struggled to his feet as Kenntnis rushed the gunman, but Grenier was running straight for a blank wall by a window.

Angela ran to Richard. Blood was pumping from a cut on the side of his head. He groaned as he pushed to a sitting position. His hand was pressed against his side, but there was no blood oozing from between his slender fingers or staining the bandages on his palm. He clutched Angela's shoulder with his free hand and used her to lever himself to his feet. She could smell sweat overlaid with the rich scent of his aftershave.

"Stop him," Kenntnis was bellowing.

Angela looked up. Grenier was clawing at the wall, and suddenly a crack appeared. Cross put on an added burst of speed. The crack lengthened and widened and Grenier turned sideways and vanished through it. The rent disappeared, leaving a plain white gypsum wall. Cross smashed face first into it.

"Shit! Fuck! Hell! Piss!" Cross bellowed as he cupped his nose.

Angela became aware of Rhiana standing stiffly in the center of the room muttering to herself. A penny lay on the palm of her hand. It began spinning and glowing, throwing off copper-colored sparks. She threw it at the wall. It left a trail of sparks like a comet's tail.

The copper fire struck the wall and the wall tore open again. There was no sign of the man. There was also no sign of the parking lot of the church. Instead Angela saw a vast expanse of seething gray sand and several burning suns. *It was night in Castle Rock, Colorado*, Angela's mind provided with rare calm. Then she saw the shapes on the other side, but her mind was unable to define what her eyes perceived.

"This ain't good," said Cross in a tight, stretched voice.

Rhiana gasped and ran to Kenntnis's side. Kenntnis gathered Rhiana within the circle of his arm. Angela realized she was screaming. She never screamed.

"Sure hope you got some dandy ideas," Cross said to Kenntnis, "because they've seen us."

Angela clamped her teeth shut to silence herself. Kenntnis reached into the pocket of his overcoat, and pulled out a strange, twisting object that looked like a piece of blown gray glass. "Richard!" he called out commandingly. Richard looked up and Kenntnis tossed the object to him. Angela had a feeling that the cop caught it more by reflex than design. Richard's fingers twined through the open curves and Angela realized that it resembled nothing so much as a Klein bottle.

"Okay, now what?" Richard called, and his voice was a high tenor squeak. The shapes were moving, drawing closer.

"You've got to close the tear."

"How?" Richard interrupted desperately.

"I'm going to tell you. Just shut up and listen." Kenntnis sucked in a deep breath. "That's a sword hilt. Draw the sword." Richard stared at the man blankly. Angela didn't blame him. She was just as befuddled.

Kenntnis set Rhiana aside and mimed drawing a sword. "Pretend there's a scabbard and just draw it!"

The *things* on the other side were drawing closer.

"Boy, I sure hope my detect magic/no magic gizmo wasn't broke when we found him," muttered Cross.

Angela stared at Richard to avoid looking through the tear in the wall. His face was tight with concentration. The pale brows furrowed and he cupped his right hand at the base of the hilt. With his left hand he swept the abstractly shaped hilt away from his right hand in a smooth gesture.

Angela's gasp was involuntary. A meter-long swordblade appeared, seeming to slide out of the palm of Richard's right hand. It was profoundly black, the blackness of deep space. She felt rather than heard a deep thrumming hum as if she were leaning against the mother of all amplifiers. Everyone in the room and the *things* on the other side of the opening froze.

"Go," Kenntnis whispered and Richard launched himself at the opening. He held his torso slightly hunched, and his panting breaths were loud in the silence.

"Of course. Kevlar," Angela muttered hysterically to herself. "He was wearing a vest. Clever boy."

Richard was at the opening. He hesitated, looking from side to side as if trying to figure out how to bring them together. He lightly touched the sword's point to the floor, then with sinuous turns of the wrist he parried his way from side to side up the length of the tear. Beneath the sword the normal drywall appeared, but it was scorched and blackened. He had almost closed the rent when a bubble of coiling and pulsing colors ranging from darkest purple to bilious green pushed through the remaining gap at the top. Richard lunged and stabbed at the thing. There was a high-pitched squeal and the intruder withdrew. The gap closed.

Richard slowly turned, rested the tip of the sword on the floor, leaned on it and stared at Kenntnis. "Does everything have to be so damned operatic with you?" he asked, trying to make it sound casual and failing completely because his voice was shaking. Kenntnis threw back his head and filled the room with his booming laugh.

Angela rushed to Richard's side, and found Cross there before her, pounding the far smaller man on the back.

Cross reeked of burned material and singed hair. Angela shoved the bum away before he could drive the cop to his knees.

"Back off," she snapped. She gently pulled back the side of Richard's suit coat. "I know I normally work on the dead, but let me have a look at you."

"Not now. Not yet," Kenntnis ordered. "Grenier's people will be returning and we don't want to have to answer any awkward questions."

"Yeah," said Angela. "You're going to have enough trouble dealing with *my* awkward questions."

"I'm sorry." The strained and tearful whisper brought all their attention to Rhiana. The young girl was shivering, tears coursing down her cheeks. "I was just trying to stop him. What did I do?"

"Shhh," Kenntnis soothed and gathered her once more in the circle of his arms. "We'll sort that out later, too."

Chapter

TWELVE

The powerful jet engines on the Gulfstream GV were a muted roar and a subtle vibration through the floor and seats of the jet. The air in the plane tasted rich and thick, heavy with oxygen, and carried none of the stink of stale coffee that one found on commercial flights. Outside the window, stars shown diamond bright and diamond hard against the night sky. Beneath the wings roiled and bulked heavy white and gray clouds.

Cross, Angela and Richard sat around a small polished mahogany conference table set in the middle of the plane. The coroner and the homeless god had bottles of beer from the galley in front of them. Richard sipped hot chocolate, trying to ward off the chill air blowing across his bare chest and the stabbing burn of a Baggie filled with ice pressed against the spectacular eggplant-colored bruise blooming across his sternum. He felt exposed with his shirt unbuttoned, but Angela had insisted on examining him. He glanced nervously toward the front of the plane where Rhiana, curled up in one of the oversized, leather-covered seats, slept deeply.

Removing his shirt revealed the bandage covering the knife thrust from Cross's doppelganger. The bandages had been removed and the cut examined. Not content with stopping there, Angela was now unwrapping the bandages covering his hands. She inspected the burns, looked up and declared, "Jesus Christ, you're a walking disaster area!" Cross burst out laughing and even Richard chuckled. "What? What's so fucking funny?"

Richard shook his head. "Nothing." But in fact the amusement didn't last long. After today's events Richard was beginning to think Grenier had spoken the truth when he said Richard's life expectancy wasn't all that great.

This brought his focus back to the center of the table and The Object. His mind provided the capitals since it couldn't produce an explanation. The hilt lay on the table. Angela had called it a Klein bottle. To Richard it looked like something out of an Escher drawing.

"So, what is it?" Richard asked Cross.

The homeless god shook his head, and held out his hands palms out. "I think we should let himself tell you. He's the answer guy. I can tell you this. You're in exalted company to be able to draw it and use it."

"Like who?" asked Angela.

"Hammurabi, Tiberius and Gaius Gracchus, Justinian, Arthur—the real Arthur who tried to hold back the darkness after the Romans pulled out—Charlemagne, Franklin."

Richard sat up straight. "As in Benjamin?"

"Yep."

"Why?" asked Angela.

Cross looked at Richard like a teacher encouraging a reluctant student.

"He was the last great renaissance man," said Richard slowly. "Scientist, a publisher who valued books and learning above everything, and when asked to edit Jefferson's first draft of the Declaration of Independence, he removed the word sacred from the text."

"Where did it say sacred?" Angela asked.

"*We hold these truths to be sacred and undeniable,*" Richard quoted. "Franklin argued that our rights derived from a rational source. He changed it to read, *We hold these truths to be self-evident.*" For some reason this knowledge about one of America's founders gave greater credence and strength to Kenntnis's arguments.

Cross glanced at Richard. "And in between the famous guys it's mostly been poor, noble schmucks like you." He fell silent for a moment and shook his head. "I also now know we are really, truly fucked because Kenntnis didn't intend to arm you, which is why he never mentioned the sword to you." Cross looked depressed and took a long pull of beer. "Could be *I'm* gonna be the one to die, and not my evil twins."

"So, who carried it after Franklin?" Richard asked.

"I'm betting Darwin," Angela said.

"And you'd lose," came Kenntnis's voice. Even before takeoff in the elegantly appointed private jet he had removed himself into a small cubicle office at the back of the plane and closed the door. "No, it was no one you've ever heard of."

"One of the schmucks," Cross interjected.

Kenntnis frowned at him. "Though Jonathan did cross paths with Darwin, and touched him with the sword."

"You remember his name," Angela said.

Kenntnis bent his dark gaze on Richard. It was disconcerting because Kenntnis looked sad. "I remember all your names."

Richard pointed at the hilt, and repeated his question. "What is it?"

"A weapon that only a select few can wield." Kenntnis turned his dark-eyed gaze on Angela. "You saw what he did. You draw it."

She stood and picked up the hilt. For a moment she bounced it in her hand, then, drawing in a deep breath, she twined her fingers through the curves, and drew. Nothing happened. Frowning, she turned it and inspected it from all angles. "Okay, what's the trick? Where's the release button?"

"Coded in your genes," said Kenntnis, taking the hilt from her and handing it to Richard. "Like most humans, you possess a touch of magic. Only a human born without any magic can activate the sword."

"And now your involvement with the human genome project and stem cell research makes more sense," Richard said.

"Yes, if we could design a retro-virus to edit magic out of your DNA it would be a big help. As it is I have to wait for that particular confluence of genes to occur before I get a new paladin."

"And boy, could we have used one in the twentieth century," Cross said. He ticked off on his fingers. "World War I, World War II, Stalin, Mao, Hitler, Pol Pot—"

Kenntnis held up a hand. "Spare me the recitation." Cross subsided.

Kenntnis resumed. "Sometimes there will be a whole clump of you born. Other times we go for years without a single one."

"You mentioned touching Darwin," Richard said. "What does that mean?"

"If you touch a normal human with the sword it will

render them incapable of performing magic. And it has many other uses. It can repair the tears in reality caused by the injudicious use of magic by humans, and the judicious efforts by the Old Ones. When it's drawn it makes people sane. Unfortunately its effect can't cover the entire world."

"Okay." Angela gave the gesture for "time out." "He . . ." she pointed at Cross ". . . says you're the answer guy. Well, I need some. I've been pretty cool with this so far, but now I really need to know what the fuck is going on."

"Richard first. He's more important than you," said Kenntnis. It was rude and arrogant and put Richard in the spotlight, and he wanted to hit Kenntnis.

"Because he can use this thingy?" asked Angela.

"Precisely."

Richard raised up the hilt. "So this was why you wanted me to work for you."

"Partly."

"And what am I supposed to do? Go through the world touching everyone with this thing?"

"A daunting if not impossible task, and enlightenment can't be handed out like a magic pill."

"Meaning what?" Angela broke in.

"People have to develop a conscience. As late as the nineteeth century slavery was accepted. One hundred years ago women were property all over the world. Today only some of you are freed. Even if we erased magic from every person on Earth, our opponents would still be here, and they can still feed. Until people can give up the violence associated with bone-searing hatreds, racial, religious, ethnic—the Old Ones will continue to thrive."

The two humans present and awake sat silent, and Richard wondered if the prospect of a tolerant humanity was so remote as to be hopeless. He stirred and looked up at Kenntnis.

"So, you've told me how it affects humans. What does it

do to . . ." He had a hard time forming the words. "To magical creatures."

"It's deadly."

Richard looked at Cross. "So, I could kill him?" Cross sat up and looked hopeful.

"Yes." Kenntnis held up a restraining hand. "But you'd leave his splinters free to operate, and his presence is as much of an annoyance to them as they are to him. Right now we need Cross and his abilities on our side." The homeless god slumped back down in his seat looking glum.

The rumble of the engines changed cadence and tone. Kenntnis glanced out the window, then back. "Sounds like we're beginning our descent. If you'll excuse me, Doctor Armandariz, I need to speak to Richard in private." He beckoned and Richard followed him into the private office.

The door closed and the hum of the engines faded to mere vibration, indicating the extent of the soundproofing. It was a confining space made too small by the presence of a desk and three chairs. There was an array of office equipment and three phones cluttering the desk. The screen of a laptop computer glowed in the dim lighting.

Kenntnis settled into the chair behind the desk, the springs creaking under his bulk. "Rhiana is your backup so you're going to have to be very careful using the sword around her. We need her."

"Okay, that seems pretty self-evident. So why bring me in here to tell me that?" Richard asked.

"Cross and I are having a difference of opinion regarding Rhiana. It's pretty clear she's not completely human. The safest course would be to neutralize her, but I think she can be controlled and guided and will be useful to us."

"What do you mean she's not human?" Richard asked and felt crazy for even saying the words.

"There is no way a normal human could have opened a tear between the dimensions with such ease. I've been doing some checking on Rhiana, and discovered she was an abandoned baby in the California foster care system. Eventually she was adopted, but it's all completely consistent with her being a changeling."

Richard started edging toward the office door. "This is . . . is . . . ludicrous."

"You need to remember your legends, Richard, and remember that they're all based on fact," Kenntnis said. "In the Bible they talk of the sons of God coming down and lying with the daughters of men. In the Middle Ages it was stolen away by elves; today we've got alien abductions."

"Would you stop lecturing!" Richard snapped. "Rhiana is a living woman—not an abstract."

"You're all abstracts to me. You have to be. I've known so many of you, and I can't allow myself to be touched by any of you. Or at least not much." Kenntnis's voice softened to a bass rumble and for the first time since meeting the man, Richard sensed emotion behind the words.

Richard concluded the sentence. "You've watched so many of us die." Kenntnis nodded.

The door to the office opened and Cross entered. "You're discussing her, aren't you?" he accused. Richard followed Kenntnis's lead and remained silent. "Well, I'm warning you both I want something done about her. She can't be trusted. Nobody knows better than me what she's capable of doing."

"So, just kill her because she *might* do something?" Richard asked. Disgust was a bad taste across the back of his tongue. "I've never liked this doctrine of preemption, not nationally and not personally."

"Who said anything about killing her?" Cross replied. "Just use the damn sword on her. Neutralize her."

Richard pulled the hilt out of his coat pocket and turned it slowly in his hands. "But this thing kills magical creatures."

Cross shrugged. "She's only half magic. She'll probably survive."

"And what happens if half of her nature is destroyed?"

Growing anger had Richard's voice rising in level and pitch.

"My guess is that it would be similar to a lobotomy," said Kenntnis smoothly.

Cross glared at him. "Whose side are you on?"

"Humanity's," said Kenntnis.

Moving slowly and deliberately, Richard returned the sword hilt to his pocket and buttoned up his shirt. "That's too esoteric for me. I'll be on Rhiana's side." He looked at Cross. "If you won't work with her then we'll send her away."

Kenntnis shook his head. "No, she's far too dangerous and valuable an asset. If she's not our piece she'll be someone else's."

"She's a girl. Not a piece. And I won't harm her . . . or allow anyone else to," Richard added, stressing the final words.

"And how are you going to stop me?" Cross's normally open and pleasant expression was twisted.

"I'll go to Grenier."

"Then I'll kill you," blustered Cross.

"No, you won't," said Richard. He was oddly calm, but he'd realized this was chess and he saw the endgame. "You need me, and if you start the killing you're just giving strength to your enemies. You'll end up consumed by one of your counterparts, and you'll never achieve the peace you're seeking. So, let's accept the stalemate, and not give Rhiana any reason to turn against us."

"You're not in charge here," said Cross.

"Yes, I am. I have to be." Richard seated himself in the chair opposite Kenntnis. "Now it's my turn to give a little lecture." Resting his arms on the desk, he leaned in on Kenntnis. "You honor, almost worship, the scientific method, but you've lost sight of its most important element. Doubt is the key to everything you profess to represent; the ability to say *I don't know*, and the strength to examine and question every conclusion. But ever since I've met you, you've been giving me all the answers, and when that happens you've lost touch with humility, and that makes you no different from your opponents."

"You ballsy little bastard," Cross whispered.

Kenntnis didn't respond, he just stared at Richard. Richard forced himself to meet that dark gaze. It wasn't easy. The force of Kenntnis's personality was a physical presence in the room, making Richard feel even smaller than usual.

"You present a utopian result for your path, but there are dangers on your path as well," Richard continued.

"I'm listening." The voice rumbled out deep and dark as the eyes.

"You can end up with profoundly secular and pro-foundly evil regimes—"

"No, no, Richard." Kenntnis shook his finger at him. "You don't get to trot out the old 'intellect without human-ity' argument. It's been used by reactionaries since Hume to frighten people into obeying religious authorities. Which is not to say that your argument isn't valid. I bear watching as much as any living being. Just be intellectu-ally honest and say what you mean."

"All right." Richard slowly stood and looked down at Kenntnis. "I will not harm Rhiana. No matter how justified the end." He paused and drew in a breath. The explosion of air into his lungs made Richard realize he had been hold-ing his breath.

Cross blew out a breath, startlingly loud in the silent room. Kenntnis shook his head. "Why couldn't you have just been an ignorant flatfoot?"

Richard allowed himself a small smile. "And just done what I was told?"

The briefest of answering smiles touched Kenntnis's lips. "No, that's Grenier's way. All right, I accept your terms."

Richard walked to the door, then paused and looked

back. "By the way, I know who you are, or at least some of the names we humans have used for you." Kenntnis raised an inquiring eyebrow.

"You're the Serpent, and Prometheus, and Lucifer."

"I've always liked Prometheus the best," Kenntnis mused.

"And given your background we don't want you thinking too much about this Satan thing," said Cross, waving his hands as if to obscure the word. "Remember, we're the good guys."

"And I'm here to keep you good," Richard said softly.

Chapter

THIRTEEN

"I sn't it a little late?" Rhiana asked as Kenntnis deposited the standing rib roast in the center of the dining room table. Mashed potatoes were piped around the edge of the platter, vegetable whitecaps breaking against the dark sides of the roast. Cross followed with a basket of popovers and a bowl of green beans.

The rich smell of fresh ground black pepper and beef juices hit Angela's nose and saliva erupted in her mouth. "Food is good," she said. "Keeps the strength up. Calms jittery nerves."

"You're my kind of woman," said Cross as he seated himself and stuffed a napkin into the collar of his dirty flannel shirt.

"You shouldn't have let Richard leave," Rhiana directed at Kenntnis. Her tone was aggrieved and accusing.

"Short of sitting on him I don't know how I was supposed to stop him," Kenntnis replied mildly.

"He might be in danger," Rhiana persisted.

Got a major crush developing here, Angela thought, but she knew from the faint twinge of pique that she was also in danger. Not wanting that much self-analysis, she turned her attention to the room. She studied the art gracing the dark wood-paneled walls, the ethereal crystal chandelier looking like a frozen waterfall, the deep glow of carved and polished wood in the table, chairs and buffet.

Kenntnis opened a bottle of Merlot, and filled their glasses. He then raised his. "To the Lumina."

"About damn time we have it back," grunted Cross.

Angela tapped the rim of her glass against Cross's, and a pure ringing tone hung in the silence. Rhiana held out her glass toward the homeless god, but Cross ignored it, focusing on his plate.

So, I wonder what's up his ass? Angela mused.

The candles on the table sprang to life, their fire dancing in the crystal and reflecting in the polished wood of the table-top. Angela jumped. Kenntnis and Cross looked at Rhiana. She looked back, and her posture yelled defiance.

"I'm still here," Rhiana said.

"We're not likely to forget about you," grunted Cross, and the tone wasn't friendly.

"Don't do parlor tricks," Kenntnis ordered. "It takes energy and it puts a pinprick hole in the universe. Do magic when I tell you to."

"So, I can keep using magic?" Rhiana asked.

"Yes, of course."

"But I thought magic was baaad." Angela put a long drawl on the final word, and was pleased to see Kenntnis flash her a look of annoyance.

Her granny had always told her the way she liked to poke people was perverse, but she couldn't help herself. Even with a man who possessed this much presence and, she suspected, power, she couldn't rein in her unruly tongue.

"There are no perfect or totally harmless choices here. We're playing to win," Kenntnis replied.

"So the ends justify the means?" Angela asked and gave Kenntnis a limpid and innocent look.

The big man looked even more annoyed, and Cross gave a bark of laughter that sent popover crumbs spewing across the table. "He's already had this conversation once tonight."

"With Richard?" Rhiana asked eagerly.

Kenntnis didn't reply. Instead he picked up a carving knife and a sharpener. Steel rasped against stone. He cut into the roast, parting the seared exterior. Blood flowed and red meat showed against the bone. Angela saw Rhiana staring with repellent fascination.

"Vegetarian?" she asked the younger woman. Rhiana nodded.

Cross reached across the table and speared a slice of beef. Angela watched the blood drip onto the white damask tablecloth and had a sudden flash of Richard's blood.

"I'll take a burnt end," Angela said firmly and held out her plate to Kenntnis.

Kenntnis sent down her plate, and filled Rhiana's with potatoes, green beans and a popover. Angela broke open the hot popover, filled the hollow interior with a large pat of butter, and took a bite. It was heavenly.

Rhiana took a few tiny bites then threw down her fork. "I still don't think you should have let Richard leave," she said again.

"He needed a break from all of us."

"From you, maybe," Rhiana muttered at her plate.

Angela cast a covert glance at Rhiana's flawless profile. The line of Richard's jaw was suddenly foremost in her mind. *Why couldn't this have been like a perfect television sitcom with a perfect set of couples? Instead we've got a monster, an enigma, a man and two women. Lovely.*

She took a bite of roast, and decided to pull the attention

away from Richard. "I have a question," she said. Kenntnis and Cross looked at her. "Why did Grenier resort to a gun? Why not continue to use magic?"

"Because I took the magical blast and he didn't have enough juice for another one," Cross answered.

"But based on the universe according to you," Angela shot Kenntnis a quick ironic smile, "couldn't he have used our fear to recharge?"

"He did; it's how he got through the wall," said Kenntnis, "but a death spell takes real power. He got it by killing those college kids."

"You're not suggesting that every time someone goes postal these guys are behind it?" Angela asked.

"No, but they certainly take advantage when it happens," Kenntnis replied dryly.

Aside from the smacking as Cross wolfed food, they ate in silence for a few minutes.

Angela found she didn't like the privacy of her own head right now. She framed another question. "So in the lexicon of mythic monsters what's Grenier? Or is he just a person?"

"He's a person," Kenntnis answered.

"Yeah, he's been carrying water for one of my splinters for years," Cross grunted and crammed a popover into his mouth.

"Why? Why him and not another preacher?" Angela asked.

"Access," said Kenntnis shortly. "He hooked up with a governor who became president, and then he was in. Given the rightward tilt of recent administrations he's been able to push the Old Ones' agenda."

"He's the reason they're teaching Intelligent Design instead of evolution in six states," added Cross, but the words were blurred as he continued to masticate popover. Angela watched the homeless god's throat work as he swallowed and she was reminded of pythons and puppies.

"He's also got a lot of magical juice so it was easy for him to learn the skills."

"Are all your . . . splinters hostile to each other?" Angela asked. "Could we do a little divide and conquer action?"

"Use your brain, girl," Cross muttered. "As long as they can get Christians and Muslims, and Jews and Muslims, and Muslims and Hindus, and Protestants and Catholics killing each other they're in hog heaven. I'm the only wart in their ointment."

"So why don't they just kill you?" Angela asked sweetly. "And don't call me 'girl.' "

"They're not certain what that would do to the other fragments," said Kenntnis stepping in as if he sensed she and Cross were about to spat.

"How do angels fit into all this?" Rhiana asked.

"Ah, angels." Kenntnis shook his head. "It was a fall-back position for some of the late arrivals. People like our friend here," he indicated Cross, "had taken most of the god positions, but they found a use for their tardy companions. You get to spread a lot of destruction when you're an angel."

"Or you got to until he," Cross jerked his chin toward Kenntnis, "came up with the idea of guardian angels."

"I never thought of angels as bad," said Rhiana.

Angela looked at the girl. "In the Bible the first words out of an angel's mouth were usually—*Don't be afraid. I'm not here to kill you.* Which now makes a whole lot more sense."

"Except that usually they were going to kill you," said Kenntnis dryly.

Thoughts spinning, Angela leaned back in her chair. "So, is there anything sacred that is good?"

"No," Cross said brightly, and helped himself to another slice of beef.

"So there is no God," Angela persisted, wanting to be

sure she understood the full implications of the day's revelations.

Kenntnis dropped his chin to his chest, and pursed his lips thoughtfully. Angela counted her heartbeats as they waited. "I've been around a long, long time," Kenntnis said slowly. "I have yet to see any evidence of one."

Exhaustion dragged at his eyelids, and the various aches in various parts of his body throbbed in time to his heartbeat. Richard knew he would need to rest soon, but his apartment was still under repair. That left the Lumina headquarters, and he couldn't face them yet. No, correct that, he couldn't face Kenntnis yet, not with what he now knew.

So he drove aimlessly through the streets of Albuquerque. The light from the street lamps flickered in his fogged windshield as the blast of warm air from the Volvo's heater struck cold glass.

He had thrown out the challenge to Kenntnis hoping to be denied, but knowing his conclusions about the man . . . creature . . . were correct. It helped if Richard thought of him as Prometheus or Loki or Coyote, but the other names remained; leaden, frightful and horrifying—Satan, Lucifer, the Devil.

But he saved my life. And his arguments make sense.

But they would, wouldn't they? He's the Great Deceiver.

The mountains served as a magnet drawing him toward the frowning rock face iced now with new-fallen snow. The storm had entered the city, and he drove through swirling snow as he followed Central Avenue east. To the north Kenntnis, Cross and the women ate and talked in the elegant confines of the penthouse. He assumed they were talking about him.

Judge Robert Oort's dry voice echoed in his ears. *"Why do you think people would notice you? You have a pretty face that attracts attention, but it's fool's gold. As yet you've failed to demonstrate that there is either accomplishment or character behind it. You lack the intellectual abilities of your sisters, and you're not a woman so you can't rely on beauty and charm the way your mother has. You'd best find something to recommend you."* But now somebody had said he was special.

But that somebody had admitted he was the embodiment of ancient evil.

Richard saw the outline of a cross dark against the shifting backdrop of snow. The building came into view, a peaked profile of a church reaching toward the sky like prayerful hands. He didn't know what denomination it might be, but right then he needed the comfort of religion. Spinning the wheel, he pulled into the parking lot. With the turn of the key the engine died. Snow tapped like fingernails against the windows and body of the car. The engine pinged as it cooled.

The snow squeaked under the leather soles of his shoes as he walked to the front doors. It wasn't his church, but the Lutheran church he normally attended was far out on Montgomery and dangerously near the Lumina headquarters. Letters in brass spelled out *Saint Luke's on the Mesa* over the door. Richard didn't have much hope the church would be open, so he had to scramble to keep his balance when the door swung open in response to his tug. It was unusual in these secular and uncertain times to find a church unlocked at night. Richard wanted to take it as a sign, but it seemed a pathetic reed on which to hang his faith.

The wall at the end of the nave was an expanse of glass. The sloping walls to either side were vast fields of stained glass. The white of the snow beyond the front window gave a pale illumination to the interior of the church. There were tall candles on the draped altar and the scent of frankincense hung in the air. A red light burned over the altar. With the steps and railing separating the nave from the apse and the kneelers in each pew it felt like a Catholic church. Richard glanced down at the hymnals in the holders on the back of the pews and saw the *Book of Common Prayer* among them. He was in an Episcopalian church.

He wasn't a smoker, but Richard carried a lighter in case he found himself stranded during one of his long drives into the New Mexico back country. Because he had been raised in such a fiercely Protestant sect the barrier of the railing held no power for him. He walked to the altar and lit both candles. He then bowed his head and began to pray.

Dear God, are you there? Do you exist? I don't know what to believe anymore. Is it presumptuous to ask for a sign? Help me, Dear Lord, I'm losing myself.

The wind hissed around the building, the snow pecked at the glass and the flames on the candles shrank briefly and then elongated once more into orange-yellow flares.

"That's it?" Richard said aloud. "Your enemy is giving me wonders."

He yanked the sword hilt out of his pocket and tossed it onto the floor in front of the altar. There was the sound of a deep-throated bell as the twisted form hit the stones. For long seconds Richard heard the overtones echoing away toward the distant ceiling.

"I've only heard something similar in the baptistry in Pisa with its perfect acoustical overtones," came a deep and gravelly voice from the back of the church. Richard whirled and peered into the dimness. "This building has crappy acoustics so I have to assume that remarkable sound was produced by whatever it was you threw on the floor." The voice was getting closer.

A stocky figure dressed in faded blue jeans but topped with a black shirt and the white collar of a priest came rolling down the aisle. The candlelight gleamed on his bald pate and reflected in the deep-set eyes.

"I'm Charlie," the man said and thrust out his hand.

Richard shook it. "Father."

"Just Charlie," came the correction.

Now that the priest was in the pale circle of light provided by the candles Richard could see the gray fringe of hair just above his ears and the seamed face.

"You seem to be a man in need of a conversation," said the older man.

Richard glanced back at the embroidered altar cloth. "Yes, but God's not talking."

"Maybe he's just coming in on a different frequency," the priest said placidly. He hesitated, then said, "Look, how about coming over to the rectory for cup of something warm?"

Richard glanced toward the altar and as if the priest had read his mind he added softly, "If God can't find you next door he's not much of a God, is he?"

Angela pulled on her coat, left the penthouse and punched the elevator call button. There was a distant clunk and whine as gears began to move. She leaned her shoulder against the wall. A muffling blanket of exhaustion fell across her head and neck. The elevator arrived with a sharp ding. The doors slid open and she staggered inside. The doors were almost closed when a slender hand was thrust in. The doors bounced apart and Rhiana joined her.

The girl leaned against the wall opposite Angela. The vivid green eyes were hard and a frown disturbed the perfect line of her brow. "Why are you here?" she demanded.

Too many times in her life, in medical school, in police forces, in morgues, Angela had met resistance and handled it. This time she was pretty confident it was coming from more than just a protection of territory.

"Because Richard needed a coroner," she said placidly.

"You don't bring us anything," the girl continued. "You're just an ordinary person."

"And you don't think an ordinary person might be of help?" Angela asked and reminded herself that Rhiana was very young and you treat the young tenderly.

"No," Rhiana said bluntly.

On the other hand not too tenderly, Angela decided.

"Look, sweetie, Kenntnis can talk all he wants about using any tool to win," she said with a tight smile. "But let's remember what winning entails—banishing all magic from the world. So I'd suggest you polish up your ordinary human skills in preparation for the time when you're no longer Super Witch, and remember that politeness is one of them." There was a faint jar through the soles of her feet as the elevator came to rest on the ground floor.

The doors opened and Angela headed for the front doors fully expecting Rhiana to come in pursuit, but she heard no answering footfalls. She looked back. Rhiana slumped against the doors of the elevator. Tears leaked slowly from beneath her closed eyelids.

Two quick strides brought her back to the girl and she wrapped her arms around her. She expected resistance, but there was none. Rhiana slumped against her, crying harder now.

"I wanted to be special," came Rhiana's muffled voice. "But nobody likes smart, and now this is wrong too."

Angela knew all about being smart and female in American society, and being a bright, ambitious Hispanic woman in a culture that rejected both attributes when displayed by women.

"What happens when they take it all away from me?" Rhiana continued.

"They can't take it *all*. You're a frigging physicist. That makes medicine look easy." Rhiana shook her head. "And you're beautiful," Angela added.

"That shouldn't matter," Rhiana sniffed.

"Well it does, and if anyone ever told you otherwise . . . well, they're an idiot." Angela paused. Her joints seemed to be grinding together with weariness. "Look, there's a twenty-four-hour Carrow's just down the road. How about we get a cup of coffee and talk? I could use a crappy cup of coffee. I've spent years drinking hospital coffee or morgue coffee. Kenntnis's is just way too fancy for my plebeian tastes." Rhiana gave a watery chuckle. "That's better. Come on."

Chapter

FOURTEEN

It feels like my faith is shriveling," said Richard as he sat huddled at the breakfast table, hands cupped around a mug of tea.

The rectory was a 1950s cracker-box house and it looked like neither the cabinets nor the appliances had been replaced since then. The residual smell of boiled peas and pot roast hung in the air. There was a guilty niggling at the back of Richard's mind telling him he ought to go back into the church and recover the sword. But he didn't want to face the cold . . . or the sword.

"Why? Because of a profound disappointment? A tragedy?" the priest asked.

"No, because this man I'm working for . . . with . . . is shining a brutally cold light on it."

"Challenging faith with logic," said Charlie. He canted his chair onto its back legs and balanced his cup on his paunch.

"Yes."

"But you can't apply logic to faith. I've talked to you long enough to tell that you're a more sophisticated believer than that."

Richard hunched forward, dropping his eyes so he didn't have to meet the priest's gaze. "Recently the words haven't been able to drown out the hundreds . . . thousands of years of atrocities."

"Men commit the atrocities," said Charlie.

"Guided by religions," countered Richard.

"Religions aren't about God," said the priest.

"So they're only for crowd control? Setting a standard of behavior and demanding people obey under pain of Hell? God as daddy?"

Charlie lifted his cup and blew across the top of his coffee. "At their best. At their worst they're about influence, manipulation and power."

Richard shook his head. "You're the strangest minister I've ever met. I actually think you could talk to Kenntnis." He paused for a sip of tea and as the liquid hit his stomach he realized he was achingly hungry. "So what do you believe?"

"That faith is transcendent, exalting. It calls you to service, worship and duty," replied the priest and his face was alight with fervor. "And I also think that religion is a deeply and totally personal experience."

Richard sunk his chin into the collar of his turtleneck and tried to think how to frame the questions. But it always came back to the same question. *Did God exist?* A real God, not these masqueraders. He stared at the stains on the heavy wooden table.

"It seems like you come from a more dogmatic tradition," Charlie said.

"Meaning what?" asked Richard a bit defensively.

Charlie tapped his chest. "I teach and have always believed that Jesus wasn't kidding when he said the kingdom of God is within you. Other sects have a more arm's-length relationship. I think every human is capable of Godlike behavior, so if you believe in yourself you believe in God."

"So, by celebrating humanity . . . ," Richard said slowly.

"You celebrate God," finished Charlie.

"So it's all about people."

"For me," said Charlie simply.

"Very like Kenntnis." Richard stood and carried his mug over to the sink. He turned, resting his hands and back against the counter. "So you set no rules?"

"Only one," said Charlie. "Do unto others as you would have others do unto you. Everything else is pretty much just noise." They regarded each other for a long time. "This man who has you questioning your faith, what does he say?" Charlie asked gently.

Richard sighed and took a drink of tea. "That it's all about people, but unlike you, he demands that I reject God."

"And that would be a mortal sin."

❀

The Carrow's was noisy and lively from the invasion of a post-football game high school crowd. A large corner booth was bursting with four enormous young men whose necks were wider than their heads. Acne bloomed across their cheeks and chins. Wedged between them like slender white beeches growing among boulders were the cheerleaders still dressed in their perky little gold and white uniforms and showing a lot of skin and goose bumps.

The rest of the room was filled with exuberant fans, and at a far corner a couple of young male shitkickers were trying to set the brims of each other's cowboy hats on fire with lighters. The waitresses looked harried and the manager, a kid just a few years older than his customers, kept setting his hand on the phone as if trying to decide whether or not to call for help.

Rhiana and Angela sat next to a broad window that gave them an uninspiring view of the cars flowing past on Montgomery Boulevard. Rhiana couldn't help it; her lip curled as she regarded the chattering teenagers running between cliques at various tables with tosses of long hair and tugs at the waistbands of absurdly baggy jeans.

"Oh come on," came the coroner's voice. "You aren't that far removed. You're what, eighteen? Nineteen?"

"Eighteen . . . almost. And I only went to one football game in high school."

Angela shook open the paper napkin and placed it in her lap with a flourish. "Sounds like a traumatic experience."

"Do you always have to make fun of me?" Rhiana asked tightly.

The older woman glanced up at her quickly and looked abashed. "I'm really not. It's just my manner. I come across glib and aggressive even when I don't mean to. It was a survival technique in the family and in medical school. So what happened at the football game?"

"I took a book," said Rhiana shortly and glared at a pimply boy whose lank hair hung well into his eyes. "The popular kids grabbed it and tore all the pages out."

"You realize, of course, that we are twin sisters separated by seventeen years and nine hundred miles. I was the kind of geek who took a book to a ball game too," and Angela smiled to remove any sting.

A waitress arrived. They both ordered coffee and handed back the menus. The roar of conversation created an odd dissonance with the music leaking from the stereo speakers. The smell of frying hamburgers filled the room, adding to Rhiana's nausea.

Angela played with her utensils for a few seconds then she rushed into speech. "So, according to Kenntnis I've got a little bit of magic," said Angela. "And after watching you in action it made me wonder . . . well, if you could teach me how to do what you do. I'm really curious."

"As as experiment?" Rhiana asked.

"Yes . . . maybe . . . no. For a lot of reasons," the older woman confessed.

"It can't be tested. I've tried. Remember, I was a scientist before I became a, well, a witch for lack of a better term," said Rhiana.

"Kenntnis called you a sorceress. It think that fits you better," said Angela, and in answer to Rhiana's questioning look she elaborated. "I've got two visions of witches. One formed at an early age from watching *The Wizard of Oz* every year, and the other from the pagan communities that were around during college. You don't fit into either category."

"I don't think Kenntnis would like it if I teach you," Rhiana said slowly.

"So, do you see me asking his permission?" came the quick response.

"It could be dangerous," said Rhiana.

"We'll hide behind Richard," said Angela. Their eyes met as they considered the diminutive stature of the policeman and they both started laughing.

To be a musician it helped to have good hearing. Richard's was exceptional, so even over the whistle of the teakettle and the east winds howling through Tijeras Canyon he heard the crunch of tires on snow and the snick of a car door closing. He checked his watch—a few minutes past midnight.

"Do you often get people this late?" he asked Charlie.

Holding a tea bag in each hand, the priest turned and looked at him. "Huh?"

"Somebody's just pulled into the parking lot," said Richard as he crossed to the window and barely lifted a curtain to look out.

A couple of darkly clad figures were hurrying toward the main door of the church, and Richard realized with a sick lurch in the pit of his stomach that he should have gone back after the sword. He'd wanted a physical break from from Kenntnis's world, and tossing away the sword seemed like the best way to accomplish that. Now it just seemed foolish.

Charlie had brought them over to the house through the door in the sacristy. It wasn't immediately evident from the parking lot. "Stay here," Richard threw back at the priest as he ran out the kitchen door. He nipped across the snow-covered gravel of the southwestern style landscaping toward the side of the church.

The wind had the snow blowing horizontal. The fat, wet flakes of earlier in the evening had become ice pellets that stung the exposed skin of his face. He reached the door and slipped into the robing room beyond. He heard the creak and clunk of the heavy front doors opening and closing. For an instant he mentally struggled, then drew his gun.

The parking lot of the Carrow's had become a skating rink. The snow was now covered with a thin coating of ice. Angela and Rhiana linked arms to help balance each other and headed for Angela's robin's-egg-blue Thunderbird.

Rhiana felt Angela stiffen and she looked up from her feet. The older woman was staring at a man seated on the hood of one of the parked cars. The man lifted a hand and waved, but all his attention was focused on Rhiana. She had the impression of a narrow face with upswept eyebrows. A gust of wind carried a squall of snow. When it passed the man was gone.

Carefully Richard opened the hidden door of the sacristy and looked out. Two men were hurrying up the aisle toward the altar.

The altar was directly across from him, perhaps ten feet away. The sword hilt lay on the concrete floor in front of it.

The candles he had lit were still burning. Richard blinked, wondering if exhaustion was causing the room beyond to dim. Then he realized the flames on the altar candles were sinking. They dwindled to tiny sparks and were extinguished. Richard glanced down at his right wrist, the luminous dial on his watch was also going dark. But the darkness wasn't complete. A nimbus of white light hovered around the sword hilt as if a swirl of stars surrounded it.

Knowing from his experience with Rhiana that his pistol was now useless, Richard holstered the Firestar. The smaller of the two men was pushing through the gate at the railing, hand outstretched for the hilt. Fear was forgotten. Richard flung himself out the door running full out. It was going to be close. Memories of summer days, the ping of a metal bat on a ball, home plate shimmering before him in the heat haze, inspired him. Richard threw himself into a dive and went sliding across the floor. The other man's fingers scraped across the back of his coat. Richard swept up the hilt, tucked and rolled to his feet. The moment his hand closed around the hilt the swirl of lights spread to encompass his body.

The man Richard had beaten out for the sword stood staring at him. His panting breaths were loud in the cavernous room. He was skinny and angular and not much older than Richard. Brown hair flopped into his eyes. The eyes stopped Richard. They were flat and utterly without expression. Blackboard dark and just as daunting. His pants were shabby and despite the cold he wore only a nylon windbreaker.

The other man was younger, burlier, with a big sagging belly, and he seemed to be in charge. He wore an expensive ski parka and fancy hiking boots. Swinging loosely in his right hand was a riding crop. It was so incongruous that for an instant Richard's attention was distracted from the skinny man.

The metallic rattle of a butterfly knife opening, and the glint of light on the blade was his only warning. Richard sprang back, sucking in his gut as the tip caught on the material of his sweater. Spinning, he swept his hand away from the hilt, summoning the blade. The spin brought him around 360 degrees to face his assailant. Grimly Richard gestured with the thirty-inch blade of the sword against the six-inch blade of the butterfly knife. "Set it down and back away," he ordered. Richard kept his eyes locked on Skinny's eyes. Fencing had taught him that the eyes telegraphed the physical.

Not surprisingly the skinny man didn't respond. The burly one suddenly swept his crop through the air, crying out in a strange language. But Richard had heard it before. It was the language that Rhiana had used in the alley. Fire arced from the end of the crop heading toward Richard. He didn't have a lot of options. The knife-wielding thug blocked one direction and the heavy stone altar the other possible avenues for retreat.

Richard braced for searing pain and parried with the sword. The fire touched the black, black blade, a deafening series of chordal overtones filled the church as if ten thousand organs were playing one profound bass note. The fire vanished into the blade, but the knife man saw his opportunity and took it. He rushed Richard, knife held low and ready, the point angled up to do the maximum amount of damage to Richard's gut. Muscles do learn and remember. Richard pivoted to the side to offer a smaller target to his attacker and pushed the knife hand away. The man spun, trying to once again face Richard, but the wet soles of his shoes slipped on the polished concrete and he crashed into him. They both fell back against the altar. Richard's head rang and spun as the back of his skull connected with the stone lip of the altar.

Fingers closed around Richard's left wrist. The bones ground together under the unrelenting pressure. Fighting back nausea and the throbbing in his head, Richard headbutted his opponent in the face. Blood spattered warm and sticky across him. Struggling desperately, he flung himself from side to side trying to dislodge the man. Panic yammered in his head as he heard the approaching footfalls of the second man.

A new sound entered the equation: the harsh rasping slide of a pump shotgun being cocked. "Church or no, if you don't back off I'll blow a hole through you," came Charlie's bass growl.

The skinny man rolled quickly off Richard. "No, stupid, it won't fire," yelled the burly young man at his associate.

"Charlie, it won't work," Richard yelled at the same time.

But it's hard to believe something so outlandish, and Charlie squeezed the trigger anyway. Skinny's chest sunk in as if anticipating the pellets. Charlie stared with grim anticipation and nothing happened.

With a braying laugh Skinny threw himself toward Richard. There was a blur of motion as the wooden grip of the shotgun swept past Richard's face and smashed into the side of Skinny's head. The impact drove the attacker sideways into the altar. He sank down onto the floor moaning, one hand nursing his head, the other his ribs. The butterfly knife lay forgotten. Richard kicked it aside.

"Yeah, but inertia sure as hell works," grunted the priest.

Richard vaulted over the railing. The other man ran backward, the crop outstretched as if warding him off. The edge of the sword cut through the crop, severing it. But that wasn't the extent of the damage. The leather twisted, writhed and liquefied.

With a sob of fear the man whirled and bolted for the door. Richard pounded after him, each step sending a jar of pain through the back of his head. *If you touch a normal human it will render him or her incapable of performing magic,* Kenntnis's words filled his mind. They were at the door, the man scrabbling at the handle. Richard adjusted his grip and laid the flat of the blade across the sorcerer's back. The tearing scream echoed around the church. His arms thrust behind his back, hands reaching for the area where the sword had rested.

Charlie lumbered down the aisle. "Stop it! What are you doing to him?"

The man sank onto his knees and vomited. The smell of bile now joined the smell of sweat and incense.

"Call the police," Richard said, pulling out his cell phone, but then he realized that the flames on the candles had not returned and his phone was dark and inert. "Oh dear," Richard whispered.

There was a whisper of sound from the altar.

Chapter

FIFTEEN

The bones in his neck cracked and the muscles stretched taut as Richard whipped his head around. At the same time the priest gave a gasping moan. Behind him the front doors creaked and a blast of cold air whistled down the length of the church. He looked back. The burly man tottered out the door, but there was nothing Richard could do to prevent the escape because the spare, suffering figure on the cross was coiling, stretching, climbing down. A bare foot touched the top of the altar. Charlie crossed himself and sank to his knees. The inert form of the knife-wielding thug still huddled at the base of the altar. God didn't spare him a glance.

God lifted his head and looked at Richard. And the eyes captured him. A golden brown—like sunlight on amber. They were soft and warm and loving. Richard stood rooted, unable to turn away.

"So you do not totally deny me, Richard," said his God.

That this day, even in this night, before the cock crow twice, thou shalt deny me thrice. The words so often read and repeated suddenly had power. Guilt and fear set his gut to aching.

"There is still time before you are lost to me forever." The voice was dark velvet, low and deep and plaintive.

Richard sucked in a shuddering breath and found it breaking on a barely suppressed sob.

"Richard. My child. My son." Now the figure was draped in a gleaming white robe. The Lord stretched out his hand. The smell of lilies caressed the air.

The point of the sword dropped to the floor. The echoing chime rang through the church, but now it sounded dissonant, creating a painful pressure deep within his ears. Richard's control broke and the sobs came. He dropped to his knees, gut clenching with the force of his tears.

"Be at peace. You have struggled and been tested, but not found wanting. There, there. Hush now. Hush. I have always heard you, Richard." God approached, careful step by careful step. "When you prayed for your mother. When those men hurt you."

But like sand through the fingers the exaltation and comfort drained away because *he had never prayed for his mother.* When she had been committed, his father had brought all the children into his study and battered into them the understanding that *no one* was to know where she had gone. Friends, neighbors and schoolmates were all told of a trip to Europe. The shame was too great to be revealed. Richard, age seven, had been terrified that if God knew about his mother's drinking she would surely go to Hell. So Richard never mentioned her in his prayers, fearful that if reminded, God might go looking for her, find her wanting and punish her.

Richard remembered the file Grenier had perused. There

was no mystery here. No omnipotence. No omniscience. No omnipresence.

Just lies.

Springing back, Richard swept up the sword point, and flung himself forward in a deep lunge. But the creature was preternaturally fast. It coiled and leaped back onto the altar before the point could connect. Its feet tangled briefly in the altar cloth, toppling the candlesticks. As it swarmed up the cross a hoarse ululating cry gurgled from its throat.

Behind him, Richard heard Charlie give a gagging cough. There was a thud. Glancing back, Richard saw that Charlie had fallen onto his side. The priest gripped his left arm with his right hand.

It was a lousy time for a heart attack because Richard knew an attack of another kind was coming. He whirled and started running to Charlie. Even as he ran he studied the church, trying to determine the potential source of the danger. The heavy stone altar? The wooden pews? His eyes lifted toward the sloping expanses of stained glass that formed the walls. His heart sank. They liked glass. With a thunderclap the windows exploded inward.

The lights sprang back to life so Richard could have a really good look at the jagged, rainbow-colored death raining down on them.

It repairs rips in the fabric of reality.

That glass is pretty goddamn real! yammered another voice inside his head.

Picture it stopping.

And Richard raised the sword straight over his head. His shoulders pulled down, his head hunching between them as he waited to be impaled. Nothing. Just the cold wet touch of snow and wind. Slowly he opened his eyes, and looked up. The shards of multicolored glass hung in the air only inches above the point of the sword.

Remember it restored.

He stretched up his arms, making them as long as possible. The glass flew back into the frames.

The flicker of fire danced on the walls. The extinguished candles were burning again and had ignited the altar cloth and the Bible. For an instant Richard dithered between Charlie and the flames. The altar was stone. The fire wouldn't spread. As for the Bible . . . Richard turned his back and ran toward Charlie.

The roar of the discarded shotgun discharging caused him to jump, stagger and slam his hip against one of the pews. He limped the last few feet to the priest, and gave thanks that the muzzle had been pointed toward a wall.

Dropping the sword, Richard gripped Charlie by the shoulders and rolled him onto his back. The priest's lips were cold and slack. Richard drew in a singer's breath, deep and full, and sent the air into Charlie's lungs. The taste of the coffee Charlie had been drinking lingered on his lips and in his mouth. Richard did chest compression with one hand as he groped for his cell phone. Eventually he managed to dial 911 and call out their location.

His head was swimming by the time the ambulance arrived.

Oddly, Lieutenant Weber was with the EMTs.

It was hard to hear the ambulance's siren over the whine of the wind. Weber and Richard, standing in the parking lot of the church, watched the red glow of its taillights dwindle as it went racing down Central toward hospital row bearing the priest and the perp. Richard's muscles contracted painfully from the violence of his shivers. The lieutenant dropped an arm over Richard's shoulders and drew him in close. Twisting aside, Richard put three feet between him and Weber. The older man gave no reaction, simply saying, "Let's go back inside." The peaked roof of the church seemed to impale the pendulous snow clouds. He walked up the steps, and pulled open the door of the church.

"I'd rather not," Richard said.

"Tough. I need a statement from you."

Richard recognized a command and knew better than to argue. They skirted the pool of vomit and moved deeper into the church. Sinking down into a pew, Richard watched Weber stroll around the church. The older man pulled on surgical gloves and picked up the discarded shotgun. He examined the stock, sticky now with blood and hair.

"Who did the head-cracking?"

"Charlie . . . the priest."

"Hmm," Weber grunted. "Tough priest."

He leaned the shotgun against the altar. Shoving his hands deep into the pockets of his sheepskin coat, he stared down at the discarded butterfly knife. He prodded it with a toe, then frowned as he spotted the blood staining the blade.

"Should there have been three patients in that ambulance?" he asked.

Richard gaped at him, not fully understanding, then it clicked and he shook his head. "No, it was just a scratch."

Weber walked back to him. "Let me have a look."

"It's nothing, really," Richard remonstrated, but Weber was tall and strong. He pulled the slighter man out of the pew, pushed open his coat and parted the torn and blood-stained sweater.

It was indeed only a scratch, but the blade had cut through the bandage that supported Richard's abused ribs. The lieutenant pulled aside Angela's handiwork. Weber's brows drew together in a sharp frown, and Richard's throat was suddenly too small to accommodate a swallow.

The bandage was pulled away and the broad hands with their blunt fingers stroked across the bruise. The skin on the tips of Weber's fingers was rough. Richard sucked in a quick breath and fought back panic.

"This is the kind of bruising you get when a bullet hits body armor." Richard remained silent. "Did you get shot?" the lieutenant demanded.

He was so bad at lying. Reluctantly, Richard slowly nodded.

"Who the fuck shot you? Did this happen in Colorado? And why the hell didn't you report it?"

Richard shrugged, nodded and shrugged again.

"What the fuck is going on with you?" Weber's tone was frustrated and aggrieved.

Disgusted, his superior threw back his head and gave it a despairing shake. Richard waited for the interrogation to continue, but Weber was frozen. Following his superior's gaze, Richard's heart sank. The stained glass windows now seemed to be courtesy of Hieronymous Bosch. In one frame a palm tree sprouted from Joseph's ear. In another there was simply a jumble of eyes. Apparently lacking a photographic memory of the pictures had led to this chaos. *Why can't it be smarter than I am?* Richard thought, and touched the hilt resting in his coat pocket.

"Okay. That's it. Now you are fucking going to tell me what the fuck is going on!" Weber grabbed him by the upper arm and started marching him toward the door. "Is your apartment still all fucked up?" Richard nodded. "Okay, you're coming home with me. . . . And don't fucking argue with me!"

"I have to write up a report."

"You'll write it in the morning, and didn't I tell you not to argue?"

Needles of hot water washed through his hair and across his body digging into each cut, scrape and bruise. The water swirling around his bare feet and gurgling down the drain was rust colored with blood. Richard hoped that most of it was Skinny's washing off his face and out of his hair.

He stayed in the shower until the water ran clean. Richard rubbed himself dry with Weber's thin and faded towels, and leaned into the medicine cabinet mirror. Pale gold bristle ghosted across his jaw and upper lip. He wished he could shave.

The older officer had left a bathrobe flung across the foot of the bed. It was a typical man's robe meant to reach mid-calf. On Richard it brushed the floor. He rubbed his cheek against the soft collar and breathed in the smell of coffee and cigarette smoke. Pausing for a moment, Richard regarded the unmade bed. It was rumpled temptation. He hurriedly left the bedroom.

Weber waited in the living room of the furnished apartment, feet up on the scarred and cluttered coffee table, body slouched on the ugly brown couch. Smoke from his cigarette floated around his head, a murderous halo. Hotel-room art hung on a couple of the walls. There was a big-screen TV on the far wall. An armchair was overflowing with coats, including Richard's cashmere overcoat. Richard gathered them up and set them on the small dinette table. From that vantage point he could see into the narrow kitchen. The surfaces of the counters were covered with take-out Chinese and pizza boxes.

"Separated or divorced?" *Or single*, his mind provided, but he thought that option was unlikely.

"Separated," Weber replied. "Why I haven't bought any dishes. Keep thinking I'll be going home soon."

Well, that settled where he would be sleeping, Richard thought.

Weber paused to take a long drag on his cigarette. "You ever been married?"

Richard shook his head. He seated himself in the armchair and watched his lieutenant crush out the cigarette in an overflowing ashtray.

"Don't. At least not until you retire from the force."

"I . . . I don't mean to be rude, but do you have anything

to eat?" Richard asked, shifting his focus from one hunger to another. "I haven't had anything since . . ." He thought about it. "Well, since yesterday morning."

Weber shook out another cigarette, jammed it into his mouth, and strode into the kitchen.

The interior of the refrigerator yawned empty before them. There were a few bottles of Corona, a carton of cottage cheese, and a plain white plastic container. Weber popped the lid off the cottage cheese and surveyed the green lumps inside. He tossed it onto the counter and pulled out the white plastic tub.

"I know this will be okay. Nothing could live in this."

From a lower cabinet he pulled out a bag of tortilla chips and shoved them into Richard's chest. Snagging a beer, he led them back into the living room and set everything on the coffee table. The lid came off the container, revealing a dark red salsa.

Richard took a chip and cautiously dipped in one corner. As the salsa passed beneath his nose the acrid, smoky scent of chile set his eyes watering. The bite, modest though it was, had the edges of his tongue burning, caught in the back of his throat and exploded in his gut. He could almost feel his ulcers cringing, but he didn't care what it might do to his stomach; his hunger was too great.

Richard mopped sweat off his brow, and Weber grinned that sadistic native New Mexican's grin that translated into *we may be poor and eccentric, but our chile is kick-ass*.

Silence once more stretched between them. "So, I'm waiting for my explanation," Weber finally said.

"And what does that mean . . . exactly?" Richard hoped it would buy him a little time to think about how he was ultimately going to answer.

What it bought him was Weber's face thrust pugnaciously into his. A gust of warm, alcohol-laden breath gusted across his skin.

"Do not treat me like a fucking mushroom or so help me God I will go straight to the Captain."

Blue eyes and brown met and held. Richard broke first. He studied the faint line of acne scars peppered around Weber's eyes, the square chin losing some of its definition to incipient jowl, the straight brows now drawn together in a deep frown. Not a handsome face, but honest and totally reassuring.

"It's . . . it's complicated."

"I'll cope."

"It will sound crazy."

"I can handle that too."

Richard got up and walked over to his overcoat, reached into the pocket and touched the hilt of the sword. For a long moment he reviewed the past three days, the people he'd met, the information he'd received, and this object he'd been given. He wondered how he would explain it to Kenntnis, especially since the decision he'd just reached was based on nothing more than gut feeling.

Richard leaned back and tried to form his expression into one of cool confidence. He met Weber's gaze and said, "So, how do you feel about ancient and secret societies?"

Chapter

SIXTEEN

Richard left Weber at Lumina Enterprises. He quickly brought Kenntnis up to speed on the events of last night, and primed him that Weber needed to hear the world-according-to-Kenntnis lecture. When Kenntnis started to argue, he held up a warning finger, and reminded him that he, Richard, got to call the shots now.

He drove across Eubank Boulevard, slow going because

of the snow blanketing the streets, and paused at Golden Fried Chicken for a breakfast burrito. He rode the freeway west into downtown, double parked while he ran into APD headquarters for the jacket on Skinny aka Doug Andresson. Finally he swung back to UNMH. It was the hospital responsible for indigent care, and it was used to house injured prisoners. Pulling into the parking lot, Richard briefly wondered where Kenntnis had gotten in the lecture, and how the lieutenant was reacting.

He left the engine running so he could have heat and music while he ate his burrito, and perused Andresson's rap sheet. It detailed numerous B & Es, a few armed robberies, assaults against girlfriends, random bar fights and a car jacking. The record extended across Arizona, Colorado and Texas with most of the crimes centered in his home state of Texas.

Crumpling the foil, still warm from the burrito and redolent of green chile, Richard gathered up the file and headed into the hospital.

It had been three years since his long hospitalization, but the smells of rubbing alcohol, bedpans, and overcooked food, and the sounds of suffering had his stomach fluttering with nausea. He hurried to an elevator and rode up with a slender Hispanic male nurse and his elderly charge. Slumped in a wheelchair, his every inhale was a sonorous wheeze and every exhale a whimper. Richard couldn't bear to look at the age-spotted skin, the rheumy eyes and the sliver of saliva coursing down the corner of the old man's mouth. He wondered if he had family? If they visited him? If there was any life beyond the hospital or if this was his final stay?

He stared at the doors until a prickling made him aware of close scrutiny. He looked over and met the eyes of the nurse over the wispy white hair of the old man. The nurse's skin was a pale olive with touches of rose in the cheeks. Jet-black hair sprang thickly back from a sharp widow's peak. The interest and invitation were bold fire in the nurse's dark brown eyes. The breath caught in Richard's throat, and he looked quickly away. The elevator shuddered to a stop and he stepped out. He looked back quickly at the young man who gave him a regretful shrug. The doors closed, leaving Richard still staring at the scuffed white metal.

It had to be Rhiana. That was the only explanation for his sudden awakening, but damn it was inconvenient. *Or maybe I'm finally over it,* he thought as he walked along the ward looking for Andresson's room.

It was easy to find. It was the only one with a uniformed policeman standing outside the door. Nodding to the guard on Andresson's door, Richard put Rhiana and attractive male nurses out of his mind and asked, "Is he alone?"

"Yeah," grunted the uniform. "If he was to fall out of bed while you were talkin' to him . . . well, let's just say I wouldn't notice."

Richard gave the young man a small smile. Cops took an extremely dim view of perps who attacked cops so the remark was not unexpected, though it made Richard cringe.

Maybe Weber is right. Maybe I am too much of a boy scout to do this job, he thought as he entered the hospital room.

The head of the bed was elevated so Andresson could have a better angle on the television that hung high on the wall. It was Regis and Kelly mugging for the camera. Andresson muted the sound, but otherwise lay unnaturally still. The unblinking dark shark eyes watched as Richard approached to within a few feet of the bed. Andresson's head was bandaged.

Like any good predator he noted the stiffness of Richard's walk and how still he kept his torso. A slow smile lifted Andresson's lips. It was a disturbing expression, exposing both teeth and gums.

"Got ya, didn't I?" It was less a question than a statement of pleasure.

"Not as well as I got you," Richard responded, and nodded toward the door and the guard.

"Yeah, well," Andresson shrugged. "They always let me out."

Richard took another step toward the bed, then felt a prickling down the back of his neck because Andresson's muscles had tightened as if in preparation for a move. Acutely aware of the Firestar beneath his right armpit and the hilt of the sword resting in the holster at the small of his back, and of Andresson's penchant for physical violence, he took three steps back.

There was a flare of disappointment deep in those flat eyes, and Andresson relaxed back against the pillows. He dug between his teeth with a fingernail. "I want a lawyer."

"This isn't a formal interrogation." Richard pulled the hilt out of the holster and held it up. "You were after this, weren't you?"

"And I should talk to you why?"

"Because your buddy ran out on you, leaving you to take the rap, and believe me, assault on a police officer is just a tad more serious than your previous felonies."

The man's eyes narrowed. "You don't have Fat Boy?" Richard shook his head. "Shit." Andresson stared intently at Richard, assessing every aspect of his looks and clothing. "They told me that you and me are alike. I sure don't fucking see it."

A thrill of cold horror shot down his back, and Richard wanted to deny the possibility. But it made sense. The issue was magic—whether you had it or not. There was no moral imperative that said only good people lacked the touch of magic. It was up to the cosmic gamble of genetics. The question was whether Richard and Andresson had rolled craps.

"Why didn't you come after *me*? Why did you go into the church?"

"Fat Boy did something with his sissy little riding crop, and said the thing we were going after was in the church. He was real pleased. Said you were a dumb motherfucker."

Richard acknowledged the truth of Delay's remark, and after another look into those empty emotionless eyes, he made a fervent promise that he would never, ever, let the sword out of his sight or out of his reach again.

"Who hired you?"

"Fat Boy."

It was disappointing but not unexpected. Grenier was too smart to have his fingerprints on this.

"And to do what . . . exactly?"

"Get a hold of that weird thing, and then to go work for them. They wanted me bad, cop. They still do."

"And how do you know that?"

The only answer was a display of teeth and gums. Andresson turned back on the sound and focused on the television.

This was information that Kenntnis needed to hear.

There was still one stop before Richard could return to Lumina. Charlie was in intensive care up on the third floor. They wouldn't let him in to see the priest and they didn't want to give him any information either, but Richard showed them his badge and explained that Charlie had saved his life last night. That broke the bureaucratic barriers and a sympathetic nurse told him the priest was in a "light coma" but they hadn't given up hope.

He left with an ache in his throat and his soul.

The receptionist in the lobby gave him a wave. The security guard nodded a hello, and Richard realized that he'd become a fixture at Lumina. He wasn't entirely certain how he felt about that, but he knew one thing. If these people were going to be so accepting of him he needed to know their names.

He reversed course, walked to the receptionist and held out his hand. "Hi, I'm Richard Oort."

She had a nice smile, flawless ebony skin, and a set of elaborate corn rows forming sharp geometric patterns across her skull. "Paulette," she said.

"Nice to meet you."

"Same here."

He repeated the process with the guard whose name was Joseph, and whose handshake was crushing. There were scars across his knuckles and his nose had been broken several times, but the eyes were kind and determined. He'd fought, but it clearly hadn't been for the sake of fighting.

Richard decided to start in the office. It didn't seem like Kenntnis welcomed people into his penthouse until he'd gotten their measure, and Richard knew he'd thrown a large and unwelcome curve ball at the industrialist when he'd shown up with another recruit for the Lumina.

The final hiss of espresso machine accompanied Richard's entrance. Kenntnis garnished the coffee with foam and handed it to Weber. Angela stared critically at the lieutenant's poleaxed expression and said, "I think he needs a dollop of something a hell of a lot stronger than milk."

Kenntnis pulled open low cabinet drawers and held up a bottle of Irish whisky for Weber's consideration. The cop nodded vigorously. Kenntnis poured a shot into the coffee. Weber took a grateful sip.

"Can I make you something?" Kenntnis asked Richard.

"Tea, please."

"Milk?"

"Yes, please."

Weber lifted his face out of the soup bowl–sized cup and stared at Richard. The expression was hard to interpret and Richard got that sick feeling that he'd lost a friendship before it had even had a chance to form. Or maybe he was just being paranoid.

"I want to see this magic thingamajigger," Weber said.

"It's not magic," Kenntnis said.

"Then what is it?" Richard asked. "I confess to being a little fuzzy on the details since it certainly seems like magic to me."

"It's a little piece of the Big Bang."

"Meaning what?" Angela asked.

"Magic violates natural law. This device restores order."

"It didn't do a very good job on the windows," Richard said.

"I didn't say it did it perfectly. Quantum mechanics and chaos theory are, well . . . chaotic," Kenntnis said sharply.

Weber held up a hand. "Look, don't confuse me anymore. Just show me the damn thing."

Richard reached under his coat to the holster at the small of his back and pulled out the hilt. Before meeting Andresson he might have just tossed it over, but now he carefully carried it to Weber and handed it to the older man.

Frowning, the lieutenant turned it in his hands. "She said it was a sword."

"Richard," Kenntnis said.

Richard took back the hilt and drew the sword. Once again he felt more than heard a sound that seemed to reverberate in every cell of his body. Angela clasped her arms across her stomach and bent forward, collapsing at the intensity.

Weber spilled coffee in his crotch as he jumped. "*Shit!*" Richard wasn't sure which had elicited the yell—the sword or the hot coffee. "So, all this shit they've been telling me . . . it's true?"

"Sadly, yes," Richard said gently.

Weber looked up at Kenntnis. "And the kid here is the only person in the world who can use this thingamajig?"

"No," Kenntnis answered. "It's a genetic anomaly, and while it's very rare, there are other people in the world like Richard. Fortunately I found him first and, equally fortunate, he's a good person."

Richard felt the blood rush to his face. Angela elbowed him in the ribs and hit him right on the cut inflicted by the faux Cross. He gasped with pain, and her hands lifted to cover her mouth.

"Oh shit, sorry. That hurting thing . . . I keep forgetting about that. Probably because all my customers are dead." She gave him her imp's grin, her teeth flashing brightly in her dark face. He smiled back.

"Something other than the gunshot to the chest?" Weber asked, and he was no longer smiling.

"It's been a tough few days," Richard said in a tone he hoped would discourage any further inquiry, but to ensure a change of subject he decided to deliver his news.

"That kid who was in the church . . . I visited him in the hospital this morning, and he's like me." He told them the little he had learned from Andresson.

"We want to make sure that he doesn't end up with Grenier," Kenntnis said and his tone was grim. "If they had the sword they could destroy Cross and that would be . . . well, a terrible setback for us."

"Who's Cross?" Weber asked plaintively.

"Another member of the Lumina," Kenntnis answered.

"You know that thing about how magic is bad and we don't use magic?" Angela asked. "Well there are two big exceptions. Cross is one and our resident sorceress is another."

"Shhhh! Don't confuse him any more than necessary." Kenntnis glared at her, then turned his attention to Weber who was blotting at the front of his pants. "So how do you feel about all this? Do you want to be part of it or do you want to return to your own world?"

"Like I could pretend I hadn't heard any of this or seen

those church windows." Weber sighed and scrubbed a hand across his face. "What is it you want from me?"

"Guard Richard. Keep him safe. Keep the sword safe."

Angela's squawk kept the older cop from answering. "Hey," Angela said. "What about me? I'm in this too. I can keep an eye on Richard."

Weber stood and looked down at her. Then he looked down at Richard. "Yeah, but without me you look like the Munchkin Brigade."

"Good, that's settled," Kenntnis said while Angela glared up at Weber.

"So what do we do now?" Weber asked.

"Go back to work. Do your jobs. There are other evils in the world that you can combat until we're ready to move," was Kenntnis's answer.

"Excuse me?! Grenier is waltzing around in Virginia after killing those kids and trying to kill Richard. Aren't we going to do anything about that?" Angela demanded.

Kenntnis strolled back over to the espresso machine and poured in a carafe of water. While it heated he tossed tea leaves into a pot. "And what would you suggest?" He looked up. The delicate china teapot looked small in his massive hand. "A newspaper reported that Grenier was at a ladies' tea in the same hour he was supposedly attacking Richard in Colorado Springs. We can't prove he wasn't."

"Also, I think it was Delay who killed the kids, and I neutralized him last night," Richard said.

Angela whirled on him. "And I suppose that's enough payback for committing murder?"

The attack rocked him. For an instant anger and shame were equally balanced. Richard swallowed past a lump in his throat. "We can prove nothing." His tone was sharper than he liked, but it seemed to back her down.

Angela shook her head, but her voice was quieter as she said, "Well, for a world-spanning secret organization we're pretty damn narrow in our application."

"They're the world-spanning evil secret society," Kenntnis said as he filled the pot with boiling water. "We're rebuilding." He gave Angela one of his half-mocking smiles. "And waiting on supplies."

"I still think we ought to do something," Angela argued.

"What do you want me to do?" Richard demanded. "Go to Virginia, walk into WWCA headquarters and assault him with this?" He held out the hilt and gave it a shake.

"It'd be a start."

Kenntnis intervened. "And I'd lose my paladin, which is not in our best interests."

"Paladin?" said Weber, and grinned. Embarrassment had Richard's face burning.

Angela and Kenntnis were staring at each other. Angela broke first. She turned away with an irritated and dismissive shrug of the shoulder. "So, I guess we don't do squat."

"We don't move directly against Grenier, no. We interfere with some of his smaller operations, and look for ways to strike at him directly."

"What small operations?" Richard asked.

Kenntnis moved to his desk and gathered up a fistful of newspaper clippings. He plucked one out. "Here's a town in Ohio that's experiencing a rash of child disappearances." That page was discarded and another pulled out. "There are plans to build a prayerful subdivision in Alabama. That one really has me worried. I've got people trying to get a copy of the plans and extrapolate an aerial view." He riffled through the papers and selected another. "A minister in Clovis is planning a major book burning." He looked up at their blank faces. "The pattern people walk as they advance toward a fire at a book burning is an elaborate power rune. It weakens the fabric of space and time and starts to open a gate. The Old Ones loved the Nazis."

"That was a secular state," Angela interrupted. "They made war on the church as well as on Jews."

"Hitler was involved in an occult circle in Vienna in his youth. Most of his lieutenants dabbled with magic. Himmler aggressively revived the worship of the old Teutonic gods with the SS. Odin made a big comeback during the forties," Kenntnis countered.

"Odin?" said Weber faintly.

Suddenly Richard understood. It had been his first year at the conservatory in Rome. Robert had brought over the rest of the family for a visit, and they had all gone on a family ski trip to Switzerland. Perhaps it had been Richard's fault; five months with Italians had had an effect and his father had spoken long and harshly regarding Richard's levity and lack of decorum. It hadn't helped when Pamela took up with the French ski instructor. Robert cut short their time in Innsbruck and decreed that the family would take a trip to Dachau and Auschwitz as a reminder of the true state of man's nature. A shiver shook him as Richard remembered the cold and damp of that plain in Poland, the heaps of rubble, remnants of the ovens, the warehouse filled with the luggage of the dead, name tags in place awaiting pickup from a vanished generation.

"It was a massive blood sacrifice, wasn't it?" he forced out through a dry and constricted throat.

Kenntnis pivoted and pointed at him. "Give the man a gold star."

Angela walked over and planted herself in front of Kenntnis. "Now I'm even less inclined to go slow."

Kenntnis fanned the clippings in front of her face. "These are just the American papers and I've only had staff on the task for a day. Where would you like to start?"

With a sound like a road grader over gravel, Weber cleared his throat. "Yeah, so, well . . . okay, we're up against Nazis and televangelists, and Islamic extremists, and on our side we've got . . ." Weber looked around the room, nodding his head as he made a point of counting. "Four of us?"

The doors flew open and Rhiana, hair tumbling around her face, rushed in.

"Actually six, and here is the fifth," said Kenntnis.

"Oh, I feel so much better now," muttered Weber as Rhiana ran to Richard's side.

Her skin was cool and soft as she grabbed his hand and pressed her cheek against his. Her hair brushed across his lips and he smelled vanilla and almond.

"Where were you last night? Why didn't you come back? I was so worried."

"I'm fine," Richard soothed. "Do you remember Lieutenant Weber?" He half turned to indicate his boss and gently slipped his hand free.

"Oh, yes, hi."

"The girl from the other night," Weber said. He looked at Kenntnis. "Should I be surprised?"

"No, there is no coincidence, just convergence," Kenntnis responded.

"He says that a lot," Angela said. "I think it's supposed to make us feel better."

"Didn't work," Weber said.

"So to reiterate Angela's question . . . what do we do now?" Richard asked Kenntnis.

"What I told you. Resume your lives. Do your jobs, but be alert for activity from our foes. Between the coven, the golems, the assault on my building, and that thing in the church, it's pretty clear that the fabric of reality is pretty stretched and thin here in Albuquerque. There may be incursions." He looked back down at the stack of clippings and his shoulders dropped as if he was too weary to bear their weight. "I'll figure out when and how we tackle these. It would be so helpful to have Cross, but he shattered late last night."

"Cross? Shattered?" Weber asked plaintively.

Kenntnis looked at the older cop. "You don't want to hear that part of the lecture yet. You've got enough to chew on."

"I can't believe we're just going to lie low," Angela interrupted, preparing to resume the argument.

Richard crossed to her and placed his hands on her shoulders. It was a rare and pleasant experience to look down into a woman's face. "Kenntnis is right," he said. "We're not ready to take on Grenier, and the work we do is a worthy role for the Lumina. We hold back the darkness."

There was no warning. Suddenly Angela's face was pressed against Richard's chest, wetting his shirt with her tears. "I'm afraid they're going to kill you," came the muffled, tear-choked words.

He laid his cheek on the top of her head, feeling the crisp spring of her dark curls against his skin. "Won't happen. I've got you . . . all of you, watching my back." Looking at the others, he gave them all a smile that froze and shattered when he met the blazing fury in Rhiana's gaze.

Angela stepped out of his embrace and rubbed furiously at her cheeks. "Shit, I'm sorry. I'm tired. I get weepy and silly when I'm tired. I need to go home."

"I'll take you."

"I can give you a lift."

Richard and Weber stopped and looked at each other. Rhiana whirled and walked out of the office. Angela watched the younger woman go, then looked back at the two men.

"I think I'd better drive myself."

She hurried out and Richard suspected that she was going to try and catch Rhiana. He hoped she succeeded and that she would be able to smooth over the clash of hormones and attraction. It was a hell of a situation.

Kenntnis's voice interrupted his reverie. "Would you please just fuck that girl so we can lose the psychodramas."

Richard stiffened. "Putting aside that she is underage, that is unbelievably sexist and offensive." He could hear in his voice the echo of three hundred years of Yankee ancestors, and he knew he sounded like a prig. He hoped the underlying fear wasn't also showing.

Amusement deepened the creases in Weber's face. Kenntnis looked exasperated. "I really, really wish you were an ignorant flatfoot."

"Hey," said Weber. "Watch it."

"Apologies," Kenntnis threw to Weber. "How about this? A more typical male."

Chapter

SEVENTEEN

It was strange to be back in school. Kenntnis had insisted, pointing out that sorceress didn't constitute an acceptable career choice, and Rhiana had acquiesced because it was tough to refuse when the man provided her with room and board, bought her a car and paid off her student loan. The corner of a textbook gouged her shoulder. Rhiana shifted the backpack, and admitted that she didn't actually mind that much. She loved the play of numbers. They almost had weight and mass, like crystals of jet all sharp-edged and glittering.

The sandstone paving the quad shone golden in the setting sunlight. Rhiana cut through the Student Union building. The scent of coffee and hamburgers elicited a growl from her stomach. She wished she didn't have this late class, but Kenntnis always had a dinner waiting when she returned to the penthouse. She fought back the impulse to get a snack, but decided she'd better stop at the bathroom before class.

Her fingers ached and tingled as the warm water flowed across her cold hands. She pulled free a paper towel and rubbed vigorously, feeling the rough paper catch on hang-nails. She needed to get a manicure.

She dug through her backpack for a hairbrush and lipstick. The brush scratched and massaged her scalp and tugged free minute tangles as she swept it down through the mass of her hair. Maybe Richard preferred short hair like Angela's? Maybe she should drop by his apartment? He hadn't come around for the past three days. Rhiana tried to think of any-thing she might have done or said the last time they met that would have kept him away.

Then abruptly her frowning image shifted and what stared back at her was *her*, but a Rhiana dressed in a gown shivering and glittering with diamonds and silver thread. Her hair floated as if blown by an unseen breeze and jew-els sparkled in the black tresses. Her lips were redder, her eyes greener, the blush in her cheeks as rich and vibrant as a rose petal. The brush fell clattering into the sink. Rhiana gripped the edges of the counter so tightly that her knuck-les went white, and gazed and gazed at the vision. She was scared, but mesmerized.

The image of a perfect Rhiana shivered and dissolved into component colors. The colors swirled and surged through the glass. She had seen this before, but what coa-lesced from the colors was not the nightmare creatures from the trailer. It was an achingly handsome face, dark skinned and green eyed, and very familiar. It was the face of the man from the Carrow's parking lot. He smiled warmly and fondly at her, and lifting a hand he beckoned to her.

Rhiana fled, forgetting both brush and backpack. Be-hind her the glass of the mirror silvered and went dark, of-fering no reflection.

An ache in her throat and a sharp stitch in her side pulled her out of her run and down to a walk just in front of the doors of the library. She gulped down air, bending over her knees until her heart stopped racing. Her first instinct was to run to the car and rush to Kenntnis to seek help. But she'd left her backpack holding her books, and those physics texts cost the Earth. And he wasn't like the monsters even if he had come out of a mirror like they did. And she'd seen him before and nothing bad had happened.

Straightening, she pushed back her hair, feeling the moisture from the sweat that hugged her hairline. She started back toward the Student Union building. He flowed out of the shadows of the courtyard. He held her backpack. Against his preternatural beauty and inhuman grace the canvas bag looked as incongruous as a cigar in an angel's mouth.

"You forgot this," he said and his voice was low but with an overtone of bells carrying the soft words farther than a natural voice could carry.

Rhiana took it numbly. His smile enfolded her. "We need to have a talk some time. I can give you the answers to all of your questions." And he stepped back into the shadows and was gone.

※

Richard was in the zone, the beating of his heart providing the metronome for the music. The muscles in the backs of his hands and forearms tensed and stretched as he reached for the chords and his fingers flew across the keys for the runs. Next to him, Susanna, her face tight with concentration and the effort of holding the violin tucked beneath her chin, attacked the strings with her bow hard enough to make her muscles flex and flare. A strand of long blond hair was caught in her lips. Bob Figge nodded his gray crewcut head, keeping the count as he sawed away at the strings of his cello. Lee Titlebaum played his viola with a gentle smile. Even the most passionate music failed to pierce his superior calm. Mozart's quartet swirled in the narrow confines of Richard's apartment, undaunted by poor acoustics. They danced toward the climax, four bodies and four minds linked by music.

And the phone rang.

The perfect blending of sound faltered. "No," Richard shouted. "The machine will get it!"

They recaptured the link. Ignored the dissonance of the blaring telephone. Three rings and it was over, and they still had seven measures before the end of the quartet. The final chords wound into a perfect resolution. Richard lifted his hands from the keyboard of the big Bösendorfer. Susanna pulled the hair out of mouth and laughed from sheer joy. Figge frowned and tapped his bow on the page, resting on his music stand. Lee gave his soft, superior smile as he wiped his hands with a perfectly starched handkerchief.

"Come on, Bob," Richard said encouragingly. "That was good."

"They best we've ever played it," Susanna added.

Titlebaum pulled a pocket watch out of his vest pocket, snapped it open and checked the time. "Eight-thirty. Can we risk an encore?"

With a regretful head shake Richard closed the cover on the piano. "Better not. I don't need a noise complaint. I barely got to stay here what with the fire and all."

Figge looked around the apartment. "You'd never know anything happened."

"Yes," said Richard. "They did a good job on the repairs."

"Besides, we've got snackies," caroled Susanna in her little girl's voice, and she headed into the kitchen.

Over tea and coffee and pastries from La Chantilly they discussed their lives, books they were reading and movies they had seen. Titlebaum taught at the law school. Figge taught history at Highland High. Susanna worked at an upscale jewelry store, and kept auditioning for the New Mexico Symphony Orchestra. The general rule was that you auditioned five times before you got hired. Richard hoped she'd make it.

They were disparate people brought together out of a love of music, but they never managed to socialize outside of their bimonthly jam sessions. Titlebaum had a wife and two small children. Figge was a dedicated bachelor who liked his privacy. Susanna spent her time working, practicing and caring for her elderly parents. And Richard was a cop.

As Richard shut the door behind them a little after nine o'clock he mused that he knew a lot of people, but seemed to have few friends.

And whose fault if that? You're the one avoiding intimacy.

For a brief instant a kaleidoscope of faces whirled through his mind—Rhiana, Angela and Weber, and faces from his past—Danny and Brett, Sarah, Blythe, Rachel, Sal and Mario.

Richard shook his head to dispel the visions and the physical reaction and the sudden wave of utter loneliness. The red message light blinked on the phone. He called voice mail and started loading the plates and cups into the dishwasher.

At first there was just the sound of soft, desperate breathing. Then his mother's voice began to speak. "Richard . . . I can't lose you. . . ." He had to strain to hear, her voice was so soft and broken. "You must be good. I can't lose you to Hell." Hysteria edged the words. There were more of the panting breaths punctuated with barely audible sobs like whimpers.

The call ended and the blank voice of the voice mail server began. "Press seven to . . ."

Richard didn't bother to delete the message. He started dialing home, and then abruptly stopped. It was 11:30 in Rhode Island. His parents would be asleep by now. It didn't take much to imagine his father's anger if Richard woke them. And a call would betray his mother. He would phone tomorrow after Robert left for work.

Dinner was over. Rhiana ate in solitary state in the dining room. Kenntnis was away and Cross had taken a plate down to his shelter in the alley because it seemed likely he would shatter again before the night was over. Rhiana returned to her room, and pulled out her books to do her homework.

The tips of her fingers met something other than physics books. Frightened, she jumped up and grabbed a penny. Holding it at the ready she grasped the backpack by the bottom and upended it. Among the books was a velvet-covered scrapbook. Rhiana flipped back the front cover with her toe.

On the front page in flowing script was her name— *Rhiana*. Inside were pictures of her, from babyhood through high school graduation. From the angles and distance they seemed to have been captured with a telephoto lens. Playing on the swings at the park near their house. In her little pink tutu at the dance recital when she was five. Digging in the wet sand at the beach at Zuma when she was eleven. The final picture was her high school graduation. Hundreds of pictures detailing a life. Her life.

In the back was every clipping from every L.A. newspaper that had ever mentioned her, from the *L.A. Times* to the local Van Nuys neighborhood rag—pitching for the girl's softball team, winning the state science fair, receiving the physics scholarship. Every tiny victory carefully recorded. Nothing like it had ever been kept in the Davinovitch household.

Rhiana hugged it to her chest.

It was probably fanciful, but it seemed to Richard that the endless rings as he called home to Newport sounded hollow and distant, as if underlining the fact he had traveled far from home. The voice mail system picked up.

"Hi, Mama, what are you up to? Call me on my cell. Love you."

He had sought privacy on the front steps of the building. A strong wind howled through Tijeras Canyon and moaned around Albuquerque's few tall buildings. Richard pulled his coat closer around him. *Maybe I did abandon her,* he thought as he stowed the phone. *Maybe I should have tried Rhode Island's various police forces instead of moving so far away.*

But the lack of an answer or a callback was really starting to worry him. It had been two days since her tearful, cryptic call and he had yet to reach her and she hadn't returned any of his calls. He pulled the phone back out, jiggled it nervously on his palm, then hit the auto dial for his sister Amelia. He didn't think there was much hope of reaching her. His eldest sister was a surgeon at Mass General, but he preferred to start with her. Pamela was a defense attorney in Newport and she viewed Richard's new career choice with disapproval. In fact she'd made him feel as if he'd joined the Brown Shirts. They hadn't talked much in the past few years.

His musings were broken when, surprisingly, Amelia picked up her phone.

"Richard, what a surprise." Her voice was deep and husky and she had a habit of interrupting her words with hesitations that should have been annoying, but ended up endearing and fascinating.

"Sorry, I haven't called for while. Things have been . . . well, a little hectic out here."

"Papa said you got a promotion."

"Yes." The cold seeped up through the soles of his shoes, burning the tips of his toes in the thin dress socks. He walked in place, trying to warm up.

"Congratulations."

"Thanks."

"We missed you at Thanksgiving."

"I just couldn't leave. I'll come at Christmas. How are Brent and Paul?"

"They're fine. Paul wants to take up hockey. We're negotiating."

"Which means he'll be picking a different sport," said Richard, and couldn't help smiling. His eldest sister was formidable, and would be more than a match for an eight-year-old's tantrums.

"What is that noise? I can hardly hear you."

Richard moved into the alcove by the front doors. "The wind. Is this better?"

"Much. So, what's up?"

"Have you talked to Mama recently?"

"Last week. Why?"

"How did she seem to you?" Richard asked.

"A little hyper, but I'd rather have her bouncing than depressed." Richard agreed with the sentiment. When depression hit, Alannis Oort tended to dull the pain with alcohol and pills. It was one of many reasons why Richard tried to keep his Valium bottle closed. "Is something wrong?" Amelia asked.

"I don't know. She left a message for me a couple of nights ago, and she seemed very agitated and upset. She was crying and talking about . . . well, about me going to Hell. I keep calling, but I haven't been able to reach her."

"Oh dear. She's been very active at church chairing some fundraising committees. Maybe it's been too much for her."

"You need to tell Papa," Richard said.

"You tell him. She's calling you."

"I'd feel like I was betraying her."

"Oh, Richard, don't start. Papa isn't the enemy. She isn't easy."

"And he doesn't help."

The front doors opened and Detective Joe Torres looked out. He spotted Richard. Joe's jaw thrust out pugnaciously and set his jowls to wobbling. He pointed theatrically at his watch. Richard nodded at his temporary partner and tried to focus on what Amelia was saying.

"Look, let's not have an argument. I've got rounds in five minutes. Was there anything else?" Amelia asked.

"No, I was just worried."

"If you don't want to talk to Papa, then talk to Pamela. At least she's in town."

"Yeah, okay. See you at Christmas."

"Take care, Richard, love you."

"Love you too."

He hung up the phone and stepped back into the building. The overheated air was suffocating after the clean cold of the wind, and it carried the faint smell of sweat generated by fear, despair and grief.

"We should have been rollin' ten minutes ago," grunted Torres.

They were partners for the week as the captain and Weber tried to work out permanent assignments. So far it didn't seem to be a rousing success. Torres made fun of Richard's contemporary Castilian Spanish rather then the archaic Castilian mixed with Spanglish spoken in New Mexico. Ridiculed his East Coast accent, and his reluctance to curse. Torres's own profanities had the quality of poetry as he tried to fill every sentence with vulgarities.

"Sorry," Richard said, and ducking his head, he followed Torres toward the back doors and the parking lot.

Worried thoughts chased one another through his head. They had attended that church Richard's entire life. Not every church was evil. They had been created to foster Kenntnis's vision of a loving God. Some still served that mission. There was nothing to indicate Grenier was behind his mother's erratic behavior.

"You've been spying on me!" Rhiana pushed the outrage, hoping that her secret pleasure over the scrapbook didn't show.

She was in a deserted bathroom on the seventh stack of the library tower. It was late in the day. She wouldn't be discovered.

The man smiled out of the mirror at her. "Since the moment of your birth."

"Why?"

"You're very special to me . . . to us."

Rhiana scuttled back a few feet. "You're with *them*," she accused.

"I might say the same of you."

"What do you want?"

"Nothing very fearsome. To take you to dinner. To get to know you. That's all."

"No!" She fled toward the door.

"You know how you used to think you were special?" he called after her. "Well, you are, Rhiana. More special than you know. I can tell you why. Let me know when you're ready."

Letters and words sprang to life on the computer screen as Richard swiftly typed. On his left Snyder was laboriously hunting and pecking as he also wrote a report. Snyder caught Richard's gaze and glared. Richard quickly looked back at his screen. It seemed like everything he did, everything he was, annoyed his fellow officers.

A large, warm hand clapped onto his shoulder as a folder slapped onto the desk next to him.

"Nice work," said Weber.

"It wasn't precisely complex," Richard replied, and tried

to stifle the tingle of pride and accomplishment engendered by Weber's words. "Once his mother realized he
was in more danger from the victim's friends than from us
she told me where to find him."

"Didn't hurt that you speak Spanish."

"And maybe when he catches a real case we'll find out if
he knows fuck-all about being a detective as opposed to all
this chichi, Miss America talent competition shit," grunted
Snyder.

Richard felt himself flush, but Weber's face suffused
with blood. He looked on the verge of a stroke. Richard laid
a hand on the older man's wrist, a feather touch, begging
him not to make it worse. Weber shut his mouth, took a few
deep breaths.

Richard examined his options. Having Weber fight his
battles would be the worst, but letting Snyder's remark
pass without reaction wouldn't be much better. Sometimes
you had to hit back before a bully would stop. Richard had
learned that lesson on a succession of playgrounds and
locker rooms. His small size and handsome face had made
him an irresistible target.

"Well maybe one of my chichi talents can help you out."
He gave Snyder a thin smile. "I can touch type. Let me
know when you want me to teach you."

Hitting the print button, Richard rolled back his chair.
The hilt of the sword dug into his back, a reminder of the
two worlds he now inhabited. Standing, he walked over to
the communal printer. Weber joined him.

"Showing some teeth, little man. About damn time, but
what's gotten into you?"

"I'm tired. There are five violent crimes detectives now
that I've been promoted, but I seem to be catching every
boring, pissant case."

"Gee." Weber laid a finger against his temple. "Huh, I
wonder why that might be?"

"I won't quit."

"Another big surprise." The lieutenant's expression became serious. "You keep clearing cases at this rate, and believe me the game is going to pall. Eventually the other guys are going to realize that their solve rates look like shit and all they're doing is making you the golden boy. Hang in there. It won't go on much longer. Want to get some lunch?"

"I want to stop by the hospital and see how Charlie . . . Father Fish is doing."

"No reason we can't do both," Weber said. "Is he any better?"

"Still in a light coma. They keep saying that's encouraging. I wish I could believe them."

Gathering up his report, Richard signed it, but before they could leave Ortiz came out of his office, head craning as he looked across the squad room. His gaze fell on Richard.

"Oort, where's your partner?"

"Out sick today, sir."

"I can ride with him," Weber offered.

"Snyder's free," Ortiz mused.

"Nah, let me go," Weber said. "What have you got?"

"Missing kid. Maybe a snatch. Down at the McDonald's on Isleta."

They didn't ask for further elaboration. They went.

⚜

"Ow! Shit, shit, shit, shit," Rhiana muttered as the power arced from the Tarot cards blistering her fingertips.

"Those would be the ones." Cross nodded with approval and picked up the Tarot deck. Kenntnis was out of town, but they were under standing orders to patrol for incursions whenever the shattered god was in one piece. Since they had to limit the search in some way, absent any specific instructions from Kenntnis, they trawled through occult, New Age, and religious stores. This was the first time they'd gotten a hit.

Rhiana, sucking on her burned fingers, glared at him. The shop was in a converted house just off Central Avenue in the University area. Heavy curtains blocked out the winter sun. Light was provided by horn lanterns wired for electricity. Incense hung heavy and cloying in the overheated air. The dominant feature was cases and cases of books on the occult, but there was also a section for magical paraphernalia—crystals, athames, Tarot decks, incense burners and jewelry.

They went up to the counter to pay for the cards. The owner of the Crystal Eye Mystic Book Store was a heavyset young woman dressed in jeans and a baggy sweatshirt. Tumbling curls of beautiful auburn hair framed her pale, bloated face. She had the sulky expression of one who's been disappointed by life.

Rhiana wondered if the girl blessed or cursed her one beauty? Would it have been easier to simply be plain and have no expectations? Or had the hair led her to need to be special, to be magic?

"You ever use this deck?" Cross asked, casually wagging the cards in the air.

"Yeah, I test them all out. See which ones really spark for me. They're all different, you know. Some manufacturers are just hacks. There's no pride in the work, it's just about money. These cards seemed to really be keyed in."

"Cool," said Cross.

Out on the sidewalk Cross shoved the Tarot deck into Rhiana's coat pocket, and looked back at the building. "That gal's got some mojo. We need to get her neutralized without getting Richard arrested for assault. Otherwise she's just going to keep on powering decks." He started to walk away. Rhiana got in front of him.

"Since you see magic, would it have strained you to give me a heads-up? Or was it just more fun to let me get burned?" Her voice shook with anger.

Cross stared down at her. His eyes didn't seem very

human. Rhiana forced herself to hold the stare. "You needed the reminder."

Rhiana took two running steps and caught up. "Reminder of what?" The homeless god didn't answer. "You just wanted to see me get hurt. You don't like me, do you?"

Cross stopped so abruptly that Rhiana, unable to react quickly enough, walked on for several feet. She swung back and met the brunt of the blunt answer.

"No. I don't."

"Why? What have I ever done to you?"

"I know what you are," he said cryptically and walked on.

Rhiana stared hard at his back, fingered the pennies in her pocket, swallowed the ache in her throat, and prayed for him to shatter into a thousand pieces and never get back together again.

Chapter

EIGHTEEN

The slowly spinning lights on a couple of patrol cars marked the location, which was good because the McDonald's was missing the usual golden arches. It had been designed to meet zoning regulations requiring architectural sensitivity to historical style. That meant it looked like a runaway pueblo set among the rundown stucco and metal buildings to either side. One held a custom body shop specializing in turning your wheels into a primo low rider. The howl of tortured metal echoed over the traffic noise from Isleta Boulevard. On the other side was a check-cashing service. Richard hated them; they were a racket designed to prey on the poor.

In the parking lot the odor of grease, fries, and that peculiar boiled meat smell of McDonald's burgers was strong enough to defeat the blast of exhaust from the passing cars.

The uniforms were gathered in the outdoor play area, and cultural sensitivity hadn't extended there. It held the usual garish plastic and metal maze. It squatted on a high platform supported by thick steel pipes that could double as a jungle gym. Green, red, blue, orange and purple plastic tubes punctuated with globes snaked down from the central body, creating the impression that a psychedelic octopus had washed up to die incongruously in the New Mexico desert.

There were three round concrete tables with benches. Underfoot the dirt was covered with rubberized outdoor carpet. The playground was surrounded by a high wrought-iron fence with mesh wire between the posts. Hamburger wrappers and squeezed ketchup packets had blown up against the eastern side. It had all the charm of an exercise yard in a prison. There was a gate set in the fence. Weber and Richard chose to enter through that rather than walk through the restaurant. Curious faces peered through the windows facing out on the playground with expressions of mingled fear and excitement. *Everyone loves a tragedy as long as it's not theirs,* Richard thought.

A distraught young Hispanic woman dressed in a shabby sweat suit slumped on a concrete bench at one of the tables. She had a Madonna's face atop a deep-bosomed, wide-hipped body. The rich brown tones of her skin were blotched from crying.

"I'm telling you! I was here the whole time! I didn't go away. I wouldn't leave Miguel! Why don't you listen to me!" And she went off in a torrent of Spanish.

"Do I want a translation?" Weber asked.

"No," said Richard.

They walked up and flashed their shields. One of the uniforms joined them. He was a heavyset Anglo man whose buzz cut suggested that cop was a second career and the first had been the military. His name tag read KOPEK. He hitched up his belt and glanced back at the young woman. The look wasn't kind.

"What have we got?" Weber asked.

The uniform flipped open his notebook. "Miguel Rodriquez, age three. Wearing a Dallas Cowboys sweatshirt, jeans and tennis shoes. He was out here playin' in the maze. She . . ." Another disgusted glance. "Says he went in and never came out. I think she went inside to pack on another Quarter Pounder with fries and some creep grabbed the kid."

Perhaps it was the sniping from Snyder that had reduced his tolerance, but Richard found the insensitivity of the cop's remark breaking through his usual polite reserve. "Why, thank you for that insight," Richard drawled. He glanced up at Weber. "I guess we don't need to ask any questions now. Shall we go on to lunch?"

Weber laid a quelling hand on Richard's shoulder. "What's her name?"

"Maria Rodriquez," the uniform answered.

"What's the word on the dad? Any chance this is a custody snatch?" Weber asked.

"Unwed mother, big surprise," Kopek grunted.

"Do we know for certain he's not in the maze?" Richard asked, disliking Kopek more and more with each word out of his mouth.

"You hear a kid cryin' in there? If he was stuck we'd fuckin' know it. It's been an hour and a half since he's gone missing according to the mother."

"So in fact you haven't checked," Richard demanded.

"You want to go crawl through it and check, detective? 'Course you're about the right size," Kopek grunted, thrusting out his chin and chest, daring Richard to react.

Weber sighed and interposed himself between Richard and Kopek. "Okay, we'll take it from here." They walked away toward the woman.

"What a . . . ," Richard struggled with himself.

"Oh, go ahead, Richard, say it," Weber urged.

"Prick. Racist prick," Richard added thinly.

"Yeah, but remember those guys are usually first on the scene. You want them working *with* you, not *against* you."

"I know, I know," Richard said. They reached the young mother.

Maria Rodriquez's hands were tightly clenched. Richard saw the tatters of a tear and snot-soaked napkin in her hand. He pulled out his handkerchief and gave it to her. On the table behind her were the half-eaten remains of a Happy Meal. It was poignant and depressing.

"Do we need an Amber alert?" Richard asked Weber quietly.

"Too early to tell. Let's ask a few questions first."

The woman's dark eyes darted back and forth between them. "He's here! I swear he's here. I *didn't* leave him. I didn't!"

Weber held up his hands and patted the air in a soothing gesture. "Okay, okay, ma'am. We understand you didn't leave the playground."

"That's right," Rodriquez said. She relaxed a bit with the indication that she might actually be believed.

"But maybe you got distracted . . . you talked to somebody or you were focusing on your food, and you took your eye off him for a few minutes," Weber suggested.

"No! He wanted me to watch him climb inside. Last week he was scared and some other kid made fun of him. So this time he was going to do it." Her voice had the musical cadences of her distant Spanish ancestors. "He was real proud when he went in. He turned around and smiled and waved to me. I told him how brave he was. I watched his little feet as he climbed farther up." Her voice broke and she mopped at the sudden stream of tears with the handkerchief. She threw back her magnificent mane of black hair, cleared her throat and began again. "So I waited. I

thought I'd see him in some of those little window things."
She indicated the gray plastic portholes and one large
bulge set in the side of the squat body of the maze as if the
octopus were in the process of ingesting a bathyscaphe.
"But I never saw him. I waited for awhile and then I went
over and called. He didn't answer, and he didn't come out,
and that's the truth."

Weber glanced over at Richard and raised his eyebrows.
When you're a cop you get an instinct when somebody is
laying a story on you. This didn't sound like a story. The
problem was, it didn't make any sense.

"And no one's been in?" Richard asked.

"Well, I won't fit." She laid her hands self-consciously
on her wide hips. "But one of the clerks, she's a little thing,
she went in."

Richard glanced over at Kopek. "Would have been nice
of him to mention that."

"That's what I'm talking about," Weber said, driving
home the lesson. Richard knew he probably deserved it,
but it stung nonetheless. "Go, find her and talk to her," Weber ordered. Richard went.

Inside the restaurant, curiosity had a few people edging
close but most stayed away. He was an Anglo cop and in
this neighborhood their experiences with Anglo cops had
probably not been great. He called out, "Which one of you
went in the maze?" A tiny Hispanic girl in her late teens
raised her hand. She was behind the service counter and
wore the McDonald's uniform. Richard took her over to
one of the pre-formed, bolted-down tables and they sat.
There was a blot of ketchup on the table. He used a napkin
to wipe it clean and then leaned forward, resting his arms
on the table.

"Could you tell me what happened?"

"Well, this lady comes in and she's all excited, yelling
about how her little boy is lost in the maze. The manager,
he tells her how a lot of kids like to tease their moms, but

she's not having any of it. She's yellin' louder and wavin' her hands around, so he sends me out to look."

"And," Richard prompted.

"He wasn't in there, and I went through the whole thing."

Depressed, he walked back out to the playground. Maria Rodriquez seemed so sincere, and he hated to think his instincts were that far wrong.

Weber was continuing his questioning, taking different angles, but no matter what he tried the story stayed the same. Richard waited for a natural break, then pulled his boss aside and repeated the clerk's story.

"So that's it, then." Weber flipped closed his notebook. "Now we call the Amber alert."

"Let me check in the maze." Richard started toward it. Weber's hand fell hard on his shoulder, stopping him cold.

"No." He jerked his head toward the uniforms. "Now, you can bet Kopek has been busy bragging to his partner about how he put the gold shield in his place, and since we're a small department everybody knows you're the new kid. After the crack Kopek made you can't go in there. It will be all over APD by shift change, and you can't afford to get humiliated." Weber sensed his hesitation and reluctance. "What?"

Frowning, Richard scanned the maze. "I don't know, this just feels . . . hinky. Like something out of Kenntnis's world."

"You got anything more than a feeling?"

Richard shook his head, frustrated that Weber sounded so much like Kenntnis. It made him feel gauche and young and inexperienced. He could accept the inexperienced, but not all three.

"Okay," Richard finally said and knew he sounded churlish.

They returned to Rodriquez. "Ma'am," Weber said, "we're going to need a picture of Miguel. We'll get it up on the TV."

"Why? He's in there!" Her voice rose and she pointed a shaking hand at the maze.

Weber put a hand under her arm. "Come on now. These gentlemen are going to take you downtown and you're going to give us all the particulars."

Hands flailing, she beat at Weber's chest and face. "No, *no,* he'll hear me. He'll come back to me."

"Ma'am, ma'am." Richard caught one of her hands, only to be shoved aside as Kopek and his partner ran over and grabbed the distraught woman.

"Go easy, guys, she didn't hurt me and she's upset," Weber said.

All the fight went out of Rodriquez and her knees buckled. Her shrieking sobs accompanied the trio across the parking lot to the squad car.

Weber sighed. "Let's get started. It's going to be a long afternoon. Sorry about visiting the father."

"That's okay, I think Father Fish would understand."

But Richard took one more long look back at the maze before hurrying after Weber.

It was after nine p.m. before Richard left headquarters. There had been a lot of calls, but none of them the right call. Miguel Rodriquez remained missing. Maria's extended family turned up at six o'clock and took her back to her parents' home. There they would hold vigil. Neighbors would come with food. Possibly the priest. This was a community that rallied to any crisis or catastrophe. In his three years with APD Richard had walked into many such vigils, where tall votive candles, their glass holders imprinted with an image of the Virgin of Guadalupe, flickered in front of pictures of the Savior of the Bleeding Heart. Now that bleeding heart had a whole different meaning for Richard and he shuddered as he stepped into the parking lot.

He found himself driving past the entrance to his apartment complex and continuing up Montgomery to Lumina. But Kenntnis wasn't there—out of town on business. Rhiana was at class.

"Would you like to wait in Mr. Kenntnis's private quarters until she gets back?" Joseph asked as they stood in the black marble lobby.

"No, thanks." He stood dithering. His stomach felt hollow. He never had eaten lunch. He considered finding dinner, but quickly rejected the idea. Even a brief thought about food nauseated him. He couldn't forget the round face of Miguel Rodriquez, age three, thirty-four pounds, black hair, brown eyes. Where was he? What were they missing?

He intended to head to his car, but found himself walking behind the building instead. Golden light spilled out from the cardboard box. Cross was in and intact. He was sitting on a blanket-covered mattress on the ground, eating Beluga caviar out of a can. The tiny glistening black beads shivered on the tines of the fork and a few spilled, catching on his lower lip and beard. His tongue darted out to lick them up.

"Good evening," Richard said.

"Hey, hi." Cross held up the can. "Want some? I love the stuff."

"No, thank you."

"Yeah, I know, it's better with the chopped egg and onion and little crackers, but it's just fine this way too. Come on in."

Richard stepped into the box. Cross indicated the wooden spool that had once carried cable. Richard sat down. "I'm sorry to bother you, but if you're not too busy, I was wondering if you would come with me and check something out."

"Let me check my Palm and see if I'm available." He

stared down into the smooth palm of one hand. "You're in luck." Richard flushed and Cross laughed. "You are the funniest little guy," the homeless god said. He tossed the nearly empty caviar can out the crude doorway, wiped his hands down his dirty jeans and stood up. "Where we going?"

Since it was a weeknight, the McDonald's closed at 10:00 p.m. They waited in the parking lot of the thrift store across the street, watching the night crew scrubbing down the floor and the tables. Finally the last trash can was emptied and the lights turned out. The taillights of the clerk's cars went off north and south on Isleta. Two of three had a taillight either busted out or burned out. Richard wondered if there was a special assembly plant where they made cars intended for the state. *Yeah, Fred, that one's going to New Mexico so bust out a headlight and make sure the turn signals don't work.* He immediately felt guilty for his whimsical little thought because the truth was that most of the citizens of New Mexico were poor. They kept their cars running, but there wasn't usually anything left for elective repairs.

They gave it a few more minutes, just in case someone had forgotten something and returned. Then Cross and Richard left the Volvo and ran across Isleta. There were small bouquets of flowers resting against the fence. Votive candles flickered among them. Yellow ribbons had been twined through the bars. Richard tried the gate, but it was locked. Richard eyed the eight-foot-high fence. He backed up and trotted forward, testing the distance he would need. Cross tapped him on the shoulder as he passed, and twining his fingers together offered his hand. Richard shrugged, placed his foot in the cupped hands, and Cross boosted. Richard caught the narrow strut at the top and swung over. Since he thought he might like to sire children someday, he cautiously lowered himself onto the top rail with a leg on either side. He reached down, offering his hand. Cross scrambled up to join him. They dropped down inside. Richard didn't even need to cue the homeless god.

Cross warily circled the maze. "Oh, that is uuuugly."

Richard heard a crunch of gravel beneath a shoe. He whirled, drawing his pistol. A dark form loomed behind the iron bars of the fence.

"Whoa, whoa, watch where you point that thing," came Weber's voice.

"Damon," breathed Richard, weak with relief. "Why are you here?"

"I went by your place. Didn't find you home. Thought you might come back here because you can't seem to let anything go. You know you're breaking and entering."

Cross came up and stood by Richard's shoulder. "If this is the new guy you brought in I don't think much of your choice," he said.

"Yeah, and who the fuck are you?" Weber asked.

"He's Cross," said Richard quickly before the Old One could launch into his Jesus lecture. "He sees magic."

"And there is a great big steaming pile of it right there," Cross said, pointing at the maze.

"I'm coming in," Weber said.

A few minutes later they all stood staring at the maze.

"It's a bad tear," Cross said. "But it's inside. They've got a glamour on this thing to hide it, but I can see it glowing through the joints. That was actually cleverer than we usually manage. Usually when we see an opening we just go balls to the wall. The mind behind this one is subtle." He looked down at Richard. "So hop to it."

"Hop to what?" asked Weber.

"Only one of us can close it, bucko, and you ain't him."

"Cross, I think the little boy went through. I've got to try and find him," Richard said.

"No, you get in there and you close it. The kid is toast."

"We don't know that. They feed on pain and fear and despair. Wouldn't they want to keep him alive?"

"It's been a long damn time on this side, and you don't know how long on the other."

Weber held up a hand. "Time out."

Cross threw him an impatient glance. "This is an opening into another universe. Time is a dimension. Natural law operates differently in different universes." He bent a dark gaze back on Richard. Richard realized that Cross's pupils had vanished. The eyes were like fragments of obsidian. "And many of the folded dimensions are inimical to your little fleshy life."

Richard shrugged out of his suit coat. "Still, I've got to try. I'll only be a step into their world. I can step back."

"I'll go with him," Weber said. He unbuckled his belt and pulled it off. "Give me yours," he ordered Richard. He hooked them together. "We'll loop it around your waist. I'll keep the other end."

"Okay. Good." Richard slipped off his shoulder rig.

"You don't want to keep your piece?" Weber asked.

"I don't want to get snagged on anything, and if this is something . . . unnatural, I don't think a gun is going to help." Weber shrugged then nodded and took off his coat and unclipped his holster from his belt.

"How come a bunch more kids didn't disappear?" Weber asked as Richard pulled the hilt out of its holster.

"It takes a lot of power to keep one of these dimensional tears open. They come and go," Cross answered.

"So what if it's not there now?" Weber pressed.

"Richard will find it," Cross replied.

"How?" Richard drew the sword. Weber pressed a hand against his chest. "Jesus. I'm never going to get used to that," he gasped.

"Because of *that*." Cross thrust a finger at the sword.

Richard studied the maze. Weber shifted from foot to foot. "Maybe if he just cuts it open . . . ," he suggested.

"The kid's not gonna fall out like candy out of a piñata," grunted Cross.

"I could hope," said Weber.

"Let's do it," Richard ordered.

Squaring his shoulders he took a breath, and climbed into the maze. Weber followed. There were little blue plastic wedges to serve as handholds and foot rests snaking up and away. Despite his slenderness Richard had broad shoulders from the years of gymnastics. He hoped he would fit, and he wondered if there was any chance of Weber making it. But as they climbed the tube expanded. *Like a throat widening to accommodate a big bite,* Richard thought and shuddered.

They continued up. Richard blinked and realized the glittering spots swirling before his eyes were caused by the aura off the sword. "I think we're getting close," he whispered.

He cleared the tube and was in the central core of the maze. Against one wall was what, from outside, had looked like the gray plastic diving bell. From this side it pulsed and shivered. Searing cold like a rhythmic exhalation swept across them. Weber stared at it and Richard watched the older man's Adam's apple work as he swallowed and swallowed.

"Oh shit, it's true," he croaked.

"Can you handle this?" Richard asked.

Weber gave an abrupt nod. "Let's get you tethered," and looped the belt around Richard's waist.

In the dreadful cold it was becoming hard to feel the curves and coils of the hilt. Richard brought his hands up to his mouth and breathed hard across the fingers. Weber grabbed his hands and almost bumped into the blade. Richard yanked it aside.

"Careful."

"It's okay, I'm beginning to think this 'no magic' thing is the right choice."

"Yes, probably, but the effects seem to be pretty extreme on a body," Richard replied, remembering Delay's agony. "And right now I need you watching my back."

"Fair enough. So set that thing aside, and give me your hands," Weber said. He took Richard's hands between his and briskly chafed them. His skin was rough. It was an endemic problem in New Mexico, and almost nothing had ever felt quite so comforting.

Richard pulled his hands away. "Thanks. Let's do it."

He held the sword diagonally across his body, the blade resting lightly in the palm of his right hand as if he could quell it and soothe it by touch, like a restive horse. He drew in a long breath, held it, and stepped through the rip in reality. The belt tugged against his belly but held.

Instantly his eyes flowed water from the bite of bitter cold. He could feel the moisture freezing on his cheeks. The glittering aura around the sword vanished, perhaps because there was no longer magic to react against. On this side of the barrier it wasn't magic, this was reality. The sword was a sliver of ebony in the gloom.

The light was strange. He could make out shapes but no details. The impression was as if mountains of stone had turned to regard him; a soft and shivering little flesh creature. Only one thing stood out. A flash of white from a Cowboys sweatshirt. Miguel's round fat belly strained against the ice-coated fabric. He seemed prematurely gray from the frost icing his hair. His eyes were open and staring where he lay on the ice-coated rocks.

I'm going to join him, Richard realized when his legs buckled under the implacable hatred of the watchers and the bitter cold. He collapsed onto his knees. Only the belt kept him from falling full length. The yank of the belt forced the breath out of him. He couldn't help gulping in a lungful of air. It was so cold it hurt.

Then Weber was there, wrapping his arms around

Richard's chest and pulling him to his feet. Weber's eyes scanned the unseen sky and occasionally he flinched, hunching toward the ground. Richard understood. The sky was falling. Soon the monstrous forms would crush them. They were coming. Soon they would reach them.

Richard staggered forward and twisted his free hand in the back of the sweatshirt. His shoulder joint popped from the strain, but he heaved the child up and clasped him against his chest. He turned back to Weber and the opening. One foot, another, but the intense cold, coupled with the weight of the child and his growing fear sapped his strength. He fell again, and was suddenly being dragged across the icy rocks by the belt.

Weber, jaw set with effort, was reeling them in hand over hand. Richard hugged Miguel tighter. Weber heaved Richard up, holding both Richard and Miguel in a bear hug. He dug in his back foot and threw himself backward through the opening. There was a high-pitched keening, a cry of rage.

"Jesus God, Jesus God," Weber mumbled as they lay on the floor of the maze. Richard felt the older man's breath puffing against his ear. It smelled of cigarettes and beer and was wonderful. But there was no time. A gray bulge, trailing tendrils of icy mist as it reacted with the warmer air of Earth, loomed over them. It licked toward them like a questing tongue.

Richard swung the sword up. Weber grunted as Richard's heel dug into his thigh as he pushed himself upright. The point of the sword sank deep into the center of the bubble. It shrank back undulating like a jellyfish. He pursued and swept the sword in an arc on the edge of the bubble. *Close!*

Then it was just plastic again, but perhaps because of the extremes to which it had been subjected or perhaps because of the touch of the sword, it blew out, raining shards across the playground. A pair of hands grabbed the edge of the platform and Cross's face came into view as he chinned himself up.

"Well, I'll be dipped in shit and fried for a hush puppy, you did it," said the homeless god.

Richard glanced back. Weber was bent over the boy, administering CPR. "I don't know. Have we?"

Weber gave him a wan grin and a thumbs-up.

They pretended that they'd found Miguel ten blocks away. Ortiz's expression clearly indicated that he thought they were bullshitting him, but the outcome was good and the APD looked great so he wasn't going to look too closely.

"I've got Child Protective Services meeting him at the hospital," Ortiz said.

Richard looked at him in dismay. "Why? He's got a mother."

"Yeah, and she left him alone and then lied to the police about it. They'll keep an eye on her. If she knows they're watching she'll be more careful. She screws up again she loses the kid," Ortiz said.

Richard folded his lips together to forestall any further desire to argue. But how awful for a mother who had done everything right but would be branded unfit. Still, she had her son back. It wasn't a perfect result, but probably better than they had had any right to hope for.

Ortiz pulled out a stick of gum, unwrapped it and stuffed it into his mouth. The overly sweet smell of Juicy Fruit floated in the air. The wrapper fell to the sidewalk. "Look, you two sleep in. Come in at noon. I'll handle payroll. I won't let them dock you."

Eventually they were alone except for the occasionally passing car on Isleta. Weber frowned down at the cracked and stained sidewalk and the wadded-up piece of foil.

Richard put a hand on his shoulder. "You did good. Really good."

"I was just brawn."

"And brave, and quick thinking. You didn't have to come through, and I could never have gotten him out without you."

"I didn't want it to be true," Weber said, and his face and body seemed to sag.

"Neither did I," Richard replied softly.

Chapter

NINETEEN

The clouds seemed to balance on the tops of New York's skyscrapers. They spat rain down the glass and concrete structures and onto the hundreds of jostling umbrellas in the streets below. Water dripped off the brim of Kenntnis's homburg. The crowds parted before him and closed back in a few feet behind him. It had been a long time since he'd mingled so openly among vast numbers of humans and he was still having the same effect. The trees were millennia behind them, but humans still had an animal's sense when something was different, powerful and potentially dangerous. Individually, humans seemed to handle him better now, but get a lot of them together and the monkey troop returned.

Despite being only three-thirty in the afternoon, the lowering cloud cover made it very dark. Light from the store windows illuminated the wares on display and formed pools of gold on the wet sidewalks. He wished he could have had Cross with him, but when he'd left, the creature was shattered. The constant assaults on his Jesus were evidence that Grenier was planning something big. That meant Richard became even more critical and that Kenntnis had to resolve the mystery of the missing months.

He had to know if it hid something damaging for the Lumina.

Up ahead Kenntnis spotted the neon sign for City Sushi. Briefly Kenntis longed for another time and eras long past when he could have walked into a deli and ordered a bowl of chicken soup with a matzoball the size of a softball floating among the nuggets of meat, tangled masses of noodles, onions and carrots, and a sandwich piled high with chicken liver and pastrami. Sushi always left him feeling hungry.

The private detective waited for him at a table. Kenntnis was grateful; with his bulk, the Washitsu rooms were pure torture. Josh Rosenblum was a medium-sized man with brown hair and brown eyes and a forgettable face. His attire suggested a low-level accountant or salesman and was as unremarkable as his face. In front of him was a celadon tray, its lovely green color obscured by the large amount of sushi. Kenntnis guessed sushi left Rosenblum hungry too. A bottle of saki sat in a pot of steaming hot water.

"Hope you don't mind. I didn't wait. I was hungry," Rosenblum mumbled around a bite of squid as Kenntnis slid into the chair across from him.

"No problem. I could use some fuel myself." He lifted a finger and the waitress, an exquiste Japanese girl, tripped lightly over. The silk of her kimono rustled as she moved.

"I'll have a bowl of beef udon soup." *At least it had noodles.* The girl bowed and pattered away. Kenntnis stared across at Rosenblum. "Okay, what have you got?"

Rosenblum fished out a reporter's thin notebook and flipped it open. "So, nobody at the hospital would talk— no big surprise there. I tracked down the EMTs who bought him into the hospital. One of them was willing to talk." Rosenblum glanced up, his brown eyes bright. "But it'll cost you three bills. Somebody else had already been there ahead of us and had established the base price."

Grenier, thought Kenntnis and gave voice to the next

thought. "And is there anything here that's going to hurt us?"

"Depends on what you're using this Oort for. If you're planning on running him for the Senate . . . well, in the present climate you're gonna have a problem."

The next day felt surreal. Richard and Torres were on their final day together. Just before they headed out, Richard went by Weber's desk.

"Did you get any sleep last night?" he asked quietly.

"Some. Bourbon is a great relaxer."

Valium, thought Richard, but he didn't say it.

"On a more mundane topic," Richard said, "you're not going to try pairing me with Snyder, are you?"

"Yeah, I'm really stupid about personnel and can't tell when people rub each other the wrong way. No, of course not."

"Sorry. I wish—"

"Not happening," and he was suddenly the lieutenant and Richard's superior officer. "I don't do that much street work anymore. It would make your situation here even worse, and we're partnered on this . . . other thing. That's enough."

"Yes, sir."

Richard gathered up his radio and followed Torres out to the parking lot. It was a bright December day. The sunlight glittered on the gold tinsel of the Christmas stars hung on wires across Grand. They swayed in the breeze.

"Would you like me to drive?" Richard offered.

"Hell, no. We'll take my truck."

"Okay."

"What the fuck kind of cop drives a fucking Volvo?" Torres added as they walked to the big Ford 4×4 pickup.

"A safe one?" Richard suggested.

Torres whirled back on him. "Don't fuckin' push it. So,

you were a fucking little hero last night. I say you got lucky. We're gonna be in my territory today. You keep your fuckin' mouth shut."

They were searching for witnesses to a late-night shooting that had erupted at an impromptu party over on Edith Boulevard. They spent the day on it without notable success, and it was adding to the other cop's general outrage at the world. It was now past four, and the cold winter afternoon was rapidly fading as they turned down the short street. On the north it dead-ended into the brown berm of the irrigation ditch. On the south it tee-boned into Cherokee Road and the graffiti-covered walls of an out-of-business indoor archery range.

Someone had been very hopeful or lured by low rents, thought Richard as he studied the chipped and faded sign. This section of the North Valley was known for its dingy pawnshops and rundown bars, not high-end hobbies.

He glanced over at Torres's profile. The sun through the car windows gave the Hispanic's skin the color and consistency of polished mahogany. Thick black hair sprang up and away from a low forehead and made his eyebrows look like escapees from his skull—particularly when he was frowning and he'd been frowning ever since their little exchange in the parking lot.

Richard tried to keep focused, but it had been a long, boring day. He felt like the ventriloquist's dummy standing mute on front porches and in a succession of living rooms while Torres asked questions. His thoughts kept drifting to Maria Rodgriquez and Miguel. And wondering if he'd been wrong to bring Weber into the Lumina. And wondering if he should try to get Angela out of the Lumina. He didn't want to endanger anyone. And then there was his mother and the impending conversation with the judge.

The truck rolled to a stop. Richard looked up at the house that was to be their final stop of the day. It shared half the lot with its neighbor and both were so small they had the quality of dollhouses. Richard was relieved that this house didn't have any dogs. Most of their stops this day had involved dogs. Lots of dogs.

They climbed out. The house next door had a blasted brown wasteland for a front yard, the boundary delineated by a six-foot-tall chain-link fence. Suddenly three large dogs of indeterminate breed and varying colors came flying around the corner of the neighboring house and flung themselves against the chain link, which twanged and rattled under the assault. Richard couldn't control the flinch. Unfortunately Torres caught it and rolled his eyes.

Torres walked up to the front door of their target. This house had as little vegetation as its neighbor, but no fence—and no dogs. There was a flicker of movement from the dingy drapes in the front window. All the endless stops this day had been routine, but this time Richard had a surge of disquiet as he watched Torres plowing doggedly up to the front door.

"Maybe you shouldn't just walk right up . . . ," Richard began.

Torres raised his hand to pound on the door. "Look, *pendejo*, when you do something to fucking deserve your fucking promotion," he half turned to look at Richard, "then maybe you can tell me how to do police work."

His fist hammered sharply twice, then the door flew open. Richard was smarting under the unfair attack, but then he saw the glint of sun on metal and all conscious thought ceased.

Richard found himself looking down the barrel of a gun he couldn't recall drawing. The rough rubber on the grip rasped across his sweat-slick palm. Torres, his face twisted into a rictus of terror, tried to jump sideways. There was a simultaneous roar of a .357 magnum and the sharp report from Richard's Firestar. The shooter jerked as Richard's bullet took him. His head snapped back, and his arms raised like an evangelical praising God. That lifting hand meant the round from the perp's magnum had parted Torres's hair and torn across the scalp instead of blowing the policeman's face off.

Torres lay on the ground, hands clasped over his head, blood seeping between his fingers. He was cussing but tears laced and separated the words.

For Richard, exhilaration washed up like a fierce heat, followed closely by horror. All the human-shaped targets in the world hadn't prepared him for the reality and finality of his first kill.

He had *shot* a man. He was *dead*.

But maybe he wasn't dead and Torres was helpless on his back in the dirt, while Richard's gun hung limply at his side. Training reasserted itself. Rushing up the two small discolored concrete steps, Richard drew down on the perp. The magnum's butt rested in the man's open hand. Richard kicked it away and finally looked down at his handiwork.

Where the man's throat had been was a raw wound. A bit of neck bone gleamed wet and white through the blood and torn cartilage. The smell of blood hung over the body. Richard's stomach heaved and before he could control the reaction he vomited. He managed to turn away so the bile didn't land on the body. Acid burned his throat and the foul, sour taste coated his tongue.

Officer down! Officer down! Get control!

Wiping the back of his hand across his mouth, Richard whirled, jumped off the stoop and knelt beside Torres. The other cop's curses had faded to mumbles and there were tears in his eyes. Richard pulled Torres's hands away, terrified that he'd see brain, but there was only a long bleeding gouge.

"Hang on. I don't think it's too bad." The words tumbled and rattled out as he grabbed his cell phone and called. It was only about four minutes from his call of "officer down" that he heard a converging symphony of sirens drawing ever closer.

Sergeant Danny McGowan leaned on the bar drinking a beer, shoveling peanuts into his mouth and watching the Patriots game on the TV hung over the bar. Kenntnis studied the man. The broad shoulders bled down into a wide, spreading waist. Judging by those shoulders the man had been an athlete in his youth. Now a shock of white hair crowned his head and the backs of his hands were ridged with veins and discolored by age spots. Kenntnis moved to the bar and ordered a single malt scotch. McGowan's face was pugnacious, but the brown eyes belied the thrust of the jaw; they were soft and kind.

"Sergeant McGowan?"

"Who wants to know?" the man growled. There was a lilt to the words. Kenntnis guessed an Irish grandmother who had lived long enough to bequeath the music of her island to her children and grandchildren.

In answer to the question Kenntnis slid over his business card. McGowan studied it with care, but made no effort to pick it up. He then gave Kenntnis an equally long look before pushing the card back. "I'm not retired yet, and when I do I'm stayin' here." A Puck's grin pulled at the full mouth. "I'll not be running away from the snow. I'll shovel the white shit and outlive all them pansy asses who ran away to Florida."

"I don't doubt it, sir, but I'm not, in fact, here to offer you a job. I'm seeking some information about . . ." Kenntnis broke off as McGowan came off the stool. McGowan's big hands clenched and unclenched at his sides, and they were nose to nose, for Kenntnis had not retreated.

"I sent that other bastard about his business and I'll send you about yours too."

"I'm not here to do any harm to Richard. He works for me. . . ." Again he was interrupted as McGowan roared, "Like Hell he does. He's a policeman in Albuquerque!" The bartender, face tight with concern, edged toward them. "Back off, Todd, I'll not be needing your help."

"If you would let me finish I was going to add—in a manner of speaking," Kenntnis said. "And Richard's made detective, by the way."

That broke through the anger. The old cop frowned and rubbed at his head in confusion. "Now why the devil wouldn't the boy tell me?"

"Because I helped him get the promotion," Kenntnis answered. "And therefore it's tainted and he's ashamed. Not that he'd brag anyway, it doesn't seem to be in his nature."

McGowan stepped back to the barstool and sat down. "Okay, unlike that other bastard, you actually seem to know the boy."

"I assume you didn't tell the other . . . er, bastard anything?"

"Damn right I didn't."

"Good, because unlike me he does intend to do Richard an injury." Kenntnis paused for a sip of scotch.

"What is it you're digging for?" McGowan asked after a few swallows of beer.

"Take a drive with me," Kenntnis said. "I'd feel better in a less public venue."

Out on the rain-slick sidewalk McGowan pushed back his hat and gave a soundless whistle at the sight of the stretch limo parked in front of the bar. The driver opened the back door for them.

"Just drive around until I tell you otherwise," Kenntnis said and hit the button to roll up the dividing window. "Drink?"

"Please. You got one of those single malts in there?" Kenntnis poured out a liberal shot and handed over the cut crystal glass. The cop took a sip and rolled it around in his mouth for a long moment before swallowing. He gusted out a sigh, then shook his head. "Who the fuck are you?"

"A really rich guy who has Richard's best interests at heart. I learned from the EMT what happened to Richard. Others also have this information. I expect they will use it, and . . . ," he paused, wondering how to phrase this diplomatically. He gave up and just said it. "I'm concerned about Richard's reaction."

"Then you don't know him as well as you think, mister. He's small and pretty, and you could break him with one hand, but you'll never *break* him. He has a will of steel."

"He tried to commit suicide."

"That was before he had the calling."

"Police work, you mean?"

"Aye."

"You make it sound like a religious vocation."

"It is for the good ones. They keep the monsters at bay."

Kenntnis smiled. "I think you're one of the good ones, and that you taught Richard a very great deal."

"Well, I tried, and it must have took because he was able to stand up to the old bastard."

"And who is that?"

"His father. Right old bastard, on the one hand talking about what lowlives cops were, and on the other tearing Richard down saying as how he wasn't tough enough to take it." McGowan drained the scotch in a long swallow. "Richard will never be pushed to try suicide again. You can take that to the bank."

Rhiana selected the bathroom at the Frontier Restaurant across the street from the university. It was a dive, open twenty-four hours a day, and she figured no one would notice or give a shit about a darkened mirror. The cloying smell of icing and cinnamon followed her to the back of the restaurant. The Frontier was famous for their plate-sized cinnamon rolls oozing grease.

She closed the door against the roar of conversation and dropped the flow of numbers out of her thoughts. It was as if he'd been waiting for her. The colors boiled and coalesced and he was there.

"I'll have dinner with you," she said, and left, unwilling to take part in any planning. That would make it a real betrayal. This was just . . . reconnaissance.

෴

Richard sat limply in an available wheelchair in the corridor of UNMH. Beyond the curtain a doctor and two nurses worked on Torres. The doors from the emergency waiting room burst open and Captain Ortiz strode in.

The broad hand rested heavily on Richard's shoulder. "Where is he?"

With a jerk of the head Richard indicated the curtained cubicle. "There, sir."

"You okay?"

"Yes, sir."

Ortiz walked through the curtain and the doctor's outraged squawk became a low murmur of conversation. Moments later Ortiz emerged and joined Richard.

"You're going to need to talk to IAD, and you'll be on administrative leave for a few days until the investigation is over." He smiled at Richard's look of alarm. "Relax, it looks like a totally righteous shoot. Joe said you saved his life out there." Richard couldn't respond. He just swallowed hard and nodded. "If you need to talk to somebody we've got shrinks available." Richard nodded again. "And don't think you need to be a macho asshole," the captain added. "This is no easy thing. Do you feel up to writing your report?"

Richard gathered his scattered wits. "Yes, sir."

Back at APD headquarters Ortiz kept his hand on Richard's shoulder all the way into the building, and all the way up the elevator. He probably meant it kindly, but it felt more like the big man was trying to press Richard through the floor like a tent peg.

They stepped through the doors of the bullpen, and a raucous cheer went up. Richard found his hand grabbed and pumped, his shoulders buffeted, shouts of congratulations, queries about the shooting, questions about Torres.

He was pretty certain he never managed a coherent sentence. Even Snyder grinned at him, and yelled something about "Deadeye Dick." To Richard's horror the phrase went rocketing around the room.

Then Weber was there standing in front of him. The brown eyes held worry, but he was also beaming with pride. Richard smiled shyly up at him.

He had finally been accepted.

❀

The garment bag hit the floor with a dull thud. The living room was dark and chill. Kenntnis flicked on a torchiere lamp and kicked up the heat. The penthouse held that silence in which no living thing breathes.

"Damn the girl. Where has she got to?"

He quickly unpacked his suits, while waiting for Cross to come upstairs. It didn't happen and Kenntnis took the elevator to the ground floor and out the back door. There was the sweet rotten smell of garbage in the Dumpster, and the faint hiss of a propane lantern shedding its muted light through the blanket hung over the opening in the cardboard shipping crate.

Bending almost double, Kenntnis swept aside the blanket and entered the crate. What he saw shocked him. Cross lay huddled on an old mattress, blankets clutched tightly around him. His skin was stretched so tightly across his bones that his head seemed skeletal, as if the human envelope that contained the true creature was being burned away.

Kenntnis squatted down next to the creature and laid a hand over his wrist. Cross pulled back his lips in a grotesque caricature of a smile. His gums were bleeding, staining his teeth.

"We pissed 'em off bad last night. Richard and the new guy." He coughed, spraying bloodstained spittle. "He's okay. Closed a gate. Took back a snack."

"You've got to resist," Kenntnis said.

"I'm trying, but it's beatin' me down—the breaking and the hunting, the fighting and the finding my way home."

"Do you think the girl can ward you?" Kenntnis asked.

"I doubt it, and that girl wouldn't do shit to help me."

"You haven't given her much reason to." The homeless god coughed wetly. Kenntnis held a bottle of water to the gray emaciated lips. "Where is she?"

"Fuck if I know."

"Could you find her?" Kenntnis asked.

"If my brains were made of dynamite I couldn't pop my eardrums right now."

Kenntnis gnawed at his lower lip. Something told him this was significant, but he didn't have enough of the pieces for it to make a picture.

He stood. "I'll bring you something to eat."

🔱

Three soft-footed waiters, two women and a man, orbited their table. Rhiana choked back an urge to giggle. Maybe this was the standard of service at the Artichoke Café, but she had a feeling some of it had to do with her and her companion's looks. He was dressed in a black turtleneck sweater that heightened the effect of his high cheekbones and almost slanted green eyes. A lock of blue-black hair lay across his forehead. He tossed it back with a hand, and the waitress's hand shook as she poured water into Rhiana's glass.

"So, you said you'd tell me why I was . . ." She hesitated, embarrassed to use the word.

"Special?" he provided. "I will, but let's not blunt the pleasure of a good appetite with business. May I order for you?" the man asked.

"I . . . I'm a vegetarian."

"What a shame. I was going to order foie gras and oysters Rockefeller."

An internal struggle began. She had read about food like this in books and seen it in movies. But there was principle. He seemed to sense her dilemma. His hand closed around hers.

"I won't try to tempt you out of your beliefs, but consider. You are a superior being. The bounties of this world are yours to enjoy. Or at least to try once before you reject them. Then it truly is a sacrifice, and therefore worthier."

And so it began. They shared a split of champagne with their appetizers. It was nothing like the stuff her dad sometimes brought home for New Year's. The bubbles tickled the back of her nose and the flavors exploded across her tongue.

Once she got used to the texture, the oysters, prepared with spinach, were delicious and the foie gras beyond description. She ate well at Kenntnis's but she had never experienced food like this. She had a salad with honey-toasted pecans and crumbled cheese while he sipped at lobster bisque. For her main course he selected sweet and succulent king crab. There were different wines with each course. They concluded with a chocolate mousse, brandy and coffee.

No course was rushed, providing them with plenty of opportunity to talk. He said little, using his words like keys to unlock more information from her, and she responded. Books, movies, her dreams of travel, her family, her isolation, her studies, her feelings for Richard; it all came out. Finally she wound down, replete and oddly exhausted; she leaned back in her chair, feeling as if her skin was too small to contain both her emotions and the masses of food and liquor she'd consumed. Sensation prickled across her skin. Heat blossomed at the base of her spine. Somehow she was feeding her power and she wasn't even trying.

She lifted her eyes and met the man's blazing green gaze. His look seemed to pierce through to her heart. He smiled, displaying sharp narrow teeth, and Rhiana knew he sensed the power rising within her. With an autocratic gesture he dismissed the hovering waiters. They were the last people in the restaurant.

"This is what you deserve and what you will receive if you join with me . . . us. I hope you will. I don't wish to battle you."

"And why is that? Are you afraid you'll lose?" It was pure bravado. She could sense the magic pulsing off him like a subsonic drone.

"I would hate to hurt you. You are my daughter."

The brandy caught in the back of her throat and her gasp of shock carried the hot fumes into her lungs. Coughing, she leaned over the table. Now the pictures, the care that they represented, made sense. The man came around the table and patted her on the back, and *something* merged like twining tentacles piercing her mind and soul.

And it didn't flow in only one direction. She ate his memories and recognized the kinship. Eventually the waves of pure emotion settled into images. The human woman giving herself in lust and ending in terror. Her mother's descent into drugs, drink and degradation, all of this feeding the embryo—*her*—inside. She tasted the wild flare of suffering and death that accompanied her birth. Then the human flesh had dulled and blunted the raw power bequeathed to her by her father.

Minutes or hours passed in that communion. When Rhiana finally returned to her body and surroundings she saw the wait staff and the maître'd collapsed on the floor.

"Are they . . . ?" she began.

"Merely unconscious. We needed them to forge the

bond," Madoc replied—for she had consumed his name among many other bits of knowledge and experience.

Some questions still remained and she asked one. "If I'm your child why did they . . . you try to kill me?"

"The golems would not have harmed you. They accomplished their purpose, which was to put you into Kenntnis's household."

"Why?"

He ignored her and instead asked, "Do you want your birthright? I rule a vast kingdom both in this world and in others. You have only to reach out and take it."

"And what do I have to do in return?"

Madoc smiled fondly at her. "You're no fool. Yes, you are my child." He paused to dab delicately at his mouth with his napkin. "But before we trust all our plans to you we must be a little more certain where your loyalties lie."

He stood and smiled down at her. "Now open a way for me. I need to go home."

"I'm not sure I can. I'm not sure how I did it before."

"Think of what you know of physics and combine it with your magic."

Rhiana considered all that she knew, particles versus waves, uncertainty principles, strong and weak forces, string theory. As her mind closed on the competing theories the walls of the restaurant seemed to waver, shift and flow. She pulled out a penny, and balanced it on the tip of her index finger.

"I need power."

Madoc made an expansive gesture with his arm, indicating the restaurant and its prone employees. "Feed, by all means."

And she did, watching the electrical fields surrounding their bodies dim and fade as she sucked it in, hot and vibrant. The plump waitress lying by the kitchen door gave a gasp and her breath began coming in wheezing pants. The pain of her laboring lungs and shuddering heart smashed into Rhiana and for a wild instant she did feel as if she had burst through the confines of her body and was stretching out, massive and powerful, across the night sky.

She was aware of Madoc's mind linked to hers, guiding her through the complex designs of competing universes. She knew from his feeling of satisfaction when she had reached the correct thread.

A rent appeared in the back wall. She had only a confused image of too-bright colors, some of which she couldn't identify, and a blast of icy air, and he was gone.

Stepping over the unconscious staff, she left the restaurant.

Chapter

TWENTY

Fog shrouded the winding canyon road up to the Taos ski basin, floated in ghost tendrils around the white trunks of the bare aspens and swathed the blue-green needles of the towering ponderosa pines. Along the side of the road a mountain stream frothed and bubbled between its icy edges. Angela drove the snow-packed road with nonchalant ease. Since Richard was on administrative leave she had suggested this weekday outing.

They had chatted on the long drive up from Albuquerque. The original plan had been the Santa Fe ski area, but when Angela learned he had never been to Taos the decision was made. She added with ghoulish glee that the Taos ski resort was where the U.S. Olympic ski team trained.

Now, three hours later, they were approaching their destination. Richard gazed silently out the front window, wondering if they were going to drive back tonight or if Angela would insist on staying in Taos. And if they stayed they would have to discuss sleeping arrangements. He dreaded that conversation. *Maybe she'd be okay with driving home,* he thought.

Richard sensed her gaze and looked over. Her eyes played slowly and languidly across his face, and came to rest on his crotch and thighs encased in the skin-tight ski pants, and he knew, with a sinking heart, that a return to Albuquerque was not likely. Blushing, he waved toward the road.

"It's pretty windy. Maybe it would be better if you watched the road?"

"Am I scaring you?" she challenged and he knew she wasn't talking about her driving.

"Should I be worried?"

"Absolutely."

Yes, they were going to have *the conversation.* Unless he could forestall it. And maybe he didn't want to. Desire had reentered his life. In the past month he had found himself looking and noticing and reacting, without the touch of that icy fear that had gripped him for the past few years. He stole a glance at her profile. The short upper lip and the uptilted nose and the riot of dark curls. No, she wasn't a raving beauty like Rhiana, but it wasn't about physical looks. She was warm and funny and direct and honest. She was his friend. *You could do far worse as a basis for intimacy*, he reminded himself.

Then there was his own self-confidence. Acceptance provided a sense of intense energy, and certainty informed his every action and reaction. He suspected that it sprang from the shooting incident, and that engendered a momentary flare of guilt. Had it really required a man's death to give him this sense of comfort in his own skin? But he wasn't willing to agonize too much over it. He was experiencing admiration, respect and friendship, and he liked it—a lot.

Another curve and a steep climb and they broke through

the fog bank. Sunlight glittered on the new snow. The needles of the pines were frosted white. Amazing views of distant snowcapped peaks distracted him from his self-congratulatory musings.

He smiled at her. "I'm glad you suggested this."

"So am I. It gives me a chance to see you in ski pants." She leered and then laughed at his expression. "It's so much fun to make you blush."

"You're a cold, hard woman," Richard said.

They pulled into the parking lot. Above them, nestled in the arms of the mountains, was a cluster of buildings. A couple of lodges, a beautiful condo and spa facility under construction, shops and restaurants, and above them all loomed the sheer white face of the mountain.

"Holy hell," Richard said.

Angela grinned. "Oh, that's one of the easier runs."

Two lifts were in view, the chairs trembling and swaying as they made their way up the mountain. There were a few hardy souls, dark silhouettes against the white mountain, riding the lift up to the runs, but it was a Tuesday and the crowds were thin.

They plowed through the snow to the back doors of the SUV, the snow squeaking and crunching beneath their feet. Angela explained that there were four more lifts, and you had to walk up to the top of the hardest runs. Angela threw open the doors and Richard pulled out their skis and boots.

Before long the shuttle came by, an open trailer pulled behind a snow cat, and they were driven up to the base of the lift. Soon they were booted and waiting for the chair to grind and whine toward them. It caught him behind the knees and with a swoop and a sway they were on their way up the mountain.

Angela shifted on the narrow seat to face him. "Richard, we have to talk." She drew in a quick, deep breath and he realized she was nervous. It was oddly calming for him. "Okay, here goes. I like you. I want to spend time with you, but you seem . . . elusive. Am I too old for you? Is that the problem?"

"No, you're not the problem. I am." He stopped and amended the statement. "Have been."

"Does that mean the problem has been resolved?" she asked.

"Yes . . . yes, I believe so."

"Good. God, I feel like I'm back in high school."

"What a terrible thought."

"Does anybody enjoy high school?" she asked, her words clipped and brittle and bright.

"Only jocks and cheerleaders," Richard replied.

He hesitated for a moment, then pulled off his glove and laid his hand against the side of her face. Her skin was soft and warm beneath beneath his palm. It seemed that desire and embarrassment had trumped wind chill. He leaned in and pressed his lips on hers. It began very chastely, but four years of abstinence had taken its toll. Arousal shot straight down into his groin. Richard couldn't control it, a sound somewhere between a whimper and a groan escaped. Cupping her face between his hands, he kissed her long and deeply. She responded fiercely. She closed her teeth on his lower lip.

Blackness danced before his eyes and his nostrils were filled with the smell of sweat and sperm, all overlaid with musty smell of Kouros aftershave. In memory he tasted blood from his brutally bitten lip. Fear swept away passion. Richard jerked back, his eyes snapped open and reality returned. Only the fact that the ground was thirty feet below kept him in the chairlift.

"What?"

His mind churned for some explanation, some plausible lie. "I . . . I was afraid we were getting close to the top."

"Yeah, I guess we are." With her bright red cheeks,

tumbled curls and crooked little grin, she looked like a particularly endearing and naughty elf. "So, hold that erection 'til later!" He gave her a wan smile in answer.

She grabbed her poles, and they both made it off the chairlift without mishap. Angela grabbed his face and planted a hard kiss on him. She skied off, throwing over her shoulder, "See you at the bottom."

Richard watched her small form leaning into each turn as she flew down the mountain. Richard dug in his poles and pushed off in a spray of new powder. So much for confidence. He'd opened this particular Pandora's box, and he couldn't back out now. If he tried and failed she would never believe it had nothing to do with her. He couldn't hurt her that way.

But you were wrong! *You can't do this!*

He tucked his poles, bent low over his skis and raced down the mountain, trying to outrun the doubt and fear.

❦

The Adobe and Stars B & B stood in a curve of the road some eight miles from the ski valley. There was not a room to be had at any of the ski lodges higher up the canyon, and Angela was beginning to despair, but then she spotted the vacancy sign. The building formed a shallow arc, crowned with snow and electric luminarias. Smoke spiraled up from chimneys, blurring the stars and the sharp points of the crescent moon. The rich and spicy smell of piñon perfumed the brisk night air.

The owner, a comfortably plump older woman with a muted Texan accent, had instructed them to park in back. Their room was up the stairs at the end of the building.

"This is crazy," Richard said, his words punctuated by his chattering teeth. "The room costs two hundred and fifty dollars a night! I haven't even got a toothbrush."

Angela pulled his arm tighter against her side, and hustled him toward the back door. "Yeah, and you won't be able to change your underwear either. And don't worry about the money."

For an instant Richard hung back like a recalcitrant foal on the end of the lead line. "Look, shouldn't we . . . well, plan this . . . a little?"

"Sex should never be planned," Angela responded.

Angela hoped that the quip came across as light and confident. She felt anything but. Despite the age difference, and his shy reticence, she wanted this man, and the intensity of that want frightened her.

Inside, the building smelled of fresh-baked cookies and coffee. The stairs were immediately evident on their right. Richard took a couple of steps toward the common room, but Angela reeled him back and marched him up the stairs. She shoved the key into the lock on the bright blue door and pulled him in.

A queen-size bed dominated the room. In a corner there was a kiva fireplace with logs already laid in the hearth. Eastern-facing windows framed a section of the mountains. Through a door she could see a two-person Jacuzzi and a spectacular western view of mesas. A narrow line of orange and pink marked the recent passing of the sun.

She was manic, bursting with energy. She could feel him trembling as she hugged him tight and rubbed her cold cheek against his. Excited that his passion matched hers, Angela reached down, unzipped his pants and reached for his crotch. He flinched, and she jerked back because she didn't find the expected erection.

"Are you okay?" she asked.

"Nervous," he said tightly. "How about we start with the coats?" Richard unzipped her parka and eased it off her shoulders. She was very aware of his slender hands with their long tapering fingers and perfect nails. There was no hair on them, nothing to blur the play of veins and tendons beneath the porcelain white skin. He removed his own jacket, opened the wardrobe and carefully hung them both side by side.

Angela released a pent-up breath and held up a hand. "Okay, so we slow down a little." She moved to the fireplace, snatched the book of matches off the mantel and struck a flame.

The fat wood ignited with a burst of green and orange and licked eagerly up the length of the tented logs. Within moments the dried piñon was snapping and crackling. She heard Richard draw in a long, shuddering breath, and the overhead light went out. That seemed an encouraging sign, so she stood and crossed to him.

Shadows ballooned and swayed across the whitewashed plaster walls. He looked down at her and she drank in the play of firelight across his chiseled features. Reaching up, she ran her fingers through his hair. It was soft and fine. She pulled off her sweater and silk undershirt and turned around, offering him the bra clasp. After a few seconds she felt his fingers across her back. They were icy cold. The clasp sprung free and she shrugged out of her bra. She pirouetted to face him, looking forward to his reaction. Angela knew she fell into the cute rather than beautiful category, but she also knew that her tits were dynamite and their effect on men electrifying.

She found Richard staring over her head at the far wall, his eyes wide and dark, sweat beading his forehead.

She laid a hand on his cheek. Unlike his hand, it was burning hot. "What's wrong?"

"I haven't done this . . . well, for awhile . . . a long while." He brought his focus back to her and forced a smile. "Just bear with me, okay?"

"Okay. And by the way I'm half naked and freezing, and you're still dressed. Could you get with the program!"

His teeth caught at his lower lip. Then with a jerky nod, like an inexpertly controlled puppet, he stripped off his sweater and silks and began to unlace his boots. Angela quickly stripped off the rest of her clothes. The floor felt like it had been tiled with ice cubes rather than Saltillo. She hustled over to the bed, ripped back the down comforter, and plunged between the sheets. They were colder than shit too.

"Brrrrr. Hey, body warmth helps," she said, because Richard was still standing in the middle of the small room holding his pants in front of him. "And by the way, I've seen a few penises in my time," and then added, "and no, they haven't all been on dead guys."

He carefully folded the ski pants over the arm of a wicker chair and stepped out of his jockey shorts. She watched the play of long flat muscles across his shoulders, and the way his back tapered down to his narrow hips. He straightened and turned to her, and all breath stopped in her chest.

The firelight played across his white, white skin. The cuts and bruises had faded. In the firelight they could only be guessed at, rather than seen. She folded her arms behind her head and drank in his body. He had only the faintest feathering of golden hair on his chest and the brush in his groin was a darker gold than the white gold on his head. A Greek statue given life and breath, and indeed his chest was rising and falling in quick panting breaths. Desire roiled warm and heavy in her belly, but judging from his flaccid penis he still wasn't sharing her need.

Why is the first First Time *always such a bitch?* she thought. A log snapped loudly as the flames reached the sap. Richard jumped like a runner at the starting blocks.

She smiled, and lifted the covers suggestively. Richard slid into the queen bed. With a deep breath he rolled over, arms on either side of her body, and held himself above her. There was the barest glitter of white-blond stubble along his jawline. Seconds passed. His arms began to tremble, and then lowering himself only slightly, he kissed her.

Angela reached up and pulled him down against her, skin against skin, chest to chest. The kiss deepened and there was a faint stir as his penis began to stiffen. She grabbed his hands, twining her fingers through his. There was still something separating them like a layer of ice.

Angela looked up into that beautiful face. Richard's eyes were tightly shut. His lashes were a deep amber and they brushed his cheeks, but the muscles of his face were so taut that his face seemed more like marble than pliant skin. He clearly wasn't going with the moment but rather working at the moment.

"Here," she whispered. "Let me help."

And she levered them over so she ended sitting on his thighs. Her hands swept down his torso, feeling the ribs and the bands of muscle in his belly. She took his penis in her mouth and went to work. A groan broke from between his lips. It was still slow but he was beginning to quicken. She drew her nail down his sternum and touched his navel. His hips arched beneath her.

She chuckled and lifted her head from his crotch. Richard reached up for her, but she caught him by the wrists and forced his arms back toward the wrought-iron headboard, and held him down.

She felt the puckered line of a scar on the right wrist. "Hey, what's . . . ," she started to say when a scream of sheer terror broke from his lips.

He began to thrash wildly. Bucked to the side of the bed, Angela went sliding off onto the floor. She stared up in shock as he hunched over his knees, hands clasped over his head, body shaking, guttural whimpers punctuating each breath.

"Here, here." She laid a hand on his shoulder and jumped back when he cried out in terror.

"Richard. Richard! *Richard!*" The shout penetrated. His breath caught, and he managed to look up at her. His eyes seemed dark, dark and very distant. She wished he'd stop looking at whatever he was seeing. Shudders passed through his body.

There was the sound of running footsteps and a hammering on the door. The owner's voice called out, "Is everything all right in there?"

"Fine, we're fine!" Angela shouted and then added inanely, "I'm a doctor."

"What does that mean?" the voice asked.

"That we're okay. Please, go away."

The footsteps retreated and she turned back to Richard. "Wait. Breathe. I'll be right back," she ordered.

Angela ran into the bathroom and began to fill the tub with hot water. She ran back, her bare feet slapping on the tile.

"Sorry. Sorry. Sorry," came the monotonous whisper, and Angela wasn't entirely certain for whom the apology was intended.

"I'm going to touch you," she said in her best brisk Doctor Voice.

He flinched but endured her touch. She got him to his feet, guided him into the bathroom and into the tub. She snatched down a washcloth, the thick Egyptian cotton soft against her fingers. Carefully she dipped it in the steaming water and squeezed it across his shoulders. His muscles were banded iron.

For a long time she sluiced water across his neck and back, and mentally berated herself. Not nervousness, flat-out terror, and she had missed it. Missed every cue. Missed it on the lift. Missed it outside the B & B. Missed it inside the B & B. *Because you were so hot to trot you couldn't spare a thought for him. You wanted to get past that first coitus, and get down to the lovemaking that can only happen when a lover's abilities are known. Well, congratulations, you've got a real mess on your hands now.*

Eventually the shivers subsided and his breathing slowed. The water was cooling and her fingers puckering and wrinkling. Richard hadn't looked at her once, but now he said, "I was so hot. I didn't think . . . I thought I could . . ." His voice broke. "Oh God, I'm so sorry."

Knees screaming in protest, Angela levered herself to her feet, using the cold porcelain side of the tub for balance. She stripped down a huge fluffy bath sheet and held it out to him. He climbed out, sluicing water. She wrapped the towel around him.

"Look, before you try this again you've got to set the ground rules so your partner doesn't hit . . . well, whatever button I hit." Placing her hands on his shoulders she guided him back toward the bed. He froze in place.

"No. I'll . . . I'll sit in the chair." The leather on the woven Spanish basket chair creaked under his weight. Angela pulled the down comforter off the bed and wrapped him in it.

She began throwing on her clothes. "I'm going to go downstairs and get you a brandy—"

"No, please don't. Alcohol . . . alcohol always gets me into trouble."

"Buddy, you are already in trouble." And she cursed her smart mouth because it had the same effect as if she'd hit him.

He flung himself out of the chair and headed for his clothes. "Look, I'll take a taxi or the bus back to Albuquerque."

"No, you will not. Richard, I'm a doctor. That means I did a rotation in psych. It's clear you've endured some kind of trauma. You need to talk about it."

The pale head gave a violent shake of negation. "No. It will destroy me."

"I'd say it's doing that right now."

"I've been fine as long as I didn't—" He broke off abruptly. "Sorry, sorry, that makes it sound like I blame you. It's all me. My fault."

It was hard but she said it anyway. "Richard, as of this

moment I'm assuming that we will never make love. So
we can put all that aside. But I am still, and will always be,
your friend. You can talk to me. I also think having this
bed sitting here staring at us doesn't make this the best
venue. So let's get dressed and get out of here."

But he never would talk. She ended up dropping him off
around 11:00 p.m. at his apartment. They had exchanged
not a word on the drive back from Taos. As she drove
down Montgomery headed for Rio Grande and her condo
she wondered if she should tell Weber or Kenntnis. But
that seemed like a betrayal.

   Still, she had unleashed a torrent of memory and trauma
and it was her experience that people didn't easily rebury
these kinds of memories. In this strange twilight world of
gods and monsters it was Richard who had to hold them at
bay and she was pretty damn sure it was going to take all
his strength and concentration.

   And she had just made that a whole lot harder.

Chapter

TWENTY-ONE

Richard overslept, waking near noon, and rolled out of
bed with a groan. Some of it was sore muscles from
skiing after five years away from the sport, but much of it
was due to the vivid and terrifying nightmares that had
disturbed his rest. The figure on the cross kept coiling
down, but it wore a different face, a face Richard had spent
four years trying to forget. He kept trying to talk to Angela
but she kept turning her back on him. At one point in the
confused and tumbled images and sounds, his father walked

through. Richard had tried to follow him, to catch him and talk with him, but Robert Oort always stayed just out of reach.

He forced himself out of the apartment and went to the club for a swim. The sunlight outside the wide bay windows at the end of the pool was deceptively bright, and the sky a brilliant turquoise blue. At the end of the hour his muscles didn't hurt quite so badly, but depression still dragged at his mind and body.

The message light on the phone was blinking. Tossing his keys on the small bar, Richard called the voice mail center. While he listened to the first two messages—Rhiana and Weber—he stared into the refrigerator, but the thought of food was nauseating.

He nudged the door shut with his hip and listened while the impassive and impersonal voice on the service said, "Message three received yesterday at 7:33 a.m."

We were already on the road to Taos, he thought, and the queasiness increased.

But there was no voice—just barely audible breathing, rapid and desperate. "End of message," said the computer voice. "Message four received yesterday at 9:17 a.m." Again the breathing. There were two more messages in the early afternoon. On the final one he could hear a woman crying.

Berating himself for not checking the messages last night, Richard dialed home and felt his gut clench when his father answered.

"Oort residence."

"Papa. What are you doing home?" Cringing at the inadvertent blurt, Richard closed his eyes and leaned his head against the wall.

"I might ask the same of you." Richard could hear the congestion from a cold blurring his father's voice.

"I'm on administrative leave."

"Why? What have you done?" The suspicion and obvious

implication that he was guilty of wrongdoing sunk Richard's spirits even lower.

"I was involved in a shooting."

"Oh, dear God. Did you hurt anyone?" Robert Oort asked.

A flare of anger and resentment kindled in his chest. *Why doesn't he ask if* I *got hurt?* "Actually I killed someone."

"Dear God," the judge repeated, but this time in a whisper.

"He was trying to kill my partner."

"So, you aren't in trouble?"

"No, sir."

"And you called to tell us about your cowboy moment?" his father asked lightly as if making a joke, but Richard knew better.

"No, I called to talk to Mama."

"She's out."

"Papa, is Mama all right? She's called me a couple of times and she seemed . . . upset."

"She's fine. A little tired. She's on a number of committees at church. This time of year things get very busy."

The phone shifted in his grip because his palms were slick with sweat. Richard remembered the dossier on his mother and Grenier's threats. "Has . . . has anything changed at church?"

"What do you mean?"

"Is there anyone new there?"

"Well, of course there is. Our membership is growing. Don't be so foolish," his father snapped.

"I meant like a new minister."

"What is this about?"

What indeed? How could he possibly explain, and, more to the point, warn his father? And warn him against what?

"Is there a new minister?"

"I don't understand why you are asking. But, no. We do not have a new minister. Reverend Hoffsteader is still here."

Relief made his knees sag. "Okay. Well, tell Mama I called and that I love her."

"When are you coming to visit?"

"Christmas."

"See to it that you do."

"Yes, sir. And Papa, please keep an eye on Mama."

There was a snort that could have been assent, disgust or goodbye, and Oort senior hung up.

Richard drifted back into the living room and stared out at the small patio. The flat expanse of concrete looked sterile. Only a small hibachi broke the monotony. *I don't really live anywhere, or belong anywhere,* he thought. Then he remembered the admiring faces of his coworkers and he smiled wistfully, wishing he could go back to work.

He was pouring out a glass of milk when the realization hit. *It doesn't need to be a new minister. Anyone would do. A new member of the congregation who showed an interest in her.*

Richard knew his mother was lonely. That had been the hardest part of leaving. Robert and Pamela's disdain over his new career choice and Amelia's disinterest had made it easy, but his mother's brittle cheerfulness, the books she had bought about New Mexico so she would know what it was like where he was going, and how he'd have such a wonderful adventure and come home a real cowboy—he knew it hid a bruised heart.

And suddenly Angela's face was before him. He dropped his face into his hands.

I hurt everyone I care about.

He tried the piano, but the notes hadn't been sufficient to stop the constant play and replay of the disastrous events in Taos. Richard kept searching for that one action that would have made it all turn out differently. A total waste of time, but he couldn't help it.

Finally, in desperation, he turned to the vocal repertoire. He chose Schubert. *Litanei auf das Fest Allersellen*, an *andante* lied to commemorate All Souls Day. The keys depressed softly beneath his fingers and his foot working the pedal was like a second, slower heartbeat. He played the three notes of the introduction and he began to sing.

The music wove a net of sound, filling the room and resonating in his chest and head with the shiver of overtones. Long breaths took air deep into his lungs. The strength of his diaphragm forced those breaths back out, carrying on them the glowing notes. He sang in German, but his mind provided the translation.

Rest in peace, all souls who, a fearful torment past
and sweet dream over, sated with life, scarcely born,
have departed from the world:
Rest in peace, all souls
And those who never smiled at the sun
but under the moon lay awake on thorns
to see God face to face
one day in heaven's pure light:
all who have departed hence,
rest in peace, all souls.

As he sang he mourned friendship lost and faith destroyed. The final note died away, followed by a soft knock at the door. It wasn't who he'd expected. Kenntnis stood outside, his bulk blotting out the light.

"May I come in?" he asked with great formality.

Richard stepped back. "Please." As Kenntnis entered the piano gave a soft, melodic sigh as if a wind had passed across the strings.

Kenntnis surveyed the living room, his gaze lingering

on the grand piano. "So that wasn't a CD. You play and sing extremely well."

"Thank you."

"Mourning for lost innocence?" the big man asked with an eerie omniscience.

"Four days ago I killed a man. Before that I denied my god. I think I'm entitled." *And I hurt and shamed a woman I care deeply about.* But he didn't say that. For a long moment they regarded each other, then Richard remembered his manners. "Would you like something to drink?"

"I take it the offer doesn't include coffee or liquor?"

"No, sorry. I can make hot chocolate," Richard offered.

"Sounds good."

While Richard busied himself in the kitchen, grating the Mexican chocolate and heating the milk, Kenntnis strolled about, studying the books on the shelves. There were a lot of holes. Richard had culled the religious works.

"*My Fifty Years in Baseball*; *Babe: The Legend Comes to Life*; *Lucky to be a Yankee*; *Five O'Clock Lightning*; *Damned Yankees*; *The Mick*," Kenntnis read aloud, trailing his fingers along the spines of the books. "You like baseball."

"Yes."

"I'm betting the Yankees."

"Yes." Richard knew his responses were not rising to the level of conversation, but he didn't feel much like talking. He carried the chocolate into the living room, and handed Kenntnis a mug.

"Some people say they're evil incarnate," Kenntnis said.

"Some people say that about you," Richard replied. Kenntnis gave his rich, rolling chuckle.

Richard settled into the armchair, giving Kenntnis the entire couch to accommodate his massive body. They sipped chocolate in silence for a few minutes, then Kenntnis said, "I came by yesterday evening."

They had been at the Adobe and Stars, Richard thought.

"I went skiing," is what he said. "I didn't get back until late. I'm sorry. Was it important? Stupid question; with you everything is important, right?" Richard forced a smile.

Kenntnis swirled the cup, watching the chocolate form a whirlpool, then sat it down on the glass coffee table. "I went to New York." Richard cocked his head, indicating polite interest. "I met Danny McGowan."

A constriction closed around his throat, cutting off the air. Richard coughed and hoped his tone was disinterested as he said, "Oh, and how is he?"

"Hurt that a young man he rescued didn't see fit to tell him about his promotion."

Richard wasn't aware of his hand moving, but he found himself clutching his right wrist. "Well . . . yes, but I didn't really . . . earn it."

"From what I hear from the chief you are earning it now, but I'm not here to bolster your ego." Standing, Kenntnis walked to the piano and softly stroked his hand across the keys, pulling out a whisper of sound. "Grenier's people have also been making inquiries."

"Danny wouldn't talk to them."

"He didn't, but others have. One of the EMTs who picked you up out of that alley and took you to the hospital. Our enemies know the nature of your injuries."

Panic and shame roiled corrosively through his gut. Richard bent over, clutching his stomach, fighting down nausea. A warm hand cupped the nape of his neck, the fingers gently massaging taut muscles.

"They will try to find the man who hurt you."

"I don't think he'll talk to them," Richard whispered.

"Are you sure? They can be most persuasive. They use both threats and bribes. And even if he doesn't provide them with the details they will spread the rumors, and those who hear will fill in their own details and may make it far worse than it actually was."

"That would be hard," Richard said softly.

"Who knows what happened to you?"

"No one. Well, Danny, but he doesn't know the specifics."

"You never told your parents?" Disbelief and surprise edged the words.

"No. Medical confidentiality is a wonderful thing. They just think I was mugged."

"What did you tell the police? You had clearly been raped and tortured."

"I told them I was attacked on the street. That I never got a look at them," Richard answered.

"And they believed this farrago?"

"No, of course not." Richard gripped his own wrists. "I had ligature marks, but they didn't push. Why should they? They have a lot of cases, and what was one faggot getting hurt by some rough trade? But Danny wouldn't let it go. He came and visited me almost every day, and tried to get me to tell him what really happened."

"But you didn't?"

"No."

"Have you ever talked to *anyone* about this?" Kenntnis asked. Richard shook his head. "And this man . . . he's walking free?" Richard nodded.

The heavy weight of the hand on his neck was removed. The big man knelt in front of him. The grip on Richard's chin was inexorable as Kenntnis forced his head up until their eyes met.

"Why are you protecting him?"

It was the one question no one had ever asked, and the absolutely right question. Richard found himself answering.

"Because he was . . . is . . . a very close friend of my father's." Richard ran a hand through his hair. Forced himself to continue. "And I worked for him. I was stupid. I asked for it."

"Really? You wanted to get raped and beaten? You trusted this man. He was a family friend. How does his crime reflect on you?" Kenntnis asked.

"Because I'm unnatural," Richard whispered. There was no response from Kenntnis, forcing him to elaborate. "I sleep with men as well as women. I crave sex," he burst out, his cheeks flaming with shame and disgust.

"Sex is a good thing, Richard; it's a life force. We serve and defend life. And homosexuality is natural. It's religion that's made it evil."

"*He* was evil," Richard choked out.

"Yes, because he's a sadist. Not because he found you desirable." Kenntnis paused, then asked, "How did you come to work for this man?"

"My father."

The silence hung between them. Kenntnis made a "go on" gesture. "More, please."

"I had finished my graduate work at the Conservatory in Rome, but I hadn't been offered a contract. My father wasn't willing to pay for any more college, so I came back to the States. I wanted to stay in New York, to be close to the musical scene. I worked at Macy's and gave piano lessons, and went to auditions. But I was just drifting and I was twenty-three years old. Past time I took responsibility and amounted to something."

"I take it that's a quote?"

Richard held up a hand, forestalling any further remark by Kenntnis. "Please don't say anything. He is my father."

"Which doesn't mean you're required to like him," came the surprising answer. "You can honor him and respect him, maybe even love him, and still know he's a bastard. But let's stay on this other man. What does he do?"

"He owns a boutique investment company."

Kenntnis shook his head. "Does your father know you at all?"

Despite his tension, and the growing knot of fear that

pressed hard beneath his breastbone, Richard found himself smiling faintly. "I know, it was ludicrous. I was Drew's assistant, and he was very good to me even though I showed little aptitude. It didn't take long for me to read the signals."

"So, you'd done this before?"

"Yes." Richard chose not to elaborate. He'd become sexually active at sixteen, and for an instant his mind filled with the faces of lovers—male and female. He pressed the heels of his hands against his eyes, trying to turn off the memories.

"Go on," Kenntnis ordered.

And while not certain he wanted to, Richard found himself continuing. "I went to his bed. He was far more experienced than I was, and his tastes were—" He searched for the word. "Eclectic? Exotic? Sometimes he scared me, hurt me a little, but he always apologized, and was always so complimentary and admiring of me afterward. He gave me lovely things. He made me feel good about myself . . . special." Kenntnis's eyes flicked around the room. "No, I don't have any of them anymore. Well, only one . . . as a . . . reminder." Richard paused for a shuddering breath. A thin line of sweat crawled down his cheek. He brushed it away.

"One night he invited me to dinner with a couple of 'special' clients. Men whose money he was hoping to manage. One was another American. The other Russian, I think, maybe Ukrainian, I don't know for certain. Just that he was one of those gangster billionaires coming out of the new Russia. We ate. Drew insisted that I try the wine." Richard raised his eyes to meet Kenntnis's. "I don't drink. Partly because of my mother, but partly because every time I drink I wake up in somebody's bed, and mostly because of . . . this."

"Were you drunk?"

Richard nodded. "Probably. I was certainly cheerful

and pretty unsteady on my feet. Drew started to guide me toward the bedroom. That's when I realized that I was dessert. I balked, pulled back. Drew dug his fingers into my arm, hanging onto me. Then we heard the dishes hitting the floor. The Russian had swept the table clean. He said . . . he said . . ." Richard started up out of the chair only to be pushed back down by Kenntnis. The man's hands closed on his forearms.

"No! No! Please, don't!" Richard heard the shrill terror in his voice. Kenntnis's hands sprang open. For such a large man he was quick and light on his feet. In an instant he was standing, pulling Richard up beside him. Kenntnis dropped an arm over Richard's shoulders and walked him up and down the length of the room. Back and forth, never stopping.

"I know from the EMT that your wrists and ankles were raw and torn. Was it rope or metal? How did they bind you?" Kenntnis's tone was clinical and matter-of-fact.

"C-c-cord." The sweat rolling off his brow stung his eyes. Richard dashed a hand across them.

"How did you get the bone breaks?" Kenntnis pressed.

"When they started to strip me, I punched the American." Richard looked down at his left hand, remembering the sharp snap as the bones had broken.

"I take it you never learned to box," Kenntnis said in that same matter-of-fact tone.

Richard shook his head. "Not until the academy. I'm still not very good at hand-to-hand." He fell silent.

"That's the hand. What about the rest?"

"The Russian slugged me. Broke my jaw. I went down. They kicked me. I didn't think I had any fight left . . . until they tied me on that table."

Richard quit walking. Stood shivering. The memories hung like an abstract painting—impressions but no details. He feared if he made them coherent they would tear him apart.

Kenntnis gave Richard a gentle shake. "Finish it."

Suddenly it was all there. No longer the scattered images of nightmares, or memories he refused to face, or the panic that buried him like an avalanche whenever he felt confined or someone touched his lips. He remembered it all.

The taste of blood from his badly bitten lips, the smell of sex and sweat, the taste of vomit, the pain from the cuts and burns, the blood trickling down his legs, and the screams.

"Afterwards they washed up, and sat in the living room drinking and talking while I lay on that table." His voice began to rise. Richard tried to pull it back down, but couldn't. Kenntnis reached out, and again laid a large, warm hand on the nape of Richard's neck. "They dumped me in an alley." His voice reached crescendo and broke. "Like I was garbage." The last words were scarcely audible.

Kenntnis pulled him against his shoulder. The soft nape of cashmere caressed Richard's cheek. There was the sharp rich scent of sandalwood. Everything combined to break his rigid control. The sob burst from him, a cry of grief and despair. Kenntnis made no sound, offered no platitudes. He simply held Richard and rocked him gently, as Richard wept as he had never wept since that night of terror, pain and betrayal. Eventually the paroxysms eased and finally Kenntnis spoke.

"You were not stupid and you did not ask for it. Your father placed you in evil and untrustworthy hands. You trusted and cared for this man. He betrayed you. That is his shame, not yours." Richard's hair had fallen forward over his forehead. Kenntnis brushed it back softly.

Richard looked up to meet Kenntnis's gaze, searching for any sign of disgust or contempt. He saw only affection and concern. "That's what hurt the worst," Richard said, and realized it was true. "I don't think Drew expected either the level or type of violence. But he didn't do anything to stop it, and eventually he joined in. Perhaps out of a desire not to offend his clients, or maybe he enjoyed it—maybe it was what he'd wanted all along. Hell, I don't know." Richard ran his hands across his hair. They came away damp from sweat.

"But you protected him."

"No, I protected my father. While Drew untied me he reminded me how bad it would be if any of this came out. The other men were getting nervous. Drew told them that 'shame was a great silencer.' "

"And death's an even better one," Kenntnis said quietly. "Is that why you tried to commit suicide?"

"There were a lot of reasons."

"And Danny kept your attempt quiet."

"Yes. He checked up on me even after I got out of the hospital. He found me that day." Richard pulled back the sleeve of his sweater and studied the narrow white scar. "While he sewed me up he made me realize that dying let them win. He told me to face the monsters."

The corner of Kenntnis's mouth quirked up in an impish half-smile. "Little did you know . . ."

Suddenly Richard found himself chuckling. Kenntnis joined in, and then they were both whooping with laughter.

"But why a policeman?" Kenntnis asked after they'd regained control. "Gratitude? Admiration for McGowan?"

"That was probably some of it, but I wanted to protect people." Richard glanced up shyly at Kenntnis. "Sorry, that sounds really corny."

"Yes, but it's also admirable. You told me you kept something this Drew gave you. Show it to me."

Richard went into the bedroom and opened the jewelry box on his dresser. The gold Rolex with its shattered crystal glinted among the cufflinks and tie tacks. He returned and handed the broken watch to Kenntnis.

"This. I was wearing it that night. I broke it in the struggle. I kept it to remind me."

Kenntnis pocketed the watch. "And now it's time to forget."

"No, it's inspiration for me, a goad."

"I think it's been more of a scourge. Let it go. McGowan's right. You've found your calling. Nothing will ever break you again."

"He said that?" Richard asked, absurdly pleased.

"Yes, he did." Placing his hands on Richard's shoulders, he guided him over to the piano. "Now, play something for me."

"What would you like?"

"Something more cheerful than that dismal Schubert."

Richard riffled through the stacks of music and pulled out a Mozart sonata. "Will Grenier use this to hurt me?" Richard asked as he set the music on the stand and settled onto the bench.

"Only if you let him."

Kenntnis stood at his side, turning the pages while he played.

Chapter

TWENTY-TWO

Angela looked up from her take-out container of egg foo yong. Richard stood in the doorway. It was déjà vu. He had looked just this hesitant and lost the first time she'd seen him. *God, had it only been a month ago?* Of course then he'd worn a uniform, and looked a little like a boy dressed up for Halloween. Today he wore a beautiful gray Prince of Wales windowpaned suit, and was gorgeous. The hurt over what lay between them tightened Angela's throat.

"You got more dead people for me?" she asked, keeping her tones clipped and professional.

"No, I have this for you." He pulled a bouquet of seven perfect white roses from behind his back. "Will you accept them and my apology?"

"I guess . . . maybe."

He walked behind her overladen desk, bent down and softly kissed her chastely on the lips.

"Have things changed?" she asked.

"Maybe. I don't know yet, but I wouldn't mind if we tried to find out," he said, then hastened to add, "As long as we go a little slow."

"I can do slow."

"Good." He gave her that heartbreaking smile. "So what's new in your life?"

"A stabbing from one of the homeless shelters, and according to the fire department a gas leak that laid out every person in the Artichoke Café. One girl had an undiagnosed heart condition and it killed her."

"You sound dubious."

"I didn't find any evidence of carbon monoxide in her blood work."

"What's their story?" Richard asked, moving aside a stack of papers and perching his hip on the corner of her desk.

"They were down to the last table of the night. A man and a young woman. Then they don't remember anything until one of them woke up and smelled smoke in the kitchen."

"The cook was down too?"

"Chef, please, this was the Artichoke Café. And yes, he was unconscious too. A pot had started to scorch."

"What about the customers?"

"They left. Without paying, according to the driver of the meat wagon." Angela sighed and dug out another bite of foo yong. "That seemed to piss him off more than anything else. I swear I don't know where they find these people."

"Well, it's not like they have to be sensitive to their passengers," Richard said. "I've got to get back to work. Would you like to have dinner tomorrow night?" he asked with shy formality.

"Yes, I would very much like that."

"I'll pick you up at seven."

Assistant District Attorney Jennifer Salisbury was waiting by his desk when Richard arrived at headquarters. She was an elegant woman in her mid-thirties. He was surprised to see her. Normally the lawyers in the DA's office sent for cops.

"Hi," Richard said.

"Hi. You don't need to be at the Grand Jury hearing on Thursday."

"Which one is that for?" Richard asked, only half listening as he flipped through the phone message slips on his desk.

"Andresson."

That got his attention. The papers fell from between his fingers and scattered like pink leaves across his desk. "Why? What's happened?"

"He's been extradited to Texas. Amarillo. Some B & E rap."

"We've got him on attempted murder of a police officer. What is this horseshit?"

Jennifer held up her hands. "Hey, don't yell at me. I didn't know about it until today."

"I'm sorry." Richard ran a hand through his hair. "Look, could you call the DA in Texas and at least try to keep them from pleading this out?"

"Sure," Jennifer said.

🔱

The heat from the pizza warmed the palm of Rhiana's hand, reminding her that she should have worn gloves. She shifted nervously from foot to foot and stared at the apartment door. Finally she reached up and knocked. Richard answered. He wore a heavy robe and was towel-drying his hair.

"Rhiana."

"Hi," she said brightly. "It's Friday and I thought, hey, I'll pick up a pie and a movie, and catch up. I haven't seen you in days and days." She closed her eyes briefly, cursing herself for sounding whiny.

"I . . . I apologize. Things have been . . . hectic."

"They said on the news that you were on leave or something."

He had the grace to blush. "Well, yes, I have been, but I've had a lot on my mind."

"Yeah, I guess you would. I mean shooting somebody . . . that must be weird."

"Yes," he said shortly.

"Look, me and the pizza are turning to ice," Rhiana said, forcing the words past the growing lump in her throat.

"I'm sorry. Come in."

She followed him into the apartment. The room no longer looked like a showroom. Music was scattered across the piano. A dirty mug rested on the coffee table among a tumble of pages from the *New York Times*. Rhiana set the pizza down on the breakfast bar.

"I wish you'd called me," Richard said, sounding hesitant and embarrassed. "I . . . I have plans tonight. I would have been free tomorrow."

Suspicion tightened her voice. "Who are you . . . what are you doing?"

He looked up at her and Rhiana watched the ice settle across his features and in his eyes. "I'm inclined to say that that is none of your business, but perhaps it's time we talked." He tossed aside the towel. "I'm going to dinner with Angela."

"Why her and not me!?" Rhiana cried.

"You're making too much of this," Richard said. "We're not dating."

She flung herself away, pacing the room. "What would you call it?"

"Spending time with a friend."

"I could be a friend."

"I don't think you want to be 'friends,'" Richard said and his dry tone provided the quotation marks.

"It could start that way, couldn't it? I mean, and then become . . . more."

"I'm too old for you, Rhi, and frankly I've got too much baggage that you don't need to deal with." His tone was warm and gentle, and it gave her hope.

"Oh, that's just silly. I'm going to be eighteen soon."

"Which makes you underage."

"Angela's old. A lot older than you. Why doesn't she feel weird about it?"

"Because we're not dating. We're just friends."

"Yeah, right. You didn't want to tell me what you were doing tonight. That means you're dating."

"We're not. And you need to leave now." Richard handed her the pizza box, and walked to the door.

Rhiana dropped the pizza and jammed a hand into her pocket. "I could . . ."

His expression went from exquisite embarrassment to ice and fury.

"Don't even think about it." His tone reminded her of her dad's when she'd wanted to go out on a school night. She suddenly felt grubby and stupid and young, and she hated him for it. "You know a purely magic spell won't work on me."

"You're scared I'll try, and maybe succeed."

"No. What scares me is that you'd actually consider using your power. Love can't be coerced. You know that." He kept his tone level, reasonable, like an adult remonstrating with a turbulent child. Her cheeks flamed with embarrassment and fury.

"Who said anything about loving you?"

As she stalked to the door she saw his cheeks flare with color. She had hit a nerve and she took a bitter joy in hurting him.

※

They had the cozy corner booth at Graze, one of Albuquerque's more upscale restaurants, which offered a selection of "American tapas." Since they offered half glasses of wine, Angela sampled a red or a white, depending upon the dish. Richard drank water and one of the fancy bottled teas.

"So Weber goes into the cell with a turkey baster and starts sampling the air all around the perp. The man is becoming more and more agitated, and finally he asks what Weber's doing. So Damon tells him that he's taking samples of the gentleman's pheromones and he's going to compare them with samples he took at the house."

Richard had a musical little chuckle, and Angela enjoyed just listening to it. "So what happened?" she asked.

"What you'd expect. He immediately confessed to the burglaries."

"If you think that's good, get Weber to tell you about the bunny suit and the two-by-four carrot sometime," Angela said.

"Bunny suit? Carrot?"

"You need to hear it from him."

Their waiter arrived and set down several plates with a flourish. "The Mediterranean grazing plate, French country pâté, and tilapia in banana leaves," he announced. "Enjoy."

Angela spooned some of each entree onto her plate. She looked up to find Richard gazing with amusement at her plate, and she realized that she was ending up with well more than half. Making a rueful face she said, "You should have taken me to the all-you-can-eat buffet at Bella Vista. You're going to go broke feeding me here."

"I'll risk it."

They ate in silence for a few minutes. Despite his amusement over Weber's antics, Angela could tell that something was bothering the young detective. Figuring it was lingering embarrassment over their disastrous night in Taos, she decided to take the issue head-on.

"So, I want you to know that I'm not expecting anything from you. At least not until you're ready and I have an idea how to help you with that. What you need is a good casual fuck with a total stranger."

Richard stared at her, the blood rushing to his cheeks and even to the tips of ears. Then he burst out laughing. "Angela, could we not discuss my . . ." he lowered his voice, ". . . sexual dysfunction in quite such a public forum?"

"Nobody's listening," she protested.

Richard leaned in and pressed his forehead against hers. "Well, let's hope not. I'd like to keep a shred of reputation."

༄

The fire from the pennies sent shadows dancing across the scarred pine of the study carrel and across the shelves of books. One spun on the top of the computer monitor. The other two flashed on the desk to either side. Rhiana murmured power words and swept the palm of her hand across the screen. Sullen colors began to crawl through the black surface. A picture, small and remote, appeared in the center of the screen. It was Richard and Angela. Their heads, pale and dark, were close together. Plates of food lay on the table before them.

"And by the way, I prefer to make love rather than f . . . well, you know," Richard was saying, and Angela laughed. A sob broke from Rhiana's lips and she bent forward over the hurt in her gut.

A long hand reached over her shoulder and picked up the pennies. For the first time Rhiana noticed Madoc's nails, long and very sharp. The picture on the screen vanished and there was a sharp *pop* as the motherboard, stressed by its unnatural use, died.

"He's just a human," Madoc said softly.

"But I want him." Rhiana drew her sleeve across her face and sniffed.

"There's time." His hand played in her long hair. "Why don't you come away with me?"

"Where?"

"Venice, Paris, London. What would you like?"

"I thought you meant . . ." She hesitated, then said, "Home."

His cat's smile caressed her. "I don't think you are quite ready to make that choice, or that journey. But I know your dreams. Let me answer a few of them."

ψ

Monday morning. A sad, cold rain fell outside and the room smelled of wet coats and strong coffee. The incident board was filled with new murders and assaults. Richard stood in front of it and shook his head.

"It's worse than last weekend. What is going on?" he asked Weber as the older man sauntered up to join him.

"It's just going to get worse. The holidays are hell. Disappointments, expectations and stress. Nice lethal combinations."

They walked to their desks. Weber gathered up his giant coffee mug shaped like the ass end of a horse.

"Do you think the captain is going to let me take vacation over Christmas?" Richard asked anxiously. "I put in my papers, but I haven't heard yet." Richard got out his mug and a tea bag.

"You *are* the new kid."

"So don't count on it?"

"Yep."

They headed over toward the coffeepots. There was a knot of cops, both uniform and detective, near the coffeepots. Snyder was prominent in the center. The low-voiced conversation stopped and all of them looked at him. Richard reached up and straightened a suddenly too-tight tie. He heard the single muttered word.

"Faggot."

Richard stopped. Snyder grinned nastily at him. The seconds seemed as long as hours as he faced the pack. Damon's face darkened.

"What is this shit?" Weber asked.

"Richie's *friend* came by yesterday lookin' for him," Snyder said and batted his eyelashes.

Terror and shame fluttered in his belly and his throat felt too narrow. Richard forced himself to walk over. They all seemed so tall.

"If you have something to say, say it to me," Richard said. Yankee pride kept his back straight and his words clipped.

"Okay. Your sweetie came by lookin' for you."

"Does this person have a name?"

"It's on your desk."

Richard could hear Kenntnis's voice urging him to do something outrageous, take control of the situation, but he couldn't. A few short days ago all these men had looked at him with admiration and friendship. Now disgust etched their faces.

Turning on his heel, Richard went to his desk and looked down at the yellow legal pad. In large print surrounded by hearts he read *Sal Verzzi* and a telephone number. In an instant he felt the burn of sunbaked sand beneath his feet, smelled the briny scent of seaweed and ocean water, and heard the shouts of children darting like minnows in and out of the waves. Fire Island, a few months before he started work for Drew Sandringham. The young actor he had met. It began with a glass of wine, and became a wild and passionate weekend. They had promised to stay in touch, but a few weeks later Sal had landed the leading role on a new television drama and moved to California.

Most actors hid their proclivities so something—*or someone*, Richard thought—had happened to lead to this betrayal.

He wanted to flee, but he forced himself to sit down, pulled the pad and phone close and started to dial. Richard noticed that Weber stayed in the knot of detectives around the coffeepot, listening as they talked. One young detective flung out a hand and went swishing toward the copier accompanied by raucous laughter. Cheeks burning, Richard bent to his task.

Soon he was talking to the front desk clerk at the Night Lighter Inn on Central. The Night Lighter was a rundown dump on east Central Boulevard that hadn't quite sunk to catering to whores, junkies and dealers, but it was hanging on by its fingernails. The clerk's soft voice held the lilt and song of subcontinental India and he sounded tired as he provided the information that Sal Verzzi had checked out that morning.

A growing fury hammered in Richard's temples. It wasn't strictly proper to use his status as a police officer for private use, but he figured he might as well be hung for a sheep as a lamb. A few more calls and he'd learned that Sal Verzzi was booked on a Southwest Airlines flight to L.A., departing at 10:20 a.m. Grabbing his overcoat and radio Richard headed for the door.

He couldn't help it. He looked over to Weber. The older man's eyes slid away, and he turned back to face the other officers. The broad expanse of his back said it all.

Richard flashed his badge to the TSA screeners at the security checkpoint, and was waved through. Usually he savored a walk through Albuquerque International with its Southwestern furnishings, wood-beamed ceilings, tile floors and leather chairs. It was a pleasant change from the usual sterile plastic and cheap carpet found in most airports. This day he stormed through.

Sal sat reading by one of the wide windows that offered a view of the towering mountains. Richard thought for a moment that the actor seemed huddled and hunched, but decided that was merely wishful thinking on his part.

"Hello, Sal."

Sal gasped, jumped and dropped his *Newsweek*. "Ri-Richard!"

"How nice to see you again, Sal. Pity you couldn't stick around to actually say hello after stabbing me in the back."

Four years had brought a few changes. The forehead shone high and white because of a receding hairline. There were a few etched lines around the wide mobile mouth that looked more like sorrow and disappointment than dissipation. The eyes were the same, a warm golden brown. As Richard watched, tears welled up and hung on the long dark lashes. Richard's anger faded, replaced with a weary sadness.

"They didn't tell me you were a cop," Sal whispered.

"Telling you to go to APD headquarters wasn't a clue?" Richard asked.

"They just gave me an address."

"You could have walked away once you realized." Sal shook his head. The tears left damp streaks down his cheeks. "What have they got on you?" Richard asked in a gentler tone.

"Nothing." It seemed to require an effort but Sal managed to meet Richard's eyes. "It was what they offered. I'm in terrible shape, Richard. I needed help desperately." Richard looked down into the pinched face. *AIDS?* he wondered. *Hepatitis C?*

With a sigh Richard sank into the chair next to the young actor. "Tell me."

Sal swept away the tears and rotated in the chair to face Richard. "I haven't worked in two years."

"What happened to your series?"

"Canceled after four episodes. You don't understand how tough it is out there. You're only as good as your last job and I was associated with a bomb." Resentment laced the words and flashed in his eyes. "But you've got to keep up appearances."

"What does that mean?"

"You've got to look hot. Keep the right address. Not have an area code in the Valley. Drive a nice car. Well, it's all about to collapse on top of me. And then they turned up and offered me a series. All I had to do was pay you a visit."

Richard stood up, pity fading. "This is about a *job*!"

"What else would it be?" Sal was honestly puzzled.

"I thought you were sick, or . . . or something," Richard replied.

"No."

"So you bought your life with mine. Thanks so much. And what makes you think they'll keep their promise? You're flying a cattlecar airline and staying in a fleabag motel. Doesn't look like they value your efforts much."

Sal's jaw sagged as he stared up at Richard. "You think they'll back out?"

"They don't need you anymore," Richard said coldly.

"I'll . . . I'll tell."

"Who? And tell them what? That you outed a bisexual cop? Not exactly earthshaking. Except to the cop," Richard added bitterly.

"I'm . . . I'm sorry. I didn't think," Sal began.

"Yes, yes you did. You just didn't care!"

His heel squeaked on the tile as Richard spun and walked away. He made it all the way out to the main concourse before shame over how he'd treated Sal and dread at the prospect of returning to work overwhelmed him. He dropped onto a bench behind a tall pillar to hide from everyone and everything.

But there was no escaping his thoughts.

"Look, all you have to do is give us what we want, and we'll support you in any and all of your goals. Chief of Detectives for New York? Director of the FBI? A brilliant concert career? A contract with the Met?" Grenier's liquid baritone echoed in his memory.

He had been both cruel and sanctimonious with Sal. If Richard hadn't had the memory of Naomi, Alice and Dan, their cold, mutilated bodies fresh in his heart and mind, he might well have been tempted by Grenier. All Sal had had was a driving need and massive insecurity, and nothing to temper the *wanting*.

Richard's thoughts moved on to his own situation, and he sat studying his options. *Quit and try to go to a new city and a new police force?*

How long before they locate another lover and send him in to wreck everything? Or got Snyder to make a few calls to his new job?

Try going back to music?

Work for Lumina?

But once again he would have been given *a job.*

Give up police work?

Simply thinking about it brought him even lower. The grief he felt at giving up his profession was far more profound than his dread at facing his fellow officers. Richard thought about the cases waiting on his desk.

The dead were beyond his help, but their memory could be honored by bringing their killers to justice. Their loved ones would find some small measure of comfort, and other potential victims would be protected. It was good work, honorable work, and he didn't need the approbation of his peers to accomplish it. He was good at this—

He was surprised and startled by the ringing of his cell phone.

"Hello?" Richard cautiously.

"Will you give us the sword?" came Grenier's voice.

Richard came to his feet. "You son of a bitch."

"Is that a no?"

"Is this the best you got? Because it wasn't enough," Richard shouted.

"Remember, things can always get worse."

Chapter

TWENTY-THREE

Just *bring bare necessities. I'll rig you out when we arrive.*" Rhiana smiled with anticipation, remembering Madoc's instructions, as she tossed a couple of sweatshirts and another pair of pants into the dufflebag.

"You're traveling light," Kenntnis's voice came from the doorway.

"Well, I've got stuff at home," Rhiana replied, and focused on zipping up her makeup bag while she uttered the lie. She didn't think Kenntnis had any abilities greater than those of a perceptive human to detect a lie, but she didn't want to test the theory.

Looking up, she glanced around the room and wondered if she would ever inhabit it again. It was beautiful, with peach-colored curtains draping the sleigh bed, and elegant carving on the dressing table and chest of drawers, but it wasn't hers. She had been a beggar, and now that she knew she belonged somewhere she didn't want to live on anyone's charity any longer. Maybe Madoc would actually let her come home this time.

Kenntnis entered the room and began picking up items randomly from the mantlepiece—an eighteenth-century couple in Meissen white porcelain. From the table by the deep armchair in front of the fireplace—a Limoges box. From the bedside table—the Diana Gabaldon novel she was reading. Everything seemed very small in his wide, powerful hands.

"I'm worried about you," he finally said. "These assaults on Cross are a preparation for something. I don't want you to be on the receiving end of . . . well, whatever they throw at us."

"I'll be fine. You've taught me how to hide and ward myself," Rhiana said, zipping the duffel shut. "And I haven't seen my family for months." She slung the duffel onto her shoulder and started for the door.

"You haven't seemed all that fond of them." Kenntnis's voice was dry. And maybe a little suspicious? Rhiana shook that off as nerves on her part.

"You can change your mind about things . . . people," she said.

"True." Kenntnis surprised Rhiana by pulling her into a hug. "Just be careful. I've grown quite fond of my 'roomie.'"

Rhiana felt doubt assail her. The phone on the bedside table rang. Rhiana answered, listened and handed it to Kenntnis.

"It's for you."

Rhiana could faintly hear the words from Kenntnis's secretary.

"Mr. Kenntnis, Detective Oort is in your office. He's says it's urgent."

"Tell him I'll be right down." Kenntnis hung up the phone and pointed at Rhiana. "Don't leave. We're not quite done yet."

"I have a plane to catch. I can't wait."

"And I have to go talk to Richard."

"It's always going to be about him first, isn't it?" Rhiana asked.

"For obvious reasons—yes."

She watched him walk out, and threw a surreptitious finger at his broad back. Fuck 'em. Tomorrow she'd be in Venice.

⚜

Kenntnis sat behind his desk and listened while Richard poured out the story. The young cop paced the room, flinging himself back and forth until he suddenly dropped into the armchair, as if the recitation had exhausted him.

"This wasn't entirely unexpected," Kenntnis said.

"I know, but it just seems so . . . petty. Why not just kill me and take the damn thing?"

"Because they don't leave fingerprints, metaphorically speaking. They sent golems after Rhiana, they used the gang members to 'kill' the college kids. And killing a cop brings down a hornet's nest of problems."

"Do they actually think this will work?" Richard was up and pacing again.

"Probably not, but it's going to take a toll on you emotionally, and they might get lucky and you'll fold. Remember they didn't manage to talk to McGowan. They think you're a fragile weakling. Grenier doesn't know he's just going to stiffen your backbone with this."

"Fragile." Richard covered his mouth with a hand. "Oh, God, they *are* going after my mother. I've got to get back to Rhode Island. Find out who's behind it, and stop them." He flung himself at the door. "You've got to arrange it with the chief."

"Wait. Wait. Wait. I can't have Rhiana gone, and you gone, and Cross incapacitated."

"Excuse me, how did you manage before?"

"Hid. Moved. Had Cross. Richard, they're planning something. Let's not play into their hands, shall we?"

"This is my family!"

"Yes, and the Lumina is more important."

"You have one day." The door fell shut behind Richard. Kenntnis dropped his head into his hands, and wished they could get past emotionalism.

Angela stood in the driveway, leaned on her shovel and eyed the pile of sand. She didn't seem to have made a dint in it. Beneath her sweatshirt sweat clung to her sides, rapidly becoming a clammy chill now that she wasn't working. From her complex on Rio Grande Boulevard Angela had a great view of the Sandias. The snow powdered the rocky sides of the mountain and blushed rose as the sun sank in the west. She gave herself a few more moments to contemplate the view, then opened another bag of brown paper lunch sacks and started folding down the edges to form a narrow cuff.

The electric luminarias on the condo to her left seemed to mock her. She surreptitiously threw a finger at the offensive display. At least she'd convinced the young transplant couple from Boston on the other side that going electric was tacky and if they really wanted to experience a New Mexico Christmas they needed to go all natural. They, however, had ordered five dozen luminarias from the Valley High School Marching Band, unlike Angela, who was building each luminaria from scratch.

Richard was supposed to have joined her after work, but he had called and begged off, saying he had to take a double shift. He'd sounded funny, but Angela hadn't pushed. She'd pushed once and to disastrous effect. *No,* she thought as she lined up the sacks at the rim of the sand pile, *I'm going to be a model of patience and understanding.*

Soon she had several dozen sacks prepared and her hands were cramping. They looked like squat little soldiers in their neat lines. Gathering up the shovel, she dumped scoops of sand into the sacks. Next she set votive candles inside. Pressing her hands against the ache in the small of her back, Angela straightened, groaned and sighed. This was a lot more fun with other people. She even had apple cider simmering on the stove and a plate of *biscochitos*.

She returned to the sacks. *These are supposed to light the way for the Christ Child to come to Earth,* she thought. *Not that I've ever been a believer, but it does seem pretty weird this year knowing what I now know. I sure as hell hope this isn't going to serve as runway lights for monsters.* She chuckled, trying to pretend she wasn't *really* worried, but she shivered as she remembered that *thing* seen through the wall up in C. Springs.

A car door slammed. Angela paid no attention until she heard footsteps coming up the driveway. She looked up eagerly, but it was Damon Weber, not Richard, who approached. His tread was heavy, his shoulders slumped and his broad pockmarked face seemed to be pulled down as if gravity had proved too much for flesh and bone to resist.

"Wow, you look like shit," Angela said, but he didn't crack a smile. Alarmed now, Angela jumped to her feet, dusting sand off the knees of her blue jeans. "What? What's wrong? What's happened?"

"I need to talk to you. Can I talk to you?" Weber asked. He looked strained.

"Is it Richard? Has something happened to Richard?"

He shook his head and she thought he looked embarrassed. "Not . . . exactly. Look, can I come in?"

"Sure. Okay."

The entrance hall had a white plaster barrel vault ceiling. Light was provided by two blue glass Mexican star lights. There was still enough light for the stained-glass window next to the front door to make a rainbow on the slate floor. Weber looked at the glass and gave a grunt of disapproval.

"You should pull that out. All some guy has to do is bust it, reach around and the front door's unlocked."

"And then I'll shoot him," Angela said, wondering why cops had to be so negative. "But I'm not taking out my stained-glass window."

"Okay, hope you don't live to regret it," came the comfortless reply.

She settled Weber on the sofa in the living room, and ducked into the kitchen for cider and cookies. He was studying the art that graced the walls, paying particular attention to the Doug West serigraph of the blossoming apple orchards of Velarde. Underfoot was a Navajo rug in a Two Gray Hills pattern.

"Most folks hang these," Weber said with a nod to the rug. "They don't walk on them."

"Yes, but they're *rugs* and they were woven to cover the dirt floor in hogans. I believe in using things."

He followed her over to the sofa and accepted a mug of cider. He sat warming his palms on the glass and stared frowning into the yawning black depths of the kiva fireplace. Angela noticed that he chewed his hangnails, leaving bloody trails around his cuticles. She couldn't help but contrast them with Richard's perfectly manicured hands. Nibbling on a *biscochito*, Angela kicked off her boots and tucked her feet up under her. She was striving for patience, but the thought of the waiting luminarias kept intruding. The minutes crawled past and still he didn't speak.

"Look, I don't mean to be rude, but I've got another three dozen sacks to fill and store in the garage."

Weber shot to his feet. "How about I help you?"

"Fine, but I thought you wanted to talk."

"You hold, I'll shovel, we'll talk," he said.

Once more bundled against the cold, they went to work. The western sky glowed with a pearly light. Overhead, stars glittered in a midnight blue sky. Angela didn't turn on the garage lights, wanting to use the last of this magical twilight.

The rows of completed luminarias clustered about her like chicks around a hen and still Weber hadn't spoken. "So, we got two out of three. When does the talking part happen?" Angela asked brightly.

Weber's face twisted as a complex rush of emotions passed across it. He threw the shovel violently into the sand. "He's a fag." His jaw worked as if he were biting down on an aftertaste from the words.

Angela didn't need to ask which *he* they were talking about. Dismay and anger, though at whom she couldn't say, squeezed her heart.

Weber paced, the sand grating beneath his shoes. "Christ! I had him stay at my apartment. He slept in my bed!" He ran a hand through his hair.

She forced herself to think again. "Well, unless you were in it with him, what's the problem?"

"I liked him. I trusted him," Weber said.

"And that's changed how?"

"This doesn't bother you at all?" Weber demanded. "You've had the hots for him."

"And I expect I will continue to."

"This doesn't change how you feel?" Weber asked.

"Well, first of all, how do I even know this is true?" Angela asked. She sat down on what remained of the sand pile, feeling the grains shift beneath her and the cold start seeping through her jeans.

"This guy came to headquarters. According to the guys who saw him, a real mincing pansy."

"And how do you know Grenier didn't just hire him off the street?"

"Richard's reaction," Weber replied. "He didn't deny it. He just left."

Angela bowed her head and stared at her knees. It didn't

feel like a lie. It felt like a piece of the puzzle that was Richard Oort had fallen into place. But his attraction to her was real. They had spent a long time snogging like a pair of teenagers after their last date. He couldn't have faked that.

"Why are you telling me this?" Angela finally asked.

"Because I don't think I can work with . . . around the guy now. Queers just . . . I can't work with him."

Alarmed at the defection, Angela jumped to her feet. "Look, maybe it's true, but it's not the whole story. Richard likes girls. I can promise you that. So at the worst he's bisexual—"

"Bi, gay, it's all the same to me. He fucks men. I can't handle that. I need you to tell him." He turned and walked toward the street.

"You bastard! Tell him yourself!" Angela shouted after him.

Weber's shoulders hunched as if she'd launched a blow rather than words. He jammed his hands into his pockets and increased his pace until he was almost running by the time he reached the car.

Angela sank down among the luminarias. Tears coursed across her cold cheeks like trails of bile, but whether they were for herself or for Richard, she couldn't tell.

After the tumult of the day before Richard almost skipped his ritual stop at the hospital to inquire after Father Fish, but he felt guilty, so he got off the freeway at University and stopped. Each time it had been "no change." Today when Richard asked the question, the nurse at the station outside of Intensive Care set aside the chart and took his hands between hers. His heart seemed to beat in the pit of his stomach, and the stink of bedpans and antiseptic broke through his control. Richard gagged and the nurse's hands tightened around his fingers.

She was an older woman, her face careworn but kind, and she smelled of vanilla and chocolate, as if she'd been baking cookies before coming into work.

"I'm so sorry." The musical cadence of her Hispanic heritage softened her words. "We lost the good Father last night." Tears spilled over. The nurse pulled out a tissue from the box on the desk and offered it to him. Richard wiped his eyes and cleared his throat. "It's sad, but he's with the good Lord now," the nurse added, patting his hand.

He tried not to yank it away. Richard stepped back slowly. "Was there any reason to think it wasn't natural causes?"

The nurse gave him an odd look. "No, he's been in a coma and that takes a toll on a body. Forgive me, detective, but that sounds really paranoid."

"Yes, yes, of course, you're right. I'm sorry."

"May I ask you something?"

"What?"

"You were so good, coming every day. I . . . I wondered why?"

"He saved my life."

No desert could have been more barren than the surface of Weber's desk. The sense of desolation settled onto his chest, crushing Richard's breath. Snyder looked up from his computer. His eyes were narrowed with cruel amusement, but he didn't say a word, forcing Richard to ask, "Where's Damon?"

"Transferred to the Arroyo del Oso substation, pretty boy," Snyder said.

Richard sank into his chair. There was a pile of papers on his desk. He started through them, then realized they were gay personals, and flyers about the gay and lesbian alliance of Albuquerque. He swept them all into the trash, pulled the phone close and called the DA's office.

He was lucky. Salisbury wasn't in court. "You've got to get Andresson back," Richard said without preamble.

"What? Who is this? Oh, Oort."

"Yes."

"Look, Detective. I've got twenty-three files on my desk. Why would I increase that by one?"

"Because it's a murder now."

"What?"

"The Episcopalian priest died last night."

"Oh, shit, I'm sorry." She paused. "Look, I don't mean to seem unfeeling, but he had a heart attack."

"Brought on by his exertions defending me. If they can bootstrap the driver of a getaway car into a felony murder charge you can make this stick."

"Don't throw around terms you don't understand." Her tone held the dismissive tone used by many professionals when talking to someone less educated.

"My father is a federal court judge. My sister is a public defender. I have a master's degree. Don't treat me like a lackey! I will not have it!" Richard found he'd slammed the flat of his hand down on the desk. A number of people in the squad room looked over at him. He moderated his tone. "Please, please, pull this man back."

"I'll try," Salisbury promised, and hung up.

Snyder smirked at Richard. "If butch don't work, you could always try crying."

Richard gave him a look of loathing. Ortiz came out of his office and beckoned to Richard, indicating his office.

"I'm pulling you off the street," the captain said.

Richard, standing in front of the desk, stared down at Ortiz, but the captain never looked up to meet his gaze.

"My solve rate is at ninety-four percent."

The office chair squeaked as Ortiz spun around and started rummaging in the credenza behind his desk. "So why not take a little break? Rest on your laurels." The captain's voice was muffled.

"Look, let's just come to the point." Richard was pleased to hear that his voice was steady. "I can work without a partner." He could feel another headache starting and he rubbed at his temples.

"That's not how we do things around here."

"I won't quit," Richard said, and remembered with a pang the last person to whom he'd spoken those words.

"I'm not asking you to," Ortiz grunted.

They were both surprised by the sharp knock on the frosted glass door. "Who is it? I'm in a meeting," Ortiz bawled.

But whoever it was didn't answer. Instead the door opened and Torres walked in. The crown of his head sported a bald strip where they had shaved away the hair to treat the gouge left by the bullet. There was a tiny sprouting of black fuzz, but Torres still looked like he had a racing stripe.

"Captain." He touched two fingers to his eyebrow in an almost salute.

"What do you want, Joe? I'm busy here," said Ortiz.

"This won't take long. I'll partner with Oort."

Nothing could have surprised Richard more. From the captain's expression he apparently shared the feeling.

"Excuse me?"

"It's all over the building that you're pulling Oort off the street. That's a waste, sir. He's good. Nobody knows that better than me." Richard smiled in gratitude, but Torres didn't look at him. "So, what do you say?"

Ortiz cocked an eye over at Richard. "You okay with that?"

"Yes, sir, I'll be happy to partner with Detective Torres, but after—"

"Excuse me?"

"I really have to go home to Rhode Island. It's imperative," Richard said.

"It is, huh?"

"Yes, sir," and Richard's voice sounded small.

"Do you want to continue to have a job here?"

"Yes, sir."

"Torres comes in here and gives you a fucking gift. It's two weeks before Christmas, and you're asking to leave. Are you seeing the problem here?"

"Yes, sir."

"Good. Now get out of here, and make me not regret this."

Richard followed Torres out of the office and pulled the door closed behind them. Torres stared down at him.

"I'm just going to say this once. I'll work with you because I owe you, and you are good, but keep your fucking hands to yourself, okay?" Torres pulled a piece of paper out of his pocket.

"Don't flatter yourself."

Torres looked up from the note. "Huh?"

"What makes you think you're cute enough to interest me?" Richard asked, and gave him a bland look. Torres stared hard at him and gave a sudden single crack of laughter.

"Okay. Touché. We got a dead hooker out on the West Mesa. You coming, or are you going to Rhode Island?"

Chapter

TWENTY-FOUR

Richard sat in the dark in Kenntnis's living room and gazed out at the rocks of the Sandias. The moonlight glittered off the snow. It was a motif of silver and black, and it was repeated in the sword that rested across his knees.

Kenntnis had asked him to sleep at the penthouse until

Rhiana returned. Richard had agreed because he still hadn't bought that plane ticket.

Because if he left he'd lose his job. And he couldn't go home and face the judge and tell him he'd walked away from another job. But he had to go because they were after his mother. He felt like a bug on a pin, tugged in opposing directions and therefore unable to move at all.

His thoughts skipped and jumped to the sad bundle of bone and flesh, the platinum wig askew, the sand from the West Mesa caked in the bloody wounds that he'd looked at earlier in the day. They had a solid lead. He and Torres would pick the guy up tomorrow. Maybe if it turned out to be a righteous bust the captain would let him leave as a reward. Richard played with that happy outcome for a few moments, then put it regretfully away. Life didn't tend to work out that way.

Richard released the hilt and the blade vanished. He checked his watch. One a.m. on the East Coast. He couldn't call Amelia at this hour, wake the whole family, and she was in Boston. His father had already dismissed his fears. Which left only one person. He pulled out his cell phone and dialed.

Pamela answered on the third ring. The husky blur of sleep softened her normally sharp consonants.

"Hello?"

"Pamela, it's Richard."

He heard fumbling. "Do you know what time it is?"

"Yes, I'm sorry, but I needed to talk to you."

"Why? Do you need a lawyer?"

"No, why would you think that?" Richard felt the constriction closing down on his lungs, his own tone sharpening to match hers. It had always been this way between them.

"Papa told me you shot and killed a man."

"Who was trying to kill my partner, and then probably

would have shot me. . . . Oh, never mind, I wanted to talk to you about Mama."

"Yes, Amelia told me that you called her about Mama's latest psychodrama." That feeling of always being the outsider while his sisters discussed and dissected him returned.

"So, what have you done, other than killing someone, that would send you to Hell?" Pamela continued.

"Look, Pamela, could you not beat me up right now about my profession? I think Mama could be in danger . . . trouble," he amended. "Could you please just . . ." Richard hesitated, trying to think of something concrete to suggest. "Take her out to lunch, or go shopping with her, be there for her. Make sure she's all right. Please."

"I have a job. I'm busy, and she doesn't talk to me—"

"Because you're always so damned unsympathetic," Richard snapped.

"Yes, yes, I am, because her problems are so damn trivial!" his sister shot back.

Richard gave a hiss of frustration. "I don't even know why I bothered. I knew you'd be like this—"

"I wish you'd figured that out before you called and woke me up. I'm going back to sleep now, Richard. Goodnight."

He forced himself to release his death grip on the cell phone, and shoved it back into his pocket.

Kenntnis padded into the room. The strings on the piano and the Celtic harp gave a ghost of sound as he entered the room. He settled onto the bench of the new addition to the furnishings, a Steinway grand piano. Richard knew it had been bought for him. It didn't change the resentment he felt toward Kenntnis. Richard glanced over at Kenntnis, then returned to his rapt contemplation of the boulders.

"Send Angela," Kenntnis suddenly said.

Richard cranked around in his chair. "I beg your pardon?"

"Send Angela to check on your mother."

"I haven't seen Angela since the latest . . . psychodrama, and I really don't want to have to go into another humiliating explanation."

"You think she doesn't know? Cops are the biggest gossips in the world, at least with each other. She's the coroner and she's popular."

"What if she reacts like Weber?"

"Then you get hurt again, but I'd at least try." Kenntnis rested his hands on his knees and levered himself to his feet.

✥

They sat in a booth at the Carrow's. The median age had shifted from sixteen to sixty-five since Angela's last visit. Older women, with crimped red or silver hair, wearing gaudy silver- and gold-trimmed fiesta skirts, sat with their husbands, who wore white shirts and black trousers and bolo ties. It was a square dance club, pausing for dinner after cutting a rug at the senior center up the street. They were a good deal more restrained than the high school football team, fans and cheerleaders, but one old guy insisted on reeling out a call while banging on the edge of the plastic table with his spoon.

". . . so, there it is. I have no idea how my father might react to you showing up. Mama would be fine." Angela noted that Richard gave the word a French pronunciation. "But I'd have someone there. I . . . I know it's incredibly presumptuous of me to ask—"

"Of course I'll do it," Angela interrupted. "My dad's family is still in Philadelphia. I'll tell your folks you asked me to bring their Christmas presents by since I was coming out east anyway. Then I'll conveniently come down with the flu and have to stay. Or if things are fine, and you are being paranoid, I'll head back."

He touched her hand lightly and withdrew. "Thank you."

"By the way, I don't give a shit that you're bi."

He flinched at her bluntness. "I do," he said shortly. "And do you really want to be known as a 'fag hag'?"

"Hey, not everyone thinks that's an insult." She took a sip of her coffee. "I presume you're HIV negative?"

"Yes."

"Then I really don't have a problem. We've just got to get past *your* problems. So, what *are* your problems?"

His fingers clutched at his hair, disturbing the perfect part. "Angela, please, I really can't take a session of tough love, or whatever the heck you want to call it, right now."

"Fine." She stood up. "How about we meet tomorrow noon in Old Town? We'll pick out some quaint and exotic Indian *tchotchkes* for your family."

❦

The crowds in Andrew's Pueblo Pottery were shoulder to shoulder as people dashed to buy Christmas gifts. Angela wriggled through and finally found Richard in rapt contemplation of a Hopi kachina Snow Maiden and a San Juan Pueblo Corn Maiden carved out of a delicate seashell. His hand were folded on the counter, chin resting on his hands as he studied them at eye level.

"I don't know which one she'd like better," he said as she joined him.

Angela took in a deep breath, struggled with how to say it, then settled for her usual bluntness. "Richard, I've got to go to Farmington. Some roughnecks digging a containment pit for a new natural gas well found a body dump. The coroner in San Juan can't handle this. I've been called in." The expression on his face pushed her to say more. "Look, it should only be a few days' delay. As soon as I can, I'll head east."

Richard slowly straightened, and pushed the Snow Maiden toward the clerk. "I'll take her."

"Richard, she's three grand," Angela said, then stopped at his look.

⚜

It seemed to have become all about food. Rhiana forced herself to set down the fork and contemplate the view across the water. Not that the water could be seen. This late in the year the canals and lagoon of Venice were hidden beneath swirling white fog, and the buildings floated like pastel dreams on billows of mist. It was beyond description beautiful, but the food . . .

Rhiana returned to her Venetian specialty, calves liver in a delicate wine and mushroom sauce. "I'm sorry," she said between bites. "I don't know what's wrong with me." The kerosene heaters dotted about the balcony hissed and warmth rolled off them. The scent of brine and the faintest whiff of sewage rose off the water. Voices called from the enshrouded buildings, the sound amplified by the fog and water. The liquid Italian syllables were like music.

Madoc smiled at her and sipped his wine. "It's all about sensation. You're compensating with physical feeding instead of feeding your magic. You should feed the magic."

She had a sudden image of Cross looking at her . . . looking *through* her. Her appetite deserted her. Rhiana pushed away the plate. "Kenntnis would find out. Cross would sense what I'd done," she whispered. "Unless I left," she added hopefully.

"Not yet. We went to a deal of trouble to place you there."

"Why?"

"Soon," Madoc said soothingly.

Rhiana couldn't resist the food. She pulled the plate back. "Do you actually look like," she gestured with her knife, "this?"

"No, I'm wearing a mask on a mask."

"I don't understand," Rhiana said.

There was a strange rippling as if Madoc were made of water and she found herself looking into the round face and brown eyes of a cute but ordinary looking young man who wore blue jeans and sneakers and whose backpack rested against the legs of his chair. "This is what Kenntnis's spies see."

"He watches me?" Her voice rose in indignation.

"Of course."

"Cross can see through that," she waved her fork at him.

"Which is why we neutralized him while you and I are . . . getting to know one another."

"Then that shape you show me?"

"Isn't real either. I tried to make myself attractive. Your mother thought I was."

"You are. So you wanted to be attractive to human women?"

"Yes," he answered simply.

"Why?"

"We needed a half-breed."

"Every theory suggests that aliens and humans would be sterile," Rhiana said.

"Yes, but we are masters at manipulating matter, particularly DNA. We want children, we get them."

"But you haven't done it in a long time." *Please, don't take away the specialness.* She couldn't control the pathetic little thought.

"Actually we have, but you may be what we've been seeking."

"And what is that?"

"A melding of technological understanding and magic."

"And I'm that melding?" she asked.

"We think so. We hope so. We arranged for your scholarship to see if you truly had the aptitude."

"And sent me to UNM?" Rhiana scoffed. "Not exactly the physics capital of the world."

"No, but close to Kenntnis."

"Oh," she said, no longer feeling clever. "So, how will you know? If I'm the one?"

"When you go back, take a hard look at Kenntnis. Beyond the physical. Tell me what you see. That will answer the question of whether we've succeeded or not." Madoc reached out and stroked his hand down her cheek caressingly. "I hope you are. I want my child to be the one."

"You impotent fucker!"

Even Richard shrank back, and he was prepared for the roar. The suspect seemed to be trying to push his spine through the back of the wooden chair. He was a skinny man with a protuberant Adam's apple, pasty pockmarked skin and mud-colored eyes. Sparse hair had been carefully combed across a wide bald spot. Torres slammed his hands down on the arms of the chair, penning the man. The cop's blood-congested face was only inches from the pale sweating face of the perp.

"You can't fuck a woman normally so you hurt 'em and then kill 'em!" Torres allowed spit to fly from his mouth into Cobb's face.

As the saliva struck his skin Randall Cobb let out a whistling squeak. It was what they had been waiting for. Richard flung himself forward, wrapped his arms around Torres's chest and pulled the older man away from Cobb.

"Back off, back off, man!" Richard said urgently.

The broad one-way mirror gave back their reflections. The interrogation room stank with years of fear-induced sweat. The acoustic tile ceiling was a dingy white, but in one corner the tiles were stained brown as if something had died in the crawl space and bled through.

Torres roughly shook off Richard's hands and stormed out of the room. Richard pulled a starched handkerchief from his pocket, crossed to Cobb, offered the cloth. Grimacing with distaste, the man wiped the spittle from his face. But his hand was shaking.

"I apologize for that," Richard said.

"He's a barbarian. Uncouth. Uneducated." Richard looked sympathetic.

The legs of the chair scraped across the stained and scratched linoleum as Richard pulled over a chair and sat down. "Look, Mr. Cobb . . . Randall. May I call you Randall?" The man nodded, his gaze suspicious. "Just answer a few of our questions and you'll be out of here. I don't really think you had anything to do with this woman. I can tell you're a man of taste and refinement, and she was . . . well. . . ." Richard shrugged and tried not to think about the woman's body so he could remain sympathetic. "But my partner is nervous. He needs an arrest. As long as you don't talk to him you give him a reason to suspect you." Cobb began to relax, twining the handkerchief through his fingers. There were tufts of coarse dark hair on the joints and the knuckles were enlarged. Richard swallowed his disgust and leaned in closer. "So, why don't we talk? If you talk to me he doesn't have to come back in."

"Okay."

"So where were you Thursday night around nine-thirty?"

The intercom came on with a hiss and click. "Detective, you have a phone call."

Richard's back teeth closed with an audible snap, for the wariness was back in Cobb face and he'd subtly withdrawn.

"Not now," he called back.

"They said it was urgent."

Richard looked down at Cobb and gave him the most warm and charming smile he could muster. "Excuse me just one moment. I'm very sorry."

Slipping out the door, Richard found Lucile waiting. "We told you we weren't to be disturbed!" Richard snapped. Torres was hustling down the hall, his brow thunderous.

Lucile looked guilty and defensive. "They said it was a family emergency, Rich. The woman on the phone, she was crying," she added.

Torres arrived in time to hear part of Lucile's remark. "You gotta take it. Go. I'll keep him softened up."

"He's ripe *now*. I'm afraid we're going to overplay it," Richard fretted.

"We've already broken the mood," Torres answered. "We can only do the best we can." He went through the door into the interrogation room.

Richard heard Cobb say, "You!" in a tone of loathing. "I want a lawyer. . . ." The closing door cut off any further words. Richard, raging inwardly, followed Lucile back into the main squad room.

"I'll forward it to your desk," Lucile said.

He grabbed up the phone on the first ring. "Oort!" he snapped.

"Richard." It was Pamela and she was crying.

The shock froze him. In all the years of childhood Pamela had *never* cried. Not when she broke her arm when she was eleven. Not when Zorro, the family poodle, died; not when her boyfriend, the captain of the tennis team, dumped her two days before the senior prom. Never.

"It's Mama. She's dead."

His head seemed to be ringing. The words kept repeating over and over in his mind as if the brain could not reach understanding. He didn't seem to have the breath to form words.

"Did you hear me?" Pamela said, and her basic nature reasserted itself, sharpening her tone even through the tears. "Mama has died!"

I should have gone! My fault! I should have gone! They killed her and I did nothing!

"Yes . . . yes." His voice was trembling. It spread to his limbs and Richard groped for the chair before his legs collapsed. "How . . . what . . . happened?"

"She committed suicide," Pamela said, her voice thick with shame and anger. "Come home." She hung up.

That revelation shook his certainty of Grenier's involvement. Slowly Richard replaced the receiver in the cradle. His mother had been fragile since Pamela's birth. Postpartum depression, the doctors had said, and recommended that the Oorts not have any more children. But they had tried again for that elusive and necessary son. *The son who had let her down.*

Logic whispered all the rational explanations, and couldn't trump his certain knowledge. Kenntnis would never approve, but Richard *knew* that Grenier was behind this suicide.

Finally the reality penetrated. His mother was dead. Hands clasped tightly between his thighs, Richard leaned forward and tried to fight back the tears. They won, but he did manage not to make a sound.

Her hands on his shoulders helping him stay upright as he learned to skate on the pond at the Vermont cabin. Curled up in his bed, chest hot and reeking with Vicks mentholated rub, the down comforter and feather pillows forming a cocoon while she read The Wind in the Willows. *Her bell-like laughter breaking up the words as she read of Mr. Toad's delight on having seen his first motorcar. Leaning across the table in the big kitchen to hand him a beater covered with chocolate batter from his birthday cake, her gray eyes warm and sparkling. Teaching him to waltz before he became an escort at the debutante ball. Turning the pages of his sheet music as he practiced before a concert.*

"Ah, itty boo Richie's crying." And the ring of phones and smell of old burned coffee and damp clothes, and microwave popcorn was back. "What happened, Richie? Your boyfriend got AIDS? Or is it you?" The words, delivered in Snyder's nasal tones, added to the ugliness and sarcasm.

It wasn't a conscious decision. Suddenly Richard was

moving, leaping up so abruptly that the chair went skittering and squealing across the floor. He rested one hand on his desk and vaulted across to land in front of his tormentor. Files flew off the desk like startled birds breaking from cover.

He watched his fist slicing through the air, smashing into Synder's nose. The mushy feeling followed by the crunch of cartilage giving way. The nose flattening and slipping sideways, the blood cascading hot and sticky across Richard's knuckles, staining the front of Snyder's shirt.

Snyder went down hard, landing on his butt, hands clasped across his face. Arms grabbed Richard and held him back. There was a confused babble of voices all around, but it was just sound, not words.

Then the captain was there. Richard, and half of downtown, heard his words. *"What in the fuck is going on?!"*

Richard twitched his shoulders and was released. Because of the broken nose Snyder's words were thick and phlegmy. "I was just askin' what was wrong, and he attacked me."

While Snyder spun out his bullshit Richard removed the handkerchief from his breast pocket and wiped away the blood. He straightened his suit coat, and smoothed out the wrinkles on the sleeves where sweating hands had gripped him.

"Is that true?"

Richard turned to face Ortiz. "I need to take personal leave, sir. My mother has died."

All the excited chatter, query and commentary died. One of the other cops muttered out of the corner of his mouth to Snyder. "Smooth, dude, very smooth."

"You hit a fellow officer. I can't just ignore that." Richard shook his head, refusing to answer. Ortiz opened his mouth, but before he could respond rescue came from an unexpected source.

Lucile sailed across the squad room, her enormous bosom separating the gathered crowd like the prow of an icebreaker. "Captain, sir, as far as I'm concerned Rich should have hit this *pendejo* days ago. Snyder's been accidentally," she made quote marks in the air, "spillin' coffee all over Rich's reports and then hoggin' the printer so Rich has to stay late. And sayin' things."

Again Ortiz started to speak, only to be struck dumb by Lucile's forefinger. It was tipped with a long bloodred nail set with a rhinestone. She wagged it under his nose. "And you know the kinds of things. You're not on another planet when you're in that office. And if hittin' a fellow officer is against the rules then discriminating against one ought to be, too. You're damn lucky Rich didn't bring in his delegate or file a lawsuit."

She folded her arms across her breast and glared at Ortiz, and such was the complexity of male and female relationships in Hispanic culture that he wilted.

"You should have said something, Oort," the captain muttered. He rounded on Snyder and the clip of command was back in his voice. "Snyder, I'll see you in my office."

The tension ebbed. People returned to their desks though their heads still craned, trying to hear. Ortiz sighed and scrubbed a hand across his face. "Mom, huh?"

"Yes, sir."

"Sorry."

"Thank you, sir."

"Yeah, you can go. Just let us know when you'll be back. It's gonna be hell to cover for you this time of year."

"Sorry, sir."

Ortiz just waved Richard off. It was all the encouragement he needed. Richard quickly loaded up his briefcase and bolted. A few of the other detectives started to say something to him, but he froze them with a look.

ψ

The fifth skull was surfacing when Angela's cell phone rang. The local coroner, standing next to her, had a poleaxed expression as he stared down at a tarp covered with a jig-saw puzzle of tumbled bones. Angela had maintained a clinical aloofness, but she couldn't help wondering if serial killers were somehow linked to the Old Ones.

"Maybe that's the Fucking Big Idiots," Angela said to him. The bitter cold and dry wind hissing across the high plateau had leached all the moisture out of her skin. She felt one of the cracks on her chapped lips break open as she spoke, and tasted salt and copper as she licked away the bead of blood.

"They gotta take over. I can't handle this," the man said plaintively.

"They'll take over," Angela said, and answered.

But it was Richard. "You don't need to go to Rhode Island." His normally lyric tenor was clipped and tight. "My mother . . ." There was a cough, then the voice resumed, tight with control. "My mother has died."

"Oh, God, Richard, I'm . . . I'm sorry."

"Yeah, me too. I'll see you when I get back."

"I can come out as soon as—"

"*No.* Leave me alone. Please. I know it's not fair, but I'm pretty angry with all of you right now. Just give me some time and some space."

"I understand," she said quietly, but she was talking to a dead phone.

TWENTY-FIVE

It had been a hellish trip. As he sat at O'Hare, delayed by snow and ice, Richard briefly regretted refusing Kenntnis's offer of the plane. But the Lumina corporate jet might have been grounded as well, and he would have had to accept charity from Kenntnis, whom he blamed for his mother's death. When he wasn't blaming himself.

He finally reached T.F. Green Airport at 3:00 a.m. after catching a connecting flight at Boston's Logan Airport. Exhaustion dragged at every muscle as he shuffled down the Jetway. Behind him the young couple who had sat in the row in front of him were still squabbling, and their tiny baby still whooped out his distress. Ahead an elderly couple kept everyone moving at their own snail's pace. The husband, face sagging with weariness, pushed his walker like a man moving boulders. His wife, her seamed face soft with concern and love, kept touching his shoulder as if to feed him energy. Richard wondered if the young couple would last to loving old age.

My parents won't, now, he thought. *And did they ever really love each other?*

Luggage collected, he made his way out on the sidewalk in front of the airport. The air was damp and carried a hint of brine from Narragansett Bay. Richard turned toward the taxi stand. It held only two cars. Behind their steering wheels the drivers dozed. A horn honked once. Richard looked back and saw a green Mercedes sedan rolling toward him. Amelia was driving and she was alone. Relief flooded through him. He wasn't ready to face his father yet.

She pulled up to the curb, jumped out and hugged him fiercely. He could feel her shoulders shaking. A security guard began to drift toward them. In the seemingly endless war on terrorism even family reunions had to be cut short. Amelia opened the trunk and Richard dumped in his suitcases. He noted the bag of soccer balls and the set of golf clubs. One was clearly for Paul and the other for her husband, Brent. Richard wondered if there was ever anything for Amelia.

As they drove he studied her profile. He hadn't seen either of his sisters for two years. Amelia was the eldest. Despite being only thirty-four, her dark blond hair had streaks of gray.

The question could be delayed no longer. "What happened?" Richard asked. "What drove her to do this?"

"I don't know." Amelia paused, shook her head sadly. "You seem to have been the only member of the family who sensed she was upset," she said. "I mean, you called me about it. But then the two of you were always close."

"Obviously not close enough." He discovered that guilt had a taste. He swallowed convulsively several times.

"You're living in New Mexico," she replied and her tone sharpened. Richard knew it was irritation over his profession and where it had taken him.

"And Papa lived with her," Richard said and he couldn't hide the bitterness.

"I'm not going to respond to that," Amelia said and they didn't speak again until they had left the freeway and commercial streets had given way to residential neighborhoods.

That gave him a lot of time to reflect on his conversation with Mark Grenier in Colorado Springs a lifetime ago, the phone call after Sal Verzzi's arrival, and now this. His mother's might have been the hand that acted, but he was certain Grenier's people had been there, quietly manipulating, tormenting, goading and encouraging.

So now he had to find them, and . . . *Do what?* He couldn't prove anything. Anymore than he could prove they had tried to kill him. Or killed those kids. As Kenntnis said, they never left fingerprints. Pain stabbed through the hinge of his jaw and Richard forced his tightly clenched teeth apart. Looking out the window, he drew in several long breaths to calm himself and watched the headlights illuminate their surroundings.

After New Mexico, where clean air and lack of humidity made it possible to see seventy or eighty miles, Rhode Island felt claustrophobic. Where there weren't houses, the trees pressed close to the roads. Only when they crossed over the bay heading toward Newport was there any relief from the press of humanity. No stars penetrated the smeared gray overcast. After the cumulus castles that formed over the mountains and deserts of the west it just looked dirty.

As they approached Newport the houses became more impressive. Small lots gave way to third- and even half-acre swathes of grass and trees. No walls disturbed the sweep of lawns between the houses. Snow lingered on the north side of bushes and walls.

But impressive is a relative term, and overlooking the Rhode Island Sound were the "cottages." A coy word to describe grandiose waterfront mansions built as testaments to the power and wealth of robber barons.

They were only a few turnings from home when Richard broke the silence. "How did she . . . ?" But he couldn't finish the sentence. Mercifully Amelia wasn't obtuse.

"Pills washed down with cognac."

Amelia spun the wheel, taking them into a cul-de-sac. The headlights played across red brick and glittered in mullioned windows. High up under the eaves on the third floor, a round window with long pie-shaped wedges of glass drew his eye. The long room behind it, running the length of the house, had been his room from age five until he went away to college.

The glow from the porch light reflected off the silver bells hung on the holly wreath. They rang softly as Amelia pushed open the heavy oak door. Their footsteps were loud on the parqueted marble floor of the entryway. The air was redolent with frankincense.

Footsteps came tapping toward them, but it was the rhythm of high heels, not his father's deliberate tread. Pamela appeared in the archway. She was dressed in professional woman chic, straight skirt and long flaring jacket in black wool, a scarf pinned to the lapel of her jacket with a pearl and silver pin. Her light brown hair was twisted up in a chignon. She was thirty-one and looked younger. Richard reflected that both his sisters were eighty-hour-a-week workers, but obviously a husband and child added to the toll, for Amelia looked older than her years.

His approach was wary and Pamela bent stiffly and offered a cheek. He saluted it with a quick kiss.

"Come into the kitchen. That way we won't disturb Papa," Pamela said. "Are you hungry?"

"Not really."

"Have you eaten at all today?" Amelia asked.

"Not since breakfast."

"Then hungry or not, you need to eat something," and she made it sound like doctor's orders.

The kitchen hadn't been remodeled but left as a relic of the Edwardian era. A large brick fireplace dominated the back wall. Copper pots hung from a large wrought-iron caddy. Opposite the fireplace loomed a gigantic mahogany buffet, loaded with the everyday china service and all manner of glasses. Between the two stretched a long table. Many a school project had been tackled at that table. Richard remembered making a diorama of a volcano for third grade. There had been an improbable herd of dinosaurs of all varieties grazing at the foot of that ominous peak. *Children are so willing to deal out death because they haven't experienced it*, he thought.

Someone had cooked. A turkey. It seemed a bad choice, a reminder of a blighted holiday. Under the warm grease smell of roasted flesh, vanilla added its richness to the air.

"Sandwich, or do you want it heated?" Pamela asked as she pulled a tray heaped with carved turkey slices out of the refrigerator.

"Sandwich."

Pamela began assembling it. "Well, she finally got the attention she craved," she said.

Richard didn't pretend not to understand. The same old game was starting with his nearest sibling. "For God's sake, Pamela, if you can't muster up any grief at least show a little respect!"

"I ran out of that years ago!"

They stood quivering. Amelia broke it up as she always had. "Pamela! Stop baiting! And Richard stop . . . well, just stop." Pamela hunched a shoulder and began putting away the sandwich fixings. "This isn't anyone's fault."

Yes it is. It's mine. I knew and did nothing. But Richard didn't say it aloud because it sounded nuts and would just start another fight with Pamela.

Amelia patted him on the arm. "Here, sit down and eat."

He did and even tried a bite, but the food seemed to enlarge as he chewed and a constriction in his throat kept him from swallowing. Finally he choked it down, but knew he'd never manage another. Richard shredded the sandwich, hoping the destruction would hide how little he had actually eaten.

"What are the arrangements?" he asked.

"The viewing this afternoon. Service tomorrow morning with internment at noon. Naturally we'll be home to visitors after that." The list was ticked off briskly by Pamela. "Uncle David, Aunt Mary and the kids are arriving tonight. Hollyburn's agreed to stay open a little late so David can have his chance to say good-bye since the service itself will be closed casket."

David was his mother's only sibling. Six years younger, David Claasen had been a Wall Street banker before a car crash put him in a wheelchair. He decided that life was too short, quit his job, moved to Vermont, bought a gift shop, married an Earth mother, sired six kids, and became a general embarrassment to his family, friends and in-laws. *Until I trumped him,* thought Richard.

"What about Brent and Paul?" Pamela asked

"They'll be in this morning. Probably around ten," Amelia answered.

"Tomorrow night we'll put all the kids in your old room, but you can stay there for now. We haven't got all the guest rooms ready yet," Pamela said to Richard.

"I'd . . ." Richard coughed. "I'd like to see her before." The lump tightened his throat and he blinked, hoping to keep the betraying moisture at bay.

Pamela nodded. Amelia stood and picked up his plate. "Since you aren't going to eat we should all get to bed. Grab a few hours at least."

🔱

It was strange to be back in his old bedroom, as strange as if adulthood had not intervened. From this side the stained glass gathered the light from the streetlights and flung it in multicolored shards across the hardwood floor. The antique sleigh bed was covered by a handmade quilt sewn by his great-grandmother. It echoed the colored wedges formed by the window. A marble-topped antique dresser surmounted by a tall mirror, a rocking chair built by great-great-great-grandfather Nicholas Oort, and bookcases were the only other furniture.

Only a few relics of childhood remained—the model ships he'd built and the case filled with beloved books. *The Jungle Book, The Wind in the Willows, The Chronicles of Narnia, The Lord of the Rings, Twenty Thousand Leagues Under the Sea.* Richard sank down on the floor and pulled out the Verne book. The book fell open to his favorite section, where Nemo and the Professor walked across the floor of the sea and examined the pearl in the womb of the giant clam.

Oddly, what returned weren't memories of his mother but of his father. Robert had always been the one to read from Verne. And another memory surfaced. Being buried beneath quilts in that double bed, burning with fever while his father held him and hummed a wordless song of Robert's own creation. Those baritone notes had rumbled with comfort. Richard returned to the present and accepted emotionally what he had intellectually always known; that his music came not from Alannis, but from his father.

Why had he denied it?

Richard wasn't certain which *he* he meant. The father who rejected that side of himself or the son who couldn't accept the father had ever possessed it?

His shoulders felt too high, relieved of the dragging burden of the shoulder holster and gun. He felt naked. Richard looked at the shoulder rig hung on the rocking chair. The weight of the pistol pulled the rocker backward.

He couldn't wear a gun into church, to his mother's funeral. But he was carrying the sword. How was that any different?

Because it's irreplaceable and I'm afraid. They killed her.

Richard shrugged into his coat, and paused before the mirror to straighten his tie. The black and dark gold paisley swirls seemed too bright against the material of his shirt. The charcoal gray suit and black shirt heightened the paleness of his skin and silver gilt hair, and turned his eyes into pale blue ice chips. He slipped on the family signet ring and watch, and squared his shoulders. It was time to face the day.

From the second floor the stairs became a great sweeping

curve depositing you in the living room. His sisters had descended those stairs, long gowns trailing, white gloved hands gripping the bannister as they set out for their debutante balls. Young men with inexpertly knotted white ties had waited at the foot of the stairs, clasping corsages in damp hands. Richard's memories were of sliding down the bannister until a broken wrist and the worst spanking of his life had made that game a lot less fun.

Three hours of sleep hadn't left him at his best. His eyelids felt coated with sand, and wisps of cloud had replaced cogent thought. It wasn't until he reached the foot of the stairs that he remembered Pamela's plans to put the kids in his old room. He went back upstairs for his piece. He would have the judge lock it in the safe. But before he faced his father with a gun in his hand, Richard decided to fortify himself with some food.

Unfortunately the plan didn't work. Robert wasn't in his study. He was in the kitchen, seated at the table, with the *New York Times* held up in front of him like a barricade. A cup of coffee sat near his right elbow. He wore a dark suit with a windowpane of grays and purples and dark lavender. He seemed aged far beyond his sixty-two years. Richard noticed that the judge's eyes weren't moving. The paper was just a prop.

"Good morning, sir," Richard said and the paper crackled as the judge's hands closed convulsively on the edges.

"Good morning. Amelia tells me you arrived very late."

"Yes, sir."

Robert's eyes fell on the shoulder rig and pistol and the corners of his mouth pulled down, etching lines in his thin cheeks.

Richard hurried into speech. "We need to get this into the safe before the kids arrive."

"Yes, we do, and Brent and Paul are already here, so come along." Robert took a sip of coffee and made a face. He crossed to the sink and poured it out.

Richard's stomach rumbled with hunger. "Just one minute, please." He opened the bread box and pulled out a slice. Saliva burst in his mouth as the rich yeasty smell hit his nostrils.

He devoured the bread in quick small bites as he followed Robert across the entryway and down the hall to the study. It was a man's room. The large cherrywood desk was tucked neatly in the bay window. There were two enormously tall wingbacked chairs flanking a fireplace detailed in Delft blue tiles. Underfoot was a geometric oriental carpet in deep shades of red and blue. Glass-fronted bookcases were filled with hardcover books. Most of them were legal texts.

The gun was safely stowed in the floor safe under the false flagstone on the hearth.

"Do you remember the combination?" Robert asked as he spun the dial.

"Yes, sir."

"I would prefer you leave it here during the duration of your visit."

"Yes, sir. I can't imagine I'll be needing it."

"I can't imagine why you ever wanted it," said Robert.

It was an invitation to begin anew the endless, circular discussions that had accompanied his announcement that he'd been accepted into the police academy in Albuquerque, New Mexico.

Richard ignored the verbal gauntlet and threw out one of his own. "Sir, are you certain it was suicide?" Perhaps they had made a mistake and there would be *something* with which to attack them.

Robert jumped to his feet, whirled to face Richard. His hand rested on the mantel and the knuckles were white. "Kindly don't try to play policeman games with me, Richard. It was suicide. She left a note."

"Oh. Amelia didn't tell me that." Richard slid the stone back into place and stood.

"She didn't know about the note because I destroyed it."

"Why, sir?"

"She said things about you," Robert answered.

There was that feeling that his stomach had been replaced with a small animal consisting of only teeth and claws. "What kind of things?"

"She offered no details, but wrote that you had done things which would forever condemn you to Hell." Robert walked toward Richard. "She thought, perhaps, she could buy your soul with her life." Now only inches separated them.

Richard stared up into his father's face, suffused with blood. Robert's eyes were rimmed with red, and his expression as he looked down at his son carried anger and accusation as well as profound grief.

Not sleeplessness, tears. *He's wept for her!* The fact that Robert blamed him didn't matter. Richard knew he deserved it. What mattered was the realization—*he had loved her.*

Which gave him a perverse hope. *Maybe someday he'll . . .*

The slamming of the front door reverberated dully down the hall. A deep baritone and a child's piping voice wove through Amelia and Pamela's sopranos. He never finished the thought.

Chapter

TWENTY-SIX

The viewing was held at the Hollyburn funeral home. Robert drove Richard and Pamela over in the Land Rover while Amelia, Brent and Paul followed in the Mercedes. Inside the Land Rover it was a silent journey.

Paul clung to Amelia's hand as they walked up to the white clapboard building. His voice tight with tension, he said, "Mama." From Amelia the little boy had learned the Oort practice (*or affectation*, Richard thought) of pronouncing the word with the French stress on the final syllable. "I'm scared." He was a sturdy youngster with chestnut brown hair and blue eyes. His features were his father's, square rather than the aquiline angles of the Oorts.

Amelia put an arm around his shoulders and pulled him close. "Don't be. It's natural. Just a part of life. Grandmama won't be scary. She's just sleeping until the resurrection."

Brent leaned down from his six feet and muttered into Richard's ear, "I don't know why we have to put a kid through this. Christ, he's just eight."

"Because we're Oorts. Neither age nor infirmity are excuses for not doing our duty," Richard muttered back, and ahead of him he watched his father's back stiffen as he overheard them.

"Yeah, well I'm a van Gelder and Paul's my son."

"So take him home," Richard shot back, suddenly irritated by Brent's carping when he wasn't willing to act.

"Yeah, right," said Brent, gazing at the judge as the older man held open the front door.

The lobby swirled with color and sound. The women wore saris, the men suits, and a few of them sported turbans. The liquid sounds of some Indian language wove through the occasional sob. On the other side of the long, narrow rectangular room were five doorways. Three stood open, yawning emptily and showing only floral wallpaper and paint in soothing green and rose colors. Outside the two closed doors were discrete placards. A steady stream of mourners moved through the right-hand door. Richard walked to the left-hand door.

Amelia laid a hand on Pamela's and Robert's arms, and held them back. They got it, and froze. Brent took Paul over to a bench against the far wall and they sat down together.

The floral edging around the card framed her name— ALANNIS OORT. Richard drew in a long breath, laid his hand on the door handle. With an effort he pressed it down. The door opened with a soft *click* and he entered, closing the door behind him.

Competing scents struck his nostrils. The sweetness of roses, the heavy sex scent of gardenias, the spicy tang of Easter lilies, and the delicate whisper of lily of the valley. It was either a testament to his mother's popularity or his father's clout; the room had become a garden. Wreaths curved around the coffin and there were more between the armchairs and sofa on the side wall.

The coffin rested on trestles draped with white satin. It was a heavy mahogany and brass affair. Richard walked to it and looked down on the face of his mother. She seemed very tiny within the coffin's bulk.

White gold hair flowed over her shoulders. Robert had selected a smoke gray dress that would have matched her eyes. A delicate silver cross lay on her breast just above her folded hands. The gold wedding band glinted on her hand. The tiniest of smiles curved her lipsticked mouth. For an instant Richard remembered the back room of the funeral home in Denver and those rows of brilliant fluorescent colors. A shivering began deep in his belly. She would have been fifty-three in May.

His knuckles whitened as he gripped the edge of the coffin. "Mama, I'm sorry," he whispered.

Her skin was unexpectedly pliant, but so terribly cold beneath his fingers as he touched her cheek. Richard bent and softly kissed her brow. Eyes burning, he spun away and paced the room. *No tears. No tears.* Pulling out his handkerchief, he blew his nose. He returned to the coffin.

"I'm sorry," he said softly. "I should have come. But why didn't you call me on my cell? Why didn't you come to me with your fears? Asked me if whatever it was they told you was true?" Richard realized his love for his mother was twined with a raging anger at her. The legacy of suicide.

Shocked by his anger, he turned it against another target. The cross. Reaching out, Richard scooped it up into his palm. The points bit into his skin as he closed his hand around it.

He spun the chain until the clasp showed and went to unfasten it. Then he thought of his family's reaction and hesitated. He must either confess his action, which would require impossible explanations, or see Pamela and Robert accuse the staff of theft.

And Kenntnis had created a loving, merciful god. That was certainly the god his mother had revered and served with countless acts of kindness and generosity. She was one of the millions who gave strength and physical form to Cross. Richard laid the cross back on her bosom.

And found that his anger at the beautiful, selfish, delicate, hysterical, charming, heedless, loving person had vanished. Richard no longer prayed, but he pulled a chair over to the coffin, sat down and talked to her. About how much he loved being a policeman. How good he was at it.

"And I learned something during the past few years. I'm not weak, and you weren't weak either. It might not have been rational, or make any logical sense, but you died trying to protect me. How many people actually have the guts to do that?"

He stood, leaned down and kissed her one last time.

Then it was time for the public face of mourning. He opened the door and the family took their positions. The afternoon wore on in a blur of faces, murmurs of condolence, firm handshakes, reminiscences and a few, very few, tasteful, quiet tears. In his work Richard saw a lot of grief. Among the Hispanic families there were loud and passionate lamentations. He frankly preferred that to his own WASP culture. Violent or sudden death deserved to be railed against.

He was trapped in an exchange of platitudes with Mrs. Vanowen. Hearing about Cindy's (they had dated his senior year) new venture in New York.

"She's not married yet, either," Mrs. Vanowen said with a suggestive little smile. "Maybe she can get up for a visit while you're still home."

A sharp and constant vibration in his inner breast pocket distracted him. Richard held up a finger to stem the flow of hopeful innuendo and hurried out into the lobby. He answered the phone.

"Okay, this is too weird," came Jennifer Salisbury's voice. "And I knew you'd want to know."

"This isn't a great time," Richard said in a low voice and looked anxiously over his shoulder toward the viewing room.

"It's about Andresson," Salisbury said.

"Okay, go ahead, but make it fast."

"I contacted the authorities in Amarillo to tell them our felony murder and assault on a police officer trumped their burglary, and found out he had been released to some faith-based initiative that rehabs newly released cons and places them back in society. I pointed out that Andresson hadn't even been *tried* for the crimes in New Mexico yet."

"But they are going to pick him up, right?" Richard asked and heard his voice rising.

"No, because he's not in Texas anymore."

"He was on parole in Texas. That's a violation," Richard said.

"Yeah, and so was coming to New Mexico. The difference is he's in a church program now, and nobody wants to expend money and resources for a parole violation when the guy is, in essence, under supervision."

"What churches are associated with this initiative?" Richard asked, knowing the answer but needing the proof.

"It's funded by the World Wide Christian Alliance, and the Amarillo authorities thought he'd gone to their compound in Virginia.

Blind rage can narrow your sight. Richard jumped when a hand fell onto his shoulder. He had neither seen nor heard Robert approaching.

"What the devil are you doing?" the judge hissed in his ear.

"Hold on," Richard said into the phone, and faced his father. "It's work. A case. I won't be long."

"No, you won't because you are done! This is both rude and disrespectful."

"Thank you, sir, your objection is noted. Now let me do my job," Richard said quietly and inwardly he was amazed at how firm and level his voice remained. Robert stared down at him, his expression both frustrated and quizzical. Then he spun on his heel and reentered the viewing room.

Richard returned to the call. "Sorry. Could you please contact Virginia and see if they can do anything?"

"Yeah, okay, this sort of gets my goat too," said the lawyer. "Should I not call back?"

"No, call. I'll have my phone off tomorrow morning. The service . . ." He coughed. "The service is in the morning."

"Service?" Salisbury asked, and he realized that like all people in a tragedy he'd assumed that the entire world knew of his particular and personal pain.

"Just avoid the morning," Richard said quickly.

"I'll try to get back to you this evening," she promised.

He returned to the chapel to glares from his father and siblings and another reminiscence about his mother.

⚶

"Can he die?" Rhiana asked as Kenntnis held the back door of the building open. She carried a tray stacked high with dirty dishes.

Kenntnis glanced back at the packing crate. "Yes, but not from this. This just weakens him and renders him useless to us. Fortunately humans occasionally disgust even themselves and ratchet down the level of violence. He'll have a chance to recover then."

He took the tray from her and they rode up in the elevator to the penthouse. "I admit it makes me feel more than a little vulnerable," Kenntnis said, and some of that supreme certainty that defined his personality was missing. He seemed depressed and even worried.

Rhiana followed him into the kitchen, perched on a stool at the center island, and watched as he loaded the dishes into the dishwasher. He looked up and gave her a smile. "I'm very glad you're back."

He moved to the enormous sub-zero refrigerator and pulled out the leftover tiramisu from last night's dinner. He indicated the dessert, then Rhiana, and lifted his brows in inquiry. She shook her head. He cut off a slab for himself.

"So did you enjoy Venice and your young man?" he asked.

Rhiana flushed, angry to discover that what Madoc had told her was true. But she suppressed it, saying, "You're not mad that I lied to you?"

"You're eighteen and shacking up, and whether I like it or not I probably give off that 'daddy' vibe so of course you lied to me even though I really don't care." He walked over to the breakfast nook in its glass bay and sat down.

She stared a him while he ate. Cross hated her. Richard rejected her. Kenntnis used her, dared to equate himself with her father with one breath, and tell her he didn't give a damn about her with another. She owed them nothing.

She considered Madoc's last words to her. *"Take a hard look at Kenntnis. Beyond the physical."* But what did that mean? Rhiana remembered another bit of advice from Madoc. *"Think of what you know of physics and combine it with your magic."*

Rhiana looked up at the lighting on its glass track curving across the ceiling. She watched the waves undulate. She blinked and the kitchen became a place of stark angled shapes in black while the light became flashing particles that caused the room to strobe. She held out her hand palm up and felt the prickle of the light. There was an explosion of light to her left. The edges of her vision went red. Rhiana narrowed her eyes and looked to where Kenntnis sat.

Nothing human sat at the table. It wasn't like the writhing and coiling forms from the other universes. This was a whirling dervish of diamond-bright particles. They danced, while around them tendrils of light coiled up like a golden mist. It was breathtaking. Unfathomable. Beautiful. Alien.

⚜

The snow blew out overnight, leaving a cold, white day. Richard had been relieved that Reverend Hoffsteader had agreed to a church service. Richard's memories of Hoffsteader's sermons were that they tended toward fire and brimstone. That he would consent to bury a suicide seemed out of character, but apparently he bowed to the modern church's creative dodges around the suicide problem; arguing that people weren't in their right minds, or the suicide was an act in defense of another. In this case it had actually been true, though the reverend didn't know that.

Milling about on the sidewalk in front of the plain white clapboard church with its clear glass windows and single high steeple, Paul and his eldest Claasen cousin, Steve, kept punching each other. They looked absurd and adorable in their grown-up suits and little boy faces, even as their antics irritated the hell out of the adults. Mary, her unruly red curls inexpertly confined by a barrette, wrestled with the four younger children while the limo driver pulled David's wheelchair out of the trunk.

Inside the entryway, the women, with children in tow, headed into the church to make certain the programs were in place and the flowers arranged to their satisfaction. The men went down the hall to Hoffsteader's office. While David couldn't assist in carrying the coffin he insisted on accompanying it, in tones that indicated he expected a fight and was disappointed when he didn't get one.

The study was book-lined and terribly overheated. Hoffsteader, a pink-faced fat man with light brown hair pulled across his bald spot, came bearing down on Richard.

"Richard." His palm was pillow soft as they shook hands. The minister's eyes raked up and down the length of Richard's body. Richard stiffened, wondering at the scrutiny, and suddenly worried that the dark purple shirt he'd selected was too colorful for good old-fashioned Protestant mourning.

"I didn't remember you were so short." That certainly seemed in character. Hoffsteader's lack of tact was well known to his parishioners. "I had thought it might be nice if you all carried the coffin on your shoulders rather than the handles, but that's not going to work."

"No," Richard said shortly.

He had made peace with his lack of inches years ago, but he didn't particularly like having his nose rubbed in it. Two of the pallbearers, friends of his father's, were already present. The next few moments were taken up by greetings and questions.

"New Mexico, not much sailing there," from Berksen.

"How do you find police work?" from Judge Martin.

"I hear they have an opera there. Supposed to be pretty good too," Berksen added. "Have you been?"

The questions came at Richard from all sides. He tried to answer without sounding idiotic. "No, sir. Yes, I go, and they are very good, sir. I like it very much, sir." The social platitudes felt surreal when his mother's body rested only a few hundred feet away.

"Aren't there going to be seven of you including Alannis's brother?" Richard heard Hoffsteader asking Robert.

"Oscar called early this morning. He's quite ill. I have a replacement," Robert added. "I'm certain he'll be here shortly."

The judge walked away and stood gazing out the window at the snow-covered vines snaking across a grape arbor that ran along the side of the building. It looked skeletal, the thick gnarled vines like bony fingers clutching at the rib cage of some dead behemoth.

Hoffsteader glanced at his watch as if death had a timetable that had to be met, and beckoned them over to him with a gathering gesture of his short arms. "So, we conclude with the Lord's Prayer. When that's finished you'll all come up and take the coffin straight down the aisle and out to the hearse."

Behind him Richard heard the door to the office open and close. The musky, exotic scent of Kouros hit Richard's nostrils and his gut clenched in a sudden spasm of nausea even before he heard the drawling, cultured voice.

"Robert, a thousand, thousand apologies. There was an accident on I-95."

Heat raced through Richard's body followed by a chill so deep and profound that his teeth began to chatter. His knees trembled and he seemed to have gone empty to his core. *Run, run, run!* a voice screamed in the recesses of his mind.

"Richard, dear boy."

Richard turned slowly and prepared to look into the face of his attacker, but Drew Sandringham had moved on, and gathered Robert's hands in his.

"Robert, I am so very sorry. I was shocked when you called with the news and I'm honored to serve as a pall-bearer."

"Excuse me," Richard murmured and fled the office.

The bathroom was just down the hall. Richard slipped inside, locked the door and leaned back against it. Breaths hissed between his teeth but he still felt as if he were suffocating. Stupid, he'd been so stupid. Of course Sandringham was going to attend the funeral. Why hadn't he foreseen that and prepared himself?

Because I didn't think he'd have the gall.

Moving to the sink, he splashed cold water over his face. It dripped off his hair where his forelock had fallen forward out of its careful part. He watched the silver drops and remembered watching the blood pattering from his badly bitten lip onto the polished inlaid wood floor of the dining room. Competing voices wove through his mind.

Pretty isn't he?

. . . Face the monsters.

Evil and untrustworthy hands.

Shame is a powerful silencer.

He betrayed you. . . . His shame, not yours.

. . . Use this to hurt me?

Only if you let him.

Richard slowly raised his head and studied his features in the mirror. What looked back out of his pale blue eyes was no longer fear. It was anger.

When he reentered the office the men had fallen back on the usual shield for grief, emotion and discomfort. They were talking business. Money was a good insulator.

Richard paused and forced himself to take a long, long look at Sandringham. Four years had wrought few changes. The sleek brown hair held a few more streaks of silver but the narrow face remained smooth, with only crow's feet radiating out from the tawny gold brown eyes. Sandringham had grown an Elizabethan-style beard and mustache and it suited him. He was still a very handsome man and he knew it. He sensed the close observation and looked over at Richard. He strolled slowly over.

He gazed down. "You look well." A hand started to raise.

"Touch me and I will kill you," Richard said in a low, conversational tone.

Sandringham blinked, startled, and for an instant the hand hung in the air as if the older man hated to back down. But back down he did. The hand slowly lowered and brushed across the immaculately knotted Italian silk tie as if that had been his intention all along.

"So, a policeman. Quite an eccentric choice. Not what your family had hoped for you."

"Yes, I no longer have any shame," said Richard and he laid a slight emphasis on the final word.

For an instant Richard thought that the evening had not made the indelible impression on Drew that it had upon him, and that Sandringham wouldn't remember what he had said. Then the dark straight brows drew together and the tawny eyes narrowed. His expression hardened.

"I'm very . . . *concerned* to hear that."

"You should be. I do hope you've mended your ways."

Sandringham stepped in even closer, crowding him, and said softly, "Don't be fooled by the power of your little gun and shiny badge. You've got potent enemies, Richard. You want to keep me neutral."

"Thank you for the warning," Richard said.

"Just so we understand each other. I'd hate to see you hurt."

"Really? Forgive me if I find that laughable. . . ."

Robert's voice interrupted them. "It's time," the judge said curtly.

They all filed into the church.

TWENTY-SEVEN

The handful of half-frozen mud struck the lid of the coffin. Robert stood staring down into the grave while Richard bent and gathered up his handful. He allowed it to roll off his fingers, hating the hollow, rattling sound as it struck. Amelia and Pamela added their small offerings. David struggled to lean down out of his wheelchair. Richard gathered a handful and gave it to his uncle. David threw it in and his lips moved. Richard couldn't tell what he'd said.

Their numbers were greatly reduced from the church. Brent and Mary had taken the children back to the house, and the cold and the morbidity of the cemetery had daunted most of the mourners. Only some thirty people sat on folding chairs at graveside. Hoffsteader, Bible in hand and looking like a large black buffalo in his curly wool overcoat, stood solemnly at one end of the grave. He offered the final benediction. It was finished.

Richard turned away. David caught him by his sleeve. "You should sing. She loved your voice."

Richard had considered it during the long hours when he'd tried and failed to sleep. He wasn't certain his father would approve, or if grief could be controlled enough to make a sound. Finally, what the hell would he sing? The religious repertory was closed to him now. Perhaps Kenntnis was right when he said that all music was born out of human genius, and therefore good no matter what the inspiration, but he couldn't say those words of false hope over his mother's grave. Richard was also afraid what it might summon. He would never forget that figure coming down off the cross. He looked over to Robert.

The judge didn't look at his brother-in-law or son. He

continued to contemplate the grave, then suddenly he gave a sharp nod. This sign of encouragement surprised Richard. A Schubert song came to mind. Focusing, he found the opening note, drew in a long steady breath, and sang.

I think of you when the sun's shimmer
gleams from the sea;
I think of you when the moon's glimmer
is mirrored in the streams.

I see you when dust rises
on the distant road;
at dead of night, when the traveller
trembles on the narrow footbridge.

I hear you when the waves
surge with a dull roar;
often I go and listen in the quiet wood
when all is still.

I am with you; however far away you are,
you are near me!
The sun sets, soon the stars will shine on me.
O that you were here!

As the final notes echoed into silence Richard found his father watching him. They stared at each other for a long moment, then Robert said ever so softly, "Thank you."

It seemed like all the people who had shunned the cemetery and even the funeral service came by the house that afternoon. The women carried covered dishes with some variety of casserole or platters of cookies, and even whole cakes. There was so much food that they'd added two extra leaves to the dining room table to accommodate it all.

Brent had made a run to the store for more paper plates and hot beverage cups.

Every room buzzed and rumbled with conversation. Overhead came the faint thunder of running feet as the seven kids romped up and down the length of the attic room. The hours passed. Richard assigned himself garbage detail. He kept making sweeps through the first floor of the house gathering up dirty plates, plastic utensils, crumpled napkins, cups filled with the dregs of coffee, tea or lemonade.

It was a slow process because he kept being drawn into conversations, sometimes about his mother but more often about New Mexico and his career choice. His first voice teacher and her partner were especially distressed that he'd abandoned music.

"Your voice just keeps getting better. What I heard today was lovely," Jeanne said as she towered over him. At five feet ten inches, a hundred and eighty pounds, and equipped with a Wagnerian soprano's bosom, she was an imposing figure.

"I wasn't going to be good enough," Richard said.

"Nonsense," said Sandra. She was an older woman, Jeanne's coach and accompanist and partner. "Tenors, like sopranos and fine wine, mature late."

"I'm really very happy with my choice," he said, sliding past them and escaping into the kitchen. His cheeks hurt from the effort of smiling and talking. Dumping the trash, he pulled out a fresh sack. Amelia turned from the stove and pushed back her hair with a forearm.

"I've boiled enough water to deliver several hundred babies," she announced.

Pamela looked up from the sink where she was washing dishes. "If I'd known this would happen, I would have hired a maid service."

"Can't we just tell them all to leave?" Richard asked plaintively.

"I thought we'd sit in the living room and *receive*," Pamela said grumpily.

The chimes from the doorbell came echoing down the hall. The siblings exchanged rueful looks. "I'll get it," Richard said.

The woman on the front step was plump and smiling. Her belly and breast strained against a fox-trimmed tweed coat. It had obviously been bought a lot of poundage ago. Gray curls sprang out beneath her fur hat. She held a covered Pyrex casserole pan in her gloved hands.

"You must be Richard. Your mother spoke about you so often and described you to a tee. I would know you anywhere." She shoved the pan into his hands. "Alannis and I spent such a lot of time together after I moved here. I was afraid I couldn't make friends with her so quickly, but she made it so easy."

She drew out the *so*, giving it a contemptuous twist, and that's when Richard noticed that despite the pink cheeks and broad smile the woman's eyes were cold blue and flint hard. She pushed past Richard and entered the house.

"Poor Alannis, I think she probably loved you too much," she said as she pulled off her coat and handed it to him. He juggled the pan from which rose the nauseating smell of tuna, cream of mushroom soup and potato chips. "It wasn't hard for me to plant a few doubts, and then we'd discuss your actions over the years. Your behavior takes on a whole new light when viewed through the prism of new facts. She might have been neurotic, but she wasn't stupid."

It wasn't a call. Grenier had sent an emissary.

"Get out," Richard said through lips gone stiff with anger.

"Wouldn't dream of leaving yet. I want to offer my condolences to your sisters and I understand you have a darling little nephew." Now an edge of fear gnawed, weakening Richard's anger. "I won't bother mentioning

Robert. Alannis made it pretty clear the two of you didn't get along." She glanced back at Richard and gave him a coquettish smile, grotesque on that aging face. "And the way he controlled her life! Keeping the liquor cabinet locked, doling out a glass of wine a few times a week and refusing to allow her any sleep aids when the poor thing was so clearly suffering. I'm just glad I was able to help her find relief."

Rage exploded along every nerve ending yanking his muscles into a clench that set his bones to aching. Red narrowed Richard's sight, cutting off all peripheral vision, leaving only her malicious, taunting face. The coat slid out of his hand onto the marble floor. Richard spun and launched the casserole. It smashed against the paneled wall, sending gobbits of tuna and limp potato chips sliding down the wood.

"Whoops," the woman said.

Amelia and Pamela came hurrying down the hall, drawn by the explosion of breaking glass. Robert appeared in the living room archway.

The woman stepped in close and whispered in Richard's ear. "Mr. Grenier wanted me to offer you his personal condolences and remind you that you still have so much you could lose. He hopes that you'll reconsider your position, and give him the item."

His family reached them. "What the devil?" Robert asked.

"It must have slipped," Richard said, in a flat, emotionless voice.

His sisters and father looked from the wall to Richard and the four feet that separated them.

"Mrs. Negary," said Robert, "I want to offer my apologies. It's been a long couple of days, and Richard has been under a great deal of . . . stress."

Negary patted the judge on the forearm. He moved out of touching range. "I completely understand," she said.

"Alannis told me a bit about the boy. How sensitive he is," and her tone and the mobile quirk of her eyebrows conveyed her total sympathy and complete understanding of Robert's burden.

Robert indicated the door to the living room. "Please, let me get you something to drink."

Negary tucked her arm through his. "Tea would be lovely."

Pamela set her fists on her hips and glared at Richard. "What the hell is wrong with you?"

"I guess the thought of another tuna casserole just pushed me right over the edge," Richard said.

And Amelia giggled. Pamela glared at her, but couldn't hold it. She began snorting with suppressed laughter. Richard forced a laugh, to share at least briefly in this moment of family solidarity, but the only emotion he truly felt was rage. It burned through him, but his mind was clear, diamond sharp and focused. A plan of action began falling into place like tumblers in a lock.

⁜

Winter lay lightly on the Virginia countryside. Richard, driving a rented Impala, wound his way along the curves and over the hills, following the narrow blacktop road. This was the heart of hunt country and purebred horses with high dollar prices cropped at the still green grass. Behind white fences, brick mansions, set well back from the road, loomed.

He had spent four days in Newport helping pack up his mother's personal effects and laying the groundwork for what he had to do. When Richard had gone to the airport that morning his father thought he was returning to New Mexico. Robert had probably learned the truth by now.

As the sun began to set, Christmas lights glowed in the trees surrounding many of the homes. No gauche Santas mounted on rooftops or wire and light deer raising and lowering their heads in robotic imitation of the grazing horses were to be seen. Money lived here, old money, and it had taste.

Seven days until Christmas and Richard's twenty-eighth birthday.

The houses became fewer as he moved farther south and west. The sun was completely gone by the time he pulled up in front of the gates. They swooped and arched before him. Pinpoint spotlights on the gatehouse gave everything a dazzling glow. Golden plaques set in the stone supports to either side read *World Wide Christian Alliance*. The metal of the gates had been gilded with some material that made each alternating strut appear to be either gold or pearl.

"Just in case anyone misses the symbolism," Richard murmured aloud.

No, he ordered himself. *Don't be flippant. You'll blow it!*

A man dressed in a conservative suit emerged from the gatehouse. It might be civilian dress but his function was clear—guard.

Richard rolled down the window. The man leaned in. He was young, midtwenties with a neck as wide as his head and burly shoulders bunching beneath the dark suit coat. Richard amended "guard" to "thug."

"May I help you, sir?"

"Detective Richard Oort, here to see Reverend Grenier."

"Is he expecting you?"

"Probably."

"Just one moment."

The man returned to the guard house. Through the window Richard could see him on the phone. He nodded and reached out to a control panel. The gates swung slowly open.

Don't let down your guard. There will be cameras. This is just the first hurdle.

The guard was back. "Follow this road to the fork. Go left. The house is a couple of miles farther on."

"Thank you," Richard said.

There were a number of buildings dotted along the road. Some looked like offices, others like dormitories. Judging from the enormous satellite dishes, one was a broadcasting studio. Richard reached the fork. To the right the road ran straight up the hill and ended at an enormous white stone church. In front of it stood an even taller white stone cross.

Richard spun the wheel, and sent the car up the left fork. He was driving through a mixed forest—evergreens and deciduous trees, denuded now for winter.

It seemed like a long time before Richard saw the house. It was a rustic timbered building, but huge, two stories tall with long wings running back toward a granite cliff. Most of the windows were illuminated.

A wide circular driveway brought him to the front doors. Richard parked. As he locked the door, shielded from the house by the bulk of the car, he gave himself the final instructions.

Be angry, but a tentative anger. Unsure of what they might do next. Be afraid.

As he climbed the stone steps he realized the last instruction no longer required acting. He was afraid. Deathly afraid.

The doorbell played the opening chords of a hymn, so corny and so at odds with the elegant Grenier. Perhaps playing for the believing sheep? The heavy carved wood doors, inset with stained glass, opened slowly. A pretty young woman in a plaid skirt and black turtleneck sweater smiled in welcome. Soft brown hair swung in a page boy that just brushed her shoulders. She had an English complexion of cream and roses.

"May I take your coat?" she asked. Richard handed over his overcoat. Shrugged to straighten the shoulders of his suit coat and shot his cuffs. "This way." She indicated the direction with a sweep of her hand.

The public rooms contained thick white carpet, blue

velvet furniture and crystal chandeliers. The art was overly lush, overly large landscapes or religious pictures. Everything was very expensive, and tacky in the extreme.

They left the main body of the house through a short hallway that ended at an ebony door. "Reverend Grenier said to send you to his private quarters. Just go through there." She indicated the door and gave him another smile. She turned and walked away.

Richard stared at the polished black wood. *Give me the strength.* Once that would have been asked of God. Now it rested only on him, his strength, his spirit, his will.

He opened the door and stepped through. Ahead, light spilled from an open doorway. A long runner, a carved Chinese rug, spread out before him. The art on the walls wasn't to Kenntnis's standards, but it was damn fine, tending toward American modern.

The open door brought him into a living room. The furniture was eighteenth century or very fine reproductions. An enormous oriental rug in golds, blues and creams lay on a polished slate floor. There were mirrors, but all were opaque gray like the mirrors in the South Valley trailer.

A fireplace dominated one wall. Built of river rocks with a granite mantelpiece, it looked large enough to roast an ox. Flames danced in the grate.

Richard heard the door close behind him and whirled. Mark Grenier stood, his hand on the doorknob, watching Richard. The minister's head was cocked to the side, a quizzical gesture. Grenier was dressed in a soft gray cardigan sweater over a striped dress shirt in shades of green, pink, blue, purple and yellow. Richard had a moment of both connection and dislocation. He was wearing the same shirt. Etro Milano, 360 dollars at Robert R. Bailey.

"You are the most unexpected young man," Grenier said. "To what do I owe the pleasure? Or have you reconsidered accepting my offer? Mrs. Negary didn't seem hopeful after your meeting."

"How could you possibly think I would work for you after what you did?" Outrage shook in his voice. Richard paused for breath and dialed it down.

"To avoid my doing it again," Grenier said with soft menace. "You've just had a taste of what my power can accomplish."

"Yes, well, you're not going to be able to do anything again because you're going to be in jail!" His voice sounded absurdly young.

Grenier's eyebrows lifted in delighted surprise. "Oh, really?"

With his left hand Richard removed the badge from his inside breast pocket and flipped open the leather case. With his right hand he pulled the warrant out of his coat pocket and opened it with a snap of the wrist.

"I'm here to arrest Douglas Andresson and return him to New Mexico for trial. I'm also arresting you for aiding and abetting a felon in contravention of his parole agreement and assisting in his flight to avoid prosecution. Add to that harboring a fugitive."

For a long moment Grenier just stared at him, then he threw back his head and laughed, roaring out his amusement. When he finally stopped, Grenier mopped at his streaming eyes. "Are you completely out of your mind?"

But Grenier was keeping well beyond Richard's reach, and Richard knew he was going to have to force the issue.

"I'm Mark Grenier. I pray with presidents, and make and break political candidates. One heartfelt plea on my network and I can raise five million dollars in a day. An outraged commentary can bring a network to its knees."

"And you bring monsters into our world," Richard said.

"They were already here. Since we developed a cerebral cortex they've been here. A million years of human evolution and they're still here. Kenntnis hasn't defeated them yet. You can't win and I don't back losers. When the gates finally open I won't be one of the cattle."

"No, you'll be a sonderkommando for the human race," Richard said. "Well, someone has to stop you." And Richard reached into the holster at the small of his back and pulled out the hilt.

Panic replaced contempt, and Grenier retreated behind his desk, yelling, "Doug, Bruce, Willie, get in here now!"

A door on the side of the living room opened. Two big men, one black and one white, charged through, followed by Doug Andresson.

"Get that away from him!"

Richard lifted his right hand toward the hilt, but a shovel-sized hand slammed against his wrist. His fingers went numb. He dropped the hilt. The black man slapped him along the side of the head, setting his ears to ringing. Then he was firmly gripped between them.

Andresson, grinning happily, removed the Firestar from Richard's shoulder holster, then gave him a rough, ball-grabbing pat down. "Like that, don't you, sweetie?" Andresson said.

"Doug," Grenier snapped out. "Leave that to Bruce and Willie. Get the sword."

Andresson picked up the hilt and walked over to Grenier. He pushed it at Grenier, who flinched back. "Want to inspect it?"

"Go. Work with it."

"What do you want us to do with him, sir?" the white goon asked.

"Lock him up downstairs."

"He's a cop, sir," Willie said.

"Who is well out of his jurisdiction, and who threatened me."

The two big men hustled him toward the door. Richard, feet barely touching the floor, had a moment of panic. He quelled it and forced himself to call back over his shoulder, "I guess this means you're resisting arrest?"

Chapter

TWENTY-EIGHT

E ven through the surgical mask Angela could smell the burned yeast smell of cutting bone. The saw clawed through the sternum of the body on the metal autopsy table. The wide curving light above the table threw everything into harsh relief.

Eighties rock 'n' roll blared from the radio, and the bone saw howled. Sometimes Angela imagined that the bones themselves were screaming. The voice of the receptionist came over the intercom, barely audible above the other racket.

"Angie, Lieutenant Weber is here. He wants to see you right away. Says it's urgent."

Angela turned off the saw and handed it to her assistant. "Get him open. I'll only be a minute."

She stripped off her gloves, gown and mask and dumped them in the waste receptacle.

Weber waited in the front office. "I'm in the middle of an autopsy," Angela said.

In answer he held out a piece of paper. It weighed heavy in the hand, fine stationery, cream colored, swirling with watermarks. Words flowed across the page, small and precise, with that strange vertical shape of a left-handed writer.

"This arrived this morning by Federal Express," Weber said as Angela began to read.

Dear Damon,
   I know that certain revelations have caused an estrangement between us. I'm sorry for that, and believe me when I say I understand, and I don't blame you. But I also believe that you are a good and honorable man which is why I'm writing to you now.

I need your help, and if any trace of affection or friendship still remains for me I hope you will respond.

Mark Grenier is a murderer and has attempted murder time and time again. His latest victim was my mother, driven to suicide by one of his people. And I can't prove any of it. I have to bring down both him and his organization and I have to use reason's tools, not mythic weapons to do it.

The best I have is his involvement with Andresson, removing him first from New Mexico and then from Texas. I convinced Jennifer Salisbury to have a warrant issued. A weak reed that will never survive judicial review, but it's enough to get me into his compound.

By the time you read this I will have gone to Virginia to serve the warrant and make my arrests. I'm counting on Grenier being unable to resist the chance to obtain the sword. Everything that's been done to me and mine has been done in an effort to get me to turn over the sword. Since bribes and intimidation haven't worked I think he'll resort to force.

Remember, Grenier has his own paladin in Andresson. They want the sword. That need will overrun any caution. So while the other charges—aiding, abetting and harboring a fugitive, may be bullshit—imprisoning a police offer most definitely is not.

I will try to hang on until you come. . . .

I hope you will come.

> Your friend,
> Richard

"Oh fuck," said Angela, and shoved the letter back into Weber's hands.

Boot heels clattered as she ran for the doors. She hit the bar with both hands, sending the door flying open, and went plunging out into the parking lot.

Weber, in close pursuit, called, "Wait. Where are you going?"

"To Kenntnis."

"Why him?"

"He's got a plane." Angela looked back at him. "You are coming, aren't you?"

Weber looked down at the letter still clutched in his hand. He set off toward his car with fast long strides that had Angela running to keep up.

⚜

"Who the devil are you? Why the hell are you interfering in my son's life? And what in God's name is *this*?"

The hilt landed in the center of Kenntnis's granite desk and gave its bell-like cry. Robert Oort jumped and retreated a few steps as the perfect overtones echoed and reechoed through the room then slowly faded. Oort stared at the hilt with the air of man for whom the rules had changed, the situation had become confusing, a man who resented the hell out of it.

Kenntnis also felt as if the ground had shifted when the hilt came out. He had been surprised but unperturbed to hear that Judge Robert Oort waited downstairs. Kenntnis assumed that Richard had tried to communicate something of his new understanding to his father, and now it was up to Kenntnis to make it explicable. The sight of the sword changed all that.

Resting his fists on the desk, Kenntnis levered himself to his feet and inclined his head to the judge. "I am Kenntnis. How do you do?"

"Not well," snapped Oort.

"Neither do I, now," Kenntnis said. He picked up the hilt. "How did you come by this?"

"My son left it for me, along with a first-class plane ticket to Albuquerque, and this . . . this . . . gibberish."

Oort handed over a folded piece of paper. Kenntnis unfolded it and read,

Dear Papa,

So by now you've found this object and the first-class ticket on the red-eye out of Logan to Albuquerque. And you've dismissed this as ravings by your grieving weakling of a son.

Don't. .

This thing that I've left for you is of incalculable value. It would be impossible for me to explain its powers and purpose in a letter. Kenntnis will explain it all to you just like he did for me. Just believe me when I say it holds back the darkness, and many people's fates, not the least of them mine, hinge on its safe return to its creator. I think Kenntnis made it; at any rate he is certainly its custodian.

Thanks to Kenntnis I've realized that I'm not weak. And now I'm going to prove it to you by bringing Mama's murderers to justice. They manipulated her into suicide, trying to force me to give them this thing. Obviously I can't have it when I confront them.

I know I've been a disappointment to you. Kenntnis says it's your problem, not mine, but it still affects me and makes it hard for me to ask this favor of you now. But I must. I know your character—your honor, integrity and sense of duty. Despite our differences I trust you. I'm begging you, take this object to New Mexico and return it to Kenntnis at Lumina Enterprises.

Papa, guard this thing with your life. Tell no one you have it, and give it into no one's keeping except Kenntnis's. Please do this for me.

Kenntnis says I don't have to like you, much less love you. You've certainly made it hard for me to, but I've decided that I do love you, Papa. I hope someday you'll love me too.

Richard

Kenntnis looked up from the letter and met Robert Oort's furious blue-eyed gaze. The judge made a gesture of distaste. "Richard has always had a taste for hyperbole and the overly dramatic. So did his mother." His lips twisted, a complex mix of grief and disgust.

Kenntnis dropped the letter. The paper fluttered down as broken and ephemeral as the family. "There's nothing hysterical about this. It's a masterful job of manipulation. How many times did he refer to me?" He picked up the letter and scanned it again. "Seven times. When he really didn't need to mention me by name at all. He made this about you and me. You wouldn't have come here for him, but you'd come here to kick my ass for interfering in his life." He handed the letter back to the judge.

"I think you give him too much credit," came the dismissive response.

"You really don't know this kid at all, do you?" Kenntnis asked, disgusted and amazed at the man's obtuseness.

"He's my son. I think I know him better than you," Oort said.

"You'd be wrong," Kenntnis shot back. "So, let's try another question. Richard's question. Do you love him?"

Kenntnis watched the conflicting emotions play in the dark blue eyes. Kenntnis knew the type. Usually male, terrified by emotional displays because they feared the power of their own emotions. Certain if they ever expressed their feelings they would be overpowered by them.

"I will not discuss any of this." Oort edged the words with fight. "I came here for some very specific answers." The letter crumpled as his hand clenched.

"And you're going to get some, and probably not like any of them. Now, *sit down*!" Kenntnis rarely used that voice on humans anymore. It still worked.

Oort dropped into the big armchair, the same one Richard had selected all those weeks ago. The man gripped the padded leather arms, and looked about as if wondering how he'd come to be there.

Kenntnis rested a hip on the edge of his desk. "Your son loves you. He won't permit a word to be said against you, even though you are clearly a son of a bitch and a self-righteous prick. He's also quite afraid of you because . . . Did I mention this before? You're a son of a bitch and a self-righteous prick. So he tries desperately to win your approval, and you piss on him every time."

It was clear where Richard got his guts. Oort came out of the chair and stood quivering in front of Kenntnis. "How dare you! I won't listen to this." He tried to move around Kenntnis toward the door.

"Oh, no, no you don't. I'm just getting started." Kenntnis placed a hand on Oort's chest, and pushed him back down into the chair. "First you kill his musical ambitions—"

"He kept auditioning and auditioning, and never getting hired," Oort shouted. "I asked how much longer he was going to go on with this, and then he admits to me that he didn't have the talent to succeed."

"So you demanded he quit."

"He was drifting," Oort said.

"So what? He wasn't sponging off you, was he?" Kenntnis asked.

"That's not the point. It's not what we do. We work. We're a family that serves. We gave him every opportunity; foreign travel, private schools, a fine college. He never follows through on anything." Oort gave Kenntnis a bitter smile. "And what does it say about Richard's character that he'd meekly quit on my say-so. You make him out to be a paragon. In fact, he's weak."

"Do you like that he's become a policeman?"

"No."

"Made that pretty clear, have you?" Oort didn't verbally reply, but the answer was in his face. "Hasn't quit yet, has he? And by the way, he's a damn fine policeman."

"And now he's run off to God knows where in pursuit of enemies that don't exist. My wife committed suicide!" Oort choked, clenched his jaw and looked away. "So he'll probably lose this job too."

"Ah, yes, that *other* job," Kenntnis said. "That job that *you* got him. Let's talk about that job." Oort looked up, a sharp glance, for he'd heard the threat purring in Kenntnis's voice. Then the judge's eyes were quickly veiled by lowered lashes.

"You suspected something, didn't you?" Kenntnis said. "All this bullshit about a random mugging, but the doctors wouldn't tell you anything about his injuries because Richard wouldn't let them. Easier to blame Richard, keep thinking of him as a failure. What kept you from finding out? Fear of what you might discover? Or what that discovery might say about *your* judgment and acuity?"

Oort jerked to his feet and pushed past Kenntnis, seeking open air and relief from Kenntnis's accusatory presence. Kenntnis didn't give him any respite. He closed in once more. "Let me tell you what Richard suffered at the hands of your good *friend*."

And he did. Holding back nothing. Softening none of the ugly details. Oort ended up hunched over the desk palms flat against the granite, relying on the stone to keep him upright.

"For four years your son has carried this secret, and a crushing load of guilt and shame. Never telling anyone. Until me. I held him while he cried. It should have been *you*, but he couldn't tell you. Not because he thought it would lower him in your estimation. He knows where he stands with you—the failure, the disappointment, the weakling. He kept it from you because he didn't want to hurt you!" Kenntnis swept up the letter, smoothed out the creases and glanced through it again.

"You don't deserve this boy! Despite everything he still turns to you as the person he most trusts in the world.

Though you sure as hell don't deserve it. If he says he's gone to bring your wife's killers to justice—"

The office doors flew open and Angela and Weber charged in. Kenntnis looked from the letter clutched in the policeman's hand and back down to the one he held.

"Richard's gone after Grenier," Angela panted.

"We need your plane," Weber said, then hurriedly added, "Please."

"They've got the sword," Angela concluded in a tone fraught with dismay.

Kenntnis reached around Oort and held up the hilt. "No. No, they don't."

"Sword?" came faintly from the judge.

Weber raised his eyebrows and pointed at Oort. "Richard's father," said Kenntnis shortly as he headed for the door.

"Don't we owe him an explanation?" Weber asked.

"No. He hasn't earned one yet."

"Sword?"

⚕

Richard wasn't certain how long he'd been in the basement cell since Willie had helped himself to Richard's watch and the family signet ring. It was silly, given his overall predicament, but worry over how his father would react to that loss was his foremost thought. The ring had been given to every Oort son on his twentieth birthday since 1797. Now he had lost it.

Four concrete walls surrounded him. One was pierced with a heavy metal door. Despite his fear and tension, hunger gnawed at Richard's belly, and his tongue felt swollen from thirst.

Underfoot was more concrete with a six-inch drain set in the middle of the floor. Overhead a high wattage bulb burned behind a wire grate. The light reflecting off the white-gray walls made his eyes water and his head ache.

There wasn't a stick of furniture or any sort of sanitary facility. Eventually he urinated down the drain.

They had taken his suit coat and emptied his pants pockets. It was cold in just his shirtsleeves, and the hard floor made his seat bones ache. Richard stood and walked in brisk circles, trying to beat back the damp chill.

He wondered how long he had been locked up. Hours certainly. A day? He couldn't tell. And a larger problem loomed. He was a police officer being held against his will, but right now it was his word against an internationally famous evangelical minister that the imprisonment had occurred. He needed more.

A key rattled in the lock. The door opened and Bruce entered. Richard thought he came alone, but Andresson stepped out from behind Bruce's camouflaging bulk. Andresson's full underlip protruded in a childlike pout, but the eyes were mean. Richard watched the hilt flip back and forth as Andresson tossed it from hand to hand.

Andresson closed to within inches. His breath was hot, rank and sour on Richard's face. "How the fuck do you make it work?" He shook the hilt. "Mark and me have been tryin' and tryin', and now he's checking out some books, and maybe he's even gonna talk to the faces, but I figured, what the fuck, I got you."

The door stood open behind Andresson. It seemed in character to make a break for it. Richard used his shoulder to shove Andresson aside, and bolted through the door. Stiff muscles seemed to crack as he barreled into a run. Glancing over he saw the keys hanging in the lock. Stunned by their stupidity, Richard began to swing the door closed, other hand grabbing for the keys. Even if he succeeded in locking them in, Richard didn't figure he'd get out of the house much less the compound.

The door shook and pushed back. Richard strained to hold it, but the combined weight of the two men on the other side overwhelmed him. Springing back, Richard went pelting for the basement stairs. The sudden release of pressure sent Bruce and Andresson plunging and staggering into the basement. The door banged against the wall.

The muscles in his thighs strained as Richard took the steps two at a time. He made it halfway up before a hand caught him by the ankle and jerked. He fell full length on the stairs, cracking his chin, teeth snapping together on his tongue. Pain seared through his skull. Bruce twisted a hand in the collar of Richard's shirt and dragged him to his feet.

"Bring him down here!" Andresson ordered.

Choking from the pressure on this throat, Richard was half dragged, half carried back into the basement. On one wall were racks of wine. On the other, ranks of filing cabinets.

Bruce frog-marched Richard up to Andresson. He transferred his grip from the collar to Richard's upper arms. The confinement raised old fears. Richard felt his belly muscles quivering.

"Show me how it works," Andresson repeated.

"You were in the church," Richard said, forcing insolence.

"You had your back to me. When you came around it was there. What's the goddamn trick?" Andresson demanded.

"It's really quite simple." There was a flicker of frustration and dull anger in Andresson's black eyes, and Richard knew he had the tool to release Andresson's pent-up rage. For an instant Richard hesitated because he was afraid, but it had to be done. He had to have proof. "Or at least it was for *me*." Richard laid a subtle emphasis on the pronoun. "But maybe I shouldn't be surprised *you* can't figure it out."

Snake quick, the sharp toe of Andresson's cowboy boot took Richard in the nuts. Pain exploded from his groin through the top of his head and a scream gurgled up carried

on a wave of rushing vomit. Richard clutched himself and
curled into a fetal crouch.

"Disrespect me, you little faggot. Now, you're going to
tell me what I want to know. When I go up to Mr. Grenier
again I'm going to damn well know how to use this fucking thing."

"I doubt it," Richard whispered. "You're too stupid."

Andresson shoved the hilt through his belt, and nodded
to Bruce. The big man jerked Richard upright, and held
him while Andresson laid into Richard's gut with punish-
ing, rhythmic blows. At first Richard managed to keep his
muscles taut, absorbing the punches, but pain from his
abused testicles and growing terror of those clutching
hands broke his concentration. His belly muscles softened,
and the next punch bent him double.

As Richard folded, Andresson's fist met Richard's face
in a hard upper cut, driving his lips against the edge of his
teeth. The taste and smell of blood was added to the rank
smell and sour taste of vomit and the sharp reek of sweat.

"How does it work?" Andresson asked.

"No," Richard gasped. The fist took him in the corner of
his right eye.

The beating went on. One eye was swelling shut. Blood
trickled down his chin from a cut on his lip. His cheekbones
hurt. Richard withdrew deep inside his mind, trying to
block out the escalating pain. Tried to focus on the passing
minutes. *Hang on. Hang on. Two more minutes. Five minutes. Time. I've got to buy time.*

❦

They were gathered around the coffee table in the living
room of the penthouse. Kenntnis swept several large art
books onto the floor, and set down the silver bowl. A small
bit of water sloshed over onto the elaborate wood inlay.
Angela instinctively wiped it up with the cuff of her jacket.

Rhiana huddled on the sofa, fingers writhing nervously through her long black hair. Cross, looking like a Peruvian mummy, just skin stretched on bone, sat in an armchair.

"Have you ever done a scrying?" Kenntnis asked the girl. Rhiana shook her head. "We take something of Richard's. We drop it into the water, you focus, and search for him."

"Based on this other letter, we know where he's gone," the judge said.

Angela studied the senior Oort from beneath her lashes. There were similarities. Richard had his father's jaw and there was the same slenderness of frame though Robert Oort was taller, perhaps five foot nine or ten. His blue eyes were unusual, with a dark halo around the iris. He had bequeathed that trait to his son. But unlike his son, Robert Oort's eyes didn't look like they ever showed much warmth or humor.

"Yes," said Kenntnis. "But there are fifteen buildings on the property. We don't want to have to search them all."

"Anybody got anything of Richard's?" Angela asked.

They all looked at each other. Weber started for the door. "I'll go over to his apartment. Get something. What kind of something you want?" he asked Kenntnis.

"You've got him," Cross said in a whispering croak, and pointed at Robert Oort. "Blood and bone." They all regarded the judge, whose expression went from careful control to outright confusion.

Kenntnis turned and picked up an elaborate Mogul dagger in a gold and jeweled sheath off an end table. The knife emerged with a soft shush of steel on leather. "Yes, half the DNA is probably more helpful than a psychometric object, no matter how often Richard handled it."

Angela could see the flight response struggling to overcome the judge's cool demeanor. "Are you all insane?"

Weber stepped in. "Look, Your Honor, I know it sounds crazy, but it's all true. I've seen shit that . . . well . . . that's just unbelievable, and will scare the crap out of you. Let them try."

"And if nothing happens?" Oort asked.

"Then your old lady was fucking somebody else when she got knocked up," said Cross. He pointed at Rhiana. "She's good. If Richard's your kid she'll find him."

"Or we're all crazy and you can have us arrested or committed, or whatever," Weber added.

Oort considered for a moment then walked up to the table and held out his hand for the knife. Kenntnis gave a little half bow and handed over the dagger. Oort gripped the jeweled handle, and flexed his left hand several times, preparing himself to cut.

Angela took the knife away from him. "Look, I'm trained to cut flesh with sharp objects. Why don't you let me?"

Oort looked down at her. "You're a scientist, a physician. Do you believe any of this?"

"All of it," Angela said. They looked at each other for a long time; then Oort gave a sharp nod and held his hand out over the silver bowl.

Angela tested the edge on her thumb. It was razor sharp. She weighed the balance of the blade and cut quickly, parting the skin. Drops of blood struck the water, and swirled away in slow eddies, deep red in the center fading to rose at the edges.

"That's probably enough," Cross croaked.

"Get me some bandages and antiseptic," Angela ordered.

"There's a first aid kit in the cabinet in the front bathroom," Kenntnis said to Weber. The cop went.

"Got a penny?" Cross asked Rhiana. She nodded.

Weber returned with a first aid kit. Angela went to work bandaging the judge's hand. Rhiana chanted quietly. The penny flared. The judge jumped.

"Now what?" Rhiana asked, looking from Cross to Kenntnis.

"Since you've never done this before, I'd put it in the water," Cross whispered. "Give yourself all the help you can."

Rhiana dropped in the penny. It spun beneath the water, creating a whirlpool effect. The bloodstained water glowed.

"Now find him," Cross ordered.

Rhiana, her face tight with concentration, held the edges of the bowl between her hands and bent over the water.

Angela gave the bandage a final pat, and edged closer to the table, craning to see. She felt Richard's father standing stiffly behind her, his sharp, nervous breaths ruffling her hair.

The water swirled wildly, then froze. Richard hung limply in the grip of a big man. A smaller man was delivering a brutal beating. Blood ran from a cut over Richard's eye, his nose, his lips. Both eyes were blackened.

"Oh, God, Richard," the judge said.

"Pull back," Cross instructed Rhiana. "Show us the fucking building." The water swirled and stilled again, showing a large stone and timber building.

"Cocky, cocky," murmured Kenntnis. "That's the main house. Okay, let's go."

Kenntnis began issuing orders. "Weber, contact local law enforcement and try to get a warrant and backup. Given Grenier's standing in the community it won't be easy, but try. Angela," he turned to her. "Judging from the scrying, Richard's going to be in bad shape. You need to get him on his feet . . . fast. Have something special, and I don't care if it's legal, in your black bag."

"Okay, then I'm going to have to meet you at the airport." She pointed at Weber. "And wait for me. I need to walk through under the umbrella of your badge."

"Do I want to know what you're getting?" Weber asked.

"No."

Angela turned away to grab her purse and found herself looking at Rhiana as the girl fished the penny out of the bloody water. Rhiana brought the penny up to her lips. There was a spark, and the fire jumped from the penny and vanished between her lips. Angela was dimly aware of Kenntnis telling Cross that as soon as they found Richard, Cross should get the sword into his hands, but it didn't really register because she was watching Rhiana lick the blood delicately off her fingers. It was disturbing, but before she could say anything or even ponder the significance, an altercation had begun.

Angela heard Cross say in a loud, rude and aggrieved voice, "Excuse me!" When she looked over Oort senior and the homeless god each had a hand on the hilt.

"My son left this in *my* keeping." There was a tug of war, then Kenntnis with one of his sly smiles nodded to Cross who, grumbling, released the hilt.

"Excuse me," said Rhiana and there was a catch in her voice. "I need a minute." She ran out of the room.

"I believe you said you have a plane?" the judge said.

Angela, Weber, Kenntnis and Cross exchanged glances.

"Quick learner," grunted the homeless god.

Chapter

TWENTY-NINE

What *the hell are you doing!*" It was Grenier, roaring out his fury. He seized Andresson by the hair and yanked him away from Richard. Bruce released Richard like he was toxic. It didn't even hurt to hit the floor. It was just a relief to lie there.

"I didn't want a mark on him. We were the injured party here, and now you've gone and done this!" Grenier pulled the handkerchief out of his breast pocket and fastidiously wiped his fingers and hand.

Richard realized he was wiping away the grease from Andresson's unwashed hair. He also realized that Grenier was no longer wearing the twin to Richard's now blood-stained shirt. A day had passed, and that gave him hope.

Andresson climbed to his feet, glaring hatred at Grenier. The older man gave him a look of disdain. Which Richard thought took some real guts, because Andresson frankly scared the crap out of him.

"Well, it's too late now," Grenier said. He walked over to Richard, and bending down, began to blot the blood flowing from Richard's nose. Richard felt his nose shift in a way it wasn't supposed to. He whimpered. "Richard, dear boy, please tell Doug how to use the sword."

"No," Richard said thickly.

The butterfly knife came out and opened with a rattle. Andresson lunged toward Richard's eyes. "Tell me or I'll fucking blind you."

Richard cried out, shrinking back. He threw his hands up in front of his face. The point of the knife slashed across his palm. Grenier close-lined Andresson and thrust him back. Andresson swung hard at Grenier, and popped him on the temple. Grenier couldn't seem to credit that *he* had been hit. But Richard had seen the behavior often enough. Violent criminals didn't have an edit button. Andresson wanted to hurt Richard. Grenier had gotten in his way. Andresson had struck out without thought of the consequences. But Bruce knew who paid his salary. He kicked the knife out of the young man's hand, and gathered Andresson into a bear hug.

Grenier's eyes flicked between Richard and Andresson. Richard found himself thinking about the Italian shirt again, and suddenly Richard knew what he was seeing. Even bloodied and bruised, Richard was of Grenier's class.

Andresson was a tool forced upon Grenier because of an accident of genetics.

"Do you really want to give him the sword?" Richard whispered. "He'll have the power to destroy you."

"What choice do I have?" Grenier said in an equally low tone. "You persist in playing the hero."

"Maybe you just haven't offered me the right incentive," Richard said. It was hard to look coy with his eyes swelling shut, but he tried.

"Bring Detective Oort upstairs," Grenier said to Bruce. The big man released Andresson, grabbed Richard under the arms and hauled him to his feet.

"Hey! What the fuck is this shit?" Andresson began.

Grenier walked over until he and Andresson were nose to nose. "Douglas, you are on very thin ice right now. You are proving to be a disappointment, so I suggest you not annoy me."

"Fuck you!" And Andresson flung himself away up the stairs.

"You want me to get him, boss?" Bruce asked.

"He won't go far. Tell Willie to bring him and the hilt to my office. Or just the hilt, if Doug isn't inclined to join us."

⚶

Cross, Rhiana, Oort and Kenntnis waited on the tarmac beside the Gulfstream GV. Kenntnis cocked an eyebrow at the sight of the large duffle Weber carried.

"Guns and body armor," Damon grunted.

"I do hope you had a complacent inspector."

"I went straight to the supervisor. Talked about federal judges, flashed my badge, waved the coroner at them." He patted Angela on the top of her head.

"All right, this is us going now," Cross said and started to climb the stairs into the plane.

The others followed. Kenntnis remained on the tarmac.

Rhiana looked back. Her expression was troubled. "You're not coming with us?"

"No. Cross will help you."

"Look at him! He's barely functioning. He could shatter at any moment. I need someone to help me, advise me."

Kenntnis looked up at Cross, who stood in the door of the plane. The homeless god shrugged. "Do as you please, but I told you I had a bad feeling."

Rhiana gave Kenntnis a tremulous smile. "I didn't think you could be spooked by 'I've got a bad feeling about this.' "

Kenntnis joined them on the plane.

⚕

The pretty, perky assistant provided an ice pack, aspirin and a glass of cognac. She seemed unfazed by Richard's condition. They sat in Grenier's study, an elegant room filled with glass-fronted bookcases, a Queen Anne desk and a number of opaque mirrors. Grenier sat behind the desk, his hands folded serenely on the blotter. To either side of the desk, floor-to-ceiling windows looked out on a grove of pines. A wind had risen and sang with a bass groan in the branches, shaking loose the thin layer of snow that had fallen. Judging by the light and the position of the sun, it was midmorning. Richard realized he had been imprisoned for two nights and a day. His thoughts went to the miles separating New Mexico and Virginia, and where along that route his friends might be. Assuming they were coming, of course.

The cognac stung the cuts in and on his mouth, but Richard forced himself to keep taking small sips. He needed the stimulant.

"So, what is it you want?" Grenier asked.

"I know you've been making inquiries about me," Richard said.

"Please don't state the obvious," Grenier drawled. "You don't have a lot of leeway here."

"Well, I'm assuming you found Drew."

Grenier maintained the bored tone, but Richard saw the subtle tightening of his shoulders. "Yes."

"And he's talked to you?" Richard asked.

"Yes. Your behavior at the funeral got him quite worried. He thought you were going to break your silence. Our offer to prevent that was all the incentive he needed."

"Well, that's what I want. I want to hurt Drew. I want him to go to jail. I want to wreck him financially." Richard shrugged. "If you can make and break presidents, Drew should be easy."

"Simple vengeance? And here I thought you were a little hero," Grenier said.

"Sorry to disappoint," Richard said.

Grenier keyed the intercom on his desk. "Ellie, has Willie found Doug? I want him now."

Richard held up a finger. "No, you start the ball rolling first."

"You make a lot of demands."

Richard forced a smile. He wasn't sure if it came out as cocky or just a grimace. "I'm worth it."

Grenier left the desk. "And by the way. Willie is going to be holding a gun to your head, literally, when you do draw the sword. You will not threaten me. Understood?"

"Understood."

The door opened and Andresson walked in. *No, correct that*, thought Richard, *he's swaggering. That can't be good.* Willie, his brow creased with concern, walked behind him. He was carrying a piece of newspaper. On it were small pieces of gray lucite.

There was a sudden tightness beneath Richard's breast bone.

"Mr. Grenier, Doug was out at the wood pile using the ax on that . . . hilt . . . thing. I'm sorry, sir, I hope this isn't a problem." He laid the paper gingerly on the desk in front of Grenier.

Grenier stared at the shards as if he'd just heard the market had dropped to zero.

Andresson strolled up to the desk, perched on the edge and began cleaning under his nails with the sterling silver letter opener. "Just doing a little experimentation, Mark," Andresson said with a grin. "Is it supposed to . . . uh . . . fall apart like that?" Andresson gave a braying laugh. "He played you, dude, and you never even saw it."

Grenier's hands shot out and gathered the fragments to him. When he finally looked up his expression was so cold and so hateful that Richard began to tremble.

"Let me kill him," Andresson said eagerly.

Sadness and regret closed on the back of Richard's throat. He hadn't thought he would die. He had really thought they would reach him in time.

"No," said Grenier.

"But he played you. He's gotta have the cops coming."

"His associates are coming, but they'll never be able to get help. He's a rogue cop out of his jurisdiction, they have no proof, and I'm Mark Grenier."

"And we want these people here why?" Andresson asked. Richard shared the psychopath's confusion.

"For reasons you don't need to know about. But in the meantime we may as well convince Richard to tell us where he left the sword. It will be useful even after—" Grenier broke off as if suddenly aware he was saying too much. "Where is the sword, Richard?" Richard carefully set aside the ice pack, took one final sip of cognac and remained silent. "Well, all right. Actually I'd just as soon hurt you," Grenier said cheerfully.

Richard briefly wondered if he could take what was coming. *But I manipulated Andresson into beating me, and I endured that.* And he remembered what he'd said at his mother's casket. *I'm not weak.* It sure as hell hadn't been meant for her. He had been the only person in that room who could listen and hear. Richard took a deep breath and met Grenier's eyes. He'd hold on.

⚕

Weber worked the phone from the moment they reached cruising altitude, and had gotten nowhere. No local cop was going to roll into the World Wide Christian Alliance on the say-so of an Albuquerque cop. Now, if he could get them any *evidence* that a police officer had been kidnapped, but of course he mustn't harass Reverend Grenier while obtaining that evidence.

"I won't kid you, this ain't good," Weber said to the group. "If we were rolling up with a line of cop cars there's less chance of Richard getting killed. Flunkies tend to give up when they see cops, and not want to face a capital murder charge, especially not of a police officer."

"What about the FBI?" Kenntnis said. "You're a federal judge."

"What's the allegation?" Oort asked. "I *think* my son's being held prisoner by one of the country's foremost evangelists?"

"Maybe your wife," Weber began. "We could shuck and jive about new evidence that the suicide wasn't—"

"What about nuclear terrorism," Rhiana said quietly. Everyone looked at her. She focused on the judge. "I'm a physics student. I was building a nuclear bomb for them."

"You would testify to this?" the judge asked.

"Yes."

"They'll want to take you into custody," Oort warned.

"They'll have to come to Grenier's compound to do that, won't they?" Rhiana said with a small smile.

"Will they come?" Kenntnis asked. "The current administration has close ties to Grenier."

"And after 9/11 the new FBI motto is CYA," Oort replied. "An abject apology for inconveniencing Mr. Grenier is preferable to congressional hearings over the failure to prevent a nuclear attack. Oh, they'll come."

Since they were only moments away from landing, the call had to wait. As soon as they were wheels down at the private airport in Virginia, Judge Oort turned on his cell phone. It started ringing immediately. He answered as they hustled across the tarmac.

"Hello? . . . Pamela, I can't talk right now. I have to make a call—"

Angela could faintly hear a woman's voice. She sounded stressed, panicked and pissed, but Angela couldn't distinguish any of the words.

Oort stopped walking, and as she watched, the blood flowed out of his face. Weber, Kenntnis, Cross and Rhiana closed ranks around them.

"No, I can't say when I'll be back. You handle things." He listened and two dull pink spots blossomed high on his cheeks. "What I'm doing right now is pretty damn important!" He snapped his phone shut. "That was my daughter, Pamela. My house in Newport has been burgled and set on fire. The fire department managed to save it, but when they got inside they said it had been trashed. Ripped apart." He slowly took the hilt out of his overcoat pocket and gazed down at it thoughtfully.

"Looks like those nuclear terrorists heard you were after them," Weber said. Oort met the cop's gaze and nodded. He opened his phone and called the FBI.

Weber was a rapidly dwindling figure standing next to the big Land Rover. Angela, peering down through the side door of the helicopter, thought he gave them a salute before climbing into the car.

Even with the headphones, the chatter of the blades was a bone-shaking presence.

"Poor guy," Angela said. "One of us should have gone with him."

"The FBI was not going to allow any of us to enter the compound with them. They will take Weber, even if they treat him like shit," Kenntnis replied over the comm.

"Boss," said the pilot, "the FAA is grounding air traffic around our destination."

"Damn, I thought we'd timed this better," Kenntnis grumbled. "So fly real low," he told the pilot.

The man's thumb shot up. "They'll think we're a car."

Angela could see the pilot's teeth, white and straight as he grinned beneath his helmet. She hated him for his cheerfulness. She hated helicopters. She hated Richard for taking this insane risk. She hated Grenier for making it necessary for Richard to take this insane risk.

She touched the rough material and ceramic inserts in her vest, and then the barrel of the shotgun nestled beside her seat; party favors from Weber's duffel bag of mayhem.

They swooped down the road. The bare branches of the trees trembled under the assault from the rotors, and a few withered but stubborn leaves that still clung to them were whirled away in tatters. The few cars they encountered swerved in dismay at the sight of a large helicopter skimming just above their roofs.

Oort senior had been totally silent, but he stirred, leaned into Angela and indicated for her to lift her earphones. She did. He yelled into her ear. "Who is he? How can he arrange all this?"

"Money," said Cross in a perfectly normal tone of voice that somehow carried over the noise of the motor and blades. Oort's eyes widened. "It's the real magic power."

"Boss," came the pilot's voice. "We've got an FBI helicopter closing fast. If I leave the road, I can take us over that ridge and straight down into the compound."

"Do it."

"You're going to have to get me out of the hoosegow later," the pilot warned.

"I'll handle it," Kenntnis said.

Angela forced herself to keep her eyes open, but she was sure the skids scrapped the rough granite outcropping as they roared over the top of the bluff. Suddenly another helicopter drew up next to them. The armored, helmeted and heavily armed figure in the doorway of the chopper made hand signals. The bottom fell out of Angela's stomach as their pilot took them straight down the cliff. Below her spread a beautiful snow-covered valley dotted with blue-green evergreens, bare-branched oaks and chestnut trees. Their pursuer overshot them. Their helicopter buzzed the peaked roof of a three-story house.

There was the sharp, stinging scent of an ammonia ampule being broken beneath his nose. "Richard." The voice was soft and reasonable.

Richard jerked back to awareness. The room spun around him, and slowly things came back into focus. He was tied in a chair. His ankles were tied to the chair legs. His wrists were swollen and blood slick from his maddened attempts to break free. It hadn't taken long for his confinement phobia to kick in. His pants were unzipped and his genitals pulled through the opening in his jockey shorts. His balls ached and burned. He bit back a whimper.

Grenier stood over him. "We searched your father's house. The sword isn't there." He picked up the ends of the frayed electrical wire, and brushed them against each other. Electricity arced. Richard's back arched in anticipation.

"My people were very unhappy. I'm afraid they burned the house down. It's unfortunate about your father. Now, where is the—"

A pulsating roar shook the house. Followed closely by another.

Helicopters, Richard realized. *I did it. I hung on.*

Grenier dropped the wire, walked to the study window and looked out. "Ah, they're here." He suddenly frowned. "Why are there two—"

Willie entered the office. "Boss, the front gate called. The FBI is here."

"This wasn't part of the plan," Grenier said, his frown deepening. "Stay here with him. We still don't have the sword so I'd like to keep him alive, but if it looks like they're about to rescue him—kill him."

Grenier left. Willie pulled out his .45. But he didn't look happy.

The helicopter slalomed between a couple of tall pines kicking up snow. It dropped into a clearing and landed hard.

"Go! Go! Go!" the pilot yelled, and Angela figured he was mentally back in Iraq.

Kenntnis slid the door open and they all piled out. Angela managed to remember her medical bag and the shotgun in the mad scramble.

They scurried in five different directions like quail exploding from a covey, heading into the cover of the trees. The judge stuck close to her, but she soon lost sight of Rhiana, Cross and Kenntnis.

"Great, leave the two ordinary humans on their own," she gasped, as they paused under the low sweeping branches of an evergreen. They stood on a deep carpet of richly scented needles free of any snow.

Oort carefully parted the branches and looked. "The house is only a few hundred feet to our left."

"Let's go." She glanced back at him and couldn't help adding, "Think you'll still be a judge after today?" To her surprise a small smile played across the thin mouth.

They ran for the house.

"Cross and I will scout," Rhiana said. "You wait here. That way if Cross's . . . feeling is right you'll be safe." She pulled out her cell phone. "I'll call you when we're sure it's okay."

Kenntnis hesitated and glanced over at Cross. The three of them were pressed against a thick hedge. "I'd rather stay with you," Kenntnis said.

That show of insecurity, almost fear, shook Rhiana's resolve. But if she didn't go through with it no one would ever believe that she *could* have done it. She wouldn't be the one they had worked so long to create. She fanned the embers of anger and resentment as she said, "We need to know the extent of the magical incursion. Only Cross and I can do that, and if we run into something we don't want to be trying to protect you too."

"Who made you queen? You're not in charge here," Cross snapped.

The embers became flames. She gave the homeless god a thin smile. "Well, you're pretty useless right now, but maybe you can help me a little."

Kenntnis nodded. "She's right. We need to know how far Grenier has gone."

"What about Richard?" Cross asked.

"He's got his father," Kenntnis said.

Rhiana nodded and ignited a penny. It led the way. She didn't look back at Kenntnis.

Willie hadn't raised the gun yet and that gave Richard a small flicker of hope. Also Willie seemed to be smarter and less vicious than Bruce. Richard's throat was so raw from screaming that he wasn't certain he could make a sound. He tried, a squeak emerged. He tried again, harder, for the sound had brought the Willie out of his thoughtful funk.

"Please, it's just . . . worse . . . for . . . you . . . if you . . . kill . . . me." The words were a thread of sound.

Somewhere down the hallway they heard the thunderous roar of a shotgun discharging. Willie's head snapped up. The .45 was lifting.

The door to the study flew open. Richard couldn't turn to look. There was the sound of a pump working, a steel clash that said death was coming.

The chair was solid wood, heavy. With his last strength Richard threw himself hard left. The chair listed, teetered and went over with a crash. At the same time guns bellowed. The exertion had Richard's vision narrowing to a dark tunnel. His last sight was of the front of Willie's chest, exploding into hamburger as the shotgun pellets ripped into him.

※

Rhiana ran through the thin blanket of snow toward the cliff face. The penny danced in the air in front of them.

"What the fuck is it sensing?" Cross panted behind her.

"I don't know. I guess find out when we get there. It's powerful, whatever it is." She darted through a modified shoji gate into a small dell shielded on one side by a spur of gray granite.

"Yeah, no shit, I feel like I'm swimming there's so much magic."

Wind chimes hung from the thin birches around the perimeter. Even though there was no breeze a dissonant overtone hung like a sigh in the cold air.

It was a sculpture garden of glass. Green, gray, red, purple, black, pebbled, swirled and clear monoliths, some with straight angles but more often twisted lines, stood in the dell. In front of some the snow had melted away, revealing matted brown grass, and in front of one a char of ash.

"What the fuck is this?"

Rhiana stopped, turned slowly and stared at him. Cross

looked down to where the snow was melting from beneath her feet.

"Ohhh, fuck."

Rhiana smiled, enjoying his fear. Payback time had finally come. She spread her arms wide. Cross's splinters, his deadly brethren, flowed out of the sculptures and through her body. She became the lens, focusing them into a single ribbon of power. The bands of pulsing color enveloped Cross and forced themselves between his lips. The human form bloated and swelled. The belly burst through the dirty jeans and flannel shirt. Soon it no longer resembled a human, just a mass of viscous colors, twining and coiling.

Cross's wailing fear and rage as his essence was diluted flowed hot into her. As their minds touched, Cross read the full magnitude of what they planned, and fear became despair, unleashing a jolt of power so great that it knocked Rhiana to the ground. The fractals blew apart and vanished. Cross was gone.

A shadow bubbled out of a purple-colored monolith. It resolved into Madoc.

"That was impressive," he said and held out a hand to help her to her feet.

"Thank you."

"All set?" he asked.

"Kenntnis isn't carrying the sword."

He seemed disappointed but not surprised. "You rarely achieve perfection. I do have one tiny question about another deviation from perfection. Why is the FBI at the gate?"

"It made everyone more comfortable. And deaths means more power." But Rhiana couldn't meet his eyes.

"Yes, but the components for the bomb are here," Madoc said.

Rhiana covered her mouth with a hand. "Oh, God, I'm sorry, I didn't think . . . I thought it was just a ruse."

"It was . . . partially. But we had intended to have you detonate it. You know enough now that you wouldn't have been hurt, and we could have ushered in the Armageddon that the humans are so eager to enjoy."

"Isn't that going to happen anyway?" Rhiana asked.

"Yes, but a nuclear bomb exploding in the United States would have started the wars much more quickly. Ah, well, I'm certain the monkeys will find ample reasons to kill each other." Madoc caressed her cheek and twined his hands in her hair, shaking her head from side to side. "So you want your little human alive. That's all right. You shall have him if that's really what you want." He dropped a kiss onto her forehead and laughed. "You can have anything you want if you pull this off."

Chapter

THIRTY

Hands were on his face. Richard remembered them being larger the last time they'd held him. He opened his eyes and looked up into his father's face.

"Papa," he whispered, and his voice broke. "You came. I tried not to tell them I knew you would come it hurt so bad they burned the house I lost my ring." The words ran together.

"Shhh. Quiet. Angela, help me. These cords are embedded in his skin."

Then Angela was there. "Hold the shotgun. Watch the door."

"I don't know how to use a gun," his father said.

"You don't need to. It's a shotgun. Brace your back against a wall and pull the trigger." She pumped it and handed it to the judge. "The shot disperses widely. It will hit anything in the general direction you're pointing."

Kneeling next to Richard, she opened her bag and pulled

out a scalpel. Her hands were cool on his abraded skin. He gazed unbelieving at her gamine face. She cut the cords, but relief soon gave way to new agony as blood flowed back into Richard's hands and feet.

They pulled him to his feet. Richard fumbled at his crotch, trying to tuck himself away. Angela took command, and soon had him zipped. They got him over to a couch and laid him down. Angela broke one of the darkened mirrors with the butt of the shotgun. The judge knelt next to Richard gently chafing his hands.

"You're going to be all right. The FBI is coming. These people are going to pay."

"The sword. Do you have it?"

"Yes."

The judge pulled it out, and Richard clutched it to his chest. Angela hurried over, carrying a large piece of glass. She opened her case and took out a square of folded aluminum foil and a Dairy Queen straw. The foil peeled back to reveal a small folded white paper. Richard and Robert watched, bemused, as she poured out two neat lines of cocaine onto the glass.

She positioned the straw. "Snort," she ordered.

"Are you crazy?" the judge said.

"I'm a cop," Richard said at the same time.

"Analgesic, and upper. He needs both real bad now."

"His mother," the judge began, and laid a hand on hers.

She pushed it away. "Look, if he becomes an addict I'll pay for the Betty Ford Clinic myself, okay? But he won't." She smiled warmly at him. "He's not the type."

Richard considered. Grenier was still free and powerful. He snorted.

A tingling jolt seemed to go straight up into his brain. The sore tissues of his nose went numb. A few seconds later there was a bitter aftertaste on the back of his tongue, but Richard didn't mind. He felt *great*.

Angela held up the glass. "Lick off the last of it. It'll

help your mouth." He obeyed and the same numbness pervaded the cut tissues of his mouth and tongue.

Richard found himself on his feet. "Yeah. Okay. This is good."

✤

"Kenntnis, come quickly." Rhiana's voice crackled on a bad cell connection. "We've found something, but we don't understand it."

"Where are you?"

"At the base of the cliff. We need—*It's trying to get Cross!*"

The phone went dead.

Kenntnis considered retreat, but Cross was irreplaceable.

✤

Richard, Angela and Robert reacted to the faint, distant crack and chatter of gunfire.

"The cavalry," Robert said.

Richard couldn't help it; he glanced over at Angela. She understood the unspoken question. "With Weber leading the charge," she said, and grinned.

They listened to the increasing tempo of gunfire. "And meeting some opposition from the sound of it," the judge said, frowning. "Idiots. Who resists the FBI?"

"Desperate or really confident people. Either way, we should get the hell out of here," Angela said.

"You go ahead," Richard said. "I need to find Grenier and use the sword on him." Angela put her hands on her hips and glared at him. "It's going to be a lot harder later," Richard warned.

Seeing the sense in what he had said, Angela nodded and turned to gather up her medical bag. Richard saw her eyes widen in horror.

"*Richard!*" She grabbed him and spun him around.

Now he could see what had so frightened her. Grenier stood in the door of the study. A fountain of light cascaded off the folded reading glasses that he held in his right hand.

The light splashed across Angela's booted feet. The intricate leaves and vines on the thick oriental carpet writhed and shot up out of the nap, twisting themselves around her body.

Robert cried out in shock and alarm as the vines wrapped tightly around Angela's neck, forced themselves up her nose and down her throat. Guttural noises erupted from Angela. If she hadn't moved him, it would have been Richard choking instead.

The entire rug was seething now. The judge, with admirable presence of mind, jumped up onto the desk, but it was only a momentary respite. The vines pursued.

The vines thrust into every orifice of Willie's body, and seemed to find nourishment in the dead flesh. They grew even more quickly there.

Richard leaped away from Angela's clawing hands. Her eyes showed mute desperation. He nearly fell as the vines tangled around his feet.

Richard drew the sword. The overtones climbed beyond human hearing, then began again with a bass groan and a rapidly ascending scale. He swept the star-swirling blade across the vines at his feet. They screamed and liquefied into a foul-smelling black ooze.

Angela lay on the heaving, writhing rug. Her body was almost invisible beneath the leaves and vines.

"*All of you die!*" Richard yelled as he thrust the point of the sword deep into the rug where the spell had first landed. They did.

He heard his father's careful precise voice, now carrying an uncontrollable quaver. ". . . Hallowed be thy Name. Thy Kingdom come—"

"Shut up, sir! Don't call them. There are openings

everywhere." Richard thrust the sword at one of the opaque mirrors.

Richard turned, and he and Grenier measured each other across half a room and an intellectual divide a universe wide.

"There's so much magic flowing we could drown in it," Grenier said. "And I can throw spells until whatever you took wears off. And of course you have to protect *them*." He jerked his head toward Angela, lying very still on the rug, and Robert perched on the desk. "That's the problem with being a hero."

Richard glanced over toward the abandoned shotgun. Grenier caught the look, and fire arced, struck the metal and the barrel melted. Richard cringed, waiting for the shells to explode, but amazingly they didn't. Grenier laughed and advanced a few steps into the study. They circled each other warily.

"Papa, take Angela. Leave by the window," Richard called.

Fire flared in the lenses of the glasses. The windows vanished as the walls grew closed, obliterating doorway and windows. The stench from the dead vines made Richard's gut heave. Grenier flexed his hands, grinning wildly.

It's like he's drunk, Richard thought. *What is going on? It's supposed to take enormous power to do this much magic, and he's unfazed.*

But there was no more time to ponder the problem. The lenses of the glasses were pulsing with changing colors. Richard decided to try to parry the attack rather than attacking the result of the spell. He dropped his weight, knees bent, balance evenly divided between his feet. He had fenced epee in college. The sword was more like a rapier and heavier. Richard hoped the high from the cocaine would last long enough.

Grenier's hand shot out, releasing a spell. Richard lunged and parried high left. The fire vanished into the blade, but it didn't blow back onto Grenier the way it had with Delay in the church, perhaps because this was no young apprentice but a master of sorcery, or perhaps because there was so much magic present, as Grenier had said.

Richard rushed Grenier, a swift advance ending in a long, deep groin-pulling lunge. Grenier grabbed a book off a small table and slapped the point of the sword aside. Richard pushed back onto his back leg. Grenier threw the book into his face. Richard knocked it aside with his right hand. Fire flew. Toward the judge this time. Richard parried.

Richard weighed the options. An all-out attack on Grenier, and hope he could neutralize him before the sorcerer landed a spell on Angela or his father? Or fight defensively, and try to protect them? Richard tried to reach a wall to neutralize the magic that closed the cage. If the judge and Angela were free Richard could concentrate on Grenier. The minister sensed his intent, and pushed hard, keeping Richard from ever reaching the blank walls.

They circled each other, exchanging feints, waiting for the other to attack. The attacks came in a flurry of fire and night. Golden light arced and soared across the room, and was eaten by the darkness of the sword. Once Richard missed and the spell reached the glass-fronted bookcases. Glass wasps swarmed out with an eerie chiming buzz, and headed for his father. Running full-out, Richard managed to bring the sword through them in an overhand cut. He couldn't control his momentum and slammed into the desk.

Robert grabbed Richard's shoulders, helped steady him and got him turned around. His father's lips were against his ear.

"Try to maneuver him over here," the judge whispered.

Richard gave an almost imperceptible nod and, bouncing lightly on the balls of his feet, advanced on Grenier.

Kenntnis entered the dell. The chimes stirred and echoed in one perfect chord, but his effect ended with the bells. The glass sculptures were stained red in the light of the setting sun. In the distance he could hear the real-world sounds of a very real firefight going on by the gate. Kenntnis realized he didn't recognize any of the artists in the garden, and a cold hollow formed at his core.

Rhiana stood on a small knoll in the center of the sculpture garden. Pennies spun at her feet, creating the illusion she stood in the midst of a fire. Her right hand was outstretched. Balanced on her palm was a tiny speck of darkness.

Kenntnis recognized the creature who sat on one of the smaller sculptures watching.

Oh, Richard, now would be a good time for "in the nick of time."

Rhiana flung the darkness into the air, crying out the spell. Kenntnis felt a cold more profound than any he'd experienced in the vast emptiness between the galaxies. He sensed the bosonic atoms falling into the lowest possible quantum state. It was a stunning blending of physics and magic, and he was powerless, trapped between the two forces. The matter that shaped his human body blasted into pieces. Icy claws settled into him, holding him like a butterfly on a pin. The spinning darkness released by Rhiana fell over his glittering form and swept him up in the whirlwind. Time slowed. The world became a smear and a blur as human time raced forward . . . and . . . he . . . froze. . . .

Parts of his beaten body were starting to make their presence known. Richard could feel sweat stinging in the cuts on his face and mouth. His abused testicles hated it every time he lunged, and his quads popped each time he pushed back out of the lunge. His breath was loud in his own ears.

Suddenly Grenier's reading glasses began to blaze constantly. It distracted even their owner. Grenier stared down at them.

"She did it," Grenier said in a fierce whisper.

That can't be good, thought Richard, and used Grenier's momentary inattention to rush him.

Richard came in slightly to the left. It forced Grenier to half-turn and step closer to the fallen chair, the desk and Willie's body.

The swirl of stars around the sword broadened and widened until Richard was looking through a hazy shield of stars at his foe. Out of the corner of his eye, Richard saw his father move. Hunching, Robert circled around the end of the desk, reached down and grabbed. The judge came up holding the frayed ends of an electrical wire.

Richard flung himself forward in a wild attack to keep Grenier focusing on him. Robert rushed forward, and pressed the exposed wires onto the back of Grenier's neck. The man screamed, his back arching.

Richard's parry caught the spell on the edge of his blade. He swept the sword back, spinning on his back foot as he did so, and brought the blade across Grenier's exposed right wrist. The hand dropped onto the sticky floor. The glasses went dark. Blood fountained from the severed stump. Grenier fell onto the floor and went into a violent seizure.

"Get a tourniquet on him," Richard ordered.

"Let him bleed. Demon," spat the judge.

"No. I want him alive, in jail, and robbed of his power."

Robert's normal icy control reasserted itself. He nodded, pulled off his necktie, put a knee in Grenier's chest to control him, and tied off the gushing arm.

Richard touched the wall. The windows returned.

He broke out several mullions with the hilt of the sword

and briefly breathed in the cold, pine-scented air, then he whirled, ran to Angela, and gathered her into his arms.

"Oh, Angie, sweetie." He felt beneath her jaw for a pulse. "Be all right. Be all right." He found it, but it was faint and jumping.

Richard pulled Angela's cell phone out of her pocket. He hit the call list and as expected, found Weber. He dialed.

"Yeah?!" came the sharp, beloved voice.

"Where are you?"

"Coming to rescue you, Rhode Island. You are the biggest ass—"

"Damon, we need a medic and quick. It's Angela. And Grenier could use help too."

"What did you do to him?"

"Cut off his hand."

"Great, how do I explain *that* to the FBI? Hang tough. We'll be there soon."

The connection was broken. Richard sat holding Angela. Exhaustion edged forward like the incoming tide. He felt Robert's hand on his shoulder.

Richard looked up. "Papa, thank you. You saved us."

"No, I helped."

They fell silent.

"It's yes," Robert said.

Richard shook himself out of his haze. "What?"

"The answer to your question. It's yes."

Embarrassed, the judge walked away. He skirted Willie's half-decayed corpse, perforated with holes so both bone and viscera showed. Richard wondered how he would explain *that* to the feds. His father bent down briefly then went to the window to watch for the FBI.

Richard held Angela and softly rocked her. He wondered where Kenntnis was. It was so unlike him not to be here. His father's voice broke though his reverie.

"Richard, I think you better come look at this, and tell me what it means."

ᏪᏅ

Richard felt like a brute for leaving her, but Weber and rescue were coming, and this couldn't wait. What Robert had seen through the window were bands of light thrusting into the sky off to their left along the cliff face. Where the light touched the rock it looked plastic and it seemed to be breathing.

Richard carried the drawn sword. Ahead of them was a crooked shoji gate. For some reason it felt disturbing.

"Let's not walk under that," Richard said.

He and Robert left the gravel path and walked in the snow. They passed close to a tree on whose bare branches hung a number of steel, glass and ceramic wind chimes. They had all been fused into undifferentiated lumps.

Glass sculptures glowed dark orange, red, purple, sick green, and threw their light into the night sky. The temperature was dropping, frosting the top of the snow with ice crystals that crunched beneath the soles of their shoes. There was a strange metallic smell in the air.

In the midst of the colored glass forms, a clear glass piece wove a serpentine shape across the snow. It was reminiscent of the sand eddies left in ancient sea beds by long dry waves. It stood about six feet tall and ten feet long.

At the heart of the clear glass there was a core of spinning darkness. Orbiting the darkness was a glitter of silver bright lights dancing through a swirling golden mist. It looked like someone had trapped a dust devil comprised of diamonds and gold dust. Tendrils of light were being dragged into the darkness.

Richard walked around the clear glass piece and retreated with a yelp of pain. He had never felt such profound cold. He looked down at the patch of frostbite across the back of his hand.

Next he approached the pulsing cliff. *Picture it closed.* But it was an enormous rip in reality, much larger than anything he'd faced before. He struggled, but the tear continued to solidify, the opening widening. Pillars began to form on the sides, and there was the suggestion of an arch in the rough stone of the cliff face. Realizing this was a gate, Richard retreated, exhausted.

A hand fell on his shoulder. "Richard," came his father's voice, and it held that uncertain quaver he had heard in Grenier's office.

Richard turned to find Rhiana regarding him from in front of a dark purple sculpture. She was dressed in a form-hugging dress that seemed constructed of snowflakes and spiderweb. Diamond pins glittered in her long hair, which floated up behind her and coiled around her arms and neck in defiance of the slight breeze.

"You can't close it. Not with Kenntnis gone."

"Rhiana, what have you done?" Richard asked, struggling for calm.

"I chose."

Richard held out a hand toward Rhiana. "And I choose you. Cross wanted to destroy you. I told Kenntnis I would never allow that."

"So, choose me now. I'll protect you." She held out her hand to him.

A black and purple shadow boiled out of the monolith. Robert gasped and his grip on Richard's shoulder tightened. The colors transformed into a sharp-faced man. He came up behind Rhiana, laid a hand on her shoulder, and smiled at Richard; an expression both triumphant and mocking.

"You're human, Rhiana, at least part. Don't do this," Richard pleaded.

She laid her hand over the man's. "And this part is better. I belong someplace, Richard."

"You belong to both. Why reject us?"

"Because they appreciate me. I've done something none of them could ever do. I blended magic and physics. You just wanted to use me, use my power to ultimately destroy my power. Why would I do that?"

"Because they're—"

"Evil?" Rhiana supplied. "People throw that word around too easily. And besides, we don't see it that way. Everyone's a hero in their own little personal drama. Don't be a dead hero, Richard. Come with me. I'll protect you," she said again. Richard shook his head. "You can't stand against us, not with Kenntnis trapped. He's ours. Your world is ours." She gestured at the clear glass sculpture.

Richard stared in shock at the gold and diamond swirl in the glass. Tried to square that with the huge man who had dominated his life for the past months. He crept toward the glass, but had to retreat from the unrelenting cold. Nothing human could survive it.

"You can't get close enough to use the sword. Absolute zero gives you slow glass. Slow glass traps light. That's all Kenntnis is . . . was," Rhiana said.

"Hush!" the man said. "You give them too much." Power flowed out of his hand and into Rhiana's shoulder. They began to dissolve into pulsing colors, black and purple, and vanished back through the purple glass sculpture.

"*Richard!*"

It was Weber followed by two big men. One was white, the other African-American. They all wore body armor. The two men had FBI jackets over their flak jackets. They were all running through the shoji gate.

"Damon, *don't!*" Richard yelled.

Weber and the African-American agent made it through safely, but something black and glistening, as if it had been dipped in oil, came undulating out of the crosspiece of the gate, and seized the other agent.

He was pulled, kicking and screaming into the air. We-

ber and the other FBI agent whirled, and shot. Intead of
the usual roar, the gun fire was a faint pop, and then their
guns wouldn't fire. The touch of dark magic damped the
ability of gunpowder to ignite. The captured agent's screams
echoed around the dell.

Richard charged, and barreled between Weber and the
African-American agent, knocking them off balance. He
was beneath the shoji gate. There didn't seem to be enough
air, and what was there was tainted with a harsh metallic
smell that was almost a taste. Richard knew he stood between worlds, and he had very little time. Swinging the
sword up, he managed to touch the Old One. A keening,
howling wail began. The agent fell heavily to the ground.

Weber and the black agent rushed in and dragged the
man away. Richard drew the sword across the uprights of
the gate. *Picture it closed.* This time it worked, because it
was a tear, not like the structure that was being constructed
on the far side of the dell. The gate collapsed in a jumble
of splintered wood. Richard retreated, the point of the
sword flicking from side to side. It was less a conscious
thought than a sense that he had to weave a net of protection around the humans.

The agent was administering CPR to his fallen comrade.
While he compressed the chest he kept yelling, *"What the
fuck is going on? What the fuck was that? What the fuck?"*

Weber grabbed Richard's shoulder. All around them the
glass sculptures were coiling with light. The enormous
gate in the cliff was almost complete.

"Can you stop this?" Weber demanded.

"No," Richard admitted.

"Then we've got to get out of here."

Richard pointed at the clear glass form. "That's Kenntnis. If we leave him . . ." He shrugged helplessly. "I don't
know how we ever get back."

"We worry about that later. Because if we don't get out

of here we're not going to get to worry about anything ever again. Let's *go*!"

His father grabbed Richard by the shoulders and gave him a shake. "He's right."

Richard looked around and realized that the five human men were in a circle of sanity. Beneath their feet was scuffed and dirt-stained snow and winter grass. Just beyond them was madness. Colors whirled and coiled. Viscous shadows crawled across undulating ground.

"Carry him," Richard ordered and pointed at the fallen agent. "Stay together."

Step by step they retreated from the dell. Fortunately the madness didn't follow. Beyond the ruins of the shoji gate the world was once again the world, familiar and safe.

But for how long? Richard wondered.

Chapter
THIRTY-ONE

Richard gave the nurses at the station a nervous wave as he walked past. The small package of Oreos weighed like a guilty conscience in his coat pocket. He had promised Angela cookies. He figured she deserved them after having her stomach pumped. He carried a carton of milk openly. He didn't think they would object to that.

The nurses gave him smiles that were almost grimaces. Angela was making herself nicely hated by the medical and nursing staff of Walter Reed. That meant she was probably ready to be discharged, and everyone, friends and staff alike, were fervently hoping that would occur today.

To his relief Richard avoided a stay in the hospital. They had set and packed his broken nose, clipped shut the cut over his right eye, bandaged his wrists and ankles, and given him a salve for his burns.

Then he belonged to the FBI. Fortunately the three of them, Richard, Weber and the judge, had had time to square their stories before the interrogations began.

They had questioned him for ten hours the first day and seven on the second. Richard had stuck to his story—he had come to Virginia to arrest Doug Andresson. No, he didn't know why his father had said there was a nuclear bomb on the premises. Maybe the judge had just said that to get help in rescuing his son. No, Richard didn't know what had happened to the girl who said she'd been recruited to build the bomb. No, he didn't know why Reverend Grenier had imprisoned and tortured him.

Fortunately Richard had sheathed the sword before the authorities found them. The FBI was baffled by the twisting hilt, but it never occurred to them that it was a weapon. When asked about it Richard had said it was an early Christmas present from his father. Just an objet d'art.

What saved them from closer scrutiny was Robert's status as a Federal Court judge, the fact that Richard and Weber were cops. Though local police were often viewed as lowly scum by the federal agents, they were still law enforcement officers. Weber had gone in with the strike team, and it was pretty damn clear that Richard had been a victim, and the judge had called in a few political favors from the Rhode Island senators.

Richard also suspected that the authorities were far more concerned with the dimensional gateway that had appeared in rural Virginia, though they never brought it up to him. They had been well away from the garden before the rest of the FBI strike team found them. Richard thought the black agent would have told them of his presence in the sculpture garden. Apparently he hadn't.

Richard made the turn toward Angela's room. A big

man was waiting for him, leaning against a wall. Richard recognized the African-American agent from the dell. The man stepped out and blocked Richard's way.

"Agent."

"Bob Franklin," he said, and held out his hand.

Richard shook it cautiously then asked, "I thought we were done with the questioning?"

"I'm not here . . . officially," Franklin said. His expression was blank, his dark brown eyes giving away nothing.

"Then maybe you would be willing to answer a few of *my* questions?" Richard suggested.

"No, but I will give you a heads-up."

"About what?" Richard asked.

"Why don't we go in here?" The agent gestured at the empty visitor's room.

The man shut the door. "So, Reverend Grenier says that you broke into his compound and attacked him. That you cut off his hand with a sword. Of course nobody can find a sword." The agent stared down at Richard.

"But, of course, you know differently," Richard said softly.

"Yeah, I do, but I haven't said anything."

"I had been wondering why you hadn't."

"Because I saw the monsters in that garden, but my superiors won't let me talk about that, not to anyone. And my partner, Sam, is catatonic in the psych ward, and since I can't tell the docs what he saw, about that . . . thing that grabbed him, they can't do shit for him."

"What do you want from me?" Richard asked.

"You seemed to understand what was going on there. I thought maybe you might be able to help," Franklin said.

Richard started to shake his head; then an almost forgotten conversation came back. *When it's drawn it makes people sane.* Richard heard Kenntnis's rumbling bass and was suddenly aware of the hilt resting in its holster at the small of his back. He also faced once more the grief and fear that accompanied the loss of his mentor.

"No promises," Richard said. "But I might be able to help. Can you get us in to see him?"

"Watch me." And the agent grinned like a happy wolf, his teeth white in his dark face.

Sam Marten sat in a chair in his small room. His chest rose and fell beneath the thin hospital gown. The sour smell of unwashed human hung in the tiny room. His brown gray-tipped hair hung in lank strands across his forehead. Occasionally his eyes blinked. Nothing else marked him as alive and human.

"His daughter, Samantha, is frantic. She's in the Bureau too," Franklin said as they looked down at the man.

Richard's eyes scanned the walls and ceiling. "No cameras," he said.

"No."

"Shield me in case someone looks through the window." Richard indicated the small glass pane in the door. Franklin placed his bulk between Richard and the door.

Richard drew the sword. Marten's head slowly turned toward the source of the sound.

"Jesus," Franklin breathed.

Richard gently touched the agent on the shoulder with the flat of the sword as if he were knighting him. Marten cried out in pain and shuddered. His eyes closed. When he opened them an intelligent presence had returned.

"Make them go away," he whispered through dry, chapped lips.

Richard rested his hand briefly on the man's shoulder. "I'll try."

"Sam," Franklin said, and pushing past Richard he gripped his partner's hand.

Sheathing the sword, Richard returned it to its holster and stepped back. After a moment Franklin looked back at him.

"Those questions you had. . . . What do you want to know?"

". . . they've thrown a cordon of National Guard around the garden, but they keep retreating a few feet each day. If they don't, the soldiers start hallucinating. That's how Franklin put it. They'll suddenly shoot each other or themselves, or walk off the cliff because they think they can fly, become catatonic. This is wrapped in so much secrecy that Franklin thinks he'd be sent to Gitmo if they ever found out he told me."

Richard sat cross-legged on the foot of Angela's bed. Cookie crumbs were scattered across the sheet. Angela had a milk mustache, and with her tumbled curls looked like a wicked urchin. Bouquets of roses lined the window ledge. Since Richard had been locked up with the FBI and hadn't been able to visit he'd arranged to have bouquets delivered three times a day.

His father stood near the door and occasionally peeked out into the hall. Weber sprawled in an armchair.

"And what do we think this means?" the judge asked, coming over to the bed to look down at his son.

"I think it has to do with Kenntnis. Rhiana bound Prometheus. Who knows what the effect will be?"

"What about Cross?" Angela asked. "He might be able to explain it to us." Her voice was hoarse and husky from a throat abused by the attacking vines and the stomach pump.

"I think we have to presume he's gone," Richard said. "There hasn't been any sign of him, and I have to believe he'd contact us."

"So, what happens to us?" Weber asked. "Last thing I

heard from my interviewers was 'Don't leave the area.' Are we stuck here forever, or are we on our way to being 'detainees'?"

"Franklin says we've been cleared," Richard answered. "Because the lie you told them actually turned out to be true. They found components for a nuclear bomb in one of the buildings."

Weber shook his head. "Those dumb bastards."

"No," the judge corrected. "Overconfident and supremely arrogant."

"Whatever the motivation it still comes out as dumb, *Que, no?*" Weber added in Spanish.

Robert Oort nodded. "Point."

"And falling under the *'my, isn't this ironic'* category, there's the little matter of a piece of paper with traces of cocaine on it found in Grenier's office." Richard chuckled. "Franklin said he couldn't tell which one bothered his superiors more, the bomb, the dope or the monsters."

Weber gave one of his sharp single cracks of laughter. Angela started to laugh, then abruptly stopped.

"Oh, shit, my fingerprints are all over that paper."

The judge swept the crumbs off the top sheet and into the palm of his hand. "I don't think you have to worry about a drug charge. I expect we're all going to become very big, very public heroes, very soon."

Weber and Angela stared at the older man, who stood serenely brushing the crumbs into the trash can. Their faces were a study in confusion. Richard suspected his expression mirrored theirs.

"I beg your pardon, sir?"

"Consider," said Robert in his best "from the bench" tone. "The government has evidence of a plot to construct an atomic bomb. They also have a hole in reality, disgorging demons—"

"Monsters," Richard corrected.

"Whatever, it doesn't matter what you call them. This

area of chaos is expanding every day, and driving soldiers mad. Which do you think is going to be more terrifying to the American people? The press knows something occurred at the WWCA compound. The authorities have to give them something."

Richard whistled. "And a nuclear bomb is a hell of a smoke screen for the real threat."

"Watch your language," his father said automatically.

"So, Grenier is screwed, blued and tattooed," Weber said.

"No, Grenier will get off. It will take time, but he has cash, connections and clout. He'll blame it all on out-of-control underlings," Robert said.

"Bummer," Weber said.

"I know we ought to stay close, and try to free Kenntnis," Angela said. "But . . ." She shivered. Richard took hold of her foot beneath the covers and gave it a comforting squeeze. "I want to get as far away from that place as possible."

"Maybe I ought to go to the authorities. Tell them what I know. Offer to help," Richard said.

"Not a bad idea," Weber mused, and Angela nodded.

Resistance came from an unexpected source. "No," said the judge. "I think you need to be free to respond to what, I think, is going to be a constantly changing, and probably ever more dangerous, situation. The government will lock you up tight, send that weapon off to the DOD to be researched, and in general fiddle while the world goes to Hell."

"Watch your language," Richard said, and gave his father a quick smile.

"I use the word in the literal, not the profane sense," Robert shot back, and the creases at the side of his mouth deepened briefly.

"Okay, but where's our headquarters while we try to save the world?" Weber asked.

"My house is, at present, uninhabitable," Robert said.

Richard's mind suddenly filled with the scent of piñon fires and the chest-aching bite of clean winter air, vistas of blue-gray mountains against turquoise skies.

"New Mexico," he said.

"Why?" his father asked.

"Kenntnis was there. Of all the places in the world he could have lived he chose New Mexico. There must have been reasons."

"It is a place where science and magic rub close," Angela mused. "On the one hand you've got Los Alamos and the Bell Lab at Kirtland Air Force Base, and White Sands missile range and space port, and the Santa Fe Institute, and on the other you've got sacred tortillas and kachinas, and crystal healers, and skinwalkers, and Tarot readers, and past life gurus, and mediums—"

"Whoa, whoa, whoa, I'm starting to feel totally outnumbered," Weber groaned.

"And the Lumina," Richard said softly. "Don't forget us."

✳

Ortiz stared, amazed, at Richard standing in the doorway of his office. "Oort, my God, we've been hearing about what happened. I had no idea that bombing at Lumina was part of a terrorist plot. You should have told me, but hell, I can't argue with the result. Good job. No, more than that, great job."

"Thank you, Captain."

"But what are you doing back here? I thought you'd stay out east with your family through Christmas," Ortiz said.

"No, sir. By the way, I don't mind working tomorrow. If you can use the help."

"Can I ever. Nobody wants to work Christmas Day." Ortiz stood and held out his hand. "Welcome back. Glad to have you."

They shook. "Thank you, sir."

Richard went into the bullpen. Snyder was staring in amazement at Weber, who was unpacking a box and arranging mementos and personal items on his desk. Snyder's head snapped around when he heard Richard's footfalls.

"You're back," Snyder said, and it wasn't clear which of the two men he was addressing.

Both Weber and Richard looked at him and said together, "Yes."

Richard sat down on the edge of Synder's desk. "And Dale," Richard said, leaning in. "I'm here to stay."

Snyder met Richard's cool, level gaze, and dropped his eyes down to the report he held. "Yeah, well, welcome back," he concluded weakly.

The few other detectives present had been watching with the interest a wolf pack shows in a clash for leadership. Now they came over, and offered hellos, expressed curiosity and congratulations about the events in Virginia, and offered best wishes for the season.

A few hours later Richard's phone rang. The man on the other end of the line was a lawyer. After Richard hung up, he called his father.

⚜

George Gold was a short, round man with a heavy mane of dark hair that brushed the top of his collar. Judging by the creases in his fat cheeks and the crow's feet surrounding his brown eyes, he was a man who smiled a lot. He wasn't smiling now.

They were in Kenntnis's office. The wide expanse of the granite desk held legal documents, and stacks of balance sheets and account books. Richard stood staring almost blindly around the room while the judge perused the documents.

"Mr. Kenntnis had a system whereby he would contact us every twenty-four hours. If that contact ever failed to occur, certain events followed. That contact ended four days ago. We had a little trouble contacting you initially, detective, and I didn't want to draw the attention of the press. At any rate, I apologize for the delay," Gold said.

Richard waved off the apology. "You understand that according to Mr. Kenntnis's instructions, control of Lumina Enterprises, all assets and operations, has been granted to you under a Durable Power of Attorney until such time as Mr. Kenntnis should return or be declared legally dead."

Richard scrubbed his hands across his face, and winced when he inadvertently touched his nose. Panic fluttered in his belly, and he couldn't seem to get control of his whirling thoughts. The only coherent thing he knew was, *I can't do this!*

"It's all in order," the judge said, looking up from the paper he was reading.

Gold pulled out an engraved card case, fished out a card, and offered it to Richard. "If you need anything, don't hesitate to call." The heavy door closed behind the lawyer.

Robert began examining the balance sheets. Richard trailed his hands along the edge of the desk, moved to the chair, sat down.

The judge looked up at him over the top of his reading glasses. "This company appears to be worth more than Microsoft."

"Oh, God." Richard dropped his face into his hands. "I can't even manage to balance my checkbook. Will you help me?" He looked up at his father, and felt ice forming in his belly at his presumption. He quickly backpedaled. "Sorry, sir, you have your own work, I can't expect—"

"Richard." He jumped at the peremptory tone in his father's voice. "I intend to resign from the bench. After what I've seen and experienced, hearing legal cases doesn't seem very relevant right now. As Detective Weber said, we have a world to save." The judge paused and busied himself with tapping straight the pages of the balance sheet he'd been reading. "And I have children and a grandson to protect. So, yes, I will help you. Here is my first piece of advice—get a new desk. You look all of twelve behind that monolith." There was again that deepening of the creases in his father's cheeks.

Richard smiled wanly back. He looked down at the flecks of gold in the granite, and remembered the glittering lights in Kenntnis's dark eyes.

The pressure from his father's hand on his shoulder made him look up. "I don't know why I waited, but now seems the right time." Robert reached into his pocket. When he opened his fingers the gold signet ring glinted on his palm.

"The family ring!" Richard reached out for it, then pulled his hand back. "Where did you . . . How did you . . ."

"Apparently those demon weeds only had a taste for flesh and fabric. It was on the floor next to the body." Robert took Richard's hand in his and slipped the ring onto his finger.

They were all staying at Angela's condo. It made sense. Richard had a one-bedroom apartment, and her townhouse had three bedrooms. Richard knew he had the right to the penthouse at Lumina headquarters, but he couldn't bring himself to make the move. Not yet. It felt too much like trespassing.

The only light came from the flames of the candles. The small votives sat in small triangular glass holders in gemlike colors. Flames licked across the wood in the kiva fireplace. The room was redolent with the scent of posole, piñon, and the anise in the *biscochitos*. The judge had made great-grandfather Oort's homemade eggnog. It was a big hit with Angela and Damon. Richard contented himself with a glass of milk.

Outside, the cul-de-sac was dark except for the flicker

of candles in the luminarias. The next-door neighbors had bowed to community pressure and removed the electric luminarias. Someone had even managed to get the city to turn off the streetlights for this one night.

The little sacks glowed with a golden light, but it was diffuse, softened by the snow that had begun falling. A thin layer already covered the sidewalks and yards. The luminarias wouldn't last much longer.

It was just the four of them. Amelia had refused to disrupt her family on such short notice and on the eve of Christmas. She seemed piqued that the judge had chosen New Mexico over Boston. Pamela had also refused, but surprised Richard by saying she would come west for New Year's. The prospect left him with more than a few misgivings.

Weber shook back his cuff and looked at his watch. "Shit, it's one o'clock in the morning. Merry fucking Christmas everybody."

"Happy birthday," the judge said to Richard.

"No shit," Weber said.

"Yes, I'm afraid so," Richard responded.

Weber pushed up out of the armchair. "I better head home. I've got to stop by Carol's for a little while tomorrow," referring to his wife.

"So things are looking up for the two of you?" Richard asked, and vowed to be pleased with the answer, whatever it might be.

"Nah. I just became momentarily more attractive because I've been interviewed on the *Today* show. She'll decide I'm the same old asshole soon enough."

"Don't tear yourself down," said Angela. She was prone on the couch with her head resting in Richard's lap and her feet tucked under a knitted comforter.

There was a soft knock on the front door. They all froze, then exchanged glances.

"You expecting anybody?" Weber asked.

Angela shook her head. "Certainly not at this hour."

She disentangled her feet from the comforter. It slid off the sofa with a whisper. Richard helped her up.

Weber unclipped his holster and drew his gun. Richard pulled the hilt of the sword free. He kept his hand in position to draw it as they moved cautiously to the door.

"Who is it?" Angela called.

"It's me," came a familiar, aggrieved voice. "Somebody threw away my box."

But Richard had been fooled before. He looked to his father. Robert took Angela by the arms and pulled her back into the living room. Richard drew the sword. The chords echoed in the barrel vault. Nodded to Damon. Weber yanked open the door. But it was Cross. Their Cross, and he looked better than he had in weeks.

"Hey," he said. "Thanks for putting a light in the window." He jerked a thumb back over his shoulder, indicating the luminarias. "So to speak."

"Get in here!" Richard ordered.

"So what happened after I got splintered?" the Old One asked, and while they told him, he ate his way through three bowls of posole, five butter-drenched tortillas, a dozen cookies, and four cups of eggnog.

He sat on the banco near the kiva fireplace, leaned back against warm plaster, and gave a huge belch. Angela picked up the tray.

"Fortified enough to answer a few questions?" Richard asked.

"Shoot."

"What happens with Kenntnis captured?" Richard continued.

"I'm not exactly sure. He's reason and order incarnate. It's why he couldn't use the sword. He made it. It's a part of him, but too much order is just as bad as too much chaos."

"So the sword is weakened?" Richard asked.

"Obviously, because they're building gates. There's a big one breaking through in Jerusalem, another in India, and I didn't look any further. I wanted to get back to you."

"So, what happens to our world? To reality as we know it?" the judge asked.

Cross shrugged. "I'm not sure. I guess we all find out together." His lips parted, showing teeth in a humorless grin. "Won't that be exciting?"

"Kenntnis told me at our first meeting that the Lumina's weapons are science, technology and rational thought. The Old Ones can't change scientific principles, and technology exists, but they can affect our ability to reason," Richard said.

"So the world goes nuts?" Weber asked.

"Or at least the people in it," Richard answered.

"Which would fit with what the FBI agent told you about the soldiers," his father said.

"I still can't believe Rhiana betrayed us," Angela said sadly.

Richard closed his eyes briefly, remembering all the times he'd mishandled the girl. "It's my fault."

Cross made a rude noise. "Yeah, I figured we'd get around to you feeling guilty sooner or later. Kenntnis said you have a bad habit of trying to take responsibility for every fucking thing. Get over it. And hey, ichor is thicker than water." Angela threw a *biscochito* at him. It bounced off the Old One's nose and fell onto his chest, leaving a trail of sugar crystals. He snatched it up and ate it in a single bite.

Cross looked at Richard with a bright-eyed glance and asked, "So, what do we do now, *jefe*?"

"I sort of hoped that you'd tell me."

"You're the head of the Lumina."

They were all looking at him . . . *to* him. Cross, the vessel holding the faith, hope and charity of millions of believers. Angela, scared but determined, believing in him totally, accepting and loving him. Weber, solid, and ready to act if he had a direction. Friendship restored. His father, steel incarnate with a cold, analytical mind, ready to advise him.

And support me.

And Richard realized he didn't have to do this alone. He drew in a long, steadying breath. "Rhiana said she bound Kenntnis with magic, but holds him with physics using something called 'slow glass.' So, we find some physicists. If reason is leaving the world, I need you all thinking clearly. Angela, you asked me weeks ago to use the sword on you. Well, it's time."

"For me too?" Cross said hopefully.

"Be quiet. Sit down," Richard ordered. The homeless god sat. "Okay, let's do it." He drew the sword. The tonal echoes seemed to shake the walls.

Weber stood up as Richard approached. Richard looked up at the taller man, started to raise the sword. "You want me to kneel, Short Stuff?" Weber asked, his tone whimsical. "Or you could just whack me on the leg."

"Hey," said Cross, waving his hands excitedly in the air. "You want to do this up right? It hasn't been done this way in a long, long time."

"What?" Robert asked.

"Where do you think the knighting ritual came from?" Cross asked. "Of course it's gotten garbled over the years, and there's been a lot of religious shit thrown in to undercut its power, but it worked good. None of my kind ever infiltrated the Lumina because you had to get touched with the sword, which kills us, and it strips the magic out of a human candidate. Win/win, right?"

"So, what do we have to do?" Angela asked, intrigued by the prospect.

"Say the oath. Let him touch you on the shoulder."

"And what is the oath?" the judge asked cautiously.

Cross closed his eyes as if summoning some distant memory, and recited:

"Here I do affirm my desire to serve the light. To seek knowledge and understanding in all my endeavors. To defend the world and all mankind. To close the gates and open minds. To teach what I know and learn what I can. To be true to reason and truth in each area of my life. This do I swear upon my life and my honor."

One by one they came to him. Richard hated to hurt them, and it was evident the touch of the sword was painful. He, who possessed no magic, wondered what they felt. Was it like losing dreams, or waking to cold reality without any softening and comforting veils?

Weber eventually left for his apartment. Angela, weakened from her illness and the touch of the sword, went upstairs to bed. Cross went outside to keep watch. Robert carried the dishes into the kitchen. Richard heard water running, the clink of silverware on crystal. He sat staring into the dying embers of the fire, looking forward and trying to plan, looking back and remembering. He wasn't certain when he fell asleep.

He came half-awake to find Robert leaning over him, covering him with the afghan. His father's hand brushed back a lock of hair. There was the briefest touch of lips on his forehead. A whisper of breath fluttered warm across his forehead.

He woke at first light. The townhouse was silent. He checked on Angela and his father. Found them sleeping. He cleaned up in the downstairs bathroom. Though rumpled, his suit still looked better than anything he'd ever seen his fellow officers wear. It would do for what, he hoped, would be a dull shift.

He stepped outside, the snow squeaking beneath his shoes, breath forming a white cloud in front of his lips. The storm had blown out overnight. Under the rising sun the snow glittered as if it had been frosted with diamonds.

The Sandias, their blue-gray splendor iced with snow, bridged Heaven and Earth, seeming to touch the turquoise-blue sky.

Richard went to work.

Ready to hold back the monsters.